MIND OVER MUSSELS

A Shores Mystery

Hilary MacLeod

The Acorn Press
Charlottetown
2011

ISBN 978-1-894838-60-3

ACORNPRESS

P.O. Box 22024
Charlottetown, Prince Edward Island
C1A 9J2
acornpresscanada.com

Printed and Bound in Canada
Cover illustration and interior design by Matt Reid
Editing by Sherie Hodds

Page 178 quote from *The Progress of Love* by Alfred Noyes (1919).
Page 239 quote from *somewhere i have never travelled, gladly beyond* by e. e. cummings (1931).

Library and Archives Canada Cataloguing in Publication
MacLeod, Hilary
Mind over mussels : a Shores mystery / Hilary MacLeod.
ISBN 978-1-894838-60-3

I. Title.
PS8625.L4555M56 2011 C813'.6 C2011-904774-8

Canada Council for the Arts
Conseil des Arts du Canada

The publisher acknowledges the support of the Government of Canada through the Canada Book Fund of the Department of Canadian Heritage and the Canada Council for the Arts Block Grant Program.

With deep affection to Glenn Murphy of Sea View, born Glenn Campbell of Irishtown, 1915 – 2011. Glenn inspired my love of Prince Edward Island, its people, and its stories, which she told so well herself.

"It's the human condition that keeps us apart:
Everybody's got a story that could break your heart."

– Amanda Marshall

Prologue

The cold blade of the axe sliced through the air.

The skull cracked. Human blood splattered on the fox's lips. She licked them and the taste flooded her small brain.

She was witness to a brutal murder, but she would never testify in court. Not just because she was a fox, but because she was confused, blood lust singing through her. She couldn't say what happened when. The humans. The axe. The brains, spilling on the sand. Had she seen the killer? Could she point to him…her?

No. She couldn't smell the difference between humans, except whether they were male or female. There had been both. She sniffed the air. As long as the creature was dead, what harm in tasting? For a long time, she didn't move while she debated.

She shrank back when the human came down onto the sand where the blood was. Had the person been there before? Before the blood? She couldn't remember anything before the blood.

An unreliable witness, your honour.

She crouched in the deep shadow, eyes fixed on the axe. She'd seen it kill.

The human went back up the cape. The fox relaxed, then froze at the scent of another one on the breeze, squatting down over the body. Grooming? Or preparing to eat? Did humans eat each other? The vixen wasn't sure.

The human left. The fox pulled herself erect, and then hunched down again.

Another one.

She slipped into the night. Too many of them. Too much trouble for blood gone cold and stale. A dead man's blood.

But he wasn't dead, not quite. As his blood spilled out on the sand, so did his spirit. His mind was fluid, his essence flowing out of his body, dissolving. He was torn – trying to get out of the body, trying to get back in – until death gripped him, sudden and hard. With a jolt that tore him out of himself, Lance Lord was no more.

The fox took one regretful look back, her eyes glinting in the moonlight, fixed on a mist swirling over the lifeless form, trailing up the cape. She closed her eyes, shook her head, and looked again. A living thing? No. It was nothing.

The lingering scent of blood galvanized her, and she pounced on a mouse stupid enough to dart in front of her. Soon she was carrying the small carcass to her den.

Behind her, the wind stirred across the surface of the water. The waves stilled with the turning of the tide. Just a few feet away, stripped of its soul, all its blood pulsed into a blackening pool beneath a shattered skull, Lance Lord's body lay undisturbed all night.

Until Hy McAllister tripped over it.

Chapter One

An unusual mix of gulls and crows was circling low over the shore, cawing, screaming, battling for their trophies with a greater fuss than usual.

It struck Gus Mack as odd when she lumbered to the back room, the one that used to be a porch. The sky was grey and angry. The storm was moving in. Hurricane Angus, they were calling it. Except here in The Shores it was Hurricane Gus – the neighbours teasing her because she was afraid of storms, she who'd seen so many of them, whose shock of white hair looked as if she'd been hit by lightning, her greatest fear.

There was a storm coming, no doubt of that. It had been brooding around The Shores for days. After a month of sunshine, the skies hung heavy over Red Island, encouraging carpenter Harold MacLean to pronounce: "Storm coming," every night for a week. Now people wanted it to come just to shut him up.

"The longer it takes, the worse it will be," Gus kept saying. Unlike Harold, she was usually right about the weather. She'd lived so long she'd seen it all.

Gus gazed on the green fields, the red cliffs, and the shore, washed today by steel-grey water spiked with whitecaps. Her neighbours found her fascination with the coast peculiar. They preferred to scan the road to see who was driving by, when and why.

Gus looked at the road, too. From her big purple recliner beside the large picture window that looked out on the crossroads, she saw everything that came and went through the village – what was left of it. The Hall. The empty lots where the school and General Store used to be.

One of the most dramatic moments had been when an explosion sent her husband, Abel, flying out of the old store. A drunken farmer had backed into a fuel pump after the tank had just been filled. A pop machine and several cartons of canned food cleared a path for Abel out the shop window. He landed on his feet, unharmed. That was Abel all over. Good luck stalked him.

In spite of this and other entertainments provided by the road view, Gus liked to look out the back way to see the ocean in its many moods, and to keep track of the new cottages popping up along the capes. One had literally popped up overnight.

"Have you looked out your back window?" came the call last May from her neighbour, Estelle Joudry.

To her chagrin, Gus had not.

"Go have a look. I'll hang on."

Gus went to the back porch.

"Good Godfrey!" She stared at the dome. A white dome. It had appeared overnight. It looked like a scientific research station in the Arctic, or a snack bar – definitely not a cottage.

Gus was so shocked she never did go back to the phone, leaving the old-fashioned receiver hanging on its cord for most of the day, frustrating neighbours who wanted to share their outrage at the oddity.

But when they learned there were only a few like it in the world, and one of them was "right here in The Shores," they watched with pride as the outer coating was applied over the white bladder. Before the owner moved in, most of them had been up the cape to peek in the porthole windows.

Gus stepped out onto the stoop. She'd gazed at the water, land, and sky every morning since she'd come here as a bride sixty years ago – and she didn't tire of it. She knew the shore and its wildlife as well as she knew any of her eight children. So you'd think, the way those birds were acting, she'd have known something was wrong. But, rich as her life had been, Gus Mack had very little experience of murder.

Hy McAllister almost missed him.

She was running at the water's edge, the damp air turning her red curls into a frizzy mass, a stopwatch bobbing around her neck, beach treasures swinging in a makeshift fishnet bag from a washed-up lobster trap. Her camera, slung across her chest, was thumping up and down.

There was a great photo now – a thin sun peeking through a bank of clouds, its glow reflected in pools of water. The sun – over and over and over again in the sand and water. Click. She got it. And it was gone. There had been something else. Footprints? She couldn't see them now. Odd. Who'd have been here before her?

She shivered at a gust of wind from the water, pasting her jacket to her thin body, her feet sinking into wet sand as she ran. Toby, the beach dog, a black Lab with a bleached red stripe down his back, dashed along beside her, darting back and forth, spraying up wet sand from his big feet.

When she stopped to pick up a rock, Toby tore off toward the cape. Hy went sprinting after him.

And tripped.

Thump! She came down on all fours, shells scattering in the sand. She hauled herself up, cursing. She was always falling.

Then she saw him.

He lay sprawled out, a crow pecking at the back of his head, a half-dozen gulls hovering above. He wore a lime-green bandana, an orange dashiki, and bellbottoms. An Afro wig was askew on his head. In one hand, he held a sign that read: No Trespassing.

He looked like Jimi Hendrix, but it was Lance Lord, clinging to his property even in death. Hy shuddered. She was looking at a corpse. She'd fallen on a dead man. She began to heave, and threw up all over Lord's leg.

Toby licked the vomit.

"Tobeeeeeee!" She shooed him off.

She was disoriented, the day becoming dark under black clouds, the wind whining in her ears. She grabbed her bag, and began gathering up the shells and rocks that had spilled out. She didn't know why she did it. Trying to feel normal? She clung to the bag as tightly as Lance Lord was clutching death and that pathetic sign. She looked at him again. Was that a lobster on his head?

She closed her eyes.

Opened them.

Not a lobster. A crow sat on Lord's head. A carrion eater. She almost retched again. The crow flew off, and she saw the wound, black and green.

It had to be murder. And where there was murder, there was a murderer. Her mind raced. Was he still out here on the shore? Thank God for Toby. Except he was showing as much interest as the birds in the contents of Lance Lord's head. She dragged him away with a beach rope tied to his collar, and stumbled up to Lord's cottage. She kept looking around. When had it happened? Was the murderer watching her right now?

Hy's friend Ian Simmons was not an early riser, or he would have been alerted by the strange behaviour of the gulls and crows. In the past year, he'd adopted an orphan parrot and learned everything about birds. Jasmine, a cheeky African Grey, was his constant companion, often perched on his shoulder.

She was not there now. Instead, a lock of honey-blonde hair trailed across it, as he woke from a dream. A dream come true. She'd appeared at his door last night. Suki Smythe. The only woman he'd ever loved. Suki Smythe. He kept looking at her and repeating her name silently.

Why had she come?

Hy's fear made her clumsy, her long legs ungainly as a colt's. She tripped and fell twice on the sandy slope up to the cottage. The rapier-sharp marram grass sliced at her ankles. Toby bounded beside her, running circles around her, thinking it a great game. Hy's heart was pounding so hard it felt as if it would burst through her chest. She was cold but she was sweating, wet beads on the back of her neck, trickling down her spine, her armpits soaking her shirt.

The cottage door was unlocked – and partly open.

She froze. Her throat went dry. She let Toby edge ahead, sniffing, licking at the floor. She took one slow step at a time, following the big black dog into the small dark cottage, the blinds down in every window.

"You."

It was all Ian could say when he'd opened the door last night and saw Suki. They'd met again last winter at a university reunion. More than thirty years since they'd been lab partners, when he'd lusted after her, never daring to make a move. Taking on all the work of the research reports had been his only means of seduction. It hadn't worked.

But here she was. He had dreamed about this. Daydreamed. Night dreamed... other kinds, too. But they were just dreams. Not like this.

"You." That's all he'd been able to say...

She'd tossed her thick honey hair, and thrust her suitcase at him.

"Are you just going to stand there gaping, or are you going to invite me in?"

He'd flushed pleasure and embarrassment. She always made him feel awkward.

"Invite me in. Wha'? Invite me in?" An odd voice from inside.

Suki's brow had furrowed.

"Is that the missus?" She'd peeked into the room. Anyone would have known from the computer station and the 1950s Danish modern furniture inherited from his parents.

"There is no missus." Ian had looked perplexed. She should know that.

She'd smiled. Touched his cheek with one long slender, perfectly manicured finger.

"Invite me in. Wha'? Invite me in?" This second time, the voice was closer to her own.

Suki had looked around and seen the parrot, Jasmine, perched on the iMac monitor, flicking her head from side to side.

"No missus?" Suki had pouted, pretending sympathy.

She had known that from the reunion. They had traded bios – three marriages for her, none for him. When he'd told her where he lived, in this backwater paradise, she had said she'd come visit. He had never believed she would.

Then suddenly, she was here.

"How'd you find me?"

"Well, you said The Shores. You said The Island. There's only one island, isn't there?" Her eyes were teasing.

"I mean here. The house." He hadn't known what else to say.

"You also mentioned Shipwreck Hill. How could I forget that? I just tried the first door and *voilà*."

She'd looked him up and down.

He still hadn't believed she was here.

"But you're no shipwreck." She'd placed a hand on his belly, newly flat, in spite of Moira Toombs' muffins.

Jasmine had bitten at her feathers, a sign of distress.

Suki had pecked Ian on both cheeks, and ruffled his head where the hair should have been. She'd put both arms around him.

He hadn't stood a chance. He'd melted into her softness, her warmth. He'd longed to touch every part of her.

That night he had.

Hy had expected Lord's cottage to look like they all did, with hooked rugs, quilts, antique pine furniture, but it was nothing like that. It was a bachelor pad with stark white walls, black leather furniture, and bursts of colour from psychedelic sixties posters. She scanned the kitchen for the phone. Bar stools, Guinness artifacts, and black appliances. She spotted the phone's base station on the wall by the fridge, but no phone.

Her teeth were chattering, she was chilled from the sweat of fear, the hair on her arms bristling, her movement erratic. She tripped down the stairs into the sunken living room. When her feet hit something thick and furry, she screamed. Toby growled.

A bearskin rug in a cottage by the sea. The absurdity cut through her fear. Just wait until she told Gus.

The room was littered with electric guitars – two Stratocasters, a Gibson Les Paul, several Rickenbackers. The walls were covered with posters of Jimi Hendrix at Monterey and Woodstock. A huge wall unit held stacks of Hendrix discography, in all its forms. Albums. Eight-track tapes. Cassettes. CDs, including the Teletubbies' *Purple Haze.*

Still no phone. Maybe the bedroom.

That was another surprise. Playboy pad gave way to Harlequin romance – a French provincial four-poster, with ivory linens and matching vanity and dressers.

A tube of KY jelly was by the bedside, its seal unbroken.

Hy went to the bathroom. The phone was on the marble sink. She grabbed it and dialed 911, hands shaking. She got it wrong and had to start again. Twice.

"I…I'm calling to report a death… Yes, I'm quite sure… No, I'm not a doctor. It's…a…murder… No, I'm not a police officer, but… At The Shores…the cottage at Mack's Shore… No, I'm not a neighbour… Just down from the dome."

Every islander knew where that was. Everyone had done a drive-by of the dome, the only one in the province. Many had been surprised that The Shores actually existed, and that it was so beautiful. Some had begun to check the real estate ads for available shorefront property.

Hy rang off and called Ian.

Suki stirred, and placed a long, smooth leg across Ian's. He was stimulated, but still wondering...*why?* Why was she here, with him? Hadn't she just been married when he had run into her at the reunion? *To some entertainer? Yes, an actor.* Ian hadn't been listening to her – he'd been staring at her, still beautiful past fifty. Had she said something about Quebec?

She rolled on top of him and her thick hair spilled onto his face.

"What about the French guy?" he asked.

"What French guy?"

"Your husband."

"Not French."

"No?" *Damn.*

"A Quebecer?"

"Nope."

"But not a husband anymore?"

"Oh, yes. We're still married."

Ian pushed her off and sat up. "Good Lord."

"That's right. Lord."

"What?"

"Lance Lord. My husband. Didn't I tell you that?"

He was sure she hadn't.

"Lance Lord?"

"Don't look so shocked."

"But...you're here with him?"

"I went to see him last night." She pouted. "He was no good." She nuzzled into his neck. "So I came here."

"But..." Ian threw off the sheets to get out of bed.

She grabbed him, pushed him down, and straddled him.

"But he can't – and you can."

Ian found that he could.

Later, when he woke up, the bed was empty.

She was gone. Had it been just a dream, after all?

He heard the toilet flush and brightened. Suki emerged from the bathroom, wearing his short terry robe, her long legs glistening.

The phone rang.

Suki slipped off the robe and let it drop.

He picked up the receiver.

"Ian!"

Hy.

Suki slid into the bed beside him.

He let go of the receiver.

Hy knew she sounded hysterical the minute she started to speak. It all came tumbling out. She was talking so fast she didn't realize at first that no one was listening, until Ian's absence seeped into her rattled brain. There was no one on the other end of the line – but there were sounds.

Squeaking. A bed squeaking.

A moan. Female.

A grunt. Male.

Ian was having sex.

At a time like this.

Hy rang off.

Chapter Two

Billy Pride was finishing the detail work on the inside of the RCMP community cruiser when the call came from the dispatcher.

"M-me? Okay. Yup. Secure the scene. Right away." He tossed the cloth onto the passenger seat, adjusted his position behind the steering wheel and started the car, excitement sizzling through him. This was his chance to show that he was more than an errand boy, the fetcher of vehicles, packages, dry cleaning. He wasn't a real Mountie, just an auxiliary officer, the province's idea of police presence in a remote community. Billy hadn't faced stiff competition to land the assignment. He'd been the only volunteer.

Billy had been closest to the scene, so they'd called him. Other, more senior officers would follow, but he would be there first. His first real case. He turned on the siren and went streaking down the Island Way toward The Shores, his size thirteen foot pressed hard on the accelerator. The computer screen and keyboard he'd removed for cleaning toppled off the roof of the car and smashed on the road behind him.

Jasmine got Ian out of bed. She was squawking for her breakfast with a medley of annoying sounds – gulls shrieking, crows cawing, foxes barking, and Britney Spears and Mick Jagger singing a duet of "Satisfaction."

Ian almost missed the phone ringing.

It was Hy again. She blurted it out.

"Lord's dead."

"Who?"

"Lance Lord."

"Dead?"

"Yup."

"God Almighty."

"Well he thought so…"

She started to laugh, the horror washing over her.

Ian hung on to the phone, listening to Hy and thinking about Suki. Lord's wife. *Jesus*. He'd have to tell her.

Hy used the bathroom again. When she came out, Toby had his feet on the kitchen table, licking the remains of a dinner for two.

"Tob-eee." Hy dashed over and yanked his collar. He didn't budge. She kept pulling and he gave way, and then lunged at the table again. She dragged him outside.

She didn't want to look at the body on the sand, but she did anyway. She tried to feel something, but couldn't. She was surprised. Another human being had been brutally killed and she felt nothing.

She'd fought Lord over the right of way, afraid the locals would cave in and lose it. Each time she'd gone to the beach she'd march across it, head up, eyes forward, stride confident. Lord would stand outside his cottage, watching and scowling.

She looked away, down the shore to the sea rock. Some people called it an island, but it was just a chunk worn off the cape by the wind and the waves. It was home, and a toilet, to a couple of dozen cormorants. Its top was white with their poop.

Hy turned and stared in the opposite direction, beyond Vanishing Point, at the dome. There was Big Ed, a big man with peculiar hair – a buzz cut, black, with a strip of white down the back, where he'd been wounded. He was standing like the Colossus of

Rhodes, legs apart, straddling not a Mediterranean harbour, but a hairline fracture in the cape. Where it widened, it had been formed into a staircase by beachgoers. Recently, a large chunk had come loose and made the path dangerous. People could no longer clamber past Big Ed's dome. They liked to go to the beach that way to avoid Lord, and because they were curious about Big Ed. His name was legendary in the world of physical fitness, and his personal story was extraordinary.

Hy had been up there once, when Ed had first arrived, curiosity propelling her to the dome. She'd gone on the pretext of writing an article for the Heart and Stroke website. She'd been disappointed that it hadn't been Ed, but Ed's companion, Leone, who came to the door. He wasn't handsome, but he was strangely attractive, uncomfortably so.

He hadn't invited her in. Instead, he had come outside, pulling the door nearly closed behind him, as if there were something to hide. He'd brushed against her, and she'd felt the warmth of his flesh and a spark between them. It had surprised her. He wasn't her type. She'd pulled away from him abruptly, disturbed by the intimacy.

So disturbed that she hadn't gone through with the sham of writing an article.

She'd left after trading a few remarks about the weather with Leone, thinking he must want to keep people away as badly as Lance Lord did.

She never had seen Ed, not up close. Only as she saw him now, from a distance during his morning routine on the cape.

The wind had picked up. So had the surf. The sky was so black it was now more like midnight than mid-morning. It didn't seem to bother Ed. He stuck to his morning routine and began the walk. The march, Leone thought as he watched Ed from the top of the dome – a fanciful widow's walk, made of intricate wrought iron, capped by a peaked roof that looked like the turret of a Bavarian castle. Leone, Ed's devoted factotum, the man who had nursed him back to life, was now watching him disintegrate.

Leone could see other things, too, in the hazy viewfinder of his poor vision. The Shores was, fortunately, a compact world. From here, he could see the body splayed out on the sand. He could see Lord's cottage. And the big house where *she* was staying. He could see the village centre and Shipwreck Hill, and the house where he believed the other one was.

Big Ed went back and forth, back and forth along the edge of the cape – from one end of his property to the other, enjoying the power in his limbs and the freedom of movement the morning provided him, feeling his strength – not the strength he had once had as a football hero in a small Pennsylvania high school, scouted and destined for Notre Dame University – but still strength. The strength of the mind over mere matter. Mind Over Muscle. The name of his fitness empire. There was a reason for the acronym MOM. She was always on his mind.

Just outside the village, Billy turned on the siren. It was a rude awakening for those villagers who weren't already up, and the phones began to ring as one phoned another, phoned another, to find out what was going on and where. No one knew, but speculation raged as, phones to their ears, hands parting blinds and curtains, they formed an information relay about where the police car was headed. Billy went racing down the Island Way, the sound of the siren sending a thrill through him. He was on real police business.

The woman peeked through the curtains of the big Victorian house on the Shore Lane as the police cruiser threaded its way to Lord's cottage, and then her hand, hidden inside a white lace glove, released the curtain. She smiled. There was no joy in it.

Her suitcases were still in the closet. She hadn't even begun to pack, though check-out time was ten o'clock tomorrow and she was not an early riser. She knew she wouldn't be leaving. Neither would Ed nor Leone. And Lance certainly wouldn't be going anywhere.

Or would he?

The sky was dark and angry, the wind raging, the waves thundering, the tide menacing Lord's body. Hy, her nose red, teeth chattering, arms wrapped around herself against the gusting wind and rain, was leaning against Toby, who would also have preferred indoor comforts and kept looking quizzically at his beach buddy. It was not in Toby's experience as a beach dog that a human would stand around on the sand in such awful weather. The smell was pleasant when he sniffed, though. Wet dog and puke – and something else.

Hy couldn't stay outside any longer. Let Toby eat the evidence on the table. It wasn't her job to worry about it. The dog sped ahead to the cottage, jumped at the door and pushed his way in. Hy had just stepped inside when the police siren cut through the air. She yanked up a blind and the car's lights slashed through the dark cottage.

That's when Hy saw him, standing in a corner of the room.

Every Saturday, in The Shores and everywhere across Red Island, the week's tourists left early in the morning and a fresh set arrived. But this was Labour Day weekend, and the tourists should have been leaving tomorrow morning, no fresh ones arriving. Only tomorrow the tourists wouldn't be able to get out – and Ben and Annabelle Mack wouldn't return to the rambling Shore Lane house they'd rented out all summer.

It was from the front parlour window of this house that their latest guest had peeked out between the heavy velvet curtains. They'd been closed for the past week, ever since she'd arrived. Hardly anyone had seen her – only Gus. She'd borrowed some thread from Gus, had admired her quilts, and ended up ordering one, custom-made. Gus hadn't told anyone. She'd been asked not to.

Big Ed stood at the top of the cape, looking down on the shore. He'd seen the woman and the dog. He'd seen the bright neon body of Lance Lord. He'd heard the police cruiser slash through the dark morning. And now? Now he was seeing nothing. Staring out at the rising surf, but seeing – nothing.

Ed Bullock's mind was a blank. Utterly blank. It wasn't meditation. It wasn't something he tried to do. It just happened. And he wouldn't stir. Couldn't. There were no signals in his brain telling him to do anything. Anything but stand and stare.

When he came to, the world would slowly come alive for him again. Sometimes it could be very disturbing, like this morning. Too many images to take in – the boiling sea, the waves assaulting the shore, the body lying on the sand.

Lance Lord. It came to him afresh. He was seeing the body for the first time, all over again, reliving the fact that Lord was dead. If either of them had laid odds on who would go first, it would have been him, Ed. A pity, but it was an obstacle out of the way.

Leone had seen the body, too, and knew who it was, but he didn't bother to give it more than a glance. He kept his eyes on Ed as he always did through his morning walk up and down the cape, and the inevitable blank-out. Leone knew, though he was only looking at his back, when Ed "came to." Knowing it would be moments only before he turned and came into the house, soaking wet and in need of help, his morning strength diminished. Ed was losing ground.

Leone grabbed the wrought iron railing of the circular staircase and hauled himself down a step, balancing on the other long arm as he swung his feet down to it. And then again – a bit like a monkey, swinging his way down the steps more with the aid of his long arms than his legs.

Even though, unlike Ed's, they were perfectly good legs.

Chapter Three

Mountie Jane Jamieson was always on call, even this weekend during her sister's wedding. She was afraid if she went off duty for an hour, that's when her big chance would come – and go. It had just arrived, and she wasn't prepared. She stood in these ridiculous clothes, waiting for her partner to pick her up.

Even so, Jamieson was soaring with excitement, hoping the call really was a murder, a case to catapult her out of this backwater to somewhere bigger, better, like Toronto.

She'd been glad not to be working Labour Day weekend, although she hadn't admitted it to herself. Long holiday weekends were just three days of chasing down drunks on the road, answering complaints of loud music and noise, responding to domestic disputes – all the dirty, grubby, unexciting routine of police work. If something big was going to happen – really big – something big enough to propel her out of here to Halifax or Toronto or Vancouver, it was not going to happen on a three-day weekend. She didn't know that police work in the big cities would be the same grubby tangle of drunks, loud parties, and domestic disputes, just more of them. She thought that's where the real police work was going on, not on this nowhere island on the Labour Day weekend.

She was about to be paid back for all the weekends she'd put her name in to be on call, and she was to learn to be careful what she wished for. She had been off duty when the call finally came, but she was very much on duty now. Except for what she was wearing.

Murdo Black knew enough to keep his mouth shut when

Jamieson came out the door of her sister's oceanfront home east of Winterside. If he'd said anything about how she looked, she might have killed him – if she'd had a gun on her. He'd never seen her out of uniform. Never even imagined it.

"Stop home first?" was the most he dared.

"No time," she said. "The clues are found in the first twenty-four hours – the best ones right away. We can't chance disruption of the crime scene." Or chance an actual detective being called to the case. She was lucky it was a long weekend and the Major Crime Investigation unit was in disarray. Lucky, too, it was The Shores, where no one wanted to go, especially on a holiday and in weather like this.

Murdo shrugged and eased away from the curb.

"Move it," she ordered, and he picked up speed, punching on the car radio.

"Hurricane Angus is approaching Red Island, packing winds of up to one hundred and forty kilometres. We're expecting him to hit later this morning. The storm will bring with it high winds and bands of rain, heavy at times. Thirty millimeters could fall within a few hours, and we could get a total of one hundred millimeters or more. The storm centre is over Nova Scotia, but its angle means it will smack us hard."

Murdo cast a worried eye at the sky. Grim. Black. So dark you'd think it was sunset not sunrise. He hoped they'd get to the causeway before the hurricane hit. Murdo knew his island weather, and thought the storm would come sooner than the forecaster said. The winds were getting wilder, buffeting the cruiser as it sped along the wet roads, through channels of water worn into the asphalt by farm trucks full of potatoes and agricultural vehicles with loads of hay and grain, but most of all potatoes. The cruiser drove by the Havesham Farms potato factory north of Winterside.

It was pumping out steam as the spuds were sliced, diced, cooked, and packaged as frozen French fries, making the air that once was fragrant with wild roses smell like a diner.

The worst of the storm would arrive, Murdo predicted, within the hour. He sped up in spite of the risk of hydroplaning. They had to get to the causeway soon, before it was flooded. The causeway attached The Shores to the rest of Red Island, not very securely. High tides could cut it off entirely – with no police response to what sounded like a murder.

Jamieson leaned her head back, her eyes firmly closed.

She'd been to a family wedding, Murdo knew. Had she been drinking? *Drinking? Jamieson?* It certainly looked like it. Her pale skin was even paler than usual.

A whiter shade of pale, thought Murdo. He'd always wondered what that meant. He was looking at it now.

The figure standing in the corner moved, as the beam of a car's headlights sliced through the window. Hy's heart leapt in her chest and pounded in her ears. Toby growled, a long, low growl.

Another sweep of light. The shadow loomed against the wall, then disappeared as the room went dark again.

Hy was frozen, listening for breathing besides her own, trying to still the arrhythmic thumping of her heart. Toby growled again, deeper, more menacing.

Two more flashes of light. The man did not move. Neither did Hy. Car door slamming. Toby barking. Heavy boots pounding across the deck. Loud knocking on the door, not just in her heart. She found courage, spun around, and switched on the room light.

She saw him clearly now – propped against the wall.

Very dead.

She let out a cry and dissolved in hysterical laughter.

That's how Billy Pride found her.

Jamieson and Murdo had not spoken for fifteen minutes. They were nearly halfway to The Shores, and the worst part of the trip lay ahead.

"The causeway," Jamieson murmured, head back, eyes half-closed.

"Yup," said Murdo. "The goddamn causeway."

It had been natural once, a slim kilometre of land joining The Shores to the rest of Red Island. A couple of winters back, a storm surge had ruptured it. Driven by a northeast gale, the sea ice had pushed onto the land and over the road. In thirteen minutes, it had crushed and buried five houses, killed nine people, shoved cars into the water, and pushed boats up onto the road.

The Shores had been cut off by land, the Campbell causeway torn apart at one end. The province had considered evacuating The Shores permanently but, after a protest, agreed to rebuild it. They'd made a bad job of it, and it had been washed out so frequently that the province had provided an ancient river ferry as backup. Now it crossed the tiny inlet, back and forth, eight cars at a time, as part of the provincial road system. But in a hurricane, that beat-up little ferry wouldn't be out on the water.

Murdo sneaked a sideways glance at Jamieson. She was scowling. His brow furrowed. He'd thought she'd be happy to answer this call.

She was. But she was tense with anticipation, glued to a strong need that the call would turn out to be a murder, that she'd be the only one on the case, that she'd solve it, and no longer would be sent on jobs like the last two. She and Murdo had just come off a couple of humiliating cases. A month ago they'd investigated the robbery of a truckload of seaweed. Somehow, some way, someone had made off with a one-ton truckload of Irish moss and no one had seen. Or no one was saying they'd seen.

Then, two weeks ago, they were assigned to the theft of twenty-five duck decoys. They did retrieve those – and the snickers of fellow Mounties when they brought the evidence back to the detachment. There were a few "quacks" as well.

No, she didn't want any more calls like those. Let it be murder, she thought. A murder that would get her off this godforsaken island and somewhere civilized.

So she might have been forgiven her first instinct when she saw the two cars entwined on the shoulder of the road. She nearly waved Murdo on, barely able to choke back an order to keep going.

Of course they had to stop. Check that the drivers and passengers were not injured. Take details. Make a report. Call for help. Put up with the odd looks the group gave her – the white-faced woman dressed kinda funny for a police officer.

The man in the corner of the living room had been dead for a long time. The intruder who'd terrified Hy was Jimi Hendrix himself – a life-size stand-up cardboard image of Jimi Hendrix playing his guitar. Hy was a sight – soaking wet, laughing, and gulping air uncontrollably when Billy walked in.

She looked up at the young community officer of staggering height and build. Impossibly young. Ridiculously handsome. Hy wondered if beauty as well as brawn was now required in law enforcement.

"Billypride." He said his name as if it were one word – the way he always had.

Hy was stunned. Billy Pride.

"How you've grown!"

He frowned. She shouldn't have said that.

"Miss McAllister?"

She nodded, dumb, unable to reply in any other way.

Billy Pride. A Mountie? No, not quite. She remembered he'd been recently appointed some kind of community officer.

"Someone is dead?" As he spoke, deep furrows of concern lined his forehead.

No, not a real Mountie.

She nodded her head. She wondered how he'd react to the sight of Lord on the sand. She hoped he wouldn't cry. He had always done that in school. When Hy had come to Red Island as a fresh-faced young teacher nearly twenty years before, all the one-room schoolhouses had been long closed, but the one at The Shores had been forgotten and had stayed open. When officials had finally remembered it, they'd closed it, and Hy had been out of a job. That's when she'd started "Content," her website writing and editing service.

She didn't need the money really. She had a nest egg.

"You found the body?"

She felt unreasonably guilty. Why? She hadn't done anything, just stumbled across a body and threw up on it. It was those clear eyes, the rosy complexion, his earnest, unlined face. Billy had always looked like an innocent, but he wasn't. He'd often gotten into scrapes. He tried to stay on the rails, but always seemed to veer off. Maybe it was the lack of a father figure. Billy's father had taken off as soon as he found out what his wife was really like – impossible to live with. But Billy hadn't had a choice. At his mother's beck and call, he'd rebelled with small offences. Under-age drinking behind the Hall. Smoking dope. Stealing from his mother's purse.

Hy nodded dumbly.

"I found it," she mumbled, as if she were the guilty one.

"Could you show me, please?"

Hy found her voice.

"Yes, yes, of course…"

She walked out onto the deck and into the rain. The wind was churning up the surf and whipping sand across the beach.

Hy led Billy through the marram grass slicing at their legs, with a delighted Toby panting at their heels, unable to believe his luck at finding two beach-walking companions. Once out of the dune, he pulled into the lead, and, nose down, began sniffing his way to the corpse.

"Are you sure it was murder?"

"Sure."

"Not an accident? Suicide? Perhaps he took a heart attack."

"Not with that great gaping wound in the back of his head." She pointed, but didn't look.

They'd reached the body and Billy saw what she meant. He walked around the corpse, bent over it, his brow furrowed as he examined the wound. He sniffed. What was that on the air? Salt? Yes. Seaweed? Certainly. But something...something...the smell of death?

No – vomit.

Hy saw him look at Lord's leg, covered in what was left of her midnight snack of toast and jam.

"I threw up."

Billy stood up and pulled out his notebook. It was new and blank.

"Vomit?" He scrawled down a few letters, then stopped. *V...o... two m's or one?*

Then gave up, and wrote "puke." That would change in the official report.

"You know the name of the victim?"

"Lord. Lance Lord."

"What kind of name is that?"

"Well – his." Hy looked from Billy to the lifeless body.

They would find out what sort of name Lance Lord was.

An assumed one.

It was thanks to Jamieson's twenty-twenty vision that they didn't hit the woman standing in the middle of the road. Girl, really.

Twenty, maybe. In spite of the weather and her ill-suited clothes, Jamieson ripped out of the cruiser and charged on the tiny girl in a fury. It was really anger born of relief. Relief that they hadn't plowed into her, coming around that corner blind, on the rain-slicked road.

"Are you nuts?" She shook her hands above her head as she marched on the poor creature, standing still like a surprised deer hoping to be hidden by its stillness and camouflage – a black rain cape on black tarmac. A lot of people did think Lili Acorn was nuts, some of them her friends.

The hooded cape was doing a poor job of keeping the rain off the young woman. It was flapping in the wind around her stick-thin body. The hood framed a pale face, nearly as pale as Jamieson's own. Big honey-brown eyes peered out from the white face, an odd sort of calm in them.

Jamieson took the blank stare for confirmation that the girl was nuts. She didn't think about how she must look herself, marching forward, arms raised, shaking with fury.

The girl didn't move. Jamieson came right up to her, her face just inches away.

"What the hell do you think you were doing?"

Something like a smile, not quite, passed across Lili's lips. Her eyes flicked sideways toward the shoulder of the road. There sat a bright red Volkswagen Beetle, its emergency lights flashing, a back tire flat.

Jamieson groaned.

"You might have got yourself killed," she said. "All for a flat tire."

The beatific expression remained on Lili's face. She shrugged.

"I didn't know how to change it," she said. "I didn't know what to do. I had to stop you. Who knows when anyone else would come by?"

She was right. At the height of tourist season, there would be a stream of cars to the newly discovered "Shores." Because of the dramatic events at Vanishing Point last year – the deaths and the property destruction, the lobster season shut down – the world now knew about The Shores, and tourists wanted in. Developers were beaming as they counted US dollars and sales figures they hadn't seen in years. They rhapsodized about their new discovery. "Like Long Island at the turn of the last century," said one land-grabber. Another had billed it "the last unspoiled shoreline in North America." The phrase had been used before, but this time it was the truth.

The provincial head was turned by all the attention, and politicians and their spin doctors got together to re-brand and rename The Island, the argument being there were already others – Cape Breton, for one – that considered themselves "The Island."

The powers-that-be chose Red Island, for the colour of its earth. And though the province hadn't completed the process of legitimizing the name, it had already stuck.

Yellow police tape was up around the body, fixed to pieces of wood harvested from lobster traps. Billy had tried to make the barricade look professional, but he'd done a poor job. Already one piece had given way and was flapping in the gathering storm.

So was the tarp Billy had used to cover the body. The gulls had to be stopped from breakfasting on the evidence. Billy wasn't used to answering calls like this one – "a possibly suspicious death," he'd termed it, unable to commit himself to the idea of murder here in The Shores. He'd radioed to Winterside and was told again that more experienced officers were on the way. They'd ordered him just to guard the scene, but he had a better idea. Noticing Hy's camera, he'd asked her to take photographs before he put the tarp over the body. It was a grim job but she did it, taking shots at every conceivable angle, including close-ups of the gash in Lord's head.

"What's that?" she'd asked Billy, pointing at the green in the wound.

"Maggots maybe," he said. "Forensics use the presence of maggots to help estimate the time of death, but I don't know if there's been time for this corpse to have maggots. Anyway, aren't they white and squirmy? This is greenish and not moving."

He pointed at the corpse. "Maybe pus."

Hy turned her head away and shivered at the cold and the graphic talk.

"Here. Drive home." Billy held out the keys to the cruiser.

She darted a look up at the vehicle, covered in red clay, parked outside Lord's cottage.

"But…it's a police vehicle."

"Yes, but it's out of service right now. Take it home, get cleaned up and bring it back."

Toby followed her and jumped into the car the moment she opened the door, dragging wet, sandy dog across the driver's seat, and settled into the passenger seat. As she drove off, Hy remembered she'd left her bag of beach treasures on Lord's kitchen counter.

The curtain in Annabelle and Ben Mack's front room inched open as Hy drove the cruiser up Cottage Lane, and there was someone peeking from every front window in the village all the way home, wondering what Hy McAllister was doing driving a police vehicle, and what had happened on the shore. The usual relay of calls down The Shores' internet – the Women's Institute phone chain – had turned up nothing.

Billy knew what he'd done was not procedure, but he'd been brought up to think about the comfort and convenience of women. He'd learned that from his mother. She was always finding things that he could do for her comfort and convenience.

No, it wasn't procedure, nor were a number of other things that were about to happen in this case, for which no one was prepared.

For now, Billy looked handsome, dutiful, and chilly, watching over the corpse as the storm gathered around him.

Chapter Four

Lili was sitting on a mat she'd pulled out of the back of her car. Though her legs were hidden under her rain cape, she was clearly in the lotus position, her hands visible, palms perched upward on the outside of the cape, one on each knee, thumb and middle finger delicately touching, poised to connect with the universe, like a hydro transformer, to bring goodness and light flowing into her. Murdo and Jamieson were kneeling down in the mud at the side of the road, wrenching at the tire of her Bug, trying to get the damn thing off.

Lili's face was raised to the sky, soaking in the rain, her eyes closed, her body and her mind untouched by the wind biting into Murdo's hands, his fingers red and raw. He noticed that Jamieson's dress was stuck to her body, clinging to her flesh, irritating her. She kept tugging it away. Murdo thought Jamieson was too thin. Much too thin. Needed some filling out.

"Ommmmmmmm." Lili hummed from her island of calm, her voice clear and steady.

"Ommmmmmmm..."

The lugs on the tire wouldn't budge. The last thing to touch that tire had been a machine in a factory. Human strength couldn't get it off, not in the wind and the rain and the rush they were in.

"Ommmmmmm..."

"Noooooooooo..." Murdo drew out the sound so it melded with Lili's chant.

Jamieson glared at him, stood up, and tapped Lili's shoulder, bringing the girl's eyes wide open, startled out of her serenity.

"Where are you headed?" Jamieson wiped at the mud on the front of her dress. It created a long smear. Her hair whipped around her face in the wind. She grabbed at the ponytail, and with muddy hands, braided it and coiled it into a bun. She had a patch of mud on her face. Neither Murdo nor the girl dared tell her.

"The Shores," said Lili, reaching in the back of the car for a satchel that smelled of patchouli oil. The rain intensified the scent.

"I'm to give a yoga demonstration at the Hall. To the Women's Institute."

"You'd better come with us," said Jamieson. "We can't leave you here." They had tried to summon help from town. Winterside had four tow trucks. One had answered their previous call. Two others had had to answer a call to the train tunnel that joined Red Island to the mainland. There'd been an accident not far from the tunnel. A transport truck had jackknifed, another had plowed into it, and two cars were involved as well. The remaining tow company wouldn't answer any calls. The owner had taped X's on his windows at home and business against the big blow. He said there was no way he or any of his lads would come out to The Shores today on that causeway, with its fragile grip on the land. He didn't want to be victim of another storm surge.

It certainly wasn't according to the rules to pick up a hitchhiking yogi, but nothing about this call so far was going by the book. Jamieson thought it still might be her big chance. It might be. She clung to that hope as they headed down the road and around the last curve before the causeway. Murdo had his hands tight on the steering wheel. He was never happy driving in the rain. He looked straight ahead, squinting into the gloom. He was afraid to have his eyes checked. Jamieson, beside him, with her perfect vision, was aware that his was poor, but had no idea just how poor. She wondered why he was going so slowly. Lili, in the back seat, was seeing – what was Lili seeing? A perfect world, not the potholed road. The light of life, not the grim dark sky. The harmony of the universe, not the tension bristling in the front seat between Murdo, eyes crazy-glued to the road and hands to the steering wheel, and Jamieson, wishing she were in the driver's seat. She liked to be in control. Instead, here she was, in the passenger seat, out of uniform, soaking wet, with a bloody hippie in the back seat. Where did they get it from, this generation? Their grandparents?

Lili was oblivious to it all, grabbing the chance to meditate, to reach perfect happiness. She was closer than she thought to attaining nirvana, but it would not come from meditation. She was about to meet Nathan.

Nathan Mack was tossing a five-hundred-pound barbell up in the air with no effort. He was grinning. There were five sets of weights, each heavier than the next, but all weighing the same – nearly nothing. The collection was his latest "find" at Jared MacPherson's house. Nathan had done what his aunt Gus called "a deal with the devil." He was staying at Jared's, fixing up the place instead of paying rent, while Jared was in jail for possession and suspected trafficking of cocaine. The weightless barbells and the literature that came with them had been in the back bedroom downstairs, the bedroom in which both Jared's parents, one after the other, had wasted away from cancer. Cigarettes. There had been butts in containers throughout the house. They were mostly Jared's, but in the back bedroom were his parents' butts, at least five years old. The smell of them had nearly choked Nathan when he'd first gone in, but, under the bed, he'd found these barbells. What a joke.

Nathan remembered the TV ads from years before. Mind Over Muscle. No fancy or heavy equipment needed. You could build strength with the power of your mind, just like the Vietnam vet who had patented the system. Big Ed Bullock. He was spending the summer here in that weird dome he'd built. Nathan had been twelve when those ads were all over late night TV. Big Ed had made the cover of *Business Week* as "Entrepreneur of the Year" and of *Sports Illustrated* as "Comeback of the Year." Not for anything to do with the magnificent football career that had been promised for him, but for his fight back against overwhelming odds when that career – and very nearly his life – had tragically ended. The story of his amazing comeback had won more replays in more media than any of his unrealized touchdowns might have. Like millions of others, Nathan thought Big Ed was a hero. He thought his body was amazing. Nathan had bugged and bugged his parents to buy him a system.

He shook his head now as he chucked the fake weight on the floor. Hundreds of dollars, it had cost. No wonder his dad had said, "Why buy the system, Nathan? Just pick up nothing instead. That should work." Ben had tossed him a bag of marshmallows. "Here, use these."

His dad had been right, but those ads were enticing – promising the muscular body Nathan craved. Still lean in his early twenties, he'd been a wretchedly skinny boy.

He'd gotten a kick looking through the pamphlets that had come with Jared's barbells – and realized it wasn't a lazy man's game. The trick was to mentally follow through every millisecond of every motion required to lift a real weight. No one could do that. Or almost no one. Nathan thought of Big Ed. It was the perfect scam. No one could say the system didn't work – because it was all in the mind. If a customer failed to build muscle, it was he or she who had failed, not the system. Big Ed was proof that Mind Over Muscle worked.

Just what Jared would go for, thought Nathan. Lazy as an old dog. Mean as one, too. Jared was always looking for the quick fix.

The house, when Nathan moved into it, was proof of that. Cabinet doors unhinged, or off, in the kitchen. Walls knocked out, joists exposed, bits of plaster and spider webs hanging off them. Doors that had been removed and not replaced. Windows that didn't shut tight. The projects started in different rooms – floor sanding, plastering – begun and then abandoned.

Nathan had been in the house all summer while his parents were cosied up at their "Love Shack" and tourists rented their house. He could see it from Jared's – back on the Shore Lane. He'd seen the woman who'd been staying there this past week, but only from a distance. Skinny, sickly looking thing.

Nathan himself was bursting with health. He had high colour in his cheeks, a cheeky grin, rebellious hair that he kept short because it saved fuss, and legs so long it was hard for him to find jeans that fit.

He'd been plowing through the garbage in Jared's house for two months. Garbage, strewn all over the floors, all over the house. Nathan had carved out an area in the kitchen and living room, and tidied and fixed, room by room.

The smell of coffee drew him downstairs. He dropped the weight, went down to the kitchen, and poured a thermos of coffee. He looked out the window. The wind was howling, and fat drops of rain were splashing on the window glass. It was shuttle day. How many of the old ladies would be willing to go out in this, he wondered. Still, if even one were willing, he'd be on the road. Nathan drove the shuttle bus between The Shores and Winterside once a week as a community service. There were more elderly people living in The Shores these days, their children in Charlottetown or other provinces. Even with willing neighbours to drive them, they preferred the shuttle. It appealed to their fierce island independence because they paid their own way. Nathan charged them a nominal fee, just barely enough to cover costs. Sometimes, he charged nothing at all, saying with a wink to Doris Sandler, "We'll put it on your account." And she, only pennies in her purse, would smile back at him, gratitude shining in her rheumy eyes.

He'd better have a look at the causeway to see if it could be crossed. He took the stairs two at a time, and from the upstairs window could see the surf welling up on the shore. If the causeway flooded, there'd be no trip to town today. The ferry wouldn't be running either.

He shucked off his dressing gown, pulled jeans up over his long, skinny legs, yanked on a sweatshirt, splashed water on his face, ran wet fingers through his hair, and his "toilette" was done. Hair stuck up from his head making him look as cheeky as his grin.

He grabbed his keys and the thermos off the kitchen counter, stuffed a donut in his mouth as he darted out the door, and jumped into his brand new, sparkling white Dodge Ram, bought from the proceeds of his souvenir stand and canteen at the ferry landing.

He drove with abandon into the banks of dirty black clouds billowing across the road, driven by the wind, rain spilling from them, so that his windshield wipers could not keep up, even on the fastest speed. For a kick, he did without them, and drove blind.

Murdo skidded to a halt just before they reached the causeway. Salt water was already splashing onto it. He darted a look over at the ferry, secured to the shore, not going anywhere. It should still have been running on regular hours on Labour Day weekend, the last weekend of the tourist season, but Chester Gallant had said he wasn't taking any chances with the storm. He took his responsibility for the boat and the people on it very seriously, and he would not be taking them out in "*this*," as he'd put it, even though "*this*" hadn't happened yet when he'd said it.

But it had started now, and Murdo froze. He couldn't keep driving, not with that wash of water coming over the road the way it was, every few waves crashing up over the buttress of rocks piled up to keep the water off the roadway. Murdo had had no idea, until this moment, that his fear of going over bridges included crossing this unstable causeway in a rainstorm. But it did.

Jamieson had been his partner long enough to know about Murdo's fear of bridges. He had tried to hide it from her, but she was a sharp judge of people. It was what made her a good cop. Small gestures, the cadence of the voice, were clues to the truth behind the words. She'd learned to pay attention to a sideways glance, lowered eyelids, a nervous tic – all the unconscious gestures and facial expressions that betray.

She knew about Murdo's fear, but kept quiet about it. She could have busted him, put him behind a desk, but she knew other things about Murdo. He was loyal. He'd never let you down, just so long as you weren't on a bridge. She read his fear in the set of his shoulders, the way his teeth were gnawing at his lower lip, how his hand came up to his mouth and he began gnawing on that, too. In the fact that he had stopped the car in the first place.

She unbuckled her seat belt and said, "I'll drive."

Suki dissolved in tears, her hair cascading forward and hiding her face, as she buried it in her hands. When Ian told her that Lance was dead, Suki threw herself at him, and her robe came undone. She wrapped herself around him, and he struggled to control himself, leading her gently to the couch, where he sat down beside her, patting her back and feeling useless.

He told her then that Lord might have been murdered. Her body heaved with sobs, and Ian didn't know how to comfort her. Perhaps another woman could help? He had no idea where Hy was. Gus? Should he call Gus? Even Moira Toombs might be welcome, so helpless was he with this sobbing woman, trapped in his boxer shorts and feeling ridiculous.

He'd been sleeping with a dead man's wife.

It didn't bother him that he'd slept with a married woman. Suki never took her marriages seriously, so why should he? Besides, he had come before all the others. Well, not exactly, not until last night, but he'd always wanted to, always wanted her. Those long nights he'd spent preparing their lab reports, doing all the work. He'd never said or done anything that might have changed things. He'd been afraid of losing the little he had.

Now he had her, and this had happened. Here she was, bawling her eyes out, and he was half-naked, unable to comfort her. The worst of it was, the sobbing excited him.

The dead husband. Maybe that, too.

She was free now. They were lovers.

Weren't they?

The wind had begun to blow and the waves were whipping up, dangerously close to the roadbed. The road crews had been in such a rush to get it repaired and completed before tourist season that they hadn't built it up high enough.

Murdo was gripping his seat, hands clamped fast on both sides of it, as they hurtled across the causeway. Water was hitting the tarmac from above and from below, waves crashing up and over the roadbed. The water was sluicing across the road, and the cruiser was hydroplaning.

Murdo wished Jamieson would ease up on the accelerator, but he didn't dare say so. Jamieson's feet were freezing and numb. They were bare and sliding around in the big billy boots. She drove expertly but too fast for someone in floppy footwear. A wave came up and broadsided the vehicle, and she couldn't press firmly enough to get the brake to respond. Helped by the wind, the car sailed across the road. Murdo had shut his eyes when the car had veered out of its lane, then opened them, to find the road was clear. They were still in the wrong lane, but no one was coming towards them. He crossed himself. They cleared the causeway, and Murdo relaxed.

Too soon. There was that tricky curve next to Junior Johnson's field, the one with the dung heap. It only took an instant. The curve came up seconds too quickly, Jamieson was going too fast to correct, and she drove straight into Junior's field and the pile of manure.

It had happened in an instant, but it seemed to the three in the car that the vehicle's motion had been choreographed, gliding to a stop in the heap of dung. They could smell the wet manure even before Jamieson opened her door. She had to push against the heap, and when she did get out, clumps of it fell on her. She swept them off with a few sharp motions. Murdo unpeeled himself from the car and grinned, as he flicked manure off his shoulder, and picked some out of his hair. Lili sat in the back seat of the car, her face still and serene.

Jamieson checked the trunk. It was full of stuff to help others in an emergency, but nothing that would help them here. She slammed the trunk shut, got back in the car, started it up, tried to back out, but the wheels spun in the wet muck. The car wouldn't budge. She barked at Murdo to push, but he couldn't get a good angle, and he ended up covered in more shit. It didn't seem to bother him.

Stuck, they were well and truly stuck, the wheels of the car dug deep into the wet earth. Murdo got back in the car and turned on the radio.

"My shed just got blown down..."

"I almost didn't make it up my laneway...it's running with red clay..."

"I've got the candles out and the propane camp stove. There's bound to be a power failure..."

"I never seen it this bad since...well, I never seen it this bad..."

Listeners were calling in to CBC radio, which had gone on a twenty-four hour weather watch. It consisted of taking calls from listeners, consulting occasionally with meteorologists, who said they, too, had never seen anything like it, and cut-ins from reporters flung into the storm and yelling over the wind hissing and thumping into their microphones. Jamieson drowned it all out with the police siren. Nathan heard the siren as he rounded the corner and saw the cop car stuck in the field. He stopped his truck, got out, and hollered into the rain.

"Anyone there? You okay?"

Jamieson responded by honking the horn, then leaning on it. Nathan grinned when he saw the cruiser nose deep in the manure pile. Jamieson rolled down her window. A clump fell onto her lap.

"Can you get us out of here?"

Nathan frowned. He had chains and a winch in his truck, but there was no way he was going to haul that vehicle out of there now. Not in this rain. He'd get stuck himself or cause another accident.

"No can do," he said. "You'd better come with me, back to the village."

Nathan had a healthy appreciation of feminine beauty, and a real soft spot for older women. His interest was piqued by Jamieson's severe manner, coupled with that porcelain skin. Flawless. Soft, you could tell. That raven hair, shiny, lustrous.

His attention was torn from her by the movement of a slight body emerging from the back seat. When she got out, they stared at each other through the wind and rain. Nathan and Lili, their eyes melting into each other.

He held out a hand. She took it, and he helped her through the mud, their eyes locked.

Lili and Jamieson squeezed into the cab of the truck beside Nathan, and Murdo jumped into the back. Nathan and Lili were glued together, unable to tell where one stopped and the other began. They had not yet said a word to one another.

Nathan drove into the rain down the Island Way, the main road that cut through The Shores. He was exceeding the speed limit in spite of the weather. He nearly hit a fox that dashed out ahead of him. He tried to pay attention to the road, but the girl beside him was all he could think of.

Jamieson wanted to tell him to go faster, but couldn't ask him to break the law. Anyway, in this backwater, clues probably weren't going anywhere fast.

She was wrong about that.

Chapter Five

The tarp over Lord's corpse blew away in the mounting storm, the yellow tape flapping on the wind. Billy was a wet, miserable, and lonely individual on the shore.

He was full of doubt. His stomach was grinding with anxious indecision.

They had told him to guard the body. He'd been doing that. He was tempted to pull it up and away from the water when the tide crept up within inches of the corpse, but he didn't dare. He had no idea if the water was at the high mark or not. Where were the so-called senior officers? They should be here by now.

Jamieson opened her eyes as they crested the hill to see The Shores spread out beneath them – a cluster of cedar shingle houses, mostly white with green or black roofs radiating out from the village centre, revolving around its once-strong heart. Now the eye was increasingly drawn to the new cottages along the cape. More of them every year. Soon there would be more people from away than villagers. The same as any small community on Red Island. It was happening to them all.

And no wonder. Red Island had more than its fair share of beauty and stunning coastline. Its landscape was like one of Gus's patchwork quilts – fields of yellow and green bursting out of the rich red earth, lined by spruce, meadows tumbling down to the blue waters that cradled this small jewel in the ocean. Who wouldn't want a seaside retreat here? And especially The Shores. It had the most spectacular shoreline on an island famous for them.

That wasn't the only difference.

Cut off by the unreliable causeway, it was adrift in time. It was an older island, where the ladies of the Women's Institute still wore dresses, each for a different purpose. The house dress, seen outdoors only when hanging the wash; the "good" dress, to wear to town to pick up groceries; and "Sunday Best," for church, wakes, and weddings.

Weddings. Jamieson's sister had been married yesterday.

Her head was throbbing and descending the steep hill made it worse. She was hungover. She'd got drunk last night, and had stayed at the beach house with other guests who'd overindulged. It was unlike her. She was ashamed, and hadn't dared wake anyone for a change of clothes when Murdo had called her. She'd slipped back into her dress, stuck her feet into a pair of billy boots at the door, and grabbed a man's jacket off a hook where it had hung for ten years. It smelled foul, but more fish than fowl.

She squinted into the day, dark clouds turning the sky a grim grey. Her eyes hurt. The car manoeuvred along the Island Way, one of the province's four officially designated scenic routes. Ahead of them was the village centre, which now consisted of one lonely white building with the requisite green roof. The school and the General Store were gone; the church had been converted into a smart summer home. The Hall was all that was left. Home of the Women's Institute, the Christmas Concert, and not much else. Kept up by federal and provincial grants, and the old-fashioned way – ceilidhs, flea markets, and bake sales. Pillsbury and Duncan Hines had yet to arrive in The Shores – birthday and even wedding cakes were still made from scratch. A village woman had once tried to sneak a "boughten" cake into a ceilidh, but was quickly shamed into feeding it to the local dogs. Many of the women still baked their own bread, and the ice cream at the annual strawberry social was always homemade.

Descending the hill, Jamieson felt as if she were simultaneously going back forty years in time, and facing the future. The demise of village life. The storm surges eating away at this fragile landscape. The place existed in a twilight reminder of the past.

So it was fitting that when murder came to The Shores, it was old-fashioned, too – caused by thwarted passion, love, and loss. Jamieson thought herself thoroughly modern, completely independent, but those old-fashioned passions would turn out to be something she could understand, though people thought her a cold fish. She'd had a reason to get drunk at the wedding.

"Stop! Now!" Jamieson pointed at the police cruiser parked outside Hy's house. What was it doing here?

Nathan swung the truck into the clamshell driveway and pulled to a stop behind the cruiser. He frowned. He, too, was wondering what it was doing here, and why Murdo and Jamieson were here.

Jamieson jumped out of the vehicle and hammered on the door.

Hy, just out of the shower, in terry robe and a towel wrapped around her head, answered it. She nearly burst out laughing at what she saw.

Jane Jamieson. In a dress. A dress? Jamieson?

Jamieson saw the shock reflected in Hy's look, and frowned, the expression doing little to crack the pallid smoothness of her complexion.

"You," she said.

"Uh…yes," said Hy dumbly, still stunned by the sight of Jamieson out of uniform. It was a bridesmaid's dress, that was obvious. It was purple, a colour brides instinctively choose for their bridesmaids because it looks good on nobody. This one was a soft lilac chiffon. Nothing about it, neither texture nor colours, suited Jamieson. It made her porcelain skin look green. Her flesh was mottled by cold, in spite of the jacket that smelled of – *fish?* And the billy boots.

Jamieson was trying not to shiver, to keep her usual composure.

Hy opened the door wide to let her in.

Billy was beginning to panic. The waves were coming too close. He didn't know what to do. None of his so-called training had prepared him for this. If he knew anything, it was not to disturb the crime scene. Billy kept thinking about the green pus in the wound. He kept looking at it nervously, until a wave washed up and over the body.

That did it. He had a plastic container of breath mints in his pocket. He emptied it into his mouth, squatted down, and scooped some of the pus out of the wound. He didn't know, but it might be important. And the way the water was coming up, that wound would be washed clean before help came.

He wondered where they were, the cops from Winterside. He looked at his watch. They'd had plenty of time to get here, but there was still no sign of them.

Panic shot through him. He started to head for the cape, to phone and see what was going on. No. He shouldn't leave the body. He came back. But what if no one was coming? The heat of panic turned to cold fear. He was well out of his depth.

He turned again and headed for Lord's cottage. Behind him, the waves were smashing on the shore, and sand-streaked foam gushed around the body.

Jamieson turned on the siren as Murdo drove along the Island Way. She'd asked Hy some hard questions about why she had the cruiser, but not much else. She'd wanted to get to the scene, so she'd demanded the keys to the vehicle and ordered Hy tthem to the shore when she got dressed.

The sound of the siren sliced through the village morning, waking anyone who wasn't already awake. Jamieson's stomach was jumping with excitement. Her case. She would make this her case. No one would get in her way thanks to the crisis in the crime unit. The chief had recently resigned and quickly died, for want of anything to keep him interested in life, and so couldn't be called back to duty when the crisis occurred. The crisis being that the next head of the unit was himself murdered. Or was it suicide? Were there sexual overtones? Jealousy? Passion? Rage? All the top people were on that case.

Even if they hadn't been, Jamieson might have been assigned to this one. In spite of its new popularity with tourists, her bosses didn't care about The Shores. Some doubted it existed. Most had never visited it, never gave it a thought.

The Shores had been in Jamieson's thoughts often since she'd first answered that call here last year. She liked to think it was a professional interest. It was more than that, but she didn't know it yet. The Shores had begun to claim her for its own.

April Dewey had just taken the tea cloth off her pan of fresh bread dough, two fat loaves nicely risen and ready to bake in the oven, when the RCMP cruiser screeched around the corner at the top of the road. The rain was pouring down and the vehicle laid tracks through the wet clay of the lane. There should have been clouds of pink dust billowing up behind it on an August-dry road, but it was soaked, and the car was ploughing through the clay, leaving deep ruts in its wake. Like driving through fudge, thought April, stirring up chocolate icing for her white cake. It was something new. She normally used a white butter icing, which Abel Mack had declared "the food of the gods." Instead of making April smile, it had made her frown. She was a devout Catholic. God's food was manna. If that seemed a bit boring, she tried to suppress the heretical thought.

"Wrong turn," said Jamieson as Murdo sped toward Wild Rose Lane. "We want Cottage Lane. Next one over, after the Hall."

He braked in a deep puddle. He spun his wheels in the water and murky red clay, trying to back up, until Jamieson couldn't stand it anymore. Her case. This was going to be her case, if only the fool would hurry up and get them there. Who knew what evidence might be destroyed by the delay? She grabbed the door handle, flung the door open, and stepped out into the puddle of cold, murky, red water, ankle deep. Both boots had a leak.

She strode around the car, yanked open Murdo's door, and with a sharp jerk of her head, said, "Get out."

Murdo hauled himself out of the car, and stepped into the sloppy puddle. As Jamieson leaned to get in, Murdo could see there were red clay splatters all over the back of her dress. She'd refused Hy's offer of a change of clothes, anxious to get down to the shore and the murder scene.

Hungover and in a dress. Murdo shook his head, and waded to the passenger side.

The reclusive woman who'd rented Ben and Annabelle's house was peering down at the shore from an oval-shaped attic window underneath the teardrop gingerbread that lined the gables.

She was still frowning from heaving herself up the attic stairs, steep and hard to climb. She didn't use the railing, because it might dirty her white lace gloves. She wore them to hide her right hand. There was nothing wrong with it that anyone else could see. If she'd taken the glove off, they might have noticed a small scar. A scar she couldn't stand to look at. Ugly. Imperfect. A terrible reminder.

She had gone up to the attic because she'd heard the siren – and seen the police cruiser threading down to the shore and Lance Lord's cottage. He was the reason she was here. He and Ed. She was staring now at the body on the shore.

Lance. Her face was streaked with a sort of sadness, but there was a strange satisfaction in her eyes. Lance was gone. Unexpected – but it made him hers. Forever. Now no one could take him away.

It was cold in the attic, which was insulated only by loose fill and seaweed stuffed between the rafters. The front wheel and handlebars of a fifty-year-old red tricycle stuck out of the primitive insulation, one mouse-shredded goalie pad lay on top of it, and a few rotting trunks, bulging with old clothes and books. Spiders and cobwebs clung to the beams, hundreds of dead flies ensnared in them. Her frown deepened. If she'd known she was living underneath this horror, she might not have rented the place. She had to stand up on a stool she'd found in the junk, because she was so small and the window so high. Grasping the window frame, she peered out again into the dark day, the wind and the rain and the waves, the thickening clouds. Now she could see better.

Her frown slowly turned right side up. A secret smile.

That was Lance, there on the sand. In his ridiculous get-up.

Lance. Dead. Dead.

She was sure of it. Her eyes shone with tears, and several spilled down her cheeks.

The smile remained.

Chapter Six

April Dewey watched the police cruiser pull a sloppy U-turn. Then she shrugged, turned away from the window, and put the icing in the fridge. She thought she saw a figure darting through the stand of spruce that separated her property from the elder Macks'. It would be Abel. He had an uncanny way of knowing when she was cooking, April thought. It wasn't uncanny at all. Abel knew when all the village social functions were coming up – and precisely when April would be cooking something special for any one of them. Abel had a sweet spot for April Dewey. It wasn't just her cooking. He found that odd smudge of flour on her cheek captivating. He liked the dimples, too, and her inviting, old-fashioned body. Just looking at her was a comfort to him. Pleasantly plump. Like her baked goods, rounded, well-formed, and quite delicious.

Stick-thin Moira Toombs was baking this morning, too – a dozen blueberry muffins for Ian. From her house right beside the Hall, she had a clear view of his kitchen and living room window on Shipwreck Hill. She'd seen a woman go in last night. Not Hy. As far as Moira knew, and she knew quite a bit, last night's woman had not come out. Moira was always spying on Ian, jealous of his comings and goings with Hy, of the nights Hy spent there, of the times Ian went to Hy's for dinner or took her to town and did – or didn't? – come home. Moira couldn't always stay awake to find out or get up early enough to see if Hy had slipped out of Ian's at dawn. But this morning she intended to find out if that woman, that statuesque stranger she'd seen slipping into Ian's after midnight, was still there. She popped the muffins in the oven, then went to fix her hair, its tight, permed curls already well-cemented with hairspray. She applied more against the heavy weather. She had to find out what was going on.

The wind blew up the east coast of the United States and Canada, stopping for nothing. Billy's head was down, his eyes closed, to keep the sand from his eyes as he emerged from the cottage. So he didn't see the awful thing that had happened. His world had been reduced to fighting against the wind shrieking inland, whistling through the trees as it stripped them of branches, pounding at buildings that creaked and groaned in the onslaught, battering him, punching waves up the shore, the wet salt spray dousing him as he descended the cape, the rain streaming down, so he was unable to distinguish where the water was coming from, the sky or the sea.

Where did birds go in weather like this? Gus wondered. When it stopped, perhaps there would be no birds at all.

And then it did stop. Dead calm fell on the village. The wind stalled, the rain sputtered, the sky ceased its shrieking. The houses stopped swaying and sat convincingly on their foundations once more.

Dead calm. A dread calm. Terrifying. Gus was unmoving, a statue of fear in her purple chair, coat on, handbag in her lap, worrying – where was Abel?

And then it began again, a fury unleashed, the terrible moaning, the high-pitched whistle of the wind, the hissing, pounding rain.

Billy opened his eyes and saw the most terrible thing. He ran from it, back up the cape, tripping over his feet, panic making him clumsy, dragging himself back on all fours, heading for the phone again. Dread calm. For him, it was dread calm. He dreaded the call he was going to make.

How was he going to tell them?

In the end, he didn't have to.

It was much worse.

The cruiser arrived as he reached the cottage.

He was going to have to tell Jamieson that Lord's body had disappeared.

Ian was anxious to go to the shore, but he needed a shower and Suki was in the bathroom. He was wearing just his boxers. He preened briefly in the hallway mirror, glad he'd been working out recently. His stomach was flat, his arms, legs, and chest well-muscled. If he only had just a bit more hair on his head. But Suki didn't seem to mind. She'd stroked and kissed his bald spot as enthusiastically as the rest of him.

Ian was standing in the kitchen, stuffing back a muffin, when Moira came in the door, her jacket soaked through.

She flushed red. She didn't think of him like that. Not like that.

"You cutting me off?" Suki breezed into the kitchen, wearing his terry cloth robe, loosely secured, a generous slice of cleavage showing.

It was Ian's turn to blush. Moira's face got redder, too.

Suki cupped Ian's chin in her hand and kissed him full on the lips. He crushed the muffin, and it fell in crumbs to the floor.

Moira turned to leave.

"Oh, don't go," said Suki, pushing Ian away and placing a hand on Moira's shoulder. "Ian, don't be rude. Please introduce us." Suki had seen Moira staring at her from the window when she walked up from Lance's last night.

Ian made the introductions, and the two women scanned each other.

A spinster of a certain age, Moira shopped the Sears catalogue, kept up-to-date with all the latest fashions, and wore them whether they suited her or not. She had the sallow complexion of someone who never spends time outdoors. Her hair, though damp under the hood, had kept its tight curls, texture of a steel wool pad and dull colour of a sick mouse.

Suki could see more than that. She could see hunger in Moira's eyes, hunger for Ian. Although myopic, Moira wasn't blind about Ian. She could see the way he looked at Suki, hunger in his eyes for Suki. And Suki? There was no hunger in her eyes. Only cold calculation as she looked first at Ian, then at Moira.

She grabbed a muffin, and spoke with her mouth full. "Mmm. Delicious."

This Moira might be useful.

"Gone? What do you mean gone?"

Jamieson was shuddering with cold in the flimsy dress, now wet through. Sand and salt spray were slicing at her bare legs, stinging them.

Billy was pointing towards the angry waves, grey and black like the sky, rising and seeming to rear back, before they thrust forward to attack the shore in a foaming fury.

Jamieson had never been so close to waves so high.

"Gone? On the water?"

Billy nodded numbly.

"You idiot!" Jamieson was shivering with fury and cold. She clutched the jacket around her, its smell redolent in the rain, punching up her nose, but that didn't matter. Her corpse was gone. She had a murder – but no victim.

"Get inside," she said.

She and Murdo were stunned by what they saw. The A-frame that they'd been called to last year at Vanishing Point had been full of antiquities – including a life-sized statue of Anubis, the Egyptian god of death. This – this was full of Hendrix memorabilia. Didn't people bring sand buckets, spades, and books to the beach anymore? Jamieson's eyes swept the room, from the cardboard cutout of Jimi Hendrix in the corner, to the table and the remnants of the meal. She walked over and scanned the offerings, making notes. Two place settings. Two bowls in the centre of the table. One tipped over and still containing a small portion of potato salad. The other held discarded lobster shells. She took a closer look at the dinner plates. On one, she could see clear remnants of lobster – the tiny legs sucked clean of their sweet, semi-liquid interiors, and the skin of a baked potato, greased with butter. The other plate had that dull sheen of being licked clean, so there was no evidence of what it had contained. The napkins were soiled and crumpled.

"Viagra." Murdo pulled on a plastic glove, picked up the pill bottle from the counter and slipped it into an evidence bag.

"What?" Jamieson looked up from inspecting wine glasses smudged with fingerprints, one edged with lipstick.

Plenty of evidence about who had been eating here.

"Viagra." He tossed it at her.

She caught it. Looked at it. It had a generic name on it.

"How do you know?"

Murdo blushed scarlet.

"Men know these things."

She shrugged and slipped the bag into a jacket pocket.

Hy thought Jamieson looked oddly vulnerable in the dress, bare legs, overwhelmed by the jacket. It hung over her slim shoulders. Jamieson tried to hook her thumbs into her belt, but there wasn't one.

The rain and the wind had eased off, a temporary lull in the storm's progress. They had gone down to the shore so Hy could show Jamieson where Lord's body had been, the same spot Billy had shown her, now covered in a wash of water. Scoured clean of evidence. And no body. No body, thought Jamieson. Who cared where it had been? Where was it now? Desperately, she looked out to sea, but she saw nothing, nothing but the water that had taken the body away.

"How did you find him?"

"I tripped over him," said Hy.

"Literally?"

"Yes."

"When did you find…trip over…the body?"

"Just before I called it in. As soon as I got over the shock, I called 911 right away…"

"And what were you doing here on the beach?"

"Morning run."

"Early."

"Always early."

"Do you know who he was?"

"Of course. Lord."

"No reason to swear. Who was he?"

"I mean Lance Lord."

"That's his name?"

"Yup."

"For real?" For a moment, Jamieson lost her usual professional composure.

"As far as I know, but I don't know that much about him."

"What do you know?"

"From away. Lived in the cottage there. I've never been in it before today."

"You went in?" It sounded more like an accusation than a question.

"Well, yes, to phone…" Hy's voice rose, defensive.

Jamieson nodded.

"Can you describe what you saw? The body?"

"He looked like Jimi Hendrix."

"And what's that look like?" *The cardboard cutout in the living room?*

"Bell-bottoms, an orange dashiki, lime-green bandana."

"Anything else?"

"An Afro wig."

"And?"

The two women stood, neither speaking for a moment.

"Well..." said Hy finally, wondering if she should mention it. It didn't seem credible.

"Well what?"

"I think...I thought..." Should she say? "Well, I thought I saw a lobster sticking out of the wound..."

Jamieson's eyes narrowed to slits.

"A lobster sticking out of his head? You can't have seen that."

"The seagulls and crows were pecking at it."

"At the lobster or his head?"

"Well, I guess his head, really."

Jamieson looked at Billy.

"Did you see it?"

He looked down at his large feet.

"No," he mumbled.

"What?"

"No." He looked up. His eyes shot an apology at Hy.

Hy sighed. Had she seen it?

"I'm not exactly sure...I...I..."

"This lobster," said Jamieson finally. "Where'd it go?"

"Well...it disappeared."

"Disappeared?"

Hy felt ridiculous. Jamieson doubted her and she doubted herself. What had she seen – or not seen?

"I'm just not sure."

"It was a shock."

"Yes, a shock."

Jamieson made a note of it, but didn't take it seriously. Eyewitnesses were valuable, but often unreliable, especially in the face of death, and if they were high-strung like this one.

"I have pictures."

"Of the lobster?"

"No – of the body."

Jamieson brightened. *Thank God. Something.*

"Where?"

"On my camera. Back at home. Billy asked me to take them."

He gave Hy a look of gratitude when Jamieson looked at him and said, "Good work."

"We'll be asking for those – the photos and the camera. For evidence."

"Of course."

"What else can you tell me about Lord?" Jamieson's eyes were scouring the water for any sign of the corpse. Her first bona fide murder case, and she'd lost the victim before she'd even started the investigation.

"Not a lot. He liked Jimi Hendrix."

"And who didn't he like? Any enemies?"

"Oh, yes," said Hy.

"Who?"

"Well Jim MacAdam for one."

"Jim MacAdam?"

Hy jutted her chin in the direction of the nondescript brown cottage between Lord's and the dome.

"Summer resident?"

"No, a local. Lives here summers, but has a farm back on The Way. Recent widower." And Gladys Fraser's "fancy man," Gus would say. It wasn't true, of course. What was true was that Gladys had always fancied Jim. Always. That made Hy smile, imagining Gladys Fraser, president of the Women's Institute and a bulldog of a woman, with a secret love.

"And why was this..." Jamieson looked at her notes. "...MacAdam an enemy of Lord's?"

"Well, Lord believed that the right of way down to the shore was his land. MacAdam thought it was his. They spent most of the summer fighting about it, with Lord putting up 'No Trespassing' signs and trying to stop anyone – everyone – from coming down here."

"So he had a lot of enemies."

"Well, yes, I guess. Most of the villagers..."

"Were you one of them? Ever have any confrontations with Lord?"

"A few. But nothing...you don't think...?"

"I always think. They pay me to think."

"...that I'm a suspect..."

"Everyone's a suspect," Jamieson said. It wasn't really true of Hy. But Jamieson liked to keep people offbalance.

A chill ran up Hy's back. If the last person to see a victim alive was the key suspect in a murder, the first person to see them dead was suspect number two. Surely Jamieson didn't think...?

Jamieson waited it out. Silence, she often found, brought out answers, sometimes answers to questions she hadn't even asked.

"Confrontations? Well, in a way, you could say."

"What way?"

"I never used to come to the shore by Lord's place before he started the nonsense with the signs. I came by Wild Rose Lane. I started coming this way when he began putting up those damn signs."

"Your reason?"

"Someone had to stand up to him. Some of the villagers thought he might have a right to close off the shore. I wanted to make sure that didn't happen."

Hy was torn between her fascination with the police proceedings and the desire to be sipping a tea with Gus and telling her the story, or up at Ian's, with the freshest most astonishing piece of news in the village – ever. She'd tried to phone earlier, but Gus's line was busy, as the village buzzed with speculation about what the police siren had meant. She hadn't dared call Annabelle. Annabelle would kill her if she called this early.

Kill her. It meant something different now.

"Who's in there?" There was an edge to Jamieson's voice. Hy hadn't been listening. Jamieson had asked the question twice.

"Where?"

Jamieson was pointing up the cape.

"I told you. Jim MacAdam."

"No. In that…that…dome."

"Oh, Ed Bullock."

Jamieson raised her eyebrows.

"*The* Ed Bullock?"

"Yup."

Interesting, thought Jamieson. Bullock. Order of Canada, just this year. For establishing fitness centres for crippled children across the country. Unlikely suspect, but he would still have to be questioned.

Jamieson's eyes turned from the dome back to the water. She'd been looking at the ocean most of the time she'd been talking to Hy, searching, searching for a body that wasn't there.

"He shouldn't be hard to spot," said Hy, adding, with a smile: "In those colourful clothes."

Jamieson looked at her notes. *A colourful corpse. A colourful, absent corpse*. She had to wonder, were they all nuts at The Shores? She turned back toward the cape. *Ed Bullock. What had brought him here?*

"Look!" Hy was pointing at the water.

Jamieson whirled round, her heart thumping. *The body?*

A wave washed it in, and dumped it at her feet.

A sign. "No trespassing," it said.

"Lord's sign," said Hy.

It was a sign all right, Jamieson thought as she scooped it up, of how things were going. Not well. She didn't need a sign to confirm that Lord's body was at sea. Like this case.

The rain began again. They went up to the cottage with the wind, mercifully, at their backs.

Chapter Seven

Hy was just leaving Lord's cottage, after Jamieson finished questioning her. She turned around at the door when she realized she'd almost forgotten her beach bag again. She scurried over to the kitchen counter and grabbed it.

"Just a minute," Jamieson put a hand on her arm. "What's that?"

Hy held it up. "Just my beachcombing. I left it here before."

Jamieson's eyes narrowed to a slit.

"Is that all?"

Hy looked scornful.

"Yes. Nothing of interest to police."

"Anything in there from around the body?"

"No. Absolutely not." They weren't, thought Hy. They'd spilled near him, but…well, this was ridiculous.

Jamieson held out a hand, and Hy gave her the bag. She examined the contents briefly. No, certainly not interesting. She couldn't understand picking up rocks and shells, bringing the messy outdoors in, to collect dust and make more mess. Jamieson tossed the bag back.

She let Hy go with a warning to be available for further questioning.

Hy braced herself against the filthy weather and opened the door. A gust of wind blew in and she had to force herself forward against it. Murdo had left just before, and was starting up the cruiser. He sprayed wet clay on her as he set off for Jim MacAdam's. Hy hauled her truck door open and slid in, just as Billy came out of the cottage, in tears. It seemed Jamieson had, as

Nathan liked to say, "Walked up one side of him and down the other – then did it again, she liked it so much." It was one of the reasons Nathan admired Jamieson. She'd done it to him once.

Hy rolled down her window.

"Need a lift?"

Billy shook his head.

"Got to go knocking on doors. Tell people to stay put."

It seemed inhuman in this weather.

"Climb in anyway. I'll take you up the road."

Billy got in and they passed MacAdam's lane just as Murdo was getting out of the cruiser. The outside light above the door was on. That was unusual. Jim never left it on overnight.

Hy knew MacAdam was Jamieson's prime suspect, but she couldn't believe he could be guilty of murder. She couldn't believe anyone in the village would be – not even the local thug, Jared MacPherson, and, anyway, he was in jail again. Out of trouble.

"I'll drop you off at the dome. You can start from there. Two fellas living there. Ed Bullock…"

Billy's eyes popped open.

Hy grinned. "Yes. *The* Ed Bullock, himself. And a fellow who works for him. Small, dark, suspicious-looking." Suspicious took on a whole new meaning now. But this fellow was always skulking around the dome. They were never seen in the village, either of them, and they'd been here all summer.

Billy was taking down notes only he could understand. The one word spelled correctly was "Ed."

"We don't see much of any of them, the tourists. Those two and the woman living at Ben and Annabelle's."

They were passing that house now, a big Victorian farmhouse, with double front doors and tall windows, the blinds down and curtains drawn as they had been ever since the woman had arrived. Another one rarely seen.

Hy let Billy out at the dome. She sat and watched him struggle against the wind to the door. There was a light shining out of one of the porthole windows. She remembered Big Ed pacing the front of his property earlier in the morning. She'd seen him do it plenty of times. So had other villagers who woke early. But that was all they'd seen of him.

Moira didn't stay long. When she left, Ian made coffee.

Suki was lying prone on the couch, robe undone. Her eyes were red, traces of tears still on her cheeks. He put her coffee down on the table and took her hand in his. She guided it to her breast.

"Suki…not now." There was shock in his voice.

"Especially now," she said. "Comfort me, Ian. Comfort me."

He was doing just that when Hy came in the door.

A long, low female moan. Just like on the phone.

A male groan.

Too late. Hy had spotted them on the couch.

"Jeeee-sus." She squeezed her eyes shut, clapped her hands over them. Again. "Jee-sus."

The pair on the couch flew apart. Hy opened her eyes. Suki yanked the robe back on. Ian, thank God, was still in his boxers.

"I'm…uh…sorry. I…" Hy began to back out of the room. She and Ian had always been in and out of each other's houses. It had never been a problem. Two single people, they'd each had affairs and dry spells. Throughout, they'd maintained a friendship. A good friendship…though there had been that kiss at the Christmas ceilidh…

Suki shook her hair and the thick mane fell perfectly into place, just a bit tousled in a sexy sort of way. She pulled the robe closed and stood up, advancing towards Hy with hand outstretched.

"Suki Smythe," she said.

"The famous Suki Smythe." It was out of Hy's mouth before she could stop it.

Hy shook Suki's hand. It was soft, moist. Suki smiled at Ian.

"I guess he's told you about me? How sweet. Just an old flame."

Apparently still burning, thought Hy. One late night, drinking brandy in front of the woodstove, Ian had told Hy all about Suki and his youthful passion. Hy stared dumbly at the woman. This was his long-lost love? This creature?

"Hyacinth McAllister," said Hy, finally. "Pal of Ian's."

Suki looked from one to the other and slumped back down on the couch.

"I'm not getting in the middle of anything, am I?"

Hy stiffened. She wasn't sure how she felt about Ian, but she didn't want this woman to have him. That honey-blonde hair. Those big brown eyes. Elegant hands with perfectly manicured nails.

"Of course not." Hy and Ian spoke at the same time and Suki giggled.

Sitting on the couch in his boxers, Ian felt even more ridiculous now than when Moira had come in. Moira he didn't care about. He would have been surprised to know she kept articles clipped from *Cosmopolitan* magazine under her bed in her spartan bedroom, articles of advice on how to catch a man. Him.

Hy, he did care about. Just how much, and in what way, he wasn't sure. But he didn't want her catching him with another woman wrapped around him.

He said the only thing he could think of.

"Coffee anyone?"

Warming to her task, Jamieson had forgotten how chilled she was. She looked with distaste at the leather couch, the bearskin rug, the trappings of a bachelor pad by the sea. She'd been trained to know that you could often tell more about a person from ten minutes in their environment than from being acquainted with them for years. Lance Lord's personality was screaming at her:

Lothario. Screaming too loudly. She thought about the Viagra in her pocket. She suspected he wasn't as manly as his environment suggested. Did that have anything to do with his death? No possibility could be ignored, and she made a note of it.

Like Hy, Jamieson was surprised when she saw the bedroom – the romantic four-poster, the feminine sheets. There had been someone in the bed. Next to the bed was the tube of KY jelly. Seal intact. What did that mean? She added it to the evidence bag.

She leaned over the bed and sniffed. A strong scent. She sniffed again, gagging on it. She knew it, she hated it, but she couldn't remember the name. Toxic? Something like that. Invasive. Cloying. One more time she sniffed, inhaling the scent into her mind, storing it for later, and thinking about a woman she didn't know, who might have lain there, doused in perfume, waiting. Sulky and unsatisfied. A reason for murder? People had killed for less.

Jamieson had an analytical mind, but she was also intuitive, and her imagination would probe the evidence, fantasizing scenarios that often brought her very close to the truth. She found it a bit disconcerting and tried to keep it in check, but here she was, almost able to hear the high whine of an electric guitar slicing through the cottage. It would be the wind, of course.

She straightened up and went into the living room, down onto the bearskin rug. She picked a CD, put it in the player, and the high-pitched guitar sound was no longer just a thought in her mind, but was screeching through it. She slammed it off.

A reason to kill? Oh, yes.

She almost neglected the woodstove. The glass was streaked with black. Something recently burned? She opened the door and found a sheaf of papers, burned off at one corner before the flame extinguished. She pulled it out, dusted it off.

Lance Lord's Last Will and Testament. She leafed through it. Her eyes opened with interest. Not valid. But interesting, nonetheless. Now she was getting somewhere. She folded the papers and stuck them in her jacket pocket, a woman's shrill voice ringing in her imagination.

"You fool! You have to name me."

He had. He had inserted a name. A date. Yesterday. Jamieson would be looking for that woman. Did she have a shrill voice? Was she the same one in the bed? Or was that, maybe, a different one? Two women, a man, and a will?

A reason for murder?

That remained to be seen.

"I think I'll pass on the coffee."

Hy didn't want to sit down with the lovebirds. She told herself she didn't care what Ian did. This was his long-lost love. Well, good for him. But she was disappointed that he couldn't hang around with her as usual, and go down to the shore and see what the police were up to.

"I should bring Jamieson some clothes. She may refuse them again, but – " *Anything to get out of here.* "And, oh – " She buried her face in her hands. "I almost forgot. It's Institute day."

"Don't leave," said Ian. There was pleading in his tone. It surprised him. Surprised Suki, too. And Hy.

"We should go as well." Ian was trying to disentangle himself from Suki. She had an arm clutching his neck and her legs lay heavy on his lap. "Identify the body."

"Identify the body?"

"Suki's his wife."

"His wife?" Hy's eyebrows shot up. "Wife?" she repeated. She looked at Suki. At Ian. What on earth did he think he was up to?

Ian looked embarrassed.

"It's a bit of a story," he said.

"I bet," said Hy. "Anyway, you can't identify the body."

"Why not?" Confusion in Suki's mascara-streaked eyes.

"No one can."

Suki and Ian looked puzzled.

"It's gone."

"Gone?" they chorused.

"Washed away."

Suki's face crumpled. She wailed in distress. Ian patted her shoulder.

For the second time that day, Hy wanted to vomit.

Chapter Eight

It wasn't the best day to try to bring meditation to the women of The Shores, but neither rain, nor hurricane – nor murder, it seemed – would cancel the monthly meeting of the Women's Institute. For one thing, the speaker had already arrived. Everyone knew that, because Nathan had phoned his mother to tell her. She'd phoned Gus. Gus had phoned Estelle Joudry, glad to know something her neighbour didn't know. Once Estelle knew, everyone did.

Still, none of them knew what Hy knew.

If she hadn't booked the program, she wouldn't have gone, not this morning, with the image of Lord's corpse still in her head. Even though she'd showered earlier, she was so wet and chilled that she had a long, hot bath as soon as she got home, a bath that, when drained, left streaks of red sand in the bottom of the tub. She didn't wash it out. There was no time. No time either to take Jamieson fresh clothes, as she had told Ian she would. Hy was always running behind time. "Can't catch up with herself," Gus would say. As the one responsible for today's program, Hy had to get to The Hall before their speaker came, to greet her and introduce her.

She picked up the phone, tucking it between her shoulder and cheek as she alternately dressed and dialed, hopping around as she tugged on sweatpants for the meditation session. She was trying to reach Annabelle or Gus. She needed to tell someone about Lord. When she called Gus, she got a busy signal. There was no answer from Annabelle, and her voicemail was full.

Hy could hear the storm – the thunder of the wind, the rapping of the rain on the window panes, the house creaking, the garbage and compost bins rattling against the oil tank, the eavestrough squeaking – and the shriek of the clothesline when the wind pulled it, so it sounded like a giant, and very angry, blue jay.

She put down the phone and looked out the window. The trees were bent over, the shrubs and bushes looking as if they were getting a blow-dry at top speed. Then the rain stopped. Hy flicked on the radio. CBC was still broadcasting wall-to-wall weather.

"The rain will fall heavily at times, dumping a total of 100 millimeters or more, in short, intense periods of rain on and off throughout the day. It's the particular characteristic of Hurricane Angus. Meteorologists are calling them rain bands. You can expect them throughout the day."

For what it's worth, Hy thought, as she punched off the radio. The weather reports came from Halifax and weren't always correct about Red Island conditions. And the weather at The Shores was often different from the rest of the island, its environment sometimes out of sync, like its geology and way of life. She just hoped the next rain band would hold off until the women were in the Hall.

She was sure the ladies would be there, in spite of the weather. Duty would bring them, but more so curiosity. Hy knew they'd all be wondering why she'd been driving the police cruiser through the village that morning, but she wasn't planning to tell them, not before the meeting, and not before she'd told Gus and Annabelle everything.

Nathan had taken Lili home to clean up and dry off. He'd started to make coffee, but she'd produced organic tea. He didn't care what he was drinking. They had sat in a comfortable silence, sipping the tea, their eyes locked.

Eventually they did talk.

"Lili." The first word she spoke to him.

"Nathan." His response.

They knew then, just from hearing the other's voice. Knew it.

Another sip. Another word or two. They were the same age, twenty-something. She was the yoga instructor who'd become popular in Charlottetown for her life-altering meditation sessions. He was an entrepreneur three or four times over. In addition to the canteen and souvenir stand at the ferry, Nathan ran The Shores' only lawn-cutting and snow-plowing operation. He'd established them all before he was twenty and even had a couple of uncles working for him. He was a trained paramedic but he didn't want to leave the village for work, so he volunteered his services in a rigged-up old camper van he'd made into a makeshift ambulance, complete with a dented defibrilator.

Nathan drove Lili to the Hall for the meeting. His eyes never left her as she glided down the pathway and through the door. As for Lili, her inner calm was unbalanced from meeting Nathan, and she understood for the first time what people meant when they said they had butterflies in their stomachs. She would have to find her calm again, before the meeting, if she was to lead the women in a meaningful meditation.

She entered the Hall, unrolled her mat, and sat down in the lotus position, hands perched on her knees, and began the long, low hum.

"Ommmmmm..."

Ben Mack watched Annabelle come out of the bathroom. She was wrapped in a towel, her long slim legs glistening with moisture. He couldn't understand why she thought she needed to get fit. He thought her body was perfect. She was tall, with legs that looked great in jeans or heels, or best of all, right now, with nothing on them. He crossed the room, and slipped the towel off her. She was not thin in the popular way – she had a well-rounded figure, with well-proportioned breasts, waist, and hips. Ben loved every inch of her – and swore he'd divorce her if she ever got to look like "that Angelina Jolly." He wondered why she was called jolly. She always looked grim and determined to him.

There was little chance of Annabelle losing her curves. She loved food. Getting fit wasn't about weight, she'd told Ben. It was all about flexibility.

She didn't need to work on that either, he thought, as he bent her back onto the bed in their "Love Shack" at Big Bay Harbour. It was a fishing shed he and his son Nathan, and Nathan's buddies, had renovated in the spring as a surprise twenty-fifth anniversary gift for Annabelle. Nathan's friend Dooley kept playing the tune "Love Shack" over and over again as they did the work one long weekend. He played it so often, that by the end of the weekend even Ben knew all the words, of which there weren't many. Ben was playing the song in his truck and singing along when he drove an amused and curious Annabelle to the harbour on the eve of Setting Day, the opening of lobster season.

They had always spent that night aboard their boat, and the plan was to do the same with the shed, but it was so comfortable, so well-equipped, they'd decided to spend the entire summer there, renting their beautiful Victorian home for thousands a week during tourist season. Exactly how much they charged, they were embarrassed to say. But they needed the money, with it costing five hundred dollars, or more, a day just to put their boat on the water.

The woman who'd rented their house for the last week of August had hardly been seen. April Dewey, who lived next door, said the blinds had been closed night and day. People reported rare sightings of her – always at dusk or dawn, on the cape, near the dome or down at the shore. No one had spoken to her. Only Gus. And she'd been sworn to secrecy.

It wasn't easy for Gus to keep what she knew to herself. But she'd given her word. She'd said nothing. Not even to Hy.

The ladies had been surprisingly willing to take part in the yoga session. Some had bought track suits, others had borrowed sweatshirts and sweatpants from their daughters or granddaughters, in a bit of a giggle about what they were going to be doing this month at "Institute."

The fitness craze had finally hit The Shores right on schedule – about twenty years behind everywhere else. It had been spurred by the arrival of Big Ed Bullock, the founder and owner of the Mind over Muscle fitness empire. Some of the men, like Jared MacPherson, had bought his system. Some, like Ben, wouldn't go near it. He was a big man. Not really fat. Just bigger than anyone else. When Ed had arrived at The Shores, Annabelle Mack had put Ben on a heart-healthy diet.

He'd gained weight.

Though he loved his wife, and couldn't bear to be apart from her, Ben had begun to follow his much older brother Abel in and out of April's kitchen, the pair competing for her leftovers. Ben would leave April's, the crumbs spilling down his chest from a mouthful of muffins.

Noticing the crumbs in the cab of his truck, Annabelle realized what Ben had been up to. She didn't say a word. She went back to feeding him as she always had – a steak, mounds of potatoes slathered with butter, and a small serving of vegetables, with muffins, cookies, squares, and fudge for "lunch" before bed.

The visits to April's ended.

Ben lost weight.

Murdo was peeking in MacAdam's front window. He couldn't see much through the slit at the edge of the blind. They were all closed. He tried the door. Unusually for The Shores, the doors – front and back – were locked. He had better luck at the shed. It was unlocked. Inside were tools, a lawn tractor, overalls, various kinds of boots, and, on the wall, guns and axes. Guns and axes – wasn't that the name of a rock group? Murdo supposed they should tag the axes as evidence, although none looked as if it had been used recently. They were clean, polished, well-cared-for instruments of – what? Death? There appeared to be one missing – a space below an empty hook on the wall.

Murdo made a note of number and type, and secured the door with yellow police tape, which immediately tore free and began dancing on the wind.

Billy reached for the doorbell. He felt funny. Not just because it was a bunch of cowbells attached to a leather strap, but it felt weird to ring any kind of doorbell. In The Shores, people didn't have them. He was saved – but not by the bell. The door opened before he had a chance to ring.

There stood the strangest man Billy had ever seen. Short muscular Leone, with his deeply creased face and broad, flat nose, dark hair that started low down on his forehead and was swept back. A large mouth and teeth to match.

"Can I help you?"

"There's been a death," Billy gulped out. Through the doorway, he could see Ed Bullock, sitting at a table, eating. Like a normal human. His hero. Eating breakfast, like anyone else.

"Ah, yes," Leone nodded. "Yes, we know…"

Billy's mouth came wide open.

"How could you?"

Leone gestured up to the rooftop gazebo.

"From here, we see everything. Come in. Come in."

If Leone was the strangest human Billy had ever seen, this was the strangest cottage he'd ever been in. Not just from the outside, but inside. Like a high-tech igloo. The walls were rounded on all sides, and covering them was a gallery of photographs of beautiful, glamorous women. Big Ed sitting in the centre of it all.

Big Ed. Billy was sure he'd had all sorts of beautiful, glamorous women, every one of those photographed around the walls. But he was wrong. Ed hadn't had all these women himself. Leone had helped him have them – in his imagination. Made him believe, for a moment, that he'd come back from Vietnam whole. Leone found the photos helped fuel the fantasy.

There was only one woman either of them really wanted and had never had.

Her. They'd both just been marking time on the way to her.

The time to have her was nearly here.

She'd promised it.

To both of them.

And to Lance Lord.

Chapter Nine

The next band of rain held off, and the thirteen women of Institute – minus one – were gathered in the Hall. Hy ran in, out of breath and only just in time to introduce Lili. As she burst through the door, her eyes darted around the room, and fixed on Annabelle and Gus. They were both thinking the same thing and nodded at each other. Hy, running to catch up with herself.

Hy was desperate to tell her two friends about Lance Lord, and gave them a wild, wide-eyed look they couldn't interpret. They noticed her agitation, her stuttering introduction of Lili Acorn. They guessed something was going on, but had no idea what.

"Your body is a temple," the lithe Lili began. Hers certainly was, thought Annabelle. Boyish. Small-breasted. Not an ounce of fat on it. She had dark black hair, cut shorter at the back than front, slicing forward in perfect geometry to skim her sculptured cheeks.

"It is a sacred vessel."

Gus looked down the line of thirteen chairs upon each of which, with the exception of Hy and the well-formed Annabelle, rested a plump posterior.

"It should contain only the rich goodness of life."

April Dewey was smug. Her baked goods contained only the best quality – real butter, whole milk, heavy cream, cake flour.

"Surround it with calm."

Pink can be a soothing colour, but the pink of the Hall had been an economic choice. Treasurer Olive MacLean had bought the paint, and she erred on the side of the Institute bank book. On sale. Much too pink. Soothing? Calm? No.

"Your body – your holy vessel…"

Annabelle glanced down the line of ladies. Holy out of shape, Batman, she thought, an expression she'd picked up from her son Nathan, who was prone to spouting popular phrases, even when they were out of date. As soon as his mother picked them up, he dropped them, knowing they must be hopelessly out of date.

The women were wearing new or borrowed sweatshirts and pants, all except Gus. She'd never worn a pair of pants, apart from dungarees the odd time, picking berries, and she wasn't going to start now in her eighties. There would be no rolling around on the floor for her.

None of the women, except Annabelle and Hy, would have considered slim-fitting leggings and form-fitting tops like the little instructor wore. After her speech, Lili got them on the floor, onto mats Hy had bought when Institute president Gladys Fraser confronted her, hands on hips, asking did she expect them to roll around in the dust? Hy had been tempted to say something about the floor being clean enough to eat off, but held her tongue and bought the mats. The women grunted and groaned their way down onto them.

Lili put herself into a pretzel shape with no effort, but the ladies grimaced with each inch they bent over or tilted sideways. Annabelle was the exception. She turned out to be good at it, and began helping Lili ease the women into bending their bodies into unimagined positions. Hy followed along, but was preoccupied with wondering where Lord's body was. Wondering what Jim MacAdam had to say. Wondering who the killer was. Wondering what was going on with Ian and Suki up on Shipwreck Hill. Like a cat, Hy was curious – always poking her nose where it didn't belong. She'd been the first up to inspect the dome when it was being built, the one who'd found out Ed Bullock was coming, and the only one who'd been almost inside his house. Hy enjoyed the shocked faces when she'd told Gus and Annabelle, Gladys and April and Ian she'd seen it. She liked to be the one with the information. But she was a washout at meditation. She wasn't alone. All the women were lousy at it. They lay rigid on their mats as Lili guided them through relaxing each part of their bodies.

"Feel the relaxation spread..."

Gladys Fraser couldn't relax anything. She was wound up as tight as she always was, anger pulsing through her body. Why had she let them rope her into this fool thing? Lying down at the start of the day? And such a day. With the wind and the rain, they'd be lucky to get home, and not end up sleeping the night on these mats.

"Relax your knees...relax your knees..."

Dolly Fraser, Gladys's sister-in-law, could feel only pain in her knees. She'd been putting off surgery, but would have to do something about it soon.

"Waves of relaxation move from your thighs to your buttocks..."

Madeline Toombs went red. She was glad her sister Moira wasn't around to hear that word said out loud in the Hall. Moira had begged off attending the yoga session, claiming she was too busy, tomorrow being "changeover day," the day the cottages were cleared out and cleaned. Some were already empty and needed to be closed down for the season. The real reason she wasn't there was that she refused to wear a track suit. She'd flipped through the Sears catalogue and hadn't found anything she would wear.

"Feel the relaxation spread to your stomach..."

April's gave a small growl. She'd had only a muffin for breakfast. She started to think about the fat content of her white cake. If she was to treat her body as a temple, did that mean she should keep the butter in her icing, or substitute it with margarine? The thought sent a shiver of anxiety from her toes to her head.

"Relax your back...relax your back..."

Olive MacLean thought if she could do that, she wouldn't be here. Lili's words only made her more aware of the nagging ache in her shoulder blades.

"Relax your jaw…"

This was one of the few times Estelle Joudry had ever been silent. She spent most days, all day, on the phone gabbing. Keeping her mouth shut made her feel tense everywhere else.

"…feel your mind like a smooth lake…"

There were no lakes on the island, thought Gus. Ponds, yes. She was sitting straight up in her chair, eyes dutifully closed.

"…no ripples…no waves…calm as the ocean…"

That set Annabelle off. The ocean wasn't calm today. Would *The Annaben* be damaged? It was securely tied, but…

"…you are completely relaxed…"

Rose Rose, the minister's wife, was not relaxed. She was concerned that, as a practicing Anglican, she should not be here lying on her back, seeking solace in some heathen belief.

Hy wasn't relaxed either. All she could think about was Lord. All she could see, that pus-filled wound. Who? Who would do such a thing? MacAdam? Surely not. A bear of a man – but still a neighbour.

As they lay there for the requisite ten minutes of deep relaxation, the ladies tried not to fidget.

April Dewey had decided on butter. Definitely stick with the butter. If her body was a temple, it should contain only the best ingredients.

Gladys was wondering when this would be over.

Madeline was thinking she'd have to hide her track suit from Moira, who didn't know she'd bought one.

Olive MacLean was taking peeks at the dust on the floor of the Hall. It would have to be mopped.

Estelle Joudry was wondering whether the hero of her favourite soap was going to come back as a vampire. He'd been buried yesterday, but he'd been with the show twenty years. She was sure he wasn't going anywhere. And the ratings would soar with a Dracula on the show.

Annabelle had gone from thinking about boat repairs to the accounting she'd shoved aside all summer and would have to do soon.

Hy was still wondering about MacAdam, Jamieson's number one suspect. Could he be guilty of murder? Maybe, if riled, but the wound was in the back of the head. That wouldn't happen in an argument. That was an attack. Could Jim get mad and stay mad long enough to do something like that? To ambush Lord, to plan to kill him? What was that called? Premeditated. The word was like meditation, which she was not managing to do.

The only truly relaxed people in the Hall were Lili and Gus. Gus had gone into a light doze on her chair, only to be woken as Lili brought the women back from wherever it was they were.

"Slowly, very gently…lift your right leg…drop it down. Lift your left leg…"

When it was over, the women creaked, pushed, and pulled themselves up off the floor, then staggered around, unbending their brittle bones, and headed thankfully for the kitchen. They produced a lunch of sandwiches, squares, cookies, and tea. Lili declined it all, eating bean sprouts she'd brought and sipping a special herbal tea.

She offered some to Annabelle, who, to be polite, accepted. She sipped it, and very nearly spat it out. *Tea? Nothing like it.*

At the end of the meeting in the section of their booklets headed "What I Learned Today," April Dewey wrote:

"Use butter cream icing."

"Don't lie down after breakfast." Gladys Fraser.

"Meditation keeps you afloat." Annabelle.

"There's nothing wrong with wearing a track suit." Madeline Toombs.

And Gus: "Estelle Joudry's mind is like a smooth pond."

Most of the women didn't know what to write. They did have a lot to say about it later, when Hy wasn't around. Another one of her weird ideas. Not as bad as some in the past, but still…

Nathan was waiting for Lili when the meeting ended, as if they'd agreed on it. She got into the truck, and he drove her back to Jared's, their hands locked together on the seat of the cab. They went into the house, hand in hand. They held on to each other all afternoon. Not for an instant did either let go – until Nathan was called out on a terrible mission.

"I…I…" Billy stuttered in front of his hero.

Big Ed Bullock. Imagine. Here at The Shores.

Big Ed did not stand up. He wiped his face with a napkin, crushed it down beside the plate, and inclined his head. Then he smiled.

Billy was dazzled by the gold front tooth. It was studded with diamonds, spelling out the logo of Big Ed's fitness empire: MOM.

"Welcome. How can we help you?" The tooth glinted.

Billy tried to keep his eyes off it. They landed on the photographs. All glamour shots. Blondes. Brunettes. Redheads. You could tell the colour of their hair, even though they were black and white.

"There's been a…"

All head-and-shoulder shots. Long curly hair. Straight. Short bobs. Big smiles with rows of pearly white teeth, or coy smiles, teeth barely visible. Big generous mouths, pouting lips.

"Yes, yes, you were saying, a death. Unfortunate. Most unfortunate."

There must be dozens of them. With mischievous, sultry, seductive eyes. Perfect makeup. Elegant necks, strung with pearls and diamonds. Did Big Ed know all these women? Had he – ? Billy blushed.

"I'm to ask everyone not to leave the village until police have spoken to you."

Ed smiled. Or was it a smirk?

"I don't believe we're going anywhere." He looked at Leone, standing behind Billy.

"Did we have plans?"

"None at all," said Leone. "Look outside." The rain was pounding down so hard, there was nothing to see. "Where would we be going?" He seemed to smirk, too. Billy felt a rush of discomfort.

"Names. I need your names, please." Billy pulled out his notebook. Flushed. "Of course, Mr. Bullock, I know yours." He turned to Leone, still standing behind him and making him feel more uncomfortable.

"Leone O'Reyley."

"Leone. L…i…"

"…e…" Leone corrected him, then rapped out the rest: "o…n…e."

O'Reilly, Billy knew. Or thought he did. He hesitated. *One "l" or two? With or without a second "e?" A capital "R?"* His pen came to a halt after the "O."

Leone, too short to peer over Billy's shoulder, peeked around his arm and spelled out the rest of the name.

Leone O'Reyley. Odd, thought Billy. It was, and not just the spelling. The name was a clash of cultures, like the marriage – a fiery union between Leone's Spanish mother and Irish American father.

"If that's all – ," Leone touched Billy's arm, and motioned toward the door.

Billy hesitated. "You can expect the police to question you."

Ed inclined his head again.

"Naturally."

Billy fingered the notebook. Dare he ask for an autograph?

No. No, of course not.

He slipped the pad into his pocket and left.

When the door had closed behind him, Ed and Leone stared across the room at each other. Neither smiled. Neither spoke.

Failing to find Jim MacAdam, or any sign of him, Murdo was bumping down toward the Shore Lane, going slowly so as not to damage the cruiser.

A short woman with a square body rather like his own was marching up toward him.

Gladys Fraser was braced against the wind and the rain, breathless and still quite stiff from her exertions at the Hall. In her hands she held a baking pan, wrapped in tin foil. Normally she would not have walked, and certainly not in this weather, but Wally had taken the car, she didn't know how to drive his truck, and she never missed a morning. No, not since Jim's wife had died in July had she missed one morning. She had convinced herself that he couldn't get on without her.

She would go there as soon as she'd finished her own chores, and he would be waiting for her, seated at the yellow Formica kitchen table, with the splayed-out legs, the cushioned seats in a swirl of yellows and oranges.

She'd prepare a pot of tea and, as she put it, "do" for him – tidy, wash the dishes, sometimes the floor, do a laundry, and then she'd sit down, feeling virtuous, and have her "cuppa" with Jim. She felt responsible for him.

"He's not there," Murdo rolled the window down and called out as she approached.

"What do you mean, not there?" Gladys's mouth set in that stubborn, pugnacious way of hers, staring at Murdo to make him retract his statement. It worked with other people.

He shrugged his shoulders.

"No sign of him. No sign of anyone."

That Murdo was a police officer didn't intimidate Gladys one bit.

She hauled on the passenger door and jumped into the vehicle.

"We'll see about that. Drive back there."

He did, because she might shed some light on the case. Who knew? She might find the guy, hidden somewhere. Perhaps he'd come out for her if he hadn't for him. Taking a quick glance at Gladys, Murdo couldn't imagine why.

Gladys was frowning. She rarely smiled. She didn't have that kind of face. Or maybe it was because she'd been jutting her jaw forward so long in defiance, that it had formed that way, into the face of a bulldog. She'd been angry almost since she was born, one of a pair of twins, who hadn't received the attention she'd wanted from her mother. The other, sicklier, twin had got it all, until she died at the age of six. Looking at the two of them, people said Gladys had eaten up all the food in the womb. It hadn't given her height, but it had given her breadth. She was stocky, square. She looked like it would hurt to bump into her. It did. Not quite like a collision with a brick wall, but she was solid. Physically and mentally, it was hard to budge Gladys Fraser. If something or someone were going to give, it was not going to be her.

Her only soft spot was for Jim MacAdam.

She could be seen, every morning "on the dot," as Gus put it, making her way up the cape to Jim's house. Her husband Wally was "glad to be clear of her," Gus pronounced. It gave Wally the few peaceful moments in his life, these visits up to MacAdam's. Wally sometimes wished MacAdam had married her instead.

It was almost the only thing he and Gladys agreed on.

She'd always leave Jim's glowing – not a word you'd attach to Gladys Fraser on a normal day. But people were seeing a difference, saying she'd changed, softened.

At the moment, though, she was suffering mounting anxiety. Elmer Gallant had died last month at just sixty-two. Took a heart attack. Died in his sleep.

Jim was in his seventies. In good shape, mind. But a big man, and he didn't care what he ate. Gladys was feeling almost as if she could take a heart attack herself, so hard was it pounding in her chest.

All through Jim's fifty-year marriage to Elvira, and Gladys's own to Wally Fraser, Gladys had nursed the childhood crush she'd had on him, affection that, once given, was not taken away. When Jim woke one morning to find his wife dead in the bed beside him, Gladys had stepped into the breach. Wally kept busy making duck decoys and other wood carvings that had gained him an international name in folk art. And whenever Gladys made a casserole, bread, a pie, or lemon loaf for Jim, she made one for him, too – so he was a happy man.

So was Jim, even though there were lumps of cornstarch in Gladys's lemon tarts, a soft doughy middle to her breads. Elvira had never been a great cook either, and anything homemade beat something out of a can.

Jim belonged to Gladys again, at least in her mind. The daily visits were pleasant for both of them. She tried to ignore his obvious grief over the woman who, she believed, had tricked Jim into marriage. Pregnant, she'd been. Or said she was. There never was a child. That was a secret grief Gladys didn't know about and couldn't understand.

And then there had been that fight with Lance Lord. Very stressful. Surely it was unthinkable that Jim might have done away with himself. Surely. He was a religious man. As Murdo pulled up to the house, Gladys shook the thought out of her head, unaware that the truth might be worse – that a man had been killed on the shore, and that her beloved Jim may have done it.

Chapter Ten

There were only three houses on the Shore Lane: Gus and Abel Mack's, the Deweys', and Ben and Annabelle Mack's, with the strange female occupant. Ben was Abel's much younger brother – ten other children separated them – but his whack of land was not, as you might expect, right next to his brother Abel's. They'd wheeled and dealed, and traded bits and pieces of land over the years, so that now April Dewey and her husband Ron, with the spiky moustache that made him look like a catfish, lived with their brood of six kids, sandwiched between the Macks. It was at Deweys' that Abel Mack could often be found when he wasn't in some secret place around his own house or land. He'd breathe in the sweet air of April's baking, accepting a few crumbs tossed his way – the scrapings from the cake tin, like the child he'd been at the beginning of the previous century, sitting at his mother's kitchen table. It wasn't that his own wife, Gus, wasn't a good cook. She still baked bread daily and turned out muffins and pies – but he enjoyed April's company.

Gus always knew when Abel had been at April's.

Hy had found that out when she once absently asked the question no one usually bothered to ask anymore: "Where's Abel?" He was never around.

"Over to Deweys'," had been Gus' reply. She peered out the window. "That'll be him comin' back now."

Hy peered out the window. She saw no one.

"How do you know where he's been, when you hardly ever know

where he is?"

"He comes back from there lookin' like the cat that stole the cream," said Gus. "Lickin' his chops. Oh, I know. I know," she said in that self-satisfied way she had.

So the Deweys were the Mack family's nearest neighbours on both sides – Abel and Gus on one, and Ben and Annabelle on the other. The three strips of land ran right alongside one another, all the way down to the pond.

From her side window, Gus could see right into April's kitchen – which was how she really knew when Abel was there. The Deweys' shed blocked a similar view of Ben and Annabelle's inside. It was just as well. Gus had lived long enough that there wasn't much that shocked her, and she knew, everyone knew, that Ben and Annabelle did not behave like the old married couple they were. Their marriage was still very much alive, with constant kissing and hugging and "all sorts," as Gus put it.

She had to content herself with the comings and goings out their front door.

It was through those doors that she had watched the latest guest move in. She thought, at first, that she was looking at a dress blowing away on the wind. But no, it was a person, a very insubstantial person, but a person nonetheless. A child.

As Gus later found out, she was no child. Just a child-size woman. Gus was quick to send Abel over with a plate of muffins and an invitation for a visit. At her age, she preferred not to go to people, but to have them come to her. And they did – paying court in her kitchen. Hy had labeled her "The Queen of The Shores." But the new tourist did not pay court that day. So Gus was left to wonder about the strange way she had of going in and out the door. She'd never seen anything like it.

Gus wasn't home when Billy knocked. There was no answer. He tried the door. It opened, and he poked his head in the "kitchen."

It was a holdover from the days when the woodstove was the focal point of any house – so that in the Macks' "modern" kitchen, there was a mustard-yellow electric stove, as well as Gus's purple chair, a moss-green sofa, coffee table, and television. All the "doings" of the kitchen were in the next tiny room, the pantry, which held the fridge, sink, and kitchen cupboards, the "new ones," installed in 1942. There was a dining room and a real living room behind the kitchen. Gus called it "the room," and never used it – only for company, big family gatherings or "putting up" a quilt. It was large and empty enough to accommodate a full-size quilt frame. It was there now. Abel had set it up, ready for the quilt Gus was working on, the Double Wedding Ring pattern of entwining circles. It wasn't ready to be "put up" yet. She hadn't finished all the patches. Piecing them was as complex as marriage itself, and it was giving Gus problems.

There was no one anywhere downstairs. Billy was reluctant to go upstairs. It seemed like snooping. What he'd just done would have been searching without a warrant anywhere else but The Shores. Here it was just what it was – looking for someone.

Billy heard the sound of a chainsaw outside. He went around the back of the house to find the shed door open. The chainsaw was on the floor. Billy touched a hand to it. Hot. But there was no sign of Abel.

Gladys could tell. She could tell as she marched toward the front door, Murdo behind her, she oblivious to the sharp wind, he with his jacket collar up around his ears, his hat pulled down, so that his cheeks bulged out and squeezed his eyes together. Gladys could tell that Murdo was right. Jim wasn't there. She would have felt his presence.

There was only emptiness.

It was funny that, knowing when he was here the way she did. She'd mentioned it to Olive, who'd laughed and said, "But he's always there. There's nothing psychic about it."

It was true. Jim was always there.

"And if he wasn't," Olive went on, "his truck would be gone."

That was true, too, but Gladys knew there was more to it. She knew, coming up the laneway every day, exactly where she would find him – in the house or shed, sitting at the table in the kitchen or lying down in the living room.

Wherever he was, she went straight to him, every time. She knew, just knew, where he was. She knew now that he was not here, but she did not accept it. As Olive said, he was always here.

Jim's truck was in the driveway, but it was no comfort to Gladys.

She looked up at the outside light. On, in the daytime. He'd never have done that. She tried the door, even though Murdo had told her it was locked. She gave him a sly look, and reached up to the overhang above the door. She held up a key. She unlocked the door and Murdo, giving a fleeting thought to search warrants, followed her in.

The kitchen was exactly as Gladys had left it the previous evening when she'd made a quick trip up, Wally being out, to see that Jim had all he needed to weather the storm.

It was exactly as she had left it. Only last night, Jim had been sitting at the table, a cup of tea in his hand. Jim was not there now. The teacup sat on the table. She picked it up. Still nearly full.

She turned to Murdo. "Something's wrong."

Murdo agreed. What was wrong was that Jim MacAdam had killed Lance Lord and now he'd got away.

Still, it didn't explain his truck in the yard.

When Murdo drove Gladys back down from MacAdam's, he told her about Lord.

"Someone killed him?"

"It seems so."

"Murder?"

"Could be." Murdo wasn't sure just how much he was free to say.

"He and Jim were not friends." It was a tentative suggestion, to get her talking.

Her face fell. Her shoulders drooped.

"It wasn't Jim," she said, fists balled up and staring at him with a fierce look, hostility in her narrowed eyes.

"I didn't say it was."

"As good as. You think it was him, don't you?" After the first shock of the realization, she had summoned her pugnacity. Murdo could feel the solid wall of her, almost as if he could touch her stubbornness.

"All's I know is, he's not here. Where is he then?"

She began to fold inward, the wall melting.

"I don't know." Her eyes lost their hard edge. For a moment, just a moment, Murdo saw fear in them, doubt.

Jamieson had scoured Lord's cottage. The sign and the will were the only evidence she had. She frowned at the red clay footprints inside the door. Too many of them, her own included, to gauge who had come and gone.

She went outside to wrap the front of the cottage in yellow tape. The wind yanked it from her hands, the tape flying free and slashing her face. She stood back for a moment, looking at the patch of sand Lord and his neighbour had fought over.

It was almost as if the sounds of their anger were whipping along on the wind.

"That's my land."

"No. Mine."

"I'll kill you."

"If I don't kill you first."

Was that how it had been?

Jamieson tried again to secure the tape. It kept lashing at her face, until finally she gave up. Hanging just inside the door, there was a key. She locked the door and slipped the key into her pocket with the document.

The wind wrapped the flimsy bridesmaid's dress around her legs. It had dried out while she was in the cottage, but the rain pelted down on her, and in a few seconds she was soaking again. The dress clung to her like grease and she kept tugging at it, pulling it away from her legs and her boots as she splashed along the lane. She didn't bother to avoid the puddles. There were too many of them.

Billy had been miserable about the task she'd given him, but Jamieson would never ask anyone else to do anything she wasn't willing to do herself. She trudged up to MacAdam's, head into the wind, the loose ponytail come undone and her hair whipping around her face. The wind blew under the jacket, inflating it so that it became like a sail, pushing her where she didn't want to go. The billy boots were blistering her heels, and she was aching to yank them off.

There was no sign of Murdo. Or MacAdam. She peeked in the glass window of the door. No sign of anyone in the house. She knocked. The door came open, and she slipped inside, though she knew she shouldn't. Jamieson went through the entire cottage. She noted the teacup on the kitchen table, the bed neatly made up, but above all, the silence of the place – different from the silence of a house whose occupant is merely out.

The silence of someone who has gone.

Was it just her imagination? MacAdam's truck was in the yard, but Jamieson's gut told her he was gone. *Where?* She gazed out over the capes, whipped by salt spray coming off the shore, the tall grasses blown flat. She looked around the room, the kitchen, and felt no presence.

Gone. He was gone.

Why? Because he had murdered Lord?

Then what did the document in her pocket mean? And why had

someone tried to burn it?

April Dewey, still dressed in her track suit, an apron shaped like a strawberry tied over it, greeted Murdo at the door. She was making pies for the ceilidh the following night. She'd invited him in, with a great fuss about the rain, flicking the water off his jacket, then removing it and hanging it up to dry off.

Murdo was soon relaxing in the comfort of a chair by the stove, a plate of fresh cookies, squares, and sliced bread in his hand. He'd told himself he had to stay because she'd been so shocked when he told her about Lord. She'd clasped her floured hands to her face and ran them through her hair when he told her how the body had been swept out to sea. Perhaps he shouldn't have told her that much, but he had, and it made him feel responsible for her, unable to leave.

Or was it the food?

No, he couldn't leave her like that. It was polite to accept her offer of "a bite of something," even though he knew he should be reporting MacAdam's disappearance to Jamieson. He hoped she was still down at Lord's cottage.

No victim. No suspect. Jamieson came out of MacAdam's and headed for the big Victorian on the Shore Lane. Part way, she slipped, and slid into a puddle. The back of her dress was covered in red clay. She tried to wring it out and made her hands filthy. She was close to tears of complete frustration at how badly this case was going, how out of control she felt. Perhaps that's why she banged as hard as she did on the next door. McAllister had told her about the reclusive tenant.

There was no answer.

Jamieson pounded again, harder this time, in case she couldn't be heard above the storm.

Still no answer.

She looked around the side and back of the house. When she turned, she missed the slight movement of a curtain in an upstairs window.

After she'd circled the house, Jamieson knocked one more time and then gave up.

She looked up at the dome, down at her clothing, into the wind and the rain and the thick black clouds rolling off the coast, and decided that call could wait. Billy would have told them not to go anywhere, and she would question them later, when she found something more respectable to wear. Ed Bullock was a recipient of the Order of Canada. He'd rubbed shoulders with the Governor General and the Prime Minister. She couldn't let the RCMP down. She couldn't question him looking like this.

The wind and the rain and the mud and the dress and the jacket that stunk of fish were taking their toll on Jamieson's confidence.

She turned away from the house and saw the police cruiser outside April Dewey's.

Murdo was still sitting by the warmth of April's old-fashioned wood range while the storm raged outside. He was comfortable, smiling between bites of food, chatting to April, and finding her absolutely charming, in spite of, or perhaps because of, the children. All six of them were in and out of the kitchen, grabbing cookies and muffins and complaining about the weather, hanging onto their mother's apron, running around her and using her as a shield from each other. She would give them an absent-minded pat on the head, shove a cookie into grabby, grubby little hands, flour dusting their faces and hair as well as her own and the floor.

Murdo found the domesticity pleasant, and April's sweetly rounded body appealing, as appetizing as the plate of food in his hand, that never seemed to empty. Every time he lifted a cookie or a slice of bread to his mouth, another would appear on the plate, like a rabbit out of a magician's hat.

"We're to tell everyone to stay put." He was talking through a cheek full of white cake and butter icing. Heaven. He was eating heaven.

"And I think you should do just that," she said, ladling soup into a bowl. "Wait the storm out. You'll only catch your death of cold. Then what good will you be to us? I'm not going anywhere, are you?" She shoved the hot bowl onto his lap. He winced. Then beamed up at her.

No. Murdo wasn't going anywhere.

Not until Jamieson appeared at the door.

Chapter Eleven

Hy, Gus, and Annabelle were in the Hall's kitchen, cleaning up after the meeting. Hy had said nothing about why she'd been driving the police cruiser, and none of the women had asked, except with their eyes. But Hy had avoided them, and they left in ones and twos, disappointed. When they had all gone, Hy told Gus and Annabelle everything – Lord was dead, his body clothed in the sixties outfit, the sign clasped in his hand, the gaping wound in the back of his head. That the body had now disappeared, stolen by the ocean.

"My Land." Gus opened her eyes wide. "Another murder."

"Well, now," said Annabelle.

"Still and all." A stock phrase Gus used to insist she was right and would not be budged. She stuffed Styrofoam plates and cups into a large green garbage bag. "I say they was murders at that cookhouse. Don't say they wasn't."

Gus loved to hear about what Hy had seen there last year. To pass the time on long winter nights, Hy had told Gus, over and over in fine detail about the dead man and the lobster eating away at him. About the crazy, dying lobster lover and the millionaire and the complicated relationship they had. Gus, who could trace the lineage of just about anybody on the island – through an endless list of aunts and uncles, cousins and nieces, nephews and grandparents – could never seem to get the relationship of those three people straight.

It was because they were strangers.

But Gus knew something about Lance Lord that Annabelle and

Hy didn't know. Was now the time to tell it?

"Jesus, it's Jamieson." Murdo scrambled to his feet, one cheek and one hand closing on a muffin.

"Jamieson?" April dusted off her hands on her apron and peered out the window – to see the bedraggled woman, fighting her way up the path in the wind.

"She's in charge of the case." Murdo spoke with his mouth still full. Was she – officially? It didn't matter. Where Jamieson was, she was in charge.

Three loud raps on the door. April skittered across the room. When she opened the door, she was impressed by Jamieson's dignity in spite of her clothes. April looked down at her own floured apron and track suit and wished she could rise above it.

Jamieson was staring at Murdo, from the hand squeezed in panic on the muffin, the crumbs going onto April's floor, to the full mouth trying to swallow.

April saw the look. "He's been questioning me," she lied.

"And you are?"

"April. April Dewey."

"About what?"

April looked puzzled.

"About what has he questioned you?"

"I…well…I…"

"No," Murdo chimed in. "I didn't have a chance yet."

Jamieson eyed the crumbs on his shirt, his jacket hung by the stove.

"So you've just been passing the time of day?"

Both Murdo and April lowered their heads.

To April, Jamieson said, "Follow us to the Hall."

"But…"

"No buts." The house had a good vantage point. This April might have seen something.

"But I have to call someone to come for the children."

Jamieson had a purpose in making things difficult for April. She didn't expect the woman would have much to tell her, but she would tell others they were dealing with a tough cop.

"Make it fast." Turning to Murdo, Jamieson held out her hand for the keys to the cruiser.

"We have a murder to solve."

And a victim and a suspect to find.

Both Jamieson and Murdo had the same thought.

Hy lifted the last dish into the drip tray. Annabelle grabbed it and began to dry it when Jamieson and Murdo came into the Hall. Billy was already there, having knocked on all the doors within walking distance and told people to stay put and wait to hear from the police. Moira Toombs had been his last stop. She had been unsure if she should go out and clean today and tomorrow or not. She'd been due to help set up the Hall for the ceilidh. She'd ordered Billy to go and help in her place. Used to taking orders from women, he had done just as she said. Now he was moving chairs and tables out of the way.

Jamieson, dripping wet, marched over to him. Her glare made him put down the chair he was shifting.

"Where's the community policing office?"

"At my house."

Jamieson rolled her eyes. "Where's that?"

"About five kilometres down the road."

Too far, she thought. Jamieson liked to be in the centre of things.

"What facilities do you have? Phone? Fax? Internet? Anything else?"

Billy looked down at the floor. "None of it."

"None of what?"

"Nothing. It's in the shed."

"What's in the shed?"

"The office," he said, his voice so low she could barely make out what he said.

"The office – in a shed?"

"It's the only room we had," he mumbled.

Jamieson looked exasperated. She'd have to set up here.

Hy, Gus and Annabelle came out of the Hall kitchen behind the main stage, from which a young Queen Elizabeth and bald but handsome Prince Philip looked down through red velvet curtains pulled to either side of a graceful arch.

The rest of the Hall was one large main room, with a hardwood floor, gleaming with layers of dance wax.

On one wall was a plaque to the brave sons of the village killed in the two great wars; on another, framed and mounted unevenly, a collection of "Best Float" certificates from the annual Harvest festival; and oddly placed at irregular intervals on another wall, various photos of celebrities – the premier, the local MP, and Shania Twain – all of whom had apparently visited The Shores.

Jamieson turned to the three women.

"Is there a phone here?"

They looked at each other.

"No." Hy reached in her pocket. "But I have my cell…"

Jamieson shook her head, irritated by the movement of hair on her shoulders. She liked to keep it pinned back in place, not straggling all over. She must look a mess to these women.

She did. Gus could barely keep her eyes off her.

A police officer? In a flimsy wet dress, revealing too much? Covered in dirt and a smelly old jacket and billy boots?

She needed a change of clothes, but Gus had none to offer that would fit.

"No, a cell won't do." There would be reports to file, McAllister's photographs to upload, backgrounds to check. Soon she would have to let the detachment know the body had disappeared.

Jamieson wasn't looking forward to that.

"I'm going to have to set up an Internet connection. I assume you don't have high speed. I'll need a land line."

"A what – ?" Gus.

"A land line."

"A what – ?" Gus repeated. Everyone knew telephone lines were up in the air, not on land. Her opinion of Jamieson dropped another notch.

"I think there was one. Yes." Annabelle pointed to the far corner of the Hall.

"Over there."

Someone once had the idea that it would be a good community gesture to install a phone for tourists staying in cottages without phones. Olive MacLean had since deemed it an unnecessary expense because everyone now had cell phones.

"It's not in service, though," Annabelle added.

The first thing Olive had done, on assuming her role as treasurer of the chapter, was to cancel the phone service and remove the phone. It was sold at their annual flea market.

Jamieson marched across the Hall to inspect the connection. It would do. A call to the company would have it in service, as long as there was nothing wrong with the line itself. She'd have to find a computer, but surely there was one in the village. She turned to look at the three women.

"Who's in charge of the Hall?"

Again, they looked at each other. Who was? No one knew who owned it. They couldn't find the deed. The building had, over the years, become the responsibility of the W.I. The women maintained it through nickel-and-dime fundraising, including bake sales, flea markets, ceilidhs and the annual Christmas pageant. There was the odd rental, too, for wedding anniversaries, family reunions, and the like. But who was in charge?

Annabelle shrugged. "Us, I guess."

"Us?"

"That would be Institute. All of us."

"I'm going to have to use it as a centre for my investigation," said Jamieson. "The Shores is cut off. I have to have somewhere to operate from."

A branch came off the old maple in the picnic area next to the Hall. It struck the large plate glass window, then flew off on the wind and lodged in the power line. The lights flickered.

"Where will you stay?"

Jamieson looked around her.

"Here, I suppose."

"Now that ain't fittin'." Gus pulled her apron over her head, suddenly conscious she was wearing it in front of an officer of the law, though this one looked like a wet rat. "We have plenty of room. My house is just across the way."

"No, thank you. It's better that I stay here if I can. It's, well – " A flush of colour appeared high on Jamieson's cheeks.

Understanding came at the same time, as it often did, to Hy and Annabelle.

Suspects. They were all suspects.

Gus didn't get it, and persisted.

"Now I'll not have it said The Shores don't know how to treat a stranger."

Hy put her hand on her friend's shoulder. "Gus, it's okay. Officer Jamieson would be more…uh…comfortable here."

"Comfortable? More than in one of my rooms? With the mattresses bought fresh for the tourists, time was."

"Time was" ten years or more since Gus had taken tourists. The beds had been well-slept-on by a succession of visiting sons and daughters and their families, nieces and nephews, and the odd stranger who stumbled in, seeking shelter from a thunderstorm. The Macks' door was always open to strangers in storms, such was Gus's fear of them.

"Them's good beds. With my good quilts atop 'em. Now talk sense."

It was Gus who wasn't making sense, thought Hy. When Gus said her "good quilts," she didn't mean any of the two hundred she'd cut and pieced and sewed and quilted herself. She meant a pair she'd bought from Sears. When youngsters came to stay with the Macks, she whipped off the "boughten ones" and substituted a couple of "old quilts" – beautiful hand-made creations of her own, less valued because she'd made them herself.

"I'm not havin' people lying on the floor here, when there's perfectly good beds…"

"No, really," Jamieson broke in. "McAllister's right. It's going to be a day and night operation. If we can just fix up a couple of cots…"

"A couple – ?" Gus looked bewildered.

"For the other officer, too," Hy propelled Gus in the direction of the kitchen.

"Come, I'll help you pack some leftovers for Abel, and we'll find some sheets and blankets."

"The other officer? That Murdo Black – and him a married man?"

"He's not a married man," said Hy.

"And him a single man? That's not fittin' either," Gus said, as Hy bustled her off.

"And who will pay the lights?" was Olive's first question, on being informed later in the day.

It wasn't just the lights, the term villagers used to refer to power in general. There was going to be the cost of the furnace. It was technically summer, but most villagers turned their heat on in August. "To take off the chill," said Gus, as her furnace pumped out an even eighty degrees on a cool August night. Gus still thought in Fahrenheit. She claimed she didn't feel warm in Celsius.

Moira loved finding out secrets. She liked knowing things about people that they didn't know she knew. It gave her a kind of power. She didn't use the information, but hugged it to her in silent satisfaction.

She knew, for instance, that April's husband Ron – he of the catfish moustache – was seeing a woman in Winterside. She knew because she'd been in town and seen them coming out of a bar in the middle of the day – *imagine, the middle of the day!* – drunk and falling all over each other. A month later, she'd been down to the shore in May for a bracing walk. She thought she'd be the only one there. It was a blustery, moody day with thick grey clouds rolling in on the waves, a sharp edge of chill on the air. There was a car parked at the end of the lane, and there was Ron, on his knees, doing something to a woman's leg sticking out the driver's door. The same woman, Moira knew instantly. She could tell from the bleached blonde hair.

Ron looked up and saw Moira. She whipped around and strode back up the lane, in righteous indignation. She didn't tell April. She liked the way Ron treated her after that – very solicitous, knowing she'd held his secret. And she liked the way it made her feel superior to April.

So Moira was happy when Suki showed up at her door. She was a rival for Ian's affections, but Moira could tell that Suki needed her, wanted to befriend her. She suspected Suki had a secret and wanted Moira to help her keep it.

The island weather had stripped Suki of her glamour. She was wearing a rain jacket of Ian's and a pair of his rubber boots. With oversized vanity bag in hand, she announced:

"Time for a makeover, Moira."

Chapter Twelve

Hy and Annabelle had made tea and offered some to Jamieson. She said no, she didn't drink on duty. Murdo and Billy were happy to have some and to inhale the muffins April had brought to her interview. Never having been called to a police investigation, she had been in a flurry about what to wear, what to bring. In the end, it didn't matter. She'd brought her blueberry muffins – they could be counted on for any social occasion. After corralling her brood to her sister's, she'd had no time to worry about her appearance.

When April gave her statement to the officers, instead of make-up, she had the usual streak of flour across her left cheekbone. Abel Mack may have found it fetching, but the fastidious Jamieson found it repellent. She declined a muffin with a frown. She didn't eat on duty either. And she didn't take bribes.

April made her statement. She had seen nothing, knew nothing. Jamieson dismissed her, having achieved her goal. April thought the policewoman was a...well, she wouldn't use that word, so how would she tell everyone? Murdo gave April an apologetic look as she left the Hall.

Hy and Annabelle sipped their tea in the kitchen.

"Suki." Hy shook her head. "Suki." She spat out the word and some of the tea with it.

"Yes?"

"Well – "

Annabelle said nothing. Maybe Hy was finally going to open up about her feelings for Ian.

"That is his long lost love? That…that…she's an absolute horror. She's…she's…" Hy was rarely at a loss for words. Then, with a big grin, she found them, "…our Lady of Lactation."

Annabelle spurted a mouthful of tea across the table. Hy laughed. Soon they were making fun of Suki in a duel of name-calling:

"Meet me in Saint Suki."

"Suki of the Bounty."

And more of the same stupidity. None of it was really funny, but their laughter gave them a much-needed release from the tension created by Lord's murder.

"Well," Annabelle said, out of loyalty, because she had not met Suki, "there's no accounting for some men's tastes. Mind you, I expect Ben would take a look at her, from the sounds of her."

"That's different," said Hy. "And you know it."

The whole village did. Ben was deeply in love with Annabelle. He had been ever since they'd met at a high school dance in Winterside thirty years before. He looked at other women – Ben liked women – but he never considered anyone but Annabelle.

"I know. He looks."

"Suki's gorgeous. But this is Ian, Annabelle. Ian. So reserved."

"He is a man."

"Oh yeah. Lust I can understand, but long-lost love? Does Ian even know the difference?"

Hy did. Hy knew the difference. For a moment, she was silent, thinking of him, her lost love. She no longer thought of him every day, and that sometimes made her feel guilty. But it had been twenty years ago, a past she'd learned to live with, a man she'd learned to live without. But Suki? How could she possibly qualify as a lost love? How could Ian's and Suki's bond compare to the tug on Hy's own heart when she thought of her own love?

Annabelle caught Hy's change in mood, saw the look in her eyes, sensed that her thoughts were somewhere else. Was she about to say something? Something about Ian? She'd never said what she felt about him, not to Annabelle.

Not to anyone. Not even herself.

But it was not about Ian that Hy was thinking.

The moment passed. Hy shrugged off the useless longing, as she had learned to do. It became easier every year.

When the women left the Hall, Jamieson began to fleece Murdo.

"Just how long were you in that woman's kitchen?" Her tone was sharp, impatient. Murdo mumbled something about meeting Gladys and going into MacAdam's house.

"Without a warrant?" Though she had done the same thing herself.

Murdo flushed bright red.

"Did you question her?"

Murdo began biting his non-existent nails.

"A bit," he mumbled through his right thumb. Gladys had scared him with her hard shell. When she softened with the fear of what Jim might have done, it scared Murdo even more.

"A bit? What's that supposed to mean?"

"Not much."

"A list. We'll have to make a list. Of suspects. People who can answer questions, like this…Mabel."

"Gladys."

"Gladys."

"Does she know where MacAdam is?"

"I don't know."

"Because you didn't ask."

"Well…no."

"Go ask now."

Murdo didn't move. He didn't know who scared him more – Gladys or Jamieson.

"Go ask," she repeated. "And then look for him – in the places she says he won't be. Billy, you go, too." She looked at Murdo. "If you don't want to get your feet wet, have him do the dog work. Then take him home to mom."

The two men looked reluctant. Jamieson tossed Murdo the car keys and stared out the window, the rain and wind pounding on it. It had a view of the road on one side, and the capes on the other. The rain dashed down on the slick asphalt of the Island Way, which ran a few kilometres past the village, beyond Big Bay with its sheltering spit of sand dunes, and then turned in on itself. One of the island's main roads and a prominent scenic route, by the time the Way ran through The Shores, it became a dead end.

The grey, metres-high waves were crashing onto the shore, mocking the ruin of her case, the case she had hoped would be the making of her. What a fool she was. She didn't even have a damn body.

Where had Jim MacAdam gone in this weather and without his truck? Perhaps he'd borrowed or stolen a vehicle. Clearly, he'd been desperate to get away. Clearly, he had done it, in a fit of testosterone-fueled rage. It was the most plausible explanation. Still she'd have to go through the tedious questioning of all these villagers and take down copious irrelevant notes, all the while waiting – for what? For the body to show up?

Her confidence was unraveling like the threads on the hem of her now torn dress. Like it, the case was shredding into pieces she might not be able to sew together. She didn't know what to do next.

She wanted a computer. She wanted her uniform. She wanted this bloody weather to let up.

"Lance Lord." Her voice startled, but did not surprise him. Hy had let herself in the door and was now pacing across Ian's living room, scratching her long bony fingers through red curls that the rain had turned into ringlets. Then she stopped. "You know who he is, right?"

"Of course I do. Mr. No Trespassing."

"But I mean, do you remember who he really is…was?"

Ian dragged his eyes away from the computer. They were blank.

"He was Lance Lord." He looked bewildered.

"Not just Lance Lord. *The* Lance Lord. I told you about him when he came here."

Sometimes, he thought, she was daft.

"Oh, Ian." She shook her head in frustration. Then smiled. She knew the perfect way to remind him who Lord was. So he wouldn't forget.

She charged across the room, shoved him aside, and rapped at the keyboard and swirled the mouse around. Alarmed, he fell back on his office chair and almost upended.

"L…a…n…c…e…L…o…r…d…" She spelled out the name as it appeared in the Google window. And up it came. Over and over again. Lance Lord. Lance Lord. There were a lot of sites.

Not all of them had anything to do with him.

"God," said Hy, "Look at this. It's some kind of sadomasochistic religious cult thing."

Now she had Ian's interest. She scrolled down quickly. He stared mesmerized at the screen, as she called up the next site.

"Lance Lord," she read, "*Kiss of the Demon Lover* 1972."

"*Planet of the Perfected People*, Art Film 1973," read Ian.

Hy: "*Futurefear. Mockumentary.* 1974."

They looked at each other. Hy pursed her lips. Ian shrugged. Neither had heard of any of them.

"Bingo!" said Hy, at the next and final entry: "'*All Around the House*. 1976-79. Popular Canadian TV series spoofing government and politicians in Ottawa. Lance Lord in minor role as cunning chauffeur to a succession of Cabinet Ministers. Gained him a small cult following.' Don't you remember?"

Ian pushed back his chair. He didn't watch television.

"I don't remember the TV show, but I guess I do remember you mentioning this."

"Guess? Mentioning?" They had been drinking brandy at the time, but still –

He noticed how Hy's green eyes darkened to emerald when she got emotional in any way. It was one of her most attractive features, next to her hair.

"So this is Lord?"

"Of course. I told you…I watched that show every week. I never missed an episode. It may have been thirty years ago, but…" Hy scrolled down as she spoke, and there he was, in full colour and thirty years younger. "Well, look."

Lord's younger but unmistakable likeness filled the screen – eyebrows and all. They were bushy, almost meeting in the middle. The full lips. The crystal blue eyes that burned with cold intensity. The teeth were different, not as white or straight.

"You're right. It's Lance Lord, all right. But what does it mean? If anything?" Ian took over the mouse, scrolling.

Hy rolled her eyes. He was acting like it was a new discovery. His discovery.

"It means he had a past and people in it we don't know. There could be something in that past that led to his murder. It might have nothing to do with anything here. I'm sure it has nothing to do with Jim MacAdam. It's much more likely to be some dark secret out of his past."

"Why must the past always have secrets, and why are they always dark?"

"That's the way the past works, dummy," Hy spoke as if it were a fact of life. And maybe it was. She hit print.

"I think it was someone we don't know, someone out of his past who killed him, for some reason we don't know yet." The photo and scant details of Lance Lord's slim acting career spit out of the printer.

Hy's eyes widened. "Or maybe someone out of his past we do

know. What about Suki?"

"I don't think that's likely." He didn't look at her. His mouth set in a grim line.

"Well how likely do you think it was Jim MacAdam? Because that's what the police think."

"Well, not at all, but…"

"No buts. I think we should be looking into Lord's past and Suki's, and forget about MacAdam."

For now, Jim MacAdam, like Lord, was missing – but he was about to make an appearance more dramatic and unforgettable than anything his rival had ever accomplished onscreen.

The rain continued on and off all day, coming as forecast in bands of rain. When it rained, it fell as a heavy curtain, slicing sideways, chased by the wind. The wind was strong enough to knock tiny Madeline Toombs off her feet when she came out her door with sandwiches and squares for the police. For Billy, really. She'd been watching him at her window. His good looks and height fascinated her. She barely scraped five feet and weighed less than a hundred pounds. Madeline picked herself up and pushed forward across the open picnic area between her house and the Hall, facing both the fury of the weather, and her sister Moira, if she found out Madeline was "giving good food away." Moira was mean, in spite of all the muffins she took to Ian. She'd been too busy to notice Madeline leave, too busy looking at herself in the mirror. She was getting all made up by that Suki woman.

The first thing Suki had noticed when Moira had let her in was the impressive grandfather clock that stood at the bottom of the stairs, grandly displaying the wrong time. Moira's father had rescued it from the garbage. Most of their furniture had come that way, but this was the best of it. It was her father's pride, even though it no longer did what it had been built to do. It looked good. He'd tried to fix it but the hands wouldn't stay in place. They drooped down, and told the time just twice a day, at six-thirty in the morning and evening.

Her father had made a point of consulting it at these times if he was home, and would smile in a satisfied way and say "right on time." Every time.

There was something of that same satisfied smile when Suki saw the clock and its obvious deficiencies. She smiled again as she watched Moira wind up the only other clock, which had run down overnight.

"I never know the time," said Moira. "That one doesn't work. This one runs down, and my computer, it's…" She searched for the word. "…digital time. I'm not used to it." The way she said it made digital time seem a personal insult.

Perfect, thought Suki.

Now, in the living room of the Toombs' modest one-and-a-half-storey home, Suki was yanking a comb through Moira's Brillo pad hair. Moira was wincing.

"You'll have to lose the perm." Suki pulled out the comb, and with it a hank of Moira's hair. Suki dropped it on the floor. "Loosen up. Let it go free. A bit of colour. Reddish."

Like Hyacinth, thought Moira. Red like Hyacinth. Of course. Why hadn't she thought of it? Perhaps that was the attraction for Ian. Still, here was this Suki, with honey-blonde hair. But no, she, Moira, could never be a blonde. Not in The Shores. Annabelle was a blonde and she looked like a tart. Anyone would think she was one.

"The hair will have to wait. We need Product." Suki said the word with a capital P. Moira felt a tingle in her spine. Product. Yes, she'd have some Product for her hair. Was Product expensive?

"Let's see the face." Suki cleansed and exfoliated Moira's dull complexion. She began to apply foundation. Foundation to Moira's face and to the story she would tell police.

"You know when I arrived, don't you?"

Like a grateful puppy, Moira nodded, causing Suki to streak the foundation.

"Oh yes, I saw you arrive."

Suki knew that. When she had passed the house last night, the upstairs light had been on and Moira's face pressed up against the window, looking in the direction of Ian's house. She'd guessed that Moira spied on him.

"And you saw me in the morning."

"Yes."

"Still there," Suki prompted.

"Yes, you were still there."

It seemed to be the right thing to say.

"Anything else?"

"No. You came about midnight…"

"Before midnight."

Moira's forehead wrinkled. Suki stopped applying the foundation and looked straight into Moira's eyes. "Well before midnight," she repeated. "I'm sure it was, aren't you?"

"Yes…uh…" She blinked her eyes as Suki painted on eye shadow. *Big eyes.*

For the first time in her life, Moira had big eyes.

"You said yourself you never know the time."

"Yes…You must be right. It must have been well before midnight."

Suki began to apply mascara. Moira couldn't believe how good she looked.

"I think it was about ten o'clock." Suki knew Lance had still been alive then. She didn't know how precise police forensics might be, but she wasn't taking any chances. Ian, she knew, had no idea when she'd come. She'd made sure of that, fogging his brain with all-night sex of a kind he likely hadn't experienced since he was a young man – if ever.

"And I was there all night?" It didn't hurt to cover all the bases.

Just in case.

"You must have been. You were there when I arrived in the morning."

"And that's what you'll say."

"Say…?"

"To the police." Suki had managed to eliminate the dark circles under Moira's eyes. She looked ten years younger. "You'll say I was there from about ten o'clock on – through the night."

"Well I didn't stay up all night checking."

Suki's eyes drilled into Moira's in the mirror. *Yes she did. That's exactly what she'd done*. Suki's eyes told Moira's eyes she knew it.

"From ten, all night – as far as you know. How's that?" Suki finished applying the foundation.

Moira looked in the mirror. She felt pretty for the first time in her life. She owed Suki.

"Of course. That's what happened."

Jealous as Moira was about Suki and Ian, the woman was fast becoming her heroine as she expertly dusted blusher across Moira's non-existent cheekbones.

Chapter Thirteen

"Excellent," said Jamieson, staring at the dead Lance Lord spread out across the screen.

Hy had brought her laptop to the Hall with the photos she had taken on the shore, and some fresh clothes for Jamieson, whether she wanted them or not. She did. She'd been shivering in the Hall, though she'd turned the furnace on, to a temperature that would have given Olive MacLean a hot flash. The dress was still wet and Jamieson was still cold. She had cleaned up in the Hall's bathroom and was wearing a pair of Hy's jeans and best Irish knit sweater, the one Gus had made her two Christmases ago. Still not very professional, but a lot better than that dress. She'd stuffed it in the garbage bin in the Institute room, giving it a fierce thrust she hoped would take all thoughts of the wedding with it.

Hy had made fresh tea, and Jamieson had broken her own rule. She'd accepted and downed most of it.

"Excellent," she said again, and squinted at the screen. That wound. Looked nasty. Like pus. Had it gone septic? That might help establish the time of death, often hard to pin down precisely enough to get a conviction.

She beckoned Hy.

"Thanks. Thanks for these." She pointed to the photos on the screen.

"Now all you need is to find the body." Hy grinned.

Jamieson frowned.

"I'd appreciate it if you didn't mention that." She realized it was probably too late. Hy's silence confirmed it. The whole village knew what senior officials didn't know – that the corpse had gone missing. Jamieson had yet to report it to the detachment. She was reluctant to admit to any weakness, even though it had happened before she arrived. She should've been here sooner.

She wasn't prepared yet to admit she'd lost the body. At least she could send photos. That would be a start. She straightened and clicked to connect to the Internet. It took forever to get on. Forever to access email. Forever again to send – a molasses slow transfer of digital data. After fifteen minutes, not even one photo had uploaded. She shoved her chair back and went over to the big window. From here, she could see the dome, like a pimple on the landscape, shining white in the black sky; and she could see the angry water and the surf surging across the sand and smashing up against the cape.

What a disaster. Her first case. A case she should own – and look what was happening. Clues had been lost, not just in the first twenty-four hours but in minutes – with the sweeping of Lord's body out to sea. The case should have been simple to crack. Jim MacAdam was her man. He had the motive, the strength, and the weapon, but he was missing. Gone like the corpse. She had no killer and no victim, no evidence – it was all gone on the wind and the waves.

Not quite all. She remembered the papers in the jacket pocket, hanging on the coat rack.

A gust of wind came slashing through the door and thrust little Madeline Toombs inside. She held her container of sandwiches and squares in front of her, the door swinging open behind her, creaking as if it would come off its hinges.

Jamieson retrieved the plate, and Madeline strained to push the door closed. She couldn't. Jamieson stuck the food on top of the clothes rack and pushed a shoulder into the door. She called Hy over. Even together they couldn't budge it. The problem was not only the wind. It was Murdo on the other side, pushing to get in.

"Give over," Murdo shouted. They only just heard him above the storm. The three women let go and a blast of wind blew the door open with such force that it hit the wall and dented it.

The four of them managed to close the door.

It opened back up again.

Ian ducked into the Hall.

All five pushed against it to close it. When it was shut, Ian smiled at Jamieson.

"Just came down to see if there was anything I could do to help."

He walked into the Hall, as if it belonged to him, as if it were not a centre of police operations. He looked at Hy's laptop with some of the distaste he usually reserved for her truck. It was a good laptop, but the set-up offended his technical sensibilities.

"You using that? Here? Better equipment at my place."

"Thank you, but no," said Jamieson crisply, returning to the desk and looking at the screen. The data transfer indicator had hardly moved at all. She frowned. Ian peeked at the screen. The image was Lord's head, a close-up on the wound.

"Good God," he said.

Then he noticed the transfer indicator. "Good God." He looked horrified. "It'll take you forever. Let me see if I can't hitchhike you onto wireless." Before Jamieson could protest, he sat down and began tapping at the keypad, staring at the gruesome photo on the screen.

Jamieson thought if she'd had her uniform, he would never have dared pull such a move. Still, he might be helpful.

"Bingo," he said. "I've got you on. You're hitchhiking on me. But get to it – it may not last long. What you can get on the hill, you can't depend on down here."

Jamieson sat down to send the photographs to the lab in Charlottetown.

"What's this one?" She'd reached the shot of the sunrise reflected in the water.

"Scenic shot. Personal stuff."

Jamieson stared at it. She stored it with the others on her flash drive, then erased the file. Hy scowled. It pissed her off, but she remembered she still had all the photographs stored on her camera that Jamieson had forgotten to ask for. Not that she was likely to want to look at them.

"Can I hang on to this?" Jamieson asked, indicating the computer.

"Well…I use it for my work."

"Just for a day, maybe two."

"All right." Hy wasn't happy about it. She'd been hoping to do some digging herself.

Jamieson turned to Murdo.

"And what of Mabel?"

Hy and Ian looked at each other. *Mabel?* The only Mabel they knew was a hundred years old, at least. Mabel Schurman. What could she have to do with it?

"Gladys," said Murdo.

"Gladys, then. What have you found out?"

"All's she said was he could be anywheres."

"And where did you look?"

"Around." He could hardly see a thing with his bad eyes through the thick sheets of rain.

"Status of the vehicle?"

"Still in the field. Nathan says the access lane's too wet to drive on."

"Status of the causeway?"

"Still flooded. Nathan says that won't change today."

"Status of the ferry?"

"Still not running. Anyway, Nathan says the operator, Chester Gallant's, stuck on this side of the causeway and the ferry's on the other."

Jamieson sighed. "Is there anything Nathan doesn't say? What about the other vehicle?"

"Billy just went off in it to knock on more doors too far to walk to."

Damn.

"We should go down to the shore again."

"I'll drive you," Hy volunteered.

"You've only got a two-seater. I'll drive as well." Ian's disdain for Hy's pick-up matched his pride in his "green" hybrid Insight. Even though it had been pulled off the market after two years. It was a manual. It was ugly. The parts were too expensive, as Ian had found out.

Jamieson sighed. She supposed she could have commandeered the vehicles, but she didn't. She felt as if events were in control of her. The loss of the body to the storm had seeped into her spirit, diluted her confidence.

The four of them left the Hall, hardly noticing Madeline was still there, sitting with her sodden tray of sandwiches, wondering if she should wait for Billy to show up.

Hy drove Jamieson. Ian took Murdo. The two vehicles navigated through the puddles and deep ruts of Cottage Lane, winding down to the shore. The rain had stopped again. They parked as close as they could to the pond.

They all saw it at the same time.

A body floating in the pond. Lord? Was it possible?

A second look.

A body floating in the pond. In colourful clothes.

Not an orange dashiki.

Blue-and-white-striped pyjamas, slightly yellowed.

They had found Jim MacAdam.

Chapter Fourteen

Ian was staring at Jamieson. She was well out of uniform now, stripped down to white cotton bra and panties, about to jump into the pond to retrieve the body. It was face down, the white polyester of the pyjamas yellowed, an old beige cardigan sweater floating on the water, the wool pilled. He was wearing socks and one ancient leather slipper. The other was bobbing on the water a few feet away. His body was tucked in behind a duck blind. He could be seen only from where they were.

They had gone as far as they could, their feet sinking into the marsh, like a giant sponge soaked in muddy clay, tugging at their shoes. Jamieson was still wearing the billy boots. First one, then the other, had been sucked off, and she had to stick a hand in the slimey muck to find them. Now Jamieson had shucked the boots, the sweater and the jeans. Hy was clutching them.

"Will you be okay?" asked Ian.

"I expect I'll be okay." Jamieson arched her back, and brought her hands above her head. She dove in.

"She's a triathlete," said Murdo.

Ian coloured, partly at Murdo's remark, partly because Hy had caught him staring as Jamieson executed her perfect dive.

She came up almost all the way across the pond, very close to the body. She couldn't budge it at first, and then realized he was hooked onto the blind by the collar of his sweater. She had to work him free, trying all the while to avoid the sight of his crushed and bloody skull. Not a drowning. The sweater had

stopped him from sinking to the bottom. Thank heaven for small mercies, thought Jamieson, as she worked to free the body. It became like a dead weight. She almost lost hold of him, but she was not going to lose another body. *No.* She used all the strength of her body and mind to roll him over and revealed the bloated blue face and cold dead eyes of Jim MacAdam, staring up into a grim sky they could no longer see. Jamieson put a hand under MacAdam's fleshy chin. She began hauling death to shore.
An eel, a large one, brushed up against her, and a wave of nausea hit her as she propelled the fat dead man through the water. Lord's rival. The man he had fought with every day over who owned the right of way.

Had it ended in murder? How had it happened? Lord taking a step forward, lifting the arm holding the sign, to strike MacAdam.

Jamieson let her imagnation run free, partly to distract her from this horrible task of hauling the corpse through the water.

Lord would have had to turn, startled by something behind him perhaps. Did MacAdam then raise the axe?

The sky rumbled as Jamieson stroked through the wind-riffled waters of the pond.

And struck Lord. Is that how it was? But then who had killed this one?

She dragged him through the pond, her mind racing with images.

Lord's body lay on the sand. MacAdam turned and ran through the tall grass toward the pond, heart pumping. Was he pursued? Had he dropped the axe and now someone else had taken it up?

It wasn't making sense. Not yet. But it would.

She reached the edge of the pond, where Murdo grabbed hold of the body and Ian and Hy helped her out.

Shaking with cold, and the aftershock of dragging the dead man through the water, Jamieson shivered back into Hy's clothes, grateful for the warmth of the wool sweater, wincing when the hard seams of the jeans scraped her wet skin.

They could not get him out. MacAdam was a big man, almost three hundred pounds, with heavy bones and a body mass index that should have killed him long before now. Their feet sank into the spongy ground, and so did the corpse, sinking further into the soft mush at the edge of the pond each time they eased up. Murdo thought it was like trying to land a big floppy fish. He'd brought in a four-hundred-pound tuna once. This was a bit like that, only without the gear.

But Ian had gear. He hurried to his car and opened the trunk. It was, like his home, equipped for a 72-hour emergency. A small generator. Flashlight. Flares. A container of dried food. A water cleansing system. Blankets. A top-of-the-line first aid kit. After what had happened the previous year with Hy and that lobster lover down at the cookhouse, Ian was determined to be ready for any emergency. Under the blankets was a fat coil of thick yellow rope with clips at both ends. He hauled it out. He attached one end to the vehicle, and unrolled the rest back to the pond.

Jamieson, recovered from her strange experience, having dismissed it as nonsense, grabbed the rope, knowing what Ian intended. Murdo and Hy had figured it out too, but they were frozen in disbelief.

"It's not elegant…" Ian and Jamieson manoeuvred the rope around the corpse, working it under both arms and tugging until it felt secure.

"Let's hope it holds." Ian gave the rope one last tug. Jamieson patted it to make sure it was tight.

Murdo crossed himself. Hy didn't know what to do. She wasn't Catholic. Not a believer of any kind – except, perhaps, in respect for the dead. Ian looked up, and caught her expression.

"Would it be better to leave him here?"

She shook her head, biting her lip, her eyes fixed on the dead face of Jim MacAdam. Pale. So pale. He'd always been so ruddy. She'd have thought a heart attack would be the end of Jim MacAdam. Not murder. Here at The Shores? It was unthinkable.

"I'll be gentle." Ian looked grim as he returned to the car.

The wind was howling and they didn't hear the engine turn over when Ian switched on the ignition, but they did hear the burbling sound of MacAdam's body being sucked out of the pond, as Ian edged the car forward, checking in his rear-view mirror for Jamieson's hand signals, encouraging him forward, forward, the body slurping up out of the pond onto land.

She kept signaling. Forward some more.

"Surely that's far enough," said Hy. She had covered and uncovered her eyes when MacAdam came out of the pond. She couldn't bear to look at him, but was too fascinated not to peek. Jim MacAdam, being hauled along like a beached whale. That's what he looked like. Only worse. Human. Covered in sludge. Pale dead face streaked with mud.

Nobody said beached whale. But they were all thinking it.

Jamieson signaled Ian to stop when the body had cleared the mushiest ground. He unhitched the rope from the car and helped Jamieson untangle it from the body. She rolled MacAdam over again. In the back of his head, there was a gaping wound, full of pond scum and marsh debris.

"Just like Lord," said Hy.

Jamieson shot her a sharp look. Hy and Billy were the only ones who'd actually seen Lord. She and Murdo had only the photographs to work from.

"Just like Lord?"

Hy nodded, slowly.

"Nearly."

"In what way – nearly?"

"This wound is muddy. The other one seemed…like it had pus

in it. You saw the photo."

Jamieson gave a quick nod, still not fully recovered from dragging the corpse out of the water.

A shadow flitted across her vision. A fox clawing up the dune? *Like MacAdam's pursuer – on all fours. MacAdam might have bent over to catch his breath, and his pursuer taking the advantage, sliced the axe down and shattered his skull.*

"What do we do with him now?" Ian was looping up the rope.

Despair clouded Jamieson's eyes. She squeezed the unwelcome images out of her head. She would never drink again. What a mess. The victim's body – missing. The key suspect, murdered himself. And the questions began again. Here by the pond? Or elsewhere? Transported here? If so, how had the murderer got MacAdam into the pond, when it had taken four people and a car to move him out? Who had killed him? Why? What connection did his death have to Lord's? If they hadn't killed each other – clearly impossible – who had killed them?

She had to answer all these questions, but the most pressing was what to do with the body.

"We can't leave him here on the ground. In this weather."

Ian shot a glance back at his car. He didn't want to transport the dead man in it. It wasn't so much that he was dead, but that he was dirty. He was fussy about his car. Besides, where could they take him?

"The cookhouse," said Jamieson, answering his unspoken question. There was a walk-in freezer in the cookhouse where the body could be stored. It was large enough. They all knew that from past experience.

In the end, they called Nathan. He had the van and the stretchers, a cot to lay out the body with dignity. Something MacAdam had not experienced in the last twenty-four hours.

Nathan came thundering down the lane, having left Lili puttering around the house, chanting "Ommmmm" as she wielded her dust rag. As he reached the bottom of the lane, a small clear break in the clouds sent a shaft of sunshine bursting through the gloom. The edge of the storm was passing almost as suddenly as it had arrived.

He saw the four of them, wet, bedraggled, and frowning, standing over the body.

"Jesus," he said. "Old MacAdam."

Then again: "Jesus."

"You said that." Hy had a grim smile on her face.

"Not about that."

Nathan pointed at the ocean. The surf was still high, but when each swell ebbed off, a strip of the sandbar rose above the water. There, in his garish outfit, was the body of Lance Lord, washed up onto the bar.

"Thank God," said Jamieson.

Nathan gave her a peculiar look. He didn't know what she was talking about. His whole world had been revolving around Lili all day, and he still had no idea there'd been a murder – two murders – at The Shores.

"Who – ?"

"Lance Lord," the other four chorused.

"But…"

"We'll have to go get him." Jamieson sighed. The last thing she wanted to do was strip down and get back in the water again. She looked at Murdo. No point. Son of a fisherman, his whole family took an odd sort of pride in the fact that they could not swim. Murdo had learned, but he wasn't good at it, and didn't like it. She looked at Hy. She was a good swimmer, but she and Ian were civilians. She couldn't ask them to retrieve the body. She began a slow walk to the water. Should she even attempt it?

On either side angry waves were raging, wave after wave crashing onto and breaking on the shore in a gush of white foam, then swirling, still angry, back into the sea. Straight ahead, where Lord's body had been tossed onto the sandbar, the waves parted at a deep hollow in the ocean floor. In front of the bar, the water was shallow, its progress slowed and the fury of the waves diminished. Yes, she could do it – she must. She couldn't lose him again.

"Now just hold on there, ma'am." Nathan had kicked off his sneakers, and was yanking his jeans off one leg at a time, hopping behind her, trying to keep up. She stopped at the edge of the water. Nathan's long skinny legs, white and covered with goose bumps, stuck out of his boxers.

"I'll go." He pulled off his sweatshirt, and, not giving her the chance to stop him, ran into the water.

"Nathan, be careful." Hy had come up behind them and yelled at him. She couldn't tell if he'd heard. He just kept plunging forward toward the sandbar.

"Be careful? It's only up to his waist." Jamieson was originally from Ontario. Most Islanders assumed that meant Toronto. But she was from further north, where there were lakes with no tide. She'd been here almost two years, but still didn't know all she should about the shore and how dangerous it could be.

"Riptide."

"But he's young, strong…"

"Doesn't matter. Riptide took a fellow down the coast a few years back. He was a Canada Games athlete and the water was only waist deep. It took him away. You can't fight it. You have to go with it. Nathan knows that. At least I hope he does."

Jamieson's brow furrowed. She squinted at the sea. Except for Newfoundland, there was nothing but water between here and Europe. She shivered. The cold? Or the enormity of the ocean and its power?

They all rolled up their pants, kicked off their footwear, and waded into the shallows to help Nathan bring Lord in.

He shook off the water like a wet dog and pulled on his clothes.

"Now what?" He looked at Jamieson. She'd been wearing a dress before. It had been a mess. So were her jeans.

Jamieson was silent, thinking about the cookhouse. Where else could the bodies go? The Hall? She didn't want to battle that one out with the women. And it was bad enough sleeping with Murdo nearby, without a couple of corpses as roommates. Besides, they'd start to rot quickly in the heated building.

"To the cookhouse," she said. "Into the freezer with both of them."

Nathan pulled a face.

"Not on," he said. "Can't do that. It's disrespectful."

"It's our only choice for now. You can't get across the causeway."

"I bet I could." Nathan's eyes sparkled at the challenge.

"Not with these two you can't." Jamieson's look dared him to defy her. Nathan admired her, but he wasn't cowed by her.

"Airlift?" He grinned into the glowering sky.

"In your dreams," said Murdo.

The five carried Lord's corpse across the shore, stiff as a plank, and laid it down beside Jim MacAdam. Joined in death were the two men who'd had murderous thoughts about each other, ferocious arguments that had broken the peace of summer, their anger now silenced on the patch of shore neither could claim anymore.

Lord had been felled with a grimace of anger on his face. MacAdam's showed fear.

"We'd better see if we can get into the cookhouse before we haul them over there. You stay here," Jamieson said to Murdo.

"I'll go with you," said Ian.

"Me, too," said Hy, though she wasn't sure why. Maybe to get away from death. Maybe to stick to Ian because of Suki – and Jamieson. She wouldn't – couldn't – call it jealousy. Ian was a friend. It was just that he had always been – if not exactly hers – well, hers.

There was a glow seeping out of the hairline crack around the door frame of the cookhouse.

Jamieson shoved open the unlocked door. Light bulbs, powered by a generator, glowed. There was no electricity anymore, no functioning freezer. None of the stainless steel appliances were working. The once gleaming kitchen was full of spider webs. The white and black ceramic tile floor and counters were dusted with red sand.

"A grow-op." Ian pointed to the back of the building, where there was a pond, dug into the earth and surrounded by natural island stone. The cookhouse had been a kitchen and the pond a place to keep lobsters happy and healthy before they were killed and eaten. The last time he and Hy had seen it, there had been a dead man, half-in and half-out of the pond, a lobster exploring his eyes and mouth for food.

Now there were thirty marijuana plants growing there. With a generator providing light and heat.

A hydroponic grow-op.

"Jared," said Hy. Jared MacPherson, the local thug who owned the cookhouse.

"But he's in jail," said Ian.

"I bet this is his hand reaching out beyond the cell."

At another time, Jamieson would have been thrilled with the discovery of a grow-op. Now, it just complicated things. Could she bring the bodies into another crime scene?

No. Anyway, the freezer wasn't working.

"Out of here." She ushered Hy and Ian through the door and into the wind.

Chapter Fifteen

"I can do it. I've done it plenty of times. Me and Dooley, we challenge each other when the road floods over..." Nathan stopped. He shouldn't be telling these things to a Mountie.

Jamieson felt herself weakening. The vehicle was right here, close to the bodies. Two cots inside. Besides, she'd crossed the causeway, hadn't she? That was before the peak of the storm, but it seemed to be easing off now. How hard could it be? Perhaps she should wait until she was able to communicate with headquarters. But she was impatient with waiting, with obstacles. She wanted to move forward. She could send Murdo along to pick up her uniform. It would be like slipping into her skin again. Jamieson wasn't a vain woman, but her uniform was a symbol to others, and herself, of her authority. She'd feel in charge, be in charge again. She examined Nathan. He seemed competent. He said he'd done it dozens of times, so why not?

Nathan had been lying. He'd done it in his all-wheel-drive truck, but never in his "ambulance," the jerry-rigged camper van almost as old as he was. And, while he and his friend Dooley did challenge each other with causeway crossings when it was flooded over, they'd never done it when it was this bad.

That's why it excited him. His eyes were bright, his grin wide, as he took off down the Island Way, the two bodies loaded into the back, and Murdo in the passenger seat, armed with a key to Jamieson's apartment and instructions to bring back her uniform. It was a maverick way to transport two murder victims to the morgue, but Jamieson couldn't see any other way. If forensics couldn't come to her, then she'd go to forensics.

The worst of the storm had passed, but the winds were still gusting to gale force and long experience told islanders that the surf would be wild for another day or two. Nathan turned on the radio to distract a visibly terrified Murdo, cringing in the seat beside him.

"RCMP advise against crossing the Campbell causeway. Police warn that it could flood over at the low point where the storm surge took it out two years ago. The entire Shores area is vulnerable in this storm. We could see another storm surge, with the ocean breeching the breakwater and flooding the roadbed."

Nathan punched off the radio. "Bloody mainlanders," he mumbled. The villagers often referred to the rest of the island as the mainland, especially since the unreliability of the causeway had cut them off and made them an island, too.

"If we get past that," he pointed at the wave of water engulfing the road ahead, "then it's clear sailing."

"Sailing?" If Murdo's fingernails weren't already bitten to the quick – working with Jamieson wasn't easy – then he'd have been biting them. Instead, he was gnawing the skin around each nail bed.

Nathan, meantime, was counting waves. It was part of his technique, learned from the movie *The Shawshank Redemption*. A group of prisoners had counted the seventh wave as the one that would sweep them to freedom. Nathan was counting for a small wave, one that wouldn't sweep them anywhere, but could be driven through.

The moment came. Nathan gunned the motor. Murdo shut his eyes tight. The camper slashed across the water-soaked road, sending spray up high on both sides, swerving from one side of the road to the other.

"Good thing no one's coming the other way." Nathan grinned.

His eyes were bright with pleasure, his cheeks flushed. His hands gripped the steering wheel. His gaze was confident, straight ahead.

"Whoaaa," he shouted and started to laugh as the truck nearly went off the road. Murdo was crouched down as low as he could go. The only thing he could see clearly was the dashboard. He didn't want to see anything more.

"That's it." Nathan yelled in jubilation. "Hang on." A wave smacked the side of the vehicle and washed over the hood. And another. And another.

Nathan was hooting with glee.

Murdo crouched down in terror.

It was the longest kilometre of his life.

When Jamieson returned to the Hall, she found Billy munching on the tray of sandwiches Madeline had brought. Madeline had lost her courage, and had shoved the tray at him when he came in, then disappeared out the door.

Jamieson dispatched Billy in the cruiser to secure the cookhouse and stand guard over the grow-op, until she decided what to do about it. Wet, worn out, and very nearly fed up, Billy dutifully did as told.

He was going from one crummy job to another. He was the dogsbody, and still in disgrace – he could tell from the way Jamieson looked at him. He hoped he would be able to resurrect his reputation.

He would, but it wasn't going to be guarding marijuana plants. That would prove too much of a temptation.

With a reluctance that showed in the stiff set of her shoulders, Jamieson had agreed to take a shower at Hy's house and borrow another change of clothes.

She allowed herself to feel grateful, as the hot water pelted down on her chilled body. She took a much longer shower than her usual short, disciplined one – luxuriating in the heat of the water, soaping until she was thoroughly clean, stepping out and wrapping herself in the generous bath towel Hy had provided, wringing out her hair in the sink and wrapping it in a smaller towel.

She slipped into a fresh pair of jeans and a wool turtleneck. Jamieson never wore jeans. She had nothing against them. She considered them practical and attractive, but had never owned a pair. She thought they looked peculiar on her. They did. Too rough for her smooth, crisp features – and not professional.

Hy had soup and hot tea waiting in the main room, which was stuffed with antiques, books spilling out of bookshelves, and a long harvest table that doubled as Hy's office. Her editorial work supplemented her nest egg from the royalties earned on her late mother's classic book about the back-to-the-land movement, *A Life on the Land*. It had been written with ink and paper that Hy's mother had made herself, and illustrated with charcoal from the embers of the woodstove. Recently, renewed interest had sparked a coffee-table version of the classic. It had been a dying mother's legacy to her daughter.

Jamieson remembered the story. It had come out when Hy had received a medal of bravery for saving the life of that lobster vigilante last year.

Jamieson had admired Hy's pluck. She relaxed. This woman was obviously not a suspect, and might be helpful in finding out who was. She knew everyone in the village, and being from away, wouldn't be as guarded as other villagers would be. Not as likely to be defensive. Yes, she could use her.

She sat down and surrendered to the soothing tea, flowing warmth through her.

"Tell me everything you know about Lord."

Hy told Jamieson what she and Ian had googled earlier in the day.

"Interesting." Jamieson took notes. "But I can check out those sites myself. I'd like you to tell me about his history here."

Suki, thought Hy. *Should I tell her?*

Suki was not history here. Not yet, much as Hy would like her to be. She was present, not past. And what did Hy know about her anyway? Jamieson would find out soon enough about Suki.

Let Ian tell her. Or Suki herself.

"I think I've told you about as much as I know. Owned that land for years I guess. It was Abel Mack's land. Sold at the same time as the land Bullock's dome is on. I forget the story about that. Abel made a bucket they say. Gus could tell you more about it."

"Or Abel?"

"If you can find him."

Jamieson's look sharpened. *Another missing person?*

Hy smiled.

"Abel's just one of those people who's always off somewhere else."

Jamieson nodded.

"Back to Lord."

"The land just sat there for years, the dune along the front slowly eroding. Ben Mack says it must have lost ten feet in as many years."

"Ben Mack?"

"Fisherman. Farmer. Abel's younger brother. He's the guy who led the protest when the government planned to evacuate The Shores after the storm surge."

Jamieson had seen the news coverage. The government had said it couldn't justify a bridge for such a small population, that fixing the causeway would be only a bandage solution. Moving a few hundred people made a lot more sense.

Not to Ben Mack, who'd spearheaded a massive protest backed by every resident of The Shores and beyond. The province had caved in. It had established ferry service as "a temporary measure," and agreed to fix the causeway.

As it turned out, everything about the route to The Shores had remained temporary.

"Would Ben know about this land deal?"

"Maybe. Maybe not. I think Gus would be your most reliable source."

Jamieson nodded.

"Go on. What else about Lord?"

"Well, after all those years, he finally came here last summer and began to build. Came back this summer and finished the job. Started sticking up signs preventing people from going down to the shore, just like I said before."

"So he could have had lots of enemies."

Hy sat down beside Jamieson. "Sure." She leaned forward. "But no one here who'd kill him."

"No one?"

"Not Jim MacAdam."

"Why not?"

"Well, he…he…he's Jim…and…"

"Also a hunter."

"Yes, but…"

"Guns in his shed."

"Lord wasn't killed with a gun. And Jim's dead, too."

"Doesn't mean he didn't do it. And there were axes in the shed."

Like a terrier, thought Hy, Jamieson was sticking to her conviction that Jim MacAdam had killed Lord, even though now it didn't make sense.

"But that would mean – "

"Yes. That we're looking for two killers."

That didn't make sense either. One killer in this tiny village was hard to believe. But two? Hy shook her head.

"No. They died the same way. Same wound."

"You said the wounds looked different."

"But I didn't mean – "

"Well, we'll let forensics figure that out for us. What more can you tell me – about possible suspects?"

"I think we should go see Gus."

Hy didn't like being the lone focus of Jamieson's questioning. She didn't want the communal village finger pointing at her for blaming anyone. Besides, Gus knew everyone. Maybe she could help Jamieson out, and set her straight about Jim MacAdam.

Ian was grateful to find Suki asleep when he got home. She lay carelessly on the bed, the sheet covering only part of her, her long legs and one breast exposed. He tiptoed through the bedroom, careful not to wake her. Not up to another encounter.

Not yet. Not ever?

Had he had his fill so quickly? Was she not the love of his life, or was she just the girl who got away? He hoped she wouldn't wake up. He wanted to shower, then get on the computer and find out more about Lord and Bullock.

"Abel never should have sold it. Soon we'll have them cottages all along the shore. The view won't be the view anymore. And look what I have to look at," Gus gestured with her thumb toward the shore.

"That dome. It was him bought the land, the two chunks." It sounded like "jonks" when she said it.

"Bullock?" Jamieson looked up from her notebook with interest.

"The muscle man. From the Boston States. Paid a good price 'n' all. Abel's canny and he knew the value of it. Not the value today, mind. Who would ever have thought lots would go so high? But it was a good price then."

"Then?"

"That was fifteen years ago, not a day less."

"And what did he pay?"

"I couldn't say. You'd have to ask Abel that, and I'm not sure he could say either. There was so much talk about the price, and Abel was keeping his mouth shut about it, which just made people think he'd made a ton of money. They kep' throwin' numbers at him. I think he forgot what he ended up gettin' for it."

"There must be papers."

"Happen there are." Gus flushed. She was the one who kept the accounts. She didn't like doing it. "The accounts" was a dime-store coiled exercise book, with spotty entries in pencil, mixed with recipes. Their legal documents were safely tucked away somewhere, possibly in a box under the stairs.

"Anyroad, it was a lot of money, we thought back then. And he paid cash. Where did a fella make that kind of money out of mussels? 'Cause that's what we thought it was. The kind you eat – if you don't know any better. Turns out it was that muscle training. Course we all know that now. That's where his money come from."

"Two chunks, you said he bought two chunks of land. His own and Lord's."

Gus nodded her head several times.

"Yes. He wanted the bit in between, but that was MacAdam's. MacAdam said he went after him every year for it. I don't know why. The fella hadn't built on his own land, and didn't until this year."

"When did Lord get hold of his piece?"

"The muscle fella give it him. Just give it him. No money. Abel never could understand that."

"When was that?"

"Mebbe when Mr. Bullock bought it, I don't know. You'd have to ask Abel that."

"And where is he?"

"I think he's gone over the road."

Her tone indicated that Jamieson would know where "over the

road" was. She didn't, but Gus just added, "He should be around shortly."

Hy snorted. If Jamieson expected Abel to be around shortly, she'd be waiting a long time.

Billy was bored. He hated being stuck here, nursemaid to a hundred thousand dollars worth of marijuana plants. Billy had done the calculation, estimating three thousand dollars per plant once they grew to maturity.

Billy smoked pot, but he hadn't since getting this position. He was tempted now. They'd never miss a few leaves. He could dry it at home in the oven.

He was sitting on one of the blocks of sandstone edging the artificial pond. He reached out a hand to pluck off a stem, but pulled back. What if he were found out? To take his mind off it, he decided to get some fresh air.

He opened the door, and what he saw made him step out and leave it banging open and shut behind him.

Gus had been working on a book about the village, containing the names and birth dates of every one of the villagers, whatever she knew about their ancestors, who they were related to and what they'd done in and for this community over a span of nearly two hundred years. She had collected historical highlights – the first car at The Shores, a set of triplets born back in the nineteen-fifties, a bean growing out of a wound in a farm worker's forehead following a fall in a field during spring planting.

The "book" was a clutch of mismatched papers, with photographs spilling out of it, pictures of sleighs and horses and buildings that no longer existed, except in the minds of the villagers. Tourists asking for directions would look puzzled when told, "Take a turn right there where the school is." The helpful villager would point to an empty lot.

Hy had been trying to get Gus to organize the book. She dove down to retrieve some papers that had floated to the floor when Gus opened the manuscript and flipped through it, rearranging papers as she went. Hy sighed. In the wrong order again. Yet Gus always seemed to be able to find what she was looking for.

Gus wanted to publish it on the community's bicentennial. That was just two years away, and Hy despaired that Gus would ever organize it in time. She'd tried to get her to keep the papers in order, by explaining, "It's like pieces of a quilt. The pages all fit in a certain pattern." Hy thought it was a brilliant explanation, but it didn't work. Gus was tidy about her sewing, but not about writing.

She was using the manuscript now to jog her memory for Jamieson, although she was unconvinced about Jamieson's authority, given her appearance. Gus eyed her over the top of her glasses. Was that the sweater she'd knitted for Hy a few years back? Well, the sweater at least was respectable, but it didn't make this woman look like a police officer.

"Elmore Gaudet." Gus pronounced it 'Goody.' "You'll not be wanting him."

Jamieson looked up from her notebook.

"He's older than me. Ninety-two next month."

It was a slow process, Gus reminiscing through the village names and bloodlines.

"Now Norah Blacquiere. She'd be the niece of Albert. Poor Albert. The woman he loved took off to the Boston States for work and never came back. He grieved for her for forty years. Then she married late in life. One day Abel found him hanging by the neck in his barn."

"Well then, he won't be a suspect," said Hy.

"'Spect not," said Gus, with a smile. "There's those two poor old souls Anna Black and Wayne MacAleer. Brother and sister – only didn't know it until their weddin' day. Both been given up for adoption different times, never met until they was older, fell in love, and then someone finds out they're brother and sister on their weddin' day. Couldn't marry, but they live together. Only knows what they get up to."

"Not much anymore," said Hy.

Gus nodded. "Yes, they upwards of eighty."

Gus was a good storyteller, but she was wearing Jamieson down.

"Let's start by eliminating everyone over seventy," she said.

After that, it went more quickly. Half the villagers were over seventy. Only a small number were of prime axe-wielding age. Young people didn't stay in the village anymore. All the potential axe murderers got out as soon as they could, and went to the big city.

Chapter Sixteen

Alyssa didn't walk; she floated, so that it seemed as if there were no stairs, only a smooth ramp that she glided down, like a model on the runway, descending with no jarring movements as each tiny foot slipped onto each step. Her dress was a loose, shapeless swath of soft-coloured fabrics that swirled around her insubstantial body, flowed with her easy movement, occasionally billowing up and then collapsing as small drafts of air caught up in the flimsy fabric.

That's what made Billy think he'd seen a piece of clothing emerge from the front door of the house, then go back in.

Then come out again. Then in, and out, once more.

Three times.

After the third time, he saw the clothing head up the lane toward the village centre, the loose fabric wet and snapping in the wind, wrapping around a small female body, and sticking to her. Gliding – she moved without effort against the wind, her movements not forced, her feet hardly seeming to touch the ground as she propelled through the storm.

His brow furrowed. What was she doing out in this weather? Why had she come in and out of the house so many times? He shook his head. Must have been deciding whether to go out at all. It was time for him to go back in. Wet and cold, and miserable at being left to guard the cookhouse, he was tempted again by the thought of all those plants. No one would miss a leaf or two.

That's when he saw it.

"Hy McAllister…Ian Simmons…Moira Toombs…"

Jamieson was reading her list of potential suspects after eliminating villagers who were too old or too young.

"…Madeline Toombs…"

"Strike her," said Hy. She's too tiny."

"How tiny?"

"Not five feet. Not a hundred pounds."

"Wouldn't hurt a fly," Gus added. "I'd swear to that on my mother's grave." It, too, would be a mess with the rain and wind, thought Gus. She'd go tidy after the storm.

"She won't even kill a mosquito feasting on her arm."

Jamieson put a question mark beside Madeline's name, and continued with her list.

"April and Ron Dewey…Ben and Annabelle Mack…"

"What about them tourists?"

"Who?"

"Them three. That Big Ed and his fella, Lee…Lee…some foreign name, and her, her, down the house."

"Which house?"

"That one," said Gus, jerking her head in the direction of Ben and Annabelle's. "It wouldn't surprise me if she did it."

"And her motive would be?" Jamieson was making notes.

"She's his wife."

"His wife? What do you mean?" Hy had a cookie halfway to her mouth.

"His real one, what I mean."

"Suki's his wife."

Jamieson looked sharply at Hy. *Suki?*

"The one afore her."

"Before Suki?" Hy wondered how Gus knew and why she hadn't said anything before. "Suki's his wife now."

"Well, not anymore, him being dead 'n' all."

Gus nodded and settled back comfortably in her chair.

Jamieson stopped writing. *Wife? Wives?* Why hadn't she been told?

"That's as may be. I say she's his wife, still 'n' all."

The "still 'n' all" meant Gus would listen, perhaps, to what you said next, but it wouldn't change her mind. In Gus's mind, the first wife was the wife. She nodded her head and pursed her lips. Case closed.

"You mean that weird woman was married to Lord before Suki?" Hy tried to put it as diplomatically as she could, knowing Gus's mind on these points of social rights and wrongs.

"Well and she was."

"Why didn't you say?"

Gus looked smug. A tiny smile began at the corners of her mouth and that gleam came to her eyes, the one she always had when she revealed a piece of news she'd been guarding until the right moment.

"No one asked."

"I'm asking now," said Jamieson. "You had both better tell me what's going on."

Alyssa had not been debating whether to stay in or go out when Billy saw her. She could not go in and out doors like other people. She had to pass through. Return. Pass through again. And then one more time.

She'd given up trying to hide or suppress it. Doing so made her head hurt and her stomach ache.

In the days when she was still trying to hide this doorway dance from others, if something so quirky could be hidden, she would pretend she had forgotten something inside and return to get it. Then "forget" something else and start all over again. She'd been doing this since the age of three, and no one was fooled. Her father had tried to stop it. So had her teachers. Her classmates at school had made fun of her. None of it stopped her. Her obsession was stronger than their attempts to mock her or discipline her. It was stronger than the discomfort and anger they caused her.

Eventually, she gave up all pretence and did just as she was compelled to.

Three times through the door. Every time. Everywhere.

Therapy could not free her from it. She couldn't curb it even though she knew why she did it.

A nun had pulled her aside on a hospital visit to her schizophrenic mother and filled her with fear of losing her virginity. At three years old. Alyssa ran off as fast as her baby legs would move, the word *chaste* ringing through her brain as her child-size footfalls echoed through the empty hall – thundering off the walls as if she were twice, no, many times her size. The sound made her dizzy, and she clasped her hands to her ears, but still the word was there. She'd heard it as *chased*. She would be chased. By what?

The adults. There they were now – following her down the hall. Chasing her. A large wood door, ornately carved with a cross and black iron hinges and handle loomed ahead of her. So great was her fear of being chased that she managed, small as she was, to haul one big door open just wide enough to slip through it.

But not quite all of her. One hand was left in the door when it came crashing closed.

Her piercing cry rang through the building, up the arched ceiling and out into the day, frightening some crows about to alight on the chapel spires. They'd flapped off, picking up her sound with their screeches.

The thundering footfalls joined in the chorus, Alyssa fell unconscious and woke much later, bandaged and in hospital.

The first face she saw was that of the same nun – and they could not stop her screeching then, until the woman left the room.

The hand healed with the help of many surgeries. Because she was so tiny when it happened, there was only a small scar left that could hardly be seen. But Alyssa still saw the wound in its raw, angry days. Ugly. Deformed. That's how it remained in her mind. It was the first of her debilitating mental wounds. After the accident, she began her threshold habit.

Once. Twice through the door. And once again.

That's how it worked in Alyssa's world.

"Here's how it works," Ian gestured toward the screen.

He had seen Hy and Jamieson leaving Gus's house, and intercepted them at the Hall, saying he had something to show them.

They were now looking at Hy's laptop screen.

"*Mind Over Muscle*. Ridiculous," Jamieson sniffed. "How could anyone buy that?"

"Plenty of people bought it, whether they believed it or not. It was sold mainly through those late-night TV infomercials."

Hy knew them well. She could even quote some of the sales pitches word for word. She was not a good sleeper, and sometimes resorted to TV to pass the sleepless hours. Once, she'd ordered a vacuum cleaner she thought would save her life, make it better in every way, as promised. It hadn't. The fancy and expensive vacuum operated just the same as her old one did – only if she took it out and used it. That didn't happen any more than before. When she did try it, it wasn't that good in spite of the claims.

"People are vulnerable at night," said Ian. "They're insomniacs, or on drugs, drinking, or feeling lonely."

"Or all of the above," said Hy. "Those marketers know what they're doing."

Ian clicked back to the home page of "Mind Over Muscle."

"But most of the claims aren't that outrageous. They usually make some kind of sense, provide some kind of evidence that the product works."

"It never does, though," said Hy.

Both Ian and Jamieson gave her sudden, quick looks. She coloured.

"I mean, I assume they don't – or why are they so desperate to sell?"

Ian shrugged.

"I don't know."

"Does his system work?" Hy asked.

"How could it?" Jamieson again.

"Well it worked for him."

It had.

Ed Bullock. High school football hero, cut down in Vietnam.

"A machete to the head, practically split his brain in two." Ian shook his own head at the thought. "Doctors gave up on him almost immediately, but not Leone O'Reyley. Fifteen-year-old kid. Brought him to life again. It took years. Endless physiotherapy. He began to talk again. To walk."

"And then he launched his physical fitness empire, based on the concept that had brought him back from the dead?" Jamieson looked skeptical.

"That was the big selling point. He made a fortune. Don't tell me you hadn't heard of it?"

Jamieson shook her head. So did Ian. She really did live in another world.

"Mind Over Muscle," Hy mumbled. " M.O.M. Mom. Is that weird? Do you think it means anything?"

It did. It was the source of Ed's problems with Alyssa. Or so he thought. The obstacle he couldn't overcome.

He closed his eyes as Leone massaged his ruined legs, closed his eyes on the sight that never left them, not even on that jungle floor in Vietnam. The sight of his father pinning his mother to the bed and raping her. Behind his closed eyes was that five-year-old boy, watching his trust shatter, his safe, secure place in shards. He'd gone tearing from the room, his father in pursuit. Pinned to the wall. Sworn to silence.

He'd been silent about it all his life, but it had simmered inside him always. Even as part of his brain had spilled out, the part that remained had re-lived that childhood scene.

So when he got everything else to work again with Leone's help, the part that made him a man wouldn't. Ed never acknowledged it. He focused on the ruin of his legs. Why couldn't he make them work as they used to?

His ghost limbs. The ones Leone was pretending to massage.

He stopped when Alyssa came to the door.

The woman they both wanted.

Murdo had never seen such a clean and well-ordered place. They'd delivered the bodies to the morgue and Nathan was waiting in the van while Murdo retrieved Jamieson's uniform from her apartment. It was just where she'd said it would be, hung up in the bedroom closet. On either side of it, clothes freshly laundered and pressed, all neatly spaced, not everything stuffed in and crushed together as in his own closet.

The bed was crisply made, as if it had never been slept in. Ever. The bedspread was pulled tight on all sides, not one wrinkle. He looked under the bed. No dust bunnies. In the kitchen, no crumbs around the toaster. The books in the living room were all about crime detection. No novels. No photographs. No knick-knacks.

He should have known. He should have known this is what Jamieson's home would look like. Not a home, more like a store showroom or hotel. Clean and crisp, just like Jamieson herself. Nothing personal.

Chapter Seventeen

Billy was in a tailspin of indecision. He'd been told to stay to guard the dope. But there, on the ground, was most likely the murder weapon. An axe, lying in the tall grass, visible because the grass had been beaten down around it by the rain.

It took him a while to pick it up. Finally, he crouched and slipped his hand under it where the blade met the wooden handle, to avoid interfering with any fingerprints or DNA. He held it poised in that difficult position, feeling his fingers go numb, his arm muscles straining as he stumbled up to the Hall, fighting the wind and the rain, hoping he was doing the right thing.

"Billy Pride! Why the hell are you here? Why aren't you where you should be?" Jamieson's tone struck fear in him. He held up the axe in explanation, misery etching his face, convinced he'd done the wrong thing.

Jamieson stared.

"The murder weapon."

"The murder weapon?" Hy asked. "Jim MacAdam's?"

Jamieson frowned. "I don't know."

Jamieson took the axe from Billy.

"Get Gladys Fraser."

When he returned with Gladys, the axe was laid out on one of the tables. It was the first thing she noticed. What was an axe doing here?

"It was found by the pond. Can you identify it?"

It was Jim's, Gladys knew right away. Any fool could tell that. There were his initials carved right into the handle. It reminded

Gladys of the day Jim had taken a penknife and carved their initials in a heart in the old willow tree by the hall. She hadn't known he was teasing her, a kid he knew had a crush on him. The willow tree hadn't lasted, as willows never do, and neither had the hint of romance. Except in Gladys's mind. She went away to teachers' college in Charlottetown, and Elvira McInnis moved in on Jim. She'd gotten herself pregnant and landed him. Gladys had never had a chance. She'd smoldered over it for years, even after she married Wally.

"She did well for herself," Gus had said, who measured such things on acreage. Wally Fraser had a hundred acres more than Jim MacAdam, although Jim did have prime waterfront. It would do him no good now.

Gladys kept staring at the axe. Should she say it wasn't his? She knew they thought he'd done it, but she knew he couldn't have.

"Yes, it's his," Gladys said finally, a small tear escaping the corner of her right eye.

A tear.

Hy couldn't believe it. Tough-as-boots Gladys, crying? Not a flood of tears. But that one single tear from Gladys was eloquent. She had loved Jim MacAdam, thought Hy. Crusty as she was, she was capable of an enduring love.

Gladys resumed her bulldog stance, grim determination etched across her face and in the thrust of her chin.

"It's his. It may be the murder weapon, but my Jim did not kill anyone. As soon as he shows up, he'll explain everything, you'll see."

Hy's mouth dropped open in shocked surprise. "She doesn't know?"

Gladys turned and shot her a sharp look, a pinpoint of fear in it.

"Jim is dead," said Jamieson, glaring at Hy. She hadn't been prepared to tell people yet. "He's been killed, too."

"By who?" The pinpoint of fear turned to horror.

"That's what we're trying to find out. That – and whether he killed Lord."

Gladys's eyes hardened.

"You don't think that anymore?"

"He's still a suspect."

Gladys was too stunned to say anything. Her shoulders drooped. Her fighting stance dissolved. She shuffled out of the Hall, like the old woman she was, to nurse her private grief.

"Jim can't be a suspect now," said Hy. She'd said it before but it had obviously had no impact.

"As I said, he's still a suspect in Lord's murder. I'm not ruling anyone out."

Jamieson wondered why she was having this conversation with Hy. She thought, with sudden irritation, that Hy had been around too much, seen and heard too much. Said too much, as well. She'd just given away that MacAdam was dead. It would be all over the village by now.

"You should go home too."

"I'm sure I can help…" She had helped, thought Hy. She'd helped a lot.

"Just stay out of police business."

That stung. Well, let Jamieson see if she could solve it on her own. It wouldn't stop Hy from trying to find out what she could. About Suki. Leone. Ed Bullock. Alyssa Lord. Hy was convinced that one of them had killed Lord and MacAdam – and that no villager had anything to do with it. She would prove she was right. She stalked out of the Hall.

Nathan brought Murdo safely back across the flooded causeway. The rain had stopped and started on their journey, coming down so hard at times that it hit the ground and jumped back up. The wind carried the rain with it, blasting up from the coast, pummeling everything in its way. Nathan sped across the causeway, faster than before, anxious to get home to Lili. Murdo cowered, his body low, Nathan grinning and laughing at him, Murdo wishing Nathan would not take his eyes off the road.

When Murdo got to the Hall, Jamieson sent him to fetch Billy and the marijuana plants from the shore. In they came – all thirty of them – filling the Hall with the scent of cannabis. After they put the plants on the table in the Institute room, Murdo drove Billy home. He bashed into the computer monitor that still lay on the road where it had fallen off the cruiser earlier in the day. Billy got out of the car, and patted his pocket to make sure his small stash of stolen pot was there. He felt something else. The breath mint box, containing evidence from the crime scene. He was going to pull it out and give it to Murdo, but Murdo was already driving slowly down the road, unable to see anything clearly in the torrent of rain. Billy could have caught up with him, but he wanted to get out of his wet clothing and have a joint. He shrugged. *Later*.

Jamieson had put on her uniform, even though it was almost time for bed. Grey shirt and dark-blue tie and trousers, pleat on the pants pressed knife sharp. Highly polished ankle boots. Nothing dared stick to them. She felt a renewed sense of command. She blamed her unprofessional behaviour, her hesitancy, and lack of resolve on not being in uniform. She felt best, most assured, happiest in uniform. If she didn't look professional, she didn't feel professional. Now she was sure she'd get the case back on track.

Jamieson and Murdo had sleeping cots that Ben and Annabelle had brought them. Jamieson had set hers up on the stage, where, by pulling the curtains, she would have privacy, and be close to the seized marijuana plants. The illicit scent wafted under the regal nose of Queen Elizabeth. Prince Philip, hand on his sword, stared down with disapproval.

Murdo had the rest of the Hall.

"You're sure you'll be all right, here?" Annabelle fussed. "Because there's plenty of room, you know..." *Where? At Gus's? Gladys's? Moira's?*

Murdo looked hopeful, but Jamieson shook her head.

"No. We'll be fine here."

Annabelle shrugged and left. It wasn't the kind of hospitality she was used to. You took people into your own home. But her home wasn't her own anymore. That strange woman was there. Lord's first wife, Hy had told her. And now here was his second, mixed up with Ian.

Like Hy, Jamieson was convinced that one or more of the four strangers in the village was behind the murder, but she still hadn't ruled out MacAdam. She'd sleep on it, hoping the weather would improve the next day and she could get down to some hard questioning.

Jamieson undressed, laying each piece of the uniform out so that it wouldn't get wrinkled, and slipped into bed.

She couldn't sleep. The storm was howling along the coast, the wind rattling the windows, and a high-pitched whistle circled the Hall, sometimes sounding like wailing guitar riffs. It was the CD she'd put on at Lord's that was torturing her brain.

Each time she began to drift off, something woke her. She got up and padded across the main room, not wanting to wake Murdo, but he was in a deep sleep. He was proving it with strong, healthy snores, interrupted by snuffling and an occasional moan. He was dreaming about April. He was in her kitchen again, warm, well-fed, and charmed.

Jamieson grabbed the laptop from the table and took it back up to her bed, hoping she'd still be able to hitchhike on Ian's wireless.

She was. She googled Big Ed Bullock again, and clicked onto an old *Time* magazine article. It said he'd volunteered to go to Vietnam. She raised her eyebrows. Not many had. That said something about him. He had been on a two-man patrol when the Vietcong had come up behind them, and even the dog hadn't heard as the guerrilla had slit his partner's throat. Ed had barely had time to hear his partner drop to the ground, when the Vietcong had sliced his head open with a machete, and part of his brain had oozed out in the jungle swamp, as he lay there, paralyzed and dying.

Up at the dome, Big Ed was dreaming that he was back in Vietnam. Only mind over matter had saved him. Somewhere in a brain struggling to function, in his deep subconscious, his mind had fixed on his mother, waiting for him back home. As his brain had shut down, closed in on itself, there had been his mother's face. He'd promised to return to her. All in one piece. Just like she'd begged him.

He had – one unmoving piece. A lump of a man, unable to lift his head, to move a finger, to do much more than blink.

He should have been brain dead, Jamieson thought, but he had been nursed back to health by his companion, Leone O'Reyley. It was Leone who had given him life the second time around. Given more than that. Success. Fame. Riches. There was something weird in such obsessive devotion, she thought.

Leone was awake, too, staring down at Ed as he slept, wondering how long he could live, fearing that his strength of mind was weakening, that he might, after all, give in to his injury all these years later. Leone had been Ed's devoted follower ever since the star quarterback of the high school football team had rescued him from a bunch of bullies.

An undersized thirteen-year-old, Leone was watching his hero from the stands when some tenth-graders grabbed him, yanked off his trousers, and pulled on a pleated cheerleader's skort and halter top. They decorated him with pompoms and tossed him up in the air, calling him monkey boy, chanting letters that spelled out his name, laughing.

Leone was squealing, more like a pig than a monkey, when Big Ed ran over and rescued him – not with muscle, but with his booming voice, which terrified Leone's tormenters. They dropped him and ran off.

Ed extended a hand, and Leone grabbed it, his eyes shining with tears and gratitude as Ed helped him to his feet. He had worshipped him before; now he adored him, and followed him around, puppy-like for the rest of the semester. Ed never called him that nasty name. He said Leone's real name in that big booming voice, so deep it was almost past hearing, softening into rich affection in Leone's ears.

Ed had helped Leone muscle up, and with the muscles came confidence, sexual confidence.

Something Leone had, now that Ed didn't.

A tear spilled down his cheek as he tucked the blanket around his hero.

Jamieson looked at a photograph of Leone in the *Time* article.

His complexion was swarthy. But in spite of this, and his name, Leone had been an all-American boy. His father had been a patriotic farmer from Nebraska. He'd named his son Leone after Sergio Leone, because he'd loved the spaghetti westerns, even though they were foreign, like his wife.

Leone had a powerful mind – a mind that brought Ed back from the netherworld he had been in. When Ed's brain was sliced open, he hadn't been in pain. The weapon had carved out his capacity for misery. He had felt only pure happiness. Floating, he had been floating. He hadn't felt his body anymore. He hadn't been able to tell where he ended and the rest of the world began. He was part of the whole, the earth and the sky.

It hadn't been easy to convince him to leave that place, to force the undamaged part of his brain to put right and left together again, to start blinking, then raising his head, moving a finger, then a toe, then his mouth – talking. Then he'd sat up. He'd regained movement of his arms and his torso.

The doctors had marveled as the fifteen-year-old boy brought Big Ed back to life. It had been a long, slow process. Leone had asked him simple questions, encouraged him to make small achievements, applauded every tiny sign of progress. And, against medical advice, had let him sleep ten, twelve, fourteen hours a day. He believed the brain needed sleep to heal, needed time. It had taken years to build Ed back up from the lump he'd become. Only Leone knew he had not been one hundred per cent successful. And only he knew something had gone terribly wrong lately.

Following Ed's recovery, the two had come up with Mind over Muscle, the body building system that built strength by "thinking" weightless barbells up and down.

Ridiculous, thought Jamieson, both the concept and the idea that it could work. Ed was obviously an exception or a fraud. What she was most interested in was the wound. The wound that Ed had suffered had been to the back of the head.

Like Lance Lord. Like Jim MacAdam.

Was there a meaning or a message in it? Did that connect the murders to Ed and Leone? Or was it just a nasty coincidence?

It didn't take much to keep Hy awake. She had good reason tonight – the wind, howling, whipping around the northeast corner of the house and tugging on the clothesline, so it gave off its blue jay shriek. The compost cart was banging up against the oil tank, and there was a new rattle in the bathroom window. Hy hated the wind. She lay firmly in bed, clutching the sheets over her head, gritting her teeth, flipping from one side to another.

She threw off the sheets and went downstairs, cursing the wind and the fact that Jamieson had her computer. She looked out the kitchen window up to Shipwreck Hill, where the lights were on at Ian's house. Normally, she'd have called him or gone up to visit, but she couldn't with Suki there. *Damn her*. Ian and she could have googled together if he weren't with Suki.

He wasn't. Suki was sound asleep and Ian had slipped out of bed and gone downstairs, where he was surfing the story of the romance between Alyssa and Lance Lord in the CBC archives. They'd met while he was in Cape Breton on tour for *All Around the House* when she was just sixteen. He was twenty years older. Unhappy at home, she'd run away with him. It had been an Elvis and Priscilla Presley type of relationship. Alyssa had lived with Lance until, at eighteen, she'd been old enough to marry. The marriage had lasted almost two decades, then come unraveled a year ago. No one knew why.

Chapter Eighteen

The computer screen flashed and went black. Jamieson hit a couple of keys. The battery was dead. She plugged in the cord. Still nothing.

Power out? She looked out the window. Lights were on at Shipwreck Hill.

She played around with the laptop some more, then got up and hit a light switch. Nothing. Power must be out. Then why were lights on up Shipwreck Hill?

Ian was fully equipped to weather any storm. He'd had a generator wired into his electrical box, and he was smiling smugly now as he continued to surf the net, uninterrupted by the gale.

Hy fell asleep on her living room couch after the power went out. Jamieson never did go to sleep. She kept getting up and checking the lights, and looking at Ian's house. He had slipped back into bed with Suki, careful not to wake her, but his computer screen tormented Jamieson when she looked out the window. She saw an eerie glow of changing colours. The planets and stars were flickering across Ian's living room walls. A comet crashing into Jupiter, ice floes on Mars, the moon with Venus rising. His screen saver. The only place the moon was visible tonight.

Down on the shore, in the spot where Lance Lord's body had lain, a dark figure was searching frantically in the sand, digging like a dog, moving from patch to patch, the movements becoming more frenzied as Leone despaired of finding what he was looking for. But his persistence had brought Ed Bullock back from the dead, and he did not let up. An hour later, he was rewarded – partly. He held up the treasure – a thin gold chain, broken. He smiled, kissed it, and began another frenzied search in the sand. Hours later, he made his way back to the dome, head down, gait slow, and disappointed.

Olive MacLean would not have to worry about "paying the lights" at the Hall. There were no lights, all night and into the morning.

"Power's out," echoed down the phone lines, where the villagers automatically retreated when the lights went. They wanted to make sure their neighbours had no power either. They wanted to complain about the power company and why it didn't just put everything underground, out of the wind that blew the poles down and dragged the lines with them. Wally Fraser was always first to reach the electric company and find out how bad the damage was. The information would be relayed and amplified down the phone lines, dubbed a province-wide disaster, whether it was or not. This time it was. It was comforting to know that plenty of others were in the same spot.

But The Shores was always last to get power back. Such a tiny community.

Was there even anyone still living out there?

It gave Ian smug pleasure to continue as usual with generated power, waiting for Hy and other neighbours to come seeking the comfort of his ingenuity. Today, he didn't wait. While Suki slept in, he went out under a black sky down to the Hall. Inside, Jamieson was doing yet another round of the place, turning the light switches on and off, impatient at this new hitch in the investigation.

Investigation. The word stuck in her mind, grinding an ache into the back of her head, threatening to balloon into a full-blown migraine.

What investigation?

She had her uniform, but no power against the elements.

There were wrinkles in her smooth complexion when Ian burst into the Hall.

"Let's get you out of here. It'll be a while before they get us back on. Quite a few lines down. I've got full power up the hill."

The creases unfolded from her face.

"You do?"

"As good as," he said, eyeing her pathetic centre of operations – a couple of tables pushed together and the laptop, battery dead, its external modem hanging down, attached to the long phone cord.

Dial-up, thought Ian. Dark ages.

"This is interesting."

Ian and Jamieson were hunched over the computer. Hy had come over, driven there by lack of both power and her laptop. She was also uneasy about having a killer in the village, so uneasy that she was willing to put up with Suki. She was lucky. Suki was still sleeping upstairs. Hy had dozed off on the floor, leaning up against the Danish modern chair with the collapsing arm. Her eyes flickered open.

"Interesting…squawk." Ian's parrot, Jasmine, was perched in her preferred place on his shoulder.

"What?" Eyes drooping, Hy propped herself up on one arm.

"What?" Jasmine repeated. "What?" Ending on a high note. She was fond of upward inflections.

"Lance Lord, modelling Stanfield underwear."

Hy sat up. "That's interesting?"

"Unusual. He has an outtie."

"So?" Jamieson frowned. "That's not unusual."

"Unusual to find in an underwear ad." Hy hauled herself up off the floor. "Advertisers like innies."

Ian zoomed in on the underwear. He pressed his face close to the screen.

"Ian!" Hy laughed.

"Look," he said.

Jamieson did – and saw it.

"One undescended testicle."

"Maybe it's one descended testicle," said Hy. "I think they scrunch them up."

"Or bulk them up?" said Jamieson, with a half-smile.

A joke. From Jamieson.

"Or tape them up."

Ian winced. "Okay. Forget the testicle. That's not unusual anyway. This is." He pulled up an ad for Mind Over Muscle. Hy and Jamieson stared at it, neither understanding what he meant. He cut and pasted both photographs side by side on the screen. Lance Lord modelling underwear. Ed Bullock showing off his physique.

It was the same physique.

"It's the same body."

Jamieson and Hy bent closer, eyes squinting on the images. Except for the faces, they were identical.

"The outtie, the undescended testicle, even the curl of the chest hair," said Ian.

"What does it mean?" asked Jamieson.

Hy straightened up. "Body double."

"Body double?"

Ian cast a look at Hy. Did Jamieson live in the same world as everyone else?

"They do it in movies. Cut to somebody else's buff body after the close-up kiss. Or to better breasts than the actress has. It's like a stunt person for appearance. Lance Lord was Ed Bullock's body double."

"Jesus," said Hy.

"No – " he grinned. She put a hand to his mouth.

"Don't say it. I've had enough Lord jokes."

"Said enough of them yourself."

"I know…I know."

"So Ed in his TV commercials wasn't Ed at all?" Jamieson was scanning the screen, fascinated.

"Right. It was Lance Lord. Give me a minute."

It was several minutes before Ian found what he was looking for.

"Here. See."

There was Ed Bullock close up, a great big diamond-dazzling smile on Ian's computer screen, spouting the virtues of his Mind Over Muscle system.

"Never lift a finger to lift weight." The MOM slogan.

"Ed," said Ian.

Cut to a muscular full-body shot.

"Not Ed," said Hy.

"Right."

"Ed. Not Ed. Ed. Not Ed," echoed Jasmine. She liked it, and started up again. "Ed. Not Ed…"

"But why?" Jamieson.

Ian shrugged. "Beats me."

All three stared at the image of Lance Lord's body with Ed Bullock's head on it.

"Maybe…" Hy broke the silence, "…the reason for the body double was something Lord knew that Ed didn't want other people to know…" she paused, leaving time for Jamieson to pick up on it.

Jamieson's face creased and then smoothed out as it dawned on her.

"The land deal."

"The land deal. Blackmail?" Hy barely concealed her pleasure at having made the connection.

"The land deal?" Ian looked puzzled. "Blackmail?"

"Interesting." Jamieson's face revealed nothing. She was good at that. She'd picked it up from her sister, who never let the sun kiss her skin, wore wide-brimmed hats, and rarely cracked a facial expression of any kind. Smile. Frown. It was all the same to her – a façade of cool neutrality. It gave her a sort of hauteur, but there was nothing special or superior about Jamieson's sister. She just didn't want wrinkles.

"Could it have been blackmail?" Hy pressed the point.

Jamieson didn't answer. She had to credit Hy with making the connection, but didn't want to encourage her.

When the lights came back on, it was a miracle. The Shores was first to have service restored. Jamieson had put pressure on the power company and they'd snapped to attention at her air of authority and mention of murder. The weather improved, too. The rain was coming straight down instead of sideways, and the wind, while still strong, had diminished.

Jamieson stepped out onto Ian's front porch. Her foot slipped across the surface, made greasy by the rain, and she steadied herself. The steps, too, were slippery, and she grabbed at the handrail.

The handrail was still in her hands when her feet flew up from under her and she spun into the air and plunged to the ground. There was a nasty cracking sound and a shot of pain seared her right ankle, twisted at a peculiar angle underneath her.

"Oh, Jesus, I'm sorry." Ian, who'd nearly slipped himself chasing down the stairs to try to break her fall. "I should have warned you the handrail was loose."

"Loose?" She grimaced and brandished the wood, rotting at one end, several nails sticking out where it had been "repaired" more than once.

He tried to help her up. She winced in pain, unable to put

weight on the foot. Hy came down, and, between them, they got Jamieson back into the house, her arms around them, hopping on her good foot.

Suki was in the kitchen in Ian's dressing gown. It seemed to be all she ever wore.

"What happened?" She was slathering butter on a big wedge of toast.

"Handrail broke," said Ian.

He and Hy took Jamieson into the living room. Suki followed and stood in the doorway, plate in hand, munching on her toast.

"This better not break," Hy said, as they lowered Jamieson onto the couch. Like the chair, it was vulnerable to the combined effects of the Red Island climate and Ian's woodstove.

"Can I help?" Suki sauntered into the room, chomping on the toast, her lips moist with butter, crumbs falling on the floor.

Ian looked up, doubtful. So did Hy. And Jamieson. Then she spoke.

"Not unless you're a nurse."

Suki scowled. "Not exactly."

Jamieson looked at Ian. "Maybe Nathan…?"

"It's okay. I can deal with this." Hy bent down and removed Jamieson's boot and sock. Her grandmother had made sure she took CPR and Red Cross courses. She'd lost her husband and daughter, and didn't want to lose anyone else, so Hy had been taught to deal with any emergency.

She felt the ankle.

"It's swollen all right." She pressed it. Jamieson squirmed. Hy pressed again. "Does that hurt?" She looked at Jamieson's face. It hurt.

"Too swollen to tell if there's a break." Hy turned to Ian. "Get an ice pack – it'll help bring the swelling down." Then she turned to Jamieson. "You'll have to stay off this foot."

Jamieson looked rebellious.

"There may be a fracture." Hy probed the ankle. Jamieson winced.

"See what I mean. Don't put weight on it. Any weight."

Jamieson grimaced. Her ankle was throbbing, a deep dull pain, mixed with a sharp stabbing that was like a needle being stuck into it and twisted around. She couldn't imagine putting weight on it, it hurt so much.

Ian brought the ice pack. "Brought this, too." He held out a gauze bandage from his seventy-two-hour emergency kit.

"I have some crutches at home," said Hy. She frowned at the smirk on Ian's face. Hy had broken a few bones herself. "I'll go get them. You stay here and keep your foot up."

Suki pouted and left the room. She wanted to lie on the couch, but Jamieson was hogging it. As she passed Jasmine, the parrot hissed. Suki jumped.

"Shut your beak," she snarled.

Hy and Ian knew Jasmine would have something to say to that. She ruffled her feathers.

"Shut your beak…squawk…shut your beak…bitch."

Jasmine always had the last word.

Gus was still working on a quilt for Alyssa. She had said she wanted it to celebrate her new relationship with Lance, that they were to remarry. She'd offered a good price for it, and sworn Gus to secrecy – a rare thing in a small place like The Shores. Now that Lord was dead, would the woman still want the quilt? Gus was well into it, an ambitious project she'd never intended to take on at her age. She'd done a few of them in her time, and they were tedious, tiny pieces all patched together in an intricate pattern, looping circles together.

Now she sat in her purple chair, with the patches scattered on the floor around her, wondering how she'd got into this fix. A quilt this complicated she usually did for family only.

And only for a wedding, not for shacking up, thought Gus. But this was to have been a wedding. Not family, but a wedding. And a good price.

She yanked at the material, pulling two patches apart. She'd sewn them together backwards so the curves of the circles went in the wrong direction. It was an easy error, but it had never happened to Gus before.

She must be getting too old for this sort of thing.

She looked up from her work, and out the window. Hy's truck going down from Ian's to the Hall. That Suki woman still up at his house. Gus sighed. Hy should just make it clear to the fellow how she felt about him. It was plain as day to everyone else.

Jamieson could not stay off her feet on Ian's couch. She refused to consider going to hospital. What, and leave her case? When Hy came with the crutches, she insisted she could walk to the Hall on them.

She was persuaded to let Hy drive her there.

Within minutes of settling in a chair and booting up the laptop, Jamieson had sent Murdo off to fetch Hy back – and bring Ian, too.

Her eyes were fixed to the screen. She had keyed in Lance Lord, and clicked to a new Google site, dated that morning. She was horrified by what she saw. She had immediately suspected Ian. Or Hy. It was their equipment, after all, that she'd been using.

When they arrived, she turned the laptop around so they could see it.

"Who's responsible for this?"

The photo of Lance Lord, his brains on the sand, was splashed on the cover of *Journal de la Cité*, a Quebec tabloid that specialized in bloody crime photos on its front page. In a play on Lord's name, the headline screamed: "Le Seigneur est Mort! – echoing

Time magazine from decades before: "God is Dead." There was a white balloon pointing to the sign in Lord's hand, with a translation of the No Trespassing warning.

Sales had been brisk. The periodical had sold out by the time Jamieson logged onto the site. Lance Lord had a cult following in Quebec, in spite of speaking not a word of French, and never having set foot in the province. Inexplicably, his fans comprised of young francophone Goths who gathered to watch the show, laugh, call him *maudit anglais*, and throw popcorn at the screen. This newspaper cover, detailing Lance Lord's fate, was the perfect ringing down of the curtain for his ghoulish fans.

Jamieson would not be able to prevent the follow-up cover that the periodical's gleeful editors planned for the next day, using another illicit shot, and promising to reveal *Les Secrets Scandaleuses de la Vie de Melvin Gruber*. The most scandalous thing that had happened in his life had been his death.

"Well?"

Ian and Hy had been too stunned to answer Jamieson's question. Besides, they didn't know who was responsible. They stood, staring at the screen.

"Melvin Gruber?" squeaked out of Hy. "Melvin Gruber," she repeated. "No wonder."

Jamieson looked up. "No wonder what?"

Ian slapped a hand to his forehead. "It should have been obvious."

"What?" asked Jamieson, impatient, her eyes now on him.

Chapter Nineteen

Alyssa opened the box, not messy as jewellery boxes often are, but neatly organized, "a place for everything and everything in its place," a refrain that had echoed in her mind since childhood. So she knew exactly where it was, tucked in the envelope that also held the appraisal for her engagement ring, a document she held in contempt. The envelope contained another document – a folded piece of paper that gave her pain. She had read and reread it dozens of times since the death last year of her father.

It was Lance's death that had made her open the box, to look at the tokens of their life together. She slipped the wedding ring she hadn't worn since their divorce on her ring finger. Now he would never belong to anyone else. The need to possess had gnawed at her like something chewing on her brain, until, finally, it was put to rest. It was what she had come for. He was hers now, forever. It did not make her any happier.

She pulled the folded paper from the sleeve of the box, the poem she had discovered amongst her father's things. She peeled it open, to his beautiful handwriting:

"In other worlds, I loved you long ago:
love that hath no beginning hath no end –"

Alyssa was twelve again. Her father was out every night. After they had supper together and she went to bed, she'd hear the front door slam behind him, leaving her alone. She'd wake to the sound of that door, opening, closing, comings and goings in the night – not just her father returning home, with someone. There were times when she swore she heard a woman's voice from her father's bedroom down the dark hallway. Laughter in the night. An unheard-of sound in that grim house.

It had ended with the return of her mother, still sick, maybe sicker than when she'd left. But her rages had been brought under control, shocked out of her. She'd spent most days sitting, listless, in the living room. Her presence had come between Alyssa and her father. He had withdrawn, slipped into a morose state, reading poetry in his library. And then there was this piece of paper. Alyssa had seen it before, when she was fifteen or sixteen, snooping in the case in which her father kept his cufflinks, seeking the source of his unhappiness. She'd found this scrap of paper then, not as yellowed, not folded in so many pieces, but the same. This proof of his love – not for her mother, not for her, but for someone else. Someone else had stolen what was hers, hers by right. Her father's love.

Now the paper was old, yellowed, decaying. It was coming apart along the folds, age eating at its edges, fraying in brittle bits, like the bitterness that was devouring her brain and stomach and heart. No, not her heart. Nothing could consume that. It had shrunk into a hard, dark knob, a weight with no feeling.

She read it again, though she knew it by her hardened heart.

"In other worlds, I loved you long ago;
love that hath no beginning hath no end – "

And then she did something unusual. Normally she would eat bitterness off the page, then fold the paper away again. It represented her father. It also represented his betrayal of her, his love for another. All the rage that had left Alyssa when Lance died now began to boil up in her again. It wasn't gone. In spite of the red tin foil shrine, the incense, the prayer mat, the photos of bald men all over the room, in spite of her trifling with Buddhist meditation, she was still angry to the core. She crushed the paper and threw it on the floor in a fury of hate – the one emotion still contained in her rock of a heart.

She kicked the ball of paper, and the love that had no beginning and no end went skittering under the bed, trailing crumbs of flaking paper in its wake. He had loved someone more than her.

She slammed the jewellery box shut. She whirled around, looking for some object upon which to unleash her hate, carve it out of her. That small hard heart had no room to contain it. It was already full – with envy, bitterness, and greed compressed, on the edge of exploding. Seeing nothing of use, she spun around, back to the box, picked it up, and flung it across the room. There was nothing precious in it.

Silver and gold chains, stud and drop earrings, small velvet boxes, went somersaulting under the dresser, catapulting to the far corners of the room, scattering to secret places in the cracks of the old board floor, hiding there for years, a trace of Alyssa that would stay at The Shores.

The paper, the scrap of poem that landed under the bed, was burned into Alyssa's tortured mind. Envy. His love had not been for her, but for someone else. Her father had loved someone else more than her and it had not been her mother, the only one woman who had been her rival for his affections, or so she had thought.

She stalked from the room. One small shard of regret at what she had done tried to follow her through the door, but she shook it off.

She thought of Ed and Leone. Now that Lance was dead, Ed was her focus. He loved her, too. So did Leone. But they were keeping a secret from her. She'd asked Leone again yesterday, but, again, he denied there was a secret.

She frowned. Then smiled.

Leone no longer had her ring on the chain around his neck.

She knew where it was. If the police found it, they'd conclude he'd done it. He'd admit to it. He'd said he would. Poor Leone. He'd go to jail. And she'd be left with Ed. She had caught Ed's eye across the room, and made a silent promise to him.

What was left of him.

"It should have been obvious Lance Lord wasn't a real name." Ian was fighting a desire to scroll down to see what else was on the front page. *More about Lord? Some other scandal?*

Hy was resisting the same urge. "I can't believe I never thought about it, then or now."

"Then?" Jamieson was still in the dark.

"When I used to watch him on TV." Hy overcame her reluctance to touch the keyboard. She reached over, clicked back to the Google page, scrolled down, and found one of the sites she and Ian had visited. Jamieson looked at it briefly, and then looked up.

"So Lance Lord's assumed name wasn't for the purposes of hiding anything, or himself, from anyone. It was a stage name."

"Yup," said Hy. "And I bet he was glad when people recognized it."

"Not many did," said Ian. "His career peaked at its beginning."

"I don't know why he was so popular in Quebec. He played that part with a really bad accent." Hy clicked back to the newspaper photo of Lance dead on the shore. Her photo.

"What part?"

Ian was staring at the wound in the back of Lord's head.

Hy took this photograph. She saw this, dead and in person. No wonder she threw up.

"He played a minor French Canadian character in a popular English Canadian TV series. Not so popular that he was ever known outside Canada, or that people who watched very little TV knew who he was, but he had a small following."

Hy stepped on Ian's toe. He was one of the people who didn't watch television very much and hadn't known who Lance Lord was. Now he was the expert. Typical. Pontificating. That was typical, too. And so was the fact that stepping on his toe didn't stop him.

"When the series ended, he went on to fewer and less significant roles in TV, film, and stage. Now almost nobody knows or remembers him."

"That just changed." Jamieson pointed at the screen.

"Melvin Gruber." Ian shook his head and smiled. "Not macho like Lance Lord. No wonder he stuck with the stage name."

"Like he's clinging to that sign," said Hy.

Melvin Gruber would never visit Quebec now, or any other province – until he was flown back in a jar to his birthplace, a small Ontario town – like him, unknown.

Googling, they found that Lord's slight notoriety had got him a mention in most of the nation's major newspapers. He got more column inches because he had been murdered. If he had merely died, he'd have been buried on the back page.

The fact that someone had taken a shot of Lord's body on the beach added to the hype. Mainstream newspapers wouldn't print the photo, and denounced papers that did, but provided detailed and very graphic descriptions of the image that sent their readers hunting the newsstands for the sleazy tabloid.

Jamieson had been sidetracked. She looked up sharply at Hy, accusation in her eyes.

"Yours?"

"Obviously," said Hy. "You've seen it."

Jamieson continued to stare, lips pressed tightly together.

"You don't think I had anything to do with this?"

"Did you?"

"Of course not."

"And why should I accept that? You didn't sell it to them?"

"No. You know I don't need the money."

"The notoriety?"

"Do you see a photo credit?"

There was not.

"Surely you know me well enough…"

Jamieson turned back to the photo. It had taken guts to take this shot. Especially in the state of shock Jamieson had found Hy that morning. It took a different kind of guts to pass it on to this rag that called itself a newspaper.

"And you?" Satisfied that Hy was telling the truth, Jamieson shifted her focus to Ian.

"Me? Of course not. I would never betray a trust in this way. I would never use the Internet for such purposes."

Jamieson could read the offended honesty in his eyes. Then how? Someone must have hacked into police communications. She'd have to pursue it. But not now. Her first duty was to find out who had killed Lord – and she was very far from that. This photo in this unfortunate publication wasn't her fault, but it wouldn't look good on her. Not this – nor any of the other things that had happened. She'd wanted the case so much just yesterday. Now she wished her sister had married in some other country, far away from all this.

Even the corpse was a joke in the wig and the bandana, the dashiki and bell-bottoms.

"What's this Jimi Hendrix obsession about?" Jamieson had been overwhelmed by Lord's Hendrix collection, which included evidence on his computer that he'd taken the online Purple Haze solo guitar lesson.

Hy and Ian both shrugged.

"He's a product of the sixties," said Hy. She was, too, in a different way. Lord had been a precocious youngster when he first discovered hash, heroin, and Hendrix. Hy herself was the end product of a night of drugs and free love on the part of her flower child mother and draft dodger father.

"Awful music," said Ian, shaking his head. "But not without merit. Hendrix pioneered the explosive possibilities of the guitar."

Here he goes, thought Hy. He'd been googling it, she knew.

"He combined fuzz, feedback, and controlled distortion to create a new musical form."

"Controlled?" Jamieson thought of the Hendrix CD she'd heard at Lord's. She'd preferred the howling of the wind.

"Doesn't sound controlled to me." She closed the file and the gruesome photo of Lord disappeared.

"What about the wife?"

"Which wife?" Hy asked, a tiny lift at the corners of her mouth, a suppressed smile.

"I'll get her," said Ian, and went home to fetch Suki.

He wondered if she'd be out of the bathroom yet, where he'd left her an hour ago.

She still wasn't ready when he got there.

"It used to take me ten minutes to put on my face," Suki said, dabbing it with a cotton ball wet with some substance out of the fourteen jars cluttering Ian's bathroom. He'd counted them.

"Now that I'm over fif…well, a certain age, it takes longer."

Ian didn't know he was supposed to protest her statement.

"Whenever you're ready." He left the room.

She stuck her tongue out at him and pouted.

Alyssa got to the Hall first.

She was all floating chiffon, slipping into the room.

A vision, thought Hy.

A vision that stepped over the threshold, retreated a few steps, and did it all again twice more. She was so focused on what she was doing, she didn't notice Hy staring at her and squinting. *Odd. Very odd.*

Alyssa moved with barely a sound across the room, so soft was her tread, her blouse and skirt a diaphanous gauze, swathed around a wraithlike body. An ethereal creature, so slight she almost wasn't there. Jamieson didn't even look up.

"Name." It was a command, not a question.

The vision's voice had no more substance than the rest of her.

"Alyssa."

The soft voice floated away on the air. She repeated it, holding on to the "s" and letting the final "a" out on a sigh of air.

"Alyssa…Lord."

Jamieson looked up sharply at the last name.

"Relationship to the deceased?" Again, not a question, but to confirm, officially, what she already knew.

"Wife."

Jamieson examined the woman in front of her. So this was the other wife. Up close the gauzy vision was gone, and with it, the loveliness. A mouse. A little mouse. That's what Jamieson saw. Nothing more. Except for the hands encased in old-fashioned white lace gloves, peeking out from the swirl of chiffon around her wrists.

Hy's eyes were fixed on Alyssa as well.

She had seen her flitting around the lanes, on the capes, down by the shore, but only from a distance. She had no substantial image of the woman, and now, close-up, she could see why. There wasn't anything substantial about her.

What a difference from Suki of the generous breasts, bountiful Suki with her hearty laugh, loud voice, and healthy appetites. Here was this other wife, this scrap of a woman with a waif's face, but not a waif's big appealing eyes. Alyssa's were small and pig-like, Hy thought.

There appeared to be two Alyssas. The one who had walked into the room had an aura, thought Hy, something otherworldly about her. Up close, nothing to her, nothing at all. No vibrancy, no glow, no visible reason why this woman would have attracted Lord.

A loud peeling laugh at the Hall door.

Suki.

She tumbling in, tickling Ian.

Ian, looking very flustered and unhappy, fended her off, trying to hang on to his dignity.

Serves him right, thought Hy. It was mean-spirited, but she didn't care.

Jamieson scowled at the interruption. Looked at her watch. Well, they were on time. It was this one who wasn't scheduled. Still, she was the more interesting at the moment.

What happened next, Jamieson found even more intriguing.

Seeing Alyssa, Suki stopped plaguing Ian. Her hands dropped to her side. She stood up straight, thrusting out her ample breast, and her mouth fell open. But she was silent.

Hearing the silence, following Jamieson's and Hy's glance, Alyssa turned around.

When she saw Suki, she squeaked.

Chapter Twenty

The police order that no one should leave The Shores had no effect on Moira's ordered schedule. Changeover day was changeover day, and Moira's on-screen calendar told her that's what it was, whatever the police might think. It was the day to clean the rentals for the last time this season. There was only Ben and Annabelle's left so she didn't need to look it up, but looking at the computer calendar pleased her. It not only appealed to her organizational sense, it brought her closer to Ian.

He'd helped her buy the computer when she'd started her cleaning business in the spring. With lots carved up for development and new cottages built or planned, Moira saw an opportunity to supplement the meagre amount her father had left them from his wages as a garbage man. Moira referred to him as a waste management supervisor, the politically correct title he'd held by the time he retired.

She'd used some of her father's savings to invest in the computer. She told herself it was a business decision, but it had more to do with getting closer to Ian. It had worked even better than she had hoped. They actually took a trip to town together, spent hours going from store to store to find the right unit at the right price. They had lunch.

Lunch. Something Moira had never had with a man.

For the entire half-hour they'd spent in the Zellers restaurant in Charlottetown, Moira had imagined that people must think they were a couple. She'd caught a group of teenagers looking at them and giggling. It had convinced her that it must be obvious she and

Ian were together. They must think they were fiancés. *Affianced.* It had a nice ring to it. She'd covered her bare left hand. She didn't know the teens were laughing at her old maid's hair.

Ian had paid the bill. That hadn't been lost on Moira. Ian was tight with his money, so she'd assumed the lunch must mean something to him, too. It had. He was like a cult leader when it came to computers, and loved luring people in and guiding them through the technological tangle. It was an outlet for his desire to teach, now that he was no longer at the high school.

She shut down the computer and dusted off the screen with the special cloth Ian insisted she buy, although the price was outrageous. *For a duster!* Ian wasn't tidy in his home, but he was fastidious about his computer. If only he would realize how much they shared.

Then there had been their time setting up her new system, here in the back room by the kitchen, where both her mother and father had spent their last days dying, tended by their dutiful daughters. She looked with satisfaction at her office, and remembered with a flush of pleasure the hours she'd spent here with Ian.

Now his interest seemed to have waned. She could occasionally tempt him here to ask his advice, but she didn't need it. Moira was a natural. She was proud of solving problems on her own, then detailing for Ian how she'd done it. He showed interest, sometimes admiration, but nothing more had come of it. And now here was that Suki woman.

Moira stood and went into the mud room to collect her cleaning supplies, stopping first to touch up her makeup in the mirror by the door.

The appearance of Suki on the scene had given Moira the gift of bright new looks. And one other satisfaction. Hy couldn't be happy about Suki.

"You killed my husband." Alyssa pointed a small accusing finger at Suki.

"*Your* husband?" Suki hurled back. She advanced a few steps into the room. Ian put a restraining hand on her shoulder.

"*Your* husband?" Suki repeated, louder this time, shaking Ian off.

Alyssa dropped her hand, but kept her composure.

"Yes, my husband."

"Past history," Suki spat out.

"And the future. You knew that. That's why you killed him. You didn't want me to have him back."

"I don't know why you would want him. Knowing what you must know about him. I assume you do know about him. You were married for years."

"Yes, years." There was a coy smile on Alyssa's face. "Wonderful years."

"Then why did you divorce him?"

Alyssa didn't answer. She turned away and pointed at Jamieson, who didn't like the gesture at all, nor Alyssa's next words.

"You must arrest her. She killed Lance. I know she did."

"It doesn't work that way. I need to take statements, examine evidence…"

"Well, my statement is, she did it. She killed Lance. I know it."

"Let's just start with the facts you do know. Where were you on the night of the murder?"

"With Lance," said Alyssa, oblivious to the shocked looks on the faces of the others in the room.

Moira let herself in the big double doors of Ben and Annabelle's home, and headed with mop, bucket, and cleaning products straight for the second floor. It was Moira's opinion that cleaning should start at the top, and all the dirt be sent down to the bottom. She headed down the long paneled hallway to begin with the bathroom, but a flash of red from the bedroom caught her eye.

She peeked in.

She had never seen anything like it.

Red foil wrapped around Annabelle's 1920s Waterfall vanity. Photographs of a fat oriental man, swathed in robes and garlands, national health glasses and a beatific smile on his face. Candles. An incense burner. Little cones of incense in a bowl.

Drugs? She'd never seen drugs, nor incense.

On the floor in front of the vanity was a prayer mat. Moira thought it was a yoga mat, like the ones she'd seen arriving at the Hall earlier in the week.

There were other photographs of other strange-looking men on the dresser, the bedside table, and the window seat.

She was appalled at the transformation of Annabelle's bedroom.

Heathen, she thought.

Unholy.

She was so undone she never saw the jewellery scattered all over the floor.

She got out as fast as she could. Down the stairs, tumbling as she went, leaving mop and bucket and cleaning supplies behind. Across the front hall, and out the door, forgetting to close it behind her. She jumped into her twenty-year-old Toyota Corolla, sped home and got on the phone.

"Ummmm," a sleepy voice responded. Annabelle was holding the receiver, her head tucked into Ben's shoulder.

"Okay. Okay. Calm down."

Annabelle sat up, and pulled the sheets over her.

Ben stirred.

"Trouble?" His voice was full of sleep, but his hands were exploring her.

Moira. Annabelle mouthed the name to Ben.

Suddenly he didn't feel so aroused.

"Yes, I'll go have a look. I don't suppose it's really any of our business. Fine. I understand. I'll do the clean-up, if you want.

No…no. Of course your work is fine." She rolled her eyes at Ben. He had begun to plant wet kisses on her stomach, more to annoy her than to arouse her. But she was aroused.

"Look, Moira, this is not a good time. Don't worry. I'll take care of it." She reached over Ben to put down the phone. He held her there.

"What's that all about?"

"I'll tell you later."

His kisses had moved up from her stomach.

"Don't stop." She slipped back under the sheets.

Jamieson had a restored sense of command. It was the uniform. And her injury had provided an unexpected benefit. Since the crutches made it hard for her to get around, she'd instructed Murdo to summon the villagers, including Ed Bullock and Leone, to the Hall for questioning. She liked the idea of taking people out of their familiar environments. She thought it unsettled them, made them more vulnerable.

But Alyssa had powers of her own. Powers of deception. As Alyssa spoke, Jamieson watched carefully for signs that she was lying, and she found none. No averted eyes. No twitching. No nervous mannerisms at all. Just calm.

"Lance was always mine. We had reconciled. We were going to re-marry after he broke the news to Suki."

"Was this part of it?" Jamieson pulled out Lord's will, the document she had found partly charred in his woodstove. She pointed to the change in it, the addition of Alyssa's name beside "my wife."

Alyssa bowed her head, so Jamieson couldn't see her eyes.

"Well, yes it was," she said. "It was always meant to be me. Lance just forgot to put in my name, and corrected it."

"Did he make the correction that night, the night when you visited?"

Alyssa lifted her head. "You mean the night he died?" Her

forehead was smooth and unworried. "The night he was murdered?" Her eyes were untroubled. "Yes. It was he who brought it up, showed me the…"

"Change?"

"Not really a change." A pause. "A correction." There was satisfaction in her voice. "Fixing a mistake. He never meant to disinherit me, even when we divorced. I belonged to him, and he…," she paused, her eyes glinting, "…belonged to me. Forever."

"You have your forever now." Jamieson's tone was grim. "So, if you belonged together…"

"To each other. We belonged to each other."

"Then why did you divorce?"

"A silly misunderstanding," she said. "I was his true love."

Whatever that means. Jamieson's cynicism kicked in, but not without a nagging doubt. *True love. Was there such a thing?* She felt an ache, more piercing than her damaged ankle, an ache in a place she couldn't identify. She set it aside, and got back to work.

"His true love – and was he yours?"

A hesitation. A smile. "Of course."

Jamieson flapped the document.

"How did it come to be burned?"

Alyssa shrugged. "Ask Suki."

"Why do you say Suki killed him? Do you have any evidence?"

Alyssa pointed at the will. "That. Because of that."

"It might just as easily have been you, for the same reason."

"Do you think I cared about the things?"

"I just hope you didn't kill him because of this." Jamieson laid the document back on the table.

Alyssa's face was blank, unreadable.

"Are you saying I killed him?"

Jamieson didn't answer. Instead, she tapped a finger on the papers. "It's not valid, you know."

"No?"

"No. It would have been automatically revoked by his marriage to Suki – with or without your name in it."

Did Alyssa pale? It was hard to say, she was so pale anyway.

"Meet me there," Annabelle had left the message on Hy's cell phone, telling her all about Moira's call. Hy had checked her messages when Jamieson kicked her out of the Hall, and went straight to Annabelle's.

Her friend was knocking on her own door just as Hy arrived. She tried the handle. Unlocked. Annabelle and Hy crept inside.

Moira had missed the changes to the living room, but they didn't. Gauzy materials in greys and greens, like the fabrics Alyssa wore, were draped, tent-like, over Ben's big armchair, held up by a sash looped through the plant holder in the ceiling.

"A throne," said Hy.

"A harem," said Annabelle.

"A spider's nest," said Hy, surprising herself.

"Why do you say that?"

Hy shook her head.

"I don't know. It just came out. You're right…it does look like a…a…harem." She grinned. "But somehow I fancy it as a spider's nest."

"Do spiders have nests?

Hy shrugged. "I don't know. Ask Ian."

"Now he's got a nest." Annabelle blurted out, not thinking.

"You mean a love nest?"

Was Hy's tone a bit arch?

"Do I ever."

The tiny moment of tension broke, and they started laughing at the thought of Ian in the clutches of the voracious Suki.

They laughed all the way up to the bedroom. Annabelle's eyes and mouth opened wide when she saw it. She began to laugh again.

"A shrine." Hy smiled.

"Our bedroom, a shrine." Annabelle snorted.

"Presumably she doesn't use this room for the same purpose you and Ben do."

Annabelle grinned and shook her head. "I guess not. Ben and I will have to desanctify it when we come home." She took a close look at the photograph on the vanity. A fat man with a bald head and a saintly smile on his face. He was clothed in a loose white robe with a garland of flowers around his neck.

"Baba," she said.

"What's with the baby talk?"

"Baba," Annabelle repeated. "Father – Buddhist word for a holy man. Don't know which Baba this is, but..."

"Is this the same guy – or a different one?" Across the room, on top of Ben's dresser, Hy picked up another photo of a holy man, balding, bespectacled, and garlanded. She stepped on something that crunched underneath her foot.

"Oh, damn." It was a crushed earring.

Annabelle saw the rest of the jewels scattered on the floor, the box on its side.

"Shit. Smokey," she said.

Smokey was the Macks' twenty-five-pound grey cat. They'd moved him to the barn for the summer, and Nathan came over to feed him. But sometimes he still slipped into the house. With a guest who had to cross the threshold multiple times when coming or going, Smokey was bound to get in.

"I'll have to apologize," said Annabelle. "This is awful."

They began retrieving chains and earrings and rings from the floor and under the furniture. Hy spied the crumpled paper under the bed. She picked it up, smoothed out the creases. Fine lines wrinkled the calligraphy. The paper was dry, bits of it flaking off as she read.

"In other worlds, I loved you long ago;
love that hath no beginning hath no end – "

This was somebody else's love, not hers, but Hy was surprised by the small sharp pain she felt. There was scar tissue there, well-formed and thick. It shouldn't hurt anymore, erupt like this after twenty years.

She had been free, single and not yet twenty. He – he had been married, with a wife and two children.

Hy read the two lines again. She folded the paper and slipped it in the box. She put her heart back where it belonged. It had been broken. It was fixed now. Pretty much fixed.

Annabelle turned.

"What's that?"

"Nothing."

From the look of her, Annabelle thought, it was very much more than nothing, but she'd learned not to pry into the secrets of her friend's heart.

Chapter Twenty-One

"Pick it up."

"Me? That?"

Alyssa was looking down at the axe with horror.

"Yes that." Jamieson pointed at it, propped against the wall.

Alyssa stuck a tentative hand forward, then recoiled.

"Is it the – ?"

"No, that's not the weapon that killed your…uh…husband. That one's been dusted for fingerprints and set aside as evidence."

Alyssa's hands came up over her face.

"Please." Jamieson used the word as a command, not a request.

"I can't. I'm sure I can't."

"I'd like to see that you can't." It was a long shot. The woman didn't appear to have the strength to wield an axe with any force, and besides, it wasn't the way women usually killed – by one brutish blow of an instrument. They were more likely to attack with a knife, stabbing repeatedly, unleashing not just hate, but thwarted love as well.

Alyssa moved forward, and put first her left hand, then her right, on the handle of the axe. She gritted her teeth and hauled it up, her face turning red.

"Higher."

Alyssa was supporting the axe with her body. She grimaced as she lifted it, waist-high. Jamieson could see her muscles straining, her face turn red, her pulse quickening in her neck, a bead of sweat forming at her temple. The effort was genuine.

"All right. You can put it down."

Alyssa sighed and dropped the axe to the floor, just missing Jamieson's foot. Jamieson hopped back and her weight came down on her injured ankle. She crumpled into her chair.

She pulled out a piece of paper. "Remove your gloves, run your hands through your hair, and press your fingerprints on the paper here."

Alyssa removed one glove, from her left hand.

"Both gloves."

Alyssa didn't move.

"Both gloves."

Reluctantly, Alyssa peeled the glove off her right hand. She was self-conscious about the scar from several reconstructions. She hated to look at it. When she did, she saw it as ugly, a deformity people would gawk at.

Like a child's, Jamieson thought. And sickly pale.

Alyssa swept her hands through her hair, plunged them onto the paper, whipped them away, and put her gloves back on.

"Okay, you can go," said Jamieson. "But be available for further questioning."

"Of course." Alyssa smiled and floated out of the Hall.

Annabelle was looking in the cracks between the boards of the old pine floor for missing earrings. Hy was organizing the jewellery case, and, curious, pulled out an appraisal envelope. It contained a photo of a modest diamond ring, probably an engagement ring, one they hadn't found in the room.

The two women searched for it, with no luck.

"She must be wearing it," concluded Hy. She put the photo back in the box.

When Alyssa returned from her interview with Jamieson, Annabelle had gone, but Hy was still there and heard the front door open. She scurried down the stairs to see Alyssa come in a final time. Thank God, she thought, that she didn't have to see the whole performance. She was getting tired of it. What must it be like to live with her?

Alyssa didn't notice Hy right away. She pulled off her gloves, wet and soiled from her excursion. Then she saw Hy, and her hands flew to her face in shock. She was paralyzed in that position, and Hy was, too, staring at Alyssa, wondering.

"What's wrong?" asked Hy.

"Fresh gloves. I need fresh gloves. In the hamper." Hy opened it to find that it was full of dozens of pairs of gloves, in every colour imaginable, but at least half of them were…

"White lace," said Alyssa, indicating her choice.

Hy fished out a pair of gloves and held them out to Alyssa, her right hand hidden in the fabric of her dress. She turned and put them on, then turned to Hy again, her face tormented.

"You won't tell anyone."

Hy was confused. "Won't tell…what?"

"That you've seen my deformity."

"I didn't. I didn't see any deformity."

An uncertain smile formed on Alyssa's strained features.

"You are kind," she said.

"No. Just truthful. I saw nothing." She hadn't. A bit of redness, some kind of scar maybe on the right hand, but nothing really.

"Very kind." Alyssa was beginning to regain her composure. When Hy offered to make her tea, she inclined her head gracefully – and gratefully accepted.

Now, Hy thought, she might be able to squeeze some information out of her. She wanted to know why Alyssa had accused Suki of killing Lord. Was it jealousy – or was there any truth to it? Could she get Alyssa to talk about it?

When the tea was ready, they took it into the double parlour. The Macks were large people and their furniture had been chosen to fit them. Alyssa was swallowed up by the big old armchair that Ben had been sitting in for the past twenty-five years. There was a permanent depression in the cushion, and when Alyssa sat in it, she sank down so deep that her feet could not touch the floor. She looked like a child, except for the fine wrinkling on her pale skin and skeletal face. Her fair hair was washed out and frizzy with split ends escaping in every direction. Her complexion was pallid, her clothes neutrals, the chair beige, and it absorbed her. The gauzy material cascaded down from the ceiling and around her, making it difficult to see her face, to see her expression.

Hy told her about finding the jewellery case upset, blamed the cat, and gave Annabelle's apologies.

Alyssa seemed unperturbed.

"I'll have to check if anything's missing," she said.

"There was a photo of a ring we couldn't find…"

"Oh that…," Alyssa said dismissively, waving her hand with the wedding ring on it, slipped on over the white glove.

And the engagement ring? Hy wondered. Some women put that on their right hand. It wasn't on Alyssa's.

"Why did you say Suki killed your husband…her husband?"

Alyssa gritted her teeth. "My husband. Who else would have done it?"

"Who else?"

"I didn't kill him, if that's what you're thinking."

"What happened that night?"

Alyssa's eyes narrowed. Should she tell this woman what she hadn't told Jamieson?

"I followed Leone. I saw him in the glow of the moon as he headed down the shore. I wondered what he was doing, so I followed him."

"In his footsteps?" Of course, thought Hy. The footsteps in the photo.

"In his footsteps. I could see where to place my feet by the light of the moon."

"Why did you do that? Were you suspicious?"

"Yes. I was."

"And what did you see when you got there? Did you see him kill Lord?"

Alyssa cast her eyes down. She fiddled with the glove that hid her scarred hand.

"No. I saw nothing. He wasn't there when I got there."

"And Lord?"

"Oh, he was there."

"Dead?"

"Dead."

"Did you want him dead?"

The glint sharpened, hardened.

"No…why would I want him dead?"

Why would she?

"The thing is…" Alyssa leaned forward confidentially, her feet now almost able to touch the worn Persian carpet. "Well, the truth is, we were about to reconcile."

"What about Suki?"

An upward shake of the head. Contempt. Eyes narrowing around the hard glint. She pushed forward in the chair. Feet hit the carpet. Suddenly Alyssa seemed larger, not the hunted but the hunter.

"What about Suki?"

Had Hy said anything Alyssa hadn't simply repeated?

"Did Suki know? Did she care? Did she care about Lord?" You wouldn't think so, thought Hy, the way she'd been fooling around with Ian.

Alyssa propped herself up, a hand on each side, pressing against the chair cushion, her chest, with its negligible breasts poking forward in the silky dress, two small cones like a pubescent girl's. She stood up. Turned halfway to look out the window, down to the shore. The surf was still pounding onto the beach. Hy couldn't see her face, her eyes, her expression.

"Suki didn't know. She doesn't care. Not about him. He didn't care about her either."

"He married her."

"Ha!" The sound was metallic, dismissive.

"He married her to make me jealous."

"Did it?"

Alyssa turned and stared straight at Hy. Hy couldn't read her eyes. They'd gone blank. Cold. They didn't match the smile that spread across Alyssa's face.

A smile of satisfaction, but cold, blank eyes. Two separate messages. But what did they mean?

"Of course not. I knew he was still mine. That he'd be mine as long as I wanted." The eyes came alive now. "He was mine when he died." Triumph.

Hy still didn't get it. What power did this woman have over Lord? He, with his good looks, with this little mouse.

"Was Suki jealous of you?"

Alyssa toyed with her wedding ring, circling her finger with it.

"Very," she said, and sat down.

"Might they have argued…is that why you said…that Suki…"

Alyssa slipped back into the chair, feet again well off the floor. She looked like a rather uninteresting doll. The fabric undulated around her.

The Black Widow spider in her nest.

"Killed Lance? Oh, I think so. Yes, I think so."

But Suki had an alibi, thought Hy, when she let herself out the big double doors with the carved St. Andrew's cross.

Ian. Ian was Suki's alibi.

It was obvious. That's all Ian was to Suki. An alibi. Ian was in the middle of a dangerous game. Hy headed for his house. It was uphill all the way, and she was out of breath when she got there. Hers wasn't the only heavy breathing, as she let herself in the kitchen door.

Not again, she thought.

Someone was having an orgasm. On the point of backing out of the house, hands over her ears, Hy heard the cries reach a peak, followed by insane laughter and a squawk.

Not Suki. Jasmine.

Jasmine was doing a perfect imitation of Suki having an orgasm.

The parrot squawked again, and then resumed the heavy breathing. Hy followed the sound into the living room, where the parrot was perched on Ian's shoulder. Ian was oblivious to the bird's carrying on, lost in his computer screen. No sign of Suki.

"Where is she?"

He jerked his head in the direction of the Hall.

"Being questioned by Jamieson."

Hy slumped down in a chair. The arm fell off.

"You know you could be sleeping with a killer."

"I could be, but I'm not." He said it in that smug way of his, but something nagged at him. Something Suki had said about Lord: *"He can't and you can."* Ian had taken it to mean that Lord was impotent, but might it be because she knew he was dead? Because she'd killed him?

"Then what was that you were doing on the couch yesterday?"

"We weren't sleeping."

"That's for sure."

"Credit me with a bit of sense. The woman is not a killer."

"And what particular sense tells you that – touch, smell, taste? Or is it what you see – or hear?" Hy let out a long, seductive moan. Jasmine copied it. Hy did it again, in a duet with the parrot. In the heightened state Ian was in, the sound stirred him.

"Don't do that unless you mean it."

She grinned.

"Mean it. Do you mean it?" asked Jasmine.

He flushed.

"You didn't see him at all? Didn't visit your husband?"

Suki shook her head and her thick hair bounced around her shoulders. Product.

But she didn't actually speak. Didn't say no.

Jamieson leaned forward, to ask the question again and press her point. Then she caught it. That scent. *Poison.* That was the name of the perfume. Jamieson choked on it, its heaviness invading her lungs. She pulled back.

"You were there." It was the scent she'd smelled at Lord's. And she could see him and Suki – Suki had been the one in the bed, a bed where she'd failed to find satisfaction. And Lance Lord was trying to give it to her in the only way he could.

"This is for you, my electric lady." He'd be balancing one of his guitars, the Fender Stratocaster, on his knee and playing a medley from "Electric Ladyland." All dressed up as Jimi Hendrix. Maybe he thought it would turn Suki on, and make up for his inadequacies.

"No. I wasn't there. I was with Ian. He'll tell you."

"In the bed. You were in the bed."

There was a long silence. Suki hadn't expected to get away with her denial, but she thought she'd try it. She had nothing to lose, and nothing to hide, as long as the police believed her story. And why shouldn't they?

"Okay, yes, I was with Lance that night. We had dinner together."

"Lobster," said Jamieson, without looking up.

"Yeah, right, lobster."

"From?"

"From? I don't remember where from. Does that matter?"

Jamieson looked up sharply.

"In a murder investigation, every detail matters."

"I don't remember. Some fish shack on a wharf. The cabbie took me there."

"You came by taxi?"

Suki nodded.

"From?"

"Charlottetown."

"Someone had something else."

"Yeah, Lance. I bought him the steak in town. He doesn't eat lobster."

Jamieson noted the details. Not particularly important, but she liked to keep track of everything.

"Okay. You had dinner. Go on."

"We ate."

Jamieson suspected Lance was at his most charming. Flashing smile. Burning blue eyes. A great body in those tight bellbottoms that showed how well-endowed he was.

"We ate – and we got..." Suki was all blushes and lowered eyelids. A small smile lit her face and eyes.

"You got?"

"...we got intimate."

"It looked like there was only one person in that bed."

"Well, Lance was...it was..."

Silence. The silence Jamieson expected would make Suki blurt out something to fill the vacuum. Suki did not. The second hand on the school clock at the back of the Hall ticked until Jamieson couldn't stand the silence.

"Didn't he use the Viagra?" Jamieson bet the Viagra had upset Suki.

Lord smiling, his matinée idol smile, the too-white teeth, too perfectly aligned, flashing at her.

"Viagra?" She jumped up, threw her napkin down on the table.

"Viagra?" Louder, as she marched the length of the table toward him.

"Viagra?" Her face within an inch of his. The smile on his gone, replaced by a perplexed look.

"I have never been so insulted."

"I have never been so insulted."

Jamieson was struck by how close she had come to the truth. Had she been insulted enough to kill?

"Did he use it?"

"What?"

"The Viagra?"

Suki shook her head.

"It was over soon?"

"He was..."

"In and out?"

Suki frowned. What did she know? Who had told her about Lance?

"More or less."

Less, thought Jamieson, clearly less. Could that have anything to do with the murder? Could Suki have killed him because he didn't satisfy her? Unlikely, but worth pursuing.

"And the KY Jelly? Yours?"

Now Suki was every bit as insulted as she had been about the Viagra.

"No. Of course not. It was for that dry little stick Alyssa. Like the bedroom. Lace and romance. I don't think they ever screwed."

Jamieson pursed her lips, rose-pink lips against a pearl complexion. Flawless. Has she ever had a man? Suki wondered.

"Enough details of your intimacy." Jamieson decided she could pursue that further at another time if necessary. "Perhaps there were events leading up to and after that might be significant. Let's go back to the supper. You're seated at the table. What did you talk about? What mood was Lord in?"

The sneaky smile again. "Well, I've told you that. We talked about getting back together, of course. That's what led to – "

"Liar..." The small high cry of a child, crossed in the playground at recess.

"Liar," Alyssa repeated, sailing across the room with a sense of purpose.

"Mrs. Lord!" cautioned Jamieson.

"Yes?" they both said.

"One at a time. I want to speak with you one at a time." She turned to Alyssa. "We have spoken, and I may wish to speak to you again, but right now I am interviewing Mrs. Lord. Please leave the Hall."

Alyssa pressed her lips together, angry that Suki was being called Mrs. Lord. Angry about being asked to leave the Hall. But she swallowed the anger – Jamieson could see her gulp it down, her larynx rising and falling. Alyssa smiled, unconvincingly, and spoke in a new, soft tone.

"It's just that I might have a piece of evidence. It may not be relevant, but I'm missing a ring."

"Lost or stolen?"

"Stolen, I believe. Yes, stolen."

"You've left it somewhere, perhaps. Taken it off to wash your hands?"

"I never wear it. It never leaves the house."

Jamieson sighed. Side issue. It was undoubtedly a side issue. Like the marijuana plants, forgotten in the Institute room. Forgotten but not gone, she thought, as she smelled the scent now, wafting into the main room. She'd have to do something about them, too.

Jamieson flipped to the back of her notebook.

"Description of the ring?"

Alyssa thrust the appraisal photo at her. Jamieson took a quick glance.

"Missing since when?"

Alyssa shrugged. "I don't know."

She didn't mention that her jewellery box had been upset. She didn't say that the ring had been gone a long time. Gone, but not missing. Not really. She smiled a sly smile.

Jamieson held up the photo. “May I keep this in the meantime?”

Alyssa nodded, smiled again at Jamieson, frowned at Suki, and headed for the door, gliding smoothly across the room.

Jamieson waited for her to cross the threshold before continuing her questioning of Suki.

“When did you leave Lord’s?”

“Quite early. I was with Ian most of the night, as he’ll tell you. Having a little…uh…reunion.”

“He’ll back you up on that?”

“Of course.”

“Time of arrival and departure?”

Suki laughed, tossing back her thick mane.

“We weren’t using a stopwatch.”

“So neither of you can confirm your time of arrival or departure?”

“Well, there hasn’t been a departure. As for the time of arrival, he wasn’t in bed yet.”

“But he might know?”

“He might…and so might Moira Toombs.”

“Moira Toombs? What’s she got to do with it?”

Suki leaned forward, her tone confidential.

“She’s sweet on him. She watches.”

“Watches?”

“From her window at night. You can see Ian’s house. You can see right into his living room.”

Jamieson sighed. The timing was too close to matter anyway. You couldn’t pin down a time of death as narrowly as these circumstances were forcing. She supposed she’d have to speak to this Moira woman sometime, but not yet.

“You had dinner with Lord, were…intimate…with him and spent the night with Ian Simmons. What am I to make of that?”

“Make what you want of it. Those are the facts.”

“Could you please elaborate on those facts?”

"Lance left me waiting. Just lying there in bed. He'd been up to his Jimi Hendrix thing. He thought it turned me on. It didn't, but it got him off."

"His Jimi Hendrix thing?"

"He'd get all dressed up and play his guitar. I peeked around the bedroom door. He looked ridiculous – wearing the bellbottom pants, the orange dashiki, and this lime-green paisley scarf." She smiled, not a kind smile. "And the Afro wig."

Jamieson clicked on the photograph of Lord. The scarf was tied around his head, the wig askew, part of it stuck into the wound by the blow of the axe. Lord's first and last front-page photo would have had him rocking and rolling in his grave.

Jamieson had to agree that it was unfortunate he was wearing the Afro wig.

Suki brought the weapon down with clear control. No trembling of the muscles, the grip of her hands sure and confident. She leaned it against the table, flipped her hair behind her shoulders, and sat down. Jamieson had no doubt that Suki had the strength to have wielded the murder weapon. She was capable, at least physically, of killing Lord.

But had she?

Jamieson lifted the will and turned it over so that Suki could see what it was.

"Do you recognize this?"

"Obviously. It says it's Lance's will."

"I didn't ask if you knew what it was. I asked if you recognized it, and..." Jamieson fingered the burned patch. "...this."

How did she find it? Where was it? Where was he?

Suki slumped down, pouting, on the living room couch. His eyes followed her, disappointment in them. Was that when he saw the flashlight out the window and Jim MacAdam at the top of the cape? On his land.

Was that when Suki saw the will on the coffee table?

His will.

Suki shrugged. What did it matter if Jamieson knew?

"I tried to burn it."

"Why?"

"I was angry. It didn't mean anything. If I'd really wanted to destroy it, I'd have made sure it burned."

"Why were you angry?"

"You must have read it. He was leaving everything to her. Even now."

"And you wanted everything?"

Suki laughed.

"No. I don't care about that. It's her I care about. Losing to her."

"But you didn't."

"What do you mean?"

"The will is not valid. It was revoked by your marriage to him."

"You mean it's no good?"

"No good to Alyssa."

"Is everything mine?"

"I suspect so. You may have a hard time collecting."

"I've told you, I don't care. It mattered to her." Suki broke into a broad smile. "So I won, after all."

Jamieson thought she was no further ahead, but she pressed on. It had happened outside. Had Suki gone out? Was he dead or alive when she got there? What did she do when she came back in?

Suki was in a panic.

She looked wildly around her. The remains of their dinner on the table. Cooking utensils piled up in the sink. Her fingerprints on everything. She couldn't think. She'd only make things worse if she cleaned up, wouldn't she?

Why should she not have had dinner here, with her husband?

Why not?

Chapter Twenty-Two

"It was dark, I know that..."

Ian was seated across the table from Jamieson. She sat upright, a no-nonsense look on her face, waiting to hear what time Suki had arrived at his house on the night of the murder. She sat rigid, pen poised over her notebook, and looked at him, unsmiling. She wasn't going to let the familiarity she had with him seep into the interview.

"Mr. Simmons," she called him to underline the official nature of their discussion. "Do you have an idea...any idea...what time she arrived?"

He did not.

"I'd been surfing the net and lost track of time. It could have been nine. It could have been midnight."

"Later?"

He shrugged, raised his hands, pressed his lips together.

"Could be, I suppose. I doubt it."

"The reason for your doubt?"

He flushed. "Well, we spent quite a lot of time together."

"You could have lost track of time then, too."

"Yes. I suppose."

He looked and sounded as if he were telling the truth.

What Jamieson would like to know was if Suki were telling the truth. Having an exact time wouldn't prove who killed Lord, but it would tell if Ian and Suki's stories matched, and if she were lying. Every bit of information helped the whole puzzle come together. Right now, the pieces were all over the place. She'd at least like to get the outline, the edges framing the whole. Then she could fill it in.

"Did Miss Smythe…Mrs. Lord…come to The Shores to see you – or her husband?"

He flushed again.

"I honestly can't say. I thought it was me, at first, but…"

"But?"

He lowered his head. Fiddled with the zipper of his slicker.

"I don't think it was."

"What do you think?"

He looked up. "I don't know what to think."

"Do you think she could kill?" Jamieson asked because he had the most intimate knowledge of Suki.

He tipped his head back, staring at the ceiling. Jamieson wasn't surprised he didn't answer. His reply could be only conjecture, but potentially damning.

There was no reply. Why hadn't he said no immediately? They were both thinking it.

She tried another tack.

"How would you describe her temperament?"

He mumbled something about passionate nature, fiery temper, regretting it as soon as he'd said it.

"A temper that could lead to murder?" Jamieson knew she was leading him on, but couldn't think of another direction.

"I suppose so," he said, adding too quickly, "but you might say that of any of us."

"You don't believe that."

After a long pause: "No. No, I don't."

He was still wondering why he'd said any of it when he left the Hall. It was true, but why did he have to say so? Jamieson had led him on. Whatever Suki might be, he was sure she was not a killer.

But she would kill him if she found out what he'd said.

"Mr. Bullock can't come."

"Why?"

"He is…unwell."

The mastermind of Mind Over Muscle ill? Jamieson wasn't sure Leone O'Reyley was telling the truth. He was hard to read – an odd individual, perhaps odder than Alyssa Lord.

"When will he not be…unwell?"

"I don't know." Never again, thought Leone. Ed might never be well again. He was deteriorating, more rapidly every day. Disintegrating. He must keep him going. For himself, for her, for all three of them. Now, more than ever. He was so close to having what he wanted.

"Of course he wants to co-operate."

"Of course." Her tone was dry.

"And, of course, he had nothing to do with it."

"Why not?"

"I can't say."

Jamieson raised an eyebrow. "Can't?"

"Shouldn't."

"Mr. O'Reyley, this is a homicide investigation. A double homicide. You could face charges for withholding information. Or it could make you a suspect."

"But I am already, am I not?"

"That I can't say – yet. Is there a reason I should suspect you? A reason I should suspect Mr. Bullock, who can't be here – or so you say."

He shrugged.

"What about the land?"

"What land?"

"The land that Mr. Bullock gave Lord."

"A gift."

"A payment for services?"

Leone inclined his head.

"For services as his body double?"

So she knew.

"You could say."

"Why wouldn't I say? Was it blackmail?"

"Not exactly."

"Unspoken blackmail?"

"Perhaps."

"How did Mr. Bullock feel about that?"

"He didn't."

Jamieson's eyebrows shot up.

"He didn't know. I protected him from the knowledge."

"Why did he need a body double?"

"He didn't like to expose himself." Lord knew the truth about Ed. The land was no gift. It was payment to a blackmailer. He knew something Ed didn't know, and Leone didn't want Ed to know. He'd threatened to tell. Leone had shut him up.

"Why did he need protection?"

Leone's eyes were distraught. His face told Jamieson that he wanted to say something, but was struggling.

"At this stage, any information you give me will be confidential. Just between us."

His tense facial muscles eased, his body relaxed into the chair. Only his hunched shoulders revealed his stress. He leaned forward.

"I beg you to keep this to yourself."

"I can't promise that it won't come out, but if it's not necessary or pertinent to the case…"

When he said it, it was almost a whisper. There was no one else in the room, but had there been, they couldn't have heard it. Jamieson could hardly make out what he was saying, and she had sharp ears. She didn't know if she should believe what he'd said. It wasn't the picture Hy had given her of Bullock striding his property at dawn.

Leone leaned back, wondering if he'd done the right thing, telling her.

"So you see he had nothing to do with it, couldn't know..."

"Except where you were that night. He could know that."

Leone's brown eyes warmed, as if she had just made a very good joke.

Jamieson didn't make jokes. She didn't always get them either.

"He takes a strong sleeping pill at nine at night," Leone explained. "After that, he is gone, gone until morning." He smiled. Jamieson frowned and continued the interview.

"Then you will have to tell me where you were that night."

"I was at home."

"With Ed, who was asleep."

Leone nodded. "Correct."

"Anyone else who might confirm that?"

"Alyssa Lord. She was there, too."

Yes. She had told Jamieson that. She'd said she'd gone there after her rendezvous with Lord, earlier in the evening. Just for a chat. They'd been friends for years, she said. She went home early. Was Alyssa a suspect? She wasn't strong enough to have inflicted the wound. The spouse was usually suspect number one in a murder investigation. But who was the spouse – Alyssa or Suki?

"Did she say anything about her meeting with Lord?"

The warmth left his eyes. The chin that jutted forward stuck out further, his mouth clamped in a grim line.

"You should ask her that."

"I have. I want your version."

Hy's beachcombing bag still lay on her table. She'd passed by it countless times, telling herself she should rinse the shells and put them somewhere.

She grabbed the bag and took it over to the kitchen, drifting sand on the floor as she went. She spilled the contents into the sink and ran the water over the rocks and shells and driftwood. Many of them had lost their charm, but there were a couple that she slid onto the windowsill above the sink, already a clutter of rocks, shells, and beach debris.

Something sharp cut her finger, and she brought it up quickly to her mouth, sucking at the blood, staring at the weapon cupped inside a mussel, like a pearl in an oyster shell.

It was a small ring, real gold and real diamonds, small, but real. She washed it off. She tried to slip it onto her ring finger. She couldn't budge it over the joint. It slipped easily onto her baby finger. She held it out. It looked nice. She smiled, pleased with herself. A real treasure. She'd found a copper bracelet before and a silver locket, but nothing as nice as this. Let Ian make fun of her now for beachcombing.

And then she recognized it.

It was the ring in the appraisal photo in Alyssa's jewellery box, the ring they hadn't been able to find.

Alyssa's ring.

She must have scooped it up beside Lord's body. This wasn't just another beach treasure. This was evidence in a murder case. She should go directly to Jamieson.

But she didn't. She called Ian.

Chapter Twenty-Three

"Stargazing." Leone looked up at the ceiling. "After I'd seen her safely home, I was stargazing."

Jamieson thought she had caught him out.

"Saw her home? You said you weren't out that night. She never mentioned it."

"I wasn't. I was up in the cupola at the top of the dome. I saw her home from there."

There was something about the way he squinted. She flipped through her notebook to the calendar. Held it up. "What's this?"

He had no idea. Shook his head.

"How well do you see?"

Leone was looking down on the shore. He squinted into the night through his blur of poor vision. He had tried glasses, but reeled back as if struck, the first time he looked through the lenses. Ugly, stark, too much definition. He went back to his half-seen world. That night, he'd been watching the blur of her make her way home, but she wasn't going home.

"You saw Alyssa."

"Alyssa, of course. I watched her all the way home. Watched over her." It was a little white lie. He had watched over her. Just not from the dome.

Jamieson looked up from her notes. She'd written: "Protective of Alyssa." *A clue?*

"And when she was home?"

"Watched the lights go on downstairs, then off. Then upstairs – on and off."

"Why such concern?"

"I just wanted to make sure she was safe."

Or safely out of the way, so you could kill Lord?

"What was your relationship with Lord?"

Silence.

"You can tell me, or I can find out."

"The relationship? Over. It was over."

"It certainly is now."

Jamieson had Leone lift the axe. He did so with ease.

He could have used it, thought Jamieson.

"I will have to speak to Mr. Bullock, you know."

Leone shrugged. "Of course. I can't stop you, but you may be disappointed. Am I free to leave?"

"Just rub your hands through your hair, and let me get your fingerprints. Then you're free to go, for now."

Olive MacLean and Gladys Fraser would not be budged.

The ceilidh must go on.

Olive sat, her mouth set in a tight line, refusing to speak a word. Gladys standing was not much taller than Olive sitting, but she was a solid wall of stubbornness. She stood, immovable, her arms crossed and balanced on her formidable bosom, her chin thrust forward.

"The ceilidh will go on." Her face was set, lips pursed, eyes squinting. The look, so successful in forcing others to back down, unnerved even Jamieson.

"I'm sorry." When had she ever apologized before? To someone like this? Over such a trivial matter?

Trivial to Jamieson, maybe, but not to Gladys, in her official capacity as President of Institute. And on a personal level, Gladys desperately needed something to take her mind off the loss of Jim MacAdam.

"Why, we often have people coming all the way from Nova

Scotia."

Jamieson doubted anyone would cross the causeway. Her latest report from Murdo was that it was still impassable, the surf crashing up and over the roadbed in the wake of the storm. Their police cruiser was a pathetic sight, its nose still firmly attached to the dung heap, the rest of it sinking deeper into the wet, red clay. The access lane, where Nathan would have to go to pull it out, looked more like a river than a farm road.

The weather had improved, but didn't clear right out, as Olive's husband Harold had predicted. That didn't surprise anyone. There were still grim black clouds scudding across the sky and rain showers spitting down. The odd shaft of sunlight knifed through the clouds. The wind had backed off, but there were still strong gusts and what Harold called a "fair breeze" – a breeze that would blow the clothes at a right angle on clotheslines, should anybody hang them out.

It wasn't a good day for laundry, but no one was going to miss the ceilidh, not anyone who could walk, and some who couldn't. No one, certainly not Gladys Fraser, would think of cancelling it, murder or not. Next to the Christmas concert, the Labour Day weekend ceilidh was the social event of the year. It couldn't go on with a cot on the stage where the musicians would play, or one down on the floor where people would dance.

"No. I'm afraid you'll have to find somewheres else to carry on your police business. It can't be here. Not tonight. We depend on these events to keep the roof over our heads."

The roof had been replaced and paid for two years before. It was a steel roof. It wasn't going anywhere. Jamieson supposed she could press her point, but it would make for ill will in the community. She needed good will, so she struck a deal. The ceilidh could go ahead, but she was to be introduced to everyone who came to the Hall and allowed to question anyone she hadn't spoken to already.

Unconventional. But what about this case so far had been conventional?

Olive and Gladys looked at each other. Tried not to smile. For Gladys, that was easy.

"All right." Her lips were tight, but there was a mean smile in her eyes.

Murdo had been knocking on doors, arranging interview times for anyone who was a suspect or possible witness. Anyone who had been at or near the shore, or knew someone who had, was at the top of the list. He'd arranged interviews well into the evening, knowing how Jamieson operated – and then had to rearrange them all when he'd reported back to her and she'd told him about the ceilidh.

"Just bump them until tomorrow." She indicated a number of names low down on his list.

"I'm not sure who will come on a Sunday." He shook his head. "Folk around here won't take kindly to police interference on the Lord's Day."

"Jesus," she said.

"Exactly," he said.

"Well, do what you can. I may be meeting all of them tonight anyway. They say the whole village will be at the ceilidh."

Murdo smiled as he left, thinking of April. April would be there.

Jamieson, meantime, was thinking about the confidence Leone had whispered in her ear. Was it true? And, if true, what did it mean? It explained the body double. But did it make Ed a killer? It made it unlikely, but she'd have to meet the man to know. He could be an accessory, or even the mastermind. Was there a reason for Leone to protect Ed, beyond what he'd told her? Did Ed need protecting? What motive did either of them have? She was determined to speak to Ed, whatever obstacles Leone put in her way. He and Leone, Alyssa and Suki, were her most likely suspects. She would speak to the rest of the villagers to find out what they'd seen or heard.

Ed Bullock, too. Maybe it wasn't about what he'd done, but what he'd seen, heard, or knew. She had to get up to the dome. She'd have to stop Murdo, get him to drop her off there. She grabbed her crutches and pulled herself up, but before she was halfway across the room, she saw the cruiser pulling out of the parking lot.

Damn. She threw the crutches down, then had to hop around, trying to pick them up, glad that no one could see her looking like an idiot.

But Moira saw, from her dining room window directly opposite the Hall's window. She smirked and hugged Jamieson's private moment.

"You make a great alibi for her."

Hy and Ian were on the phone. She hadn't had a chance to tell Ian about the ring yet. He'd been telling her about his interview with Jamieson and now they were arguing about Suki. Hy thought it was unlikely Suki had killed Lord, especially with the new evidence she now had, the ring on her hand. She knew she was being petulant, acting like a child, but she couldn't help herself. She'd pushed Ian into defending Suki.

"You make alibi sound like an excuse – suspicious, somehow."

"I think it is."

"Do you think I'm lying, covering for her?"

She didn't think that. No, she didn't believe Ian would lie to her about something so serious.

"No. I just think she might have arrived later – or slipped out during the night." Ian, once asleep, could not be woken.

"Hy – we hardly slept a wink."

"Spare me the details." It was suspicious, Suki coming for Ian after all these years, at such a convenient time for her.

"Where is she now?"

"She's having a shower." She was having a very long shower. Using all the hot water, Ian thought meanly.

Hy could hear the hiss of the water down the phone line. She said nothing.

"Can I see you – alone?" he asked.

At last. Maybe he was seeing sense.

Moira couldn't stay away. She was torturing herself over what was going on between Ian and Suki, but she just had to see if there were really something between them, or if Suki was just a guest, a guest with no manners, prancing around half-naked.

It would also give her a chance to test her new look on Ian.

Moira had baked some blueberry muffins. She didn't know that Ian was tiring of them, but didn't dare say.

She knocked on the door. She usually walked in without knocking, but Moira didn't want to while Suki was there. She didn't want to see anything she shouldn't see.

"Gotta go. Talk to you later," said Ian, hanging up, without saying when and how he and Hy could meet. He had no idea how he would wriggle away from Suki.

He was almost relieved to see Moira at the door.

"Um, delicious," he said, but he didn't grab one. He took the plate and put it on the kitchen counter.

He looked at Moira. Was there something different about her?

Suki knew what it was when she sauntered downstairs. Moiras's poorly applied mascara was smudged and made her look a bit like a raccoon.

Her blush was uneven on her cheeks.

She obviously needed more lessons. Suki took Moira in hand.

"Let's go to your place," she suggested. "For some girl talk."

Moira blushed redder than her blusher. No one had ever invited her for "girl talk" before.

Suki turned to Ian.

"I'll be a while," she said.

"Take your time."

Suki paused at the door. Did he sound eager for her to go?

As soon as she had gone, Ian called Hy.

"Come over," he said. "She's gone."

Was that relief in his voice?

"Her jewellery box was on the floor, jewels scattered everywhere. Annabelle thought it was the cat, but I'm not so sure."

"Who would have done that, if not the cat?"

They were sitting at Ian's kitchen table, drinking coffee.

"I don't know. Alyssa herself? Suki?"

He groaned. "Let's not go there."

"You have to admit it's strange her turning up now…and then this happens."

There was a long pause.

"I have thought about it, but whatever reason she's here, I don't believe she's a killer."

"If she's not the killer, she's part of the reason. There's no love lost between her and Alyssa."

"When is there between wife number one and two?"

"The point is," said Hy, "Alyssa had no strong reaction to the jewellery box being upset. Just said she'd have to check if anything was missing. And this was." She held out her hand to Ian, and wiggled her little finger.

"That's hers? What are you doing with it?"

"I found it."

"Found it?"

"Yup."

"And didn't put it back?"

"I didn't find it in the box or in the room."

He looked puzzled.

"I found it on the shore."

"The shore?"

Hy was having fun, playing it out.

"Beside Lord's body."

She was gratified by the look on his face.

"Do you think Alyssa killed him?"

"I don't know. I don't think she could do it, but the ring says she was there."

"Or someone was. Someone who could've put it there. Who?"

"That's what I plan to find out."

"Aren't you going to give it to Jamieson?"

"No. First I'm going to wear it at the ceilidh."

"Be careful, Hy."

"What's to worry about? The room will be packed."

Ian groaned. He hadn't been planning to go, because it meant he'd have to accompany Suki. The idea embarrassed him. But now that Hy might be in danger, he'd have to go to back her up.

Step by painful step, Jamieson had inched her way to the dome, propelled by a sense that she shouldn't be blinded by Bullock's social or medical status. She became better at manoeuvring the crutches, so that by the time she arrived, she was quite expert, moving freely and quickly.

It wasn't so easy to knock on the door. She needn't have bothered. Leone had been watching her from the cupola as she struggled up the cape.

He let her in. "So soon?"

"No point in waiting." She looked beyond him into the room, barbells stacked in the back – real or fake weights? In front of them, Big Ed sat playing solitaire. He was sitting, but he stood up and came with a confident stride towards her, hand extended. She was surprised, because of what Leone had whispered to her at the Hall: "*He has no legs and his mind is going.*" Could that be the reason for the body double? The world had been told Ed was fit and whole. It was the cornerstone of his fitness empire. If people found out he was missing parts…

"Welcome." Big Ed flashed a smile, his tooth with the diamonds sparkling at her. She had no idea of the effort it took him. The flash of the diamonds made what was actually a grimace look like a smile. They shook hands.

"Please, sit," he said. He sat himself with a deep sigh. Jamieson remained standing. She meant to maintain a position of control, even though the crutches made her look and feel vulnerable. Her underarms and shoulder muscles were pulsing with pain.

She didn't know where to begin. *Ed Bullock. Order of Canada.* She mustn't be dazzled by the wealth, the legend, the tooth. But how could she frame her questions so as not to offend him?

"We're tracking everyone's movements on the night of Lord's murder. Finding out if anyone might have seen something, however insignificant, that might provide a clue to who killed Lance Lord and Jim MacAdam."

"Yes…" Not quite a question, but drawn out, with an upward inflection. Like he didn't know what she was asking. As if he had nothing to offer.

"We…I…thought perhaps you could shed some light on it."

Big Ed's eyes glazed over.

"Perhaps you could tell me the nature of your relationship with Lance Lord."

He began to mumble softly. Jamieson couldn't make it out. Soft and hissy. *Alyssa? Had he said Alyssa?*

"Mr. Bullock…I don't understand…"

"I'm sorry." The eyes were clear now, no longer glazed over. "What were we talking about?"

"Lance Lord."

"Oh yes. Lord."

"Your body double."

"Yes. Don't know why. Nothing wrong with my body." He

slapped his chest. "These media things. Hard to understand."

"Was it a secret? Did he threaten to tell it?"

Ed frowned. So did Leone. And it was he who replied.

"He did."

"Had he threatened – recently – to expose you?"

Ed looked confused. He began to fiddle with the top button of his shirt, counting silently each time he flicked it. She'd lost him again.

"I know what you're thinking," said Leone, "But I can tell you that's not why Lord died. Ed didn't care about the land. I didn't either. I cared about the betrayal."

"Enough to kill him?"

"No. Not that much. Lord died for another reason."

"Which was?"

"I can't say."

"You don't know?"

"I can't say."

"I'll leave you some time to think about it. Perhaps you'll find you can say."

Leone's eyelids drooped, shading his eyes.

"I don't think so."

"Well perhaps Mr. Bullock will be better equipped to speak for himself the next time."

Leone's lids lifted. His eyes were sad.

"I doubt that, too."

"I'm interested to know something about your system. Your claims…"

"Please. Not claims."

"All right. Mind Over Muscle. How does it work?"

"Come. I will show you."

Jamieson felt the same spark of sexual energy all women felt when Leone touched them. Even though she was a Mountie, he placed a hand on her arm, and steered her to the back of the circular room where the barbells were stacked.

His touch was charged, the hand warm, almost hot, on her arm. He sat her down on a leather bench under the weights. He took her hand and strapped it in. Then the other. She didn't like it. Tried to pull out. He strapped her feet in, making her wince when he tightened the strap around her injured ankle. She began to wish she hadn't agreed to this. But had she? *No.*

"So you will be safe," he said. He turned on the power, and a steel rod with massive weights on either end eased down, coming at her. She didn't feel safe.

"How is it safe?" Her voice rose.

He watched, a gleam in his eyes as the weights descended. A foot from her. Why had she agreed to this? Just above her and still coming down. Six inches. Sweat broke out under her arms and on her forehead. Only six inches more. Her stomach rebelled, churning with fear. Three inches. Two. She tried to pull away. The leather straps bit into her. One. The weights stopped moving.

"So you won't try to get up and hurt yourself with the weights."

Jamieson felt sweat trickle down her back. Not from exertion. Sheer fear.

A clunk. Grinding. And the weights began moving up again.

"Now imagine. Imagine you are lifting them. You are not yet. This is just to train your mind to take over from the motor. Slowly. Don't skip a moment. Follow through." The weights glided up. Jamieson couldn't imagine a thing, except how she would get out.

"It is the brain that signals the limbs to move, but in the absence of limbs, it is the mind that moves. You and the objects you choose. This is what I know."

Jamieson gained nothing from the experience, except a suspicion that Leone may have been threatening her. She left, frustrated. Who was Leone protecting? Himself or Bullock – or both? Was Ed Bullock, in spite of what Leone had whispered in the Hall, actually whole and capable of killing? At times he seemed so. One moment, intelligence shone through his eyes. The next, they were blank.

Could it be an act?

Hy and Ian were looking at the photographs she had taken of Lord and retained on her camera's memory card. They clicked through the shots, looking for anything that might be a clue, and found nothing. They ended up at the first shot – the one Hy had taken of the repetitive suns in the water.

"Look at that," said Ian.

"What?" Hy was looking at the composition, quite proud of the way she'd framed the shot.

Ian zoomed in.

"That." He pointed at the screen.

"Footprints," said Hy.

"Odd footprints." Ian zoomed in tighter.

"It almost looks like two sets of prints there. One on top of the other." So had Alyssa been telling the truth?

Ian peered at the screen.

"You could be right. We better tell Jamieson."

She put a hand on his arm. "Not just yet."

"That's withholding evidence."

"So's the ring. And this isn't really." Hy hit print. "She has the photo, too."

Ian watched from the door as she left. He stared at her back as she walked all the way down Shipwreck Hill, admiring her straight posture and long, confident stride. As she rounded the corner at the bottom of the hill, he sighed and went back to his computer. Within minutes, he was lost in the machine.

"Are you still working on that? Do you think she still wants it?"

Hy had stopped to see Gus on her way home from Ian's. Gus was ripping out and re-sewing yet another of the wedding quilt squares with its tiny patches placed just so. She'd made another error and turned it the wrong way and got the whole thing twisted around.

Like relationships, Hy thought. Maybe those women from the past knew exactly what they were doing when they made the wedding quilt so complex.

"Well, she hasn't told me otherwise, and the thing must be finished. If it won't do for her, someone else can use it. Maybe she'll find another man and want it for him. One's pretty much the same as another."

"What? The quilts? No, Gus, they're absolutely unique."

"I meant men. Ain't much difference between them."

"C'mon. It's always been Abel for you."

Gus just smiled and punched the needle into the fabric.

"Gus."

Gus looked up, eyes smiling.

"When? Where? Who?"

"Up West. Afore Abel. I was a schoolgirl. He was the teacher."

"The teacher?"

"Oh, we was only two years apart. But he was a schoolteacher. Too smart for me 'n' all."

"Was he good-looking?"

Gus grinned.

"Oh yes," she said, drawing out the word and the memory. "Oh yes," she said again, looking back down at the quilt.

"Then why didn't you…didn't he…?"

Gus shrugged. "Abel gave me a ride home from pickin' potatoes one day in his truck wagon. Then it was every day. Then we was married."

Hy smiled. So matter of fact for such a long, productive marriage.

"Me and Abel, we was suited anyroad. We rubbed along well together."

Rubbed along well enough to produce eight kids. But Abel was never around, thought Hy. Maybe that's why the marriage had lasted so long.

"Why did you come here?"

He'd asked her the same thing the day before, and she had managed not to answer.

Ian was sitting at his kitchen table. Suki was stirring a pot on the stove. She ladled the contents into two large bowls.

"Made it myself," she said as she plopped a bowl in front of him, not answering his question. Hungry, he began to spoon it up, slurping as it went into his mouth.

She gritted her teeth at the slurping sound.

"I don't believe it was for me," he said between spoonfuls.

"What, the chowder?"

"No, not the – " He suddenly realized what he was eating. "The what?" His eyes opened wide. He stood up.

"What's in this chowder?" It was hard to make out what he was saying. His mouth was full. He was headed for the kitchen sink.

"Uh…I don't know…"

He spat the chowder into the sink.

"You said you made it."

He turned on the water, drank out of the faucet, rinsed, and spat again. He never drank tap water.

Suki frowned. "I did…" She smoothed the napkin on her lap. "I didn't think it was that bad."

"Mussels. Does it have mussels in it?"

"Are those the things with the purplish black shells?"

"Yes," said Ian, washing out his mouth again, this time with filtered water from the fridge.

"Yes, there were some of those."

Not too many, he decided. And he'd hardly swallowed any of it. He seemed to have had no reaction. He'd wait it out. Ian was allergic to mussels, his mouth blowing up in hives when he ate them. Each time – there had been only two occasions – it was worse. The doctor had told him that one more could be fatal.

When he told her, her hand flew to her mouth.

"Oh, I forgot. Well, no harm done."

Ian felt a thin prick of fear. She had known that about him, but could he expect her to remember all these years? Was she trying to kill him? No, she couldn't be. He was her alibi. There, he'd used the word Hy had used. *Alibi.*

"You could have killed me with your chowder."

"Do you really believe that?" She smiled. "I don't believe in allergies. I think it's all in your mind."

"You would believe if you had them. Trust me."

"If you say so." She attacked her chowder with gusto.

He sat down again, and grabbed the loaf of bread, sliced it, buttered it, and began chewing on it.

"Sorry," she said, sounding insulted, and as if he were overreacting.

Life with Suki. Bread and water – and the occasional fatal chowder.

Ian frowned.

Suki scowled.

Chapter Twenty-Four

"Do you think it was Suki killed Lord?" Gus could believe it might be. For one thing, there was the strange name. Names. Suki Smythe. What was wrong with Smith?

"I don't suppose so. I guess I'm just – "

"Jealous?"

Hy squirmed.

"Not really," she said, but Gus wasn't convinced. "It's just that she takes up so much of his time. I'd like him to help me solve the murders."

"Well, now, the police will do that."

"They don't seem to be in a hurry."

Jamieson's words still stung: *"Just stay out of police business."*

It had made Hy want to find the killer before Jamieson did. She had her own list of suspects and intended to question them. She'd spoken to Alyssa and had access to Suki. If Big Ed and Leone weren't at the ceilidh, she'd go up to the dome and speak to them there. If one of them was a killer, Hy told herself she wasn't afraid. She had to know more about the connection between Big Ed and Lance Lord. Had there been enmity as well, hate? Had there been bad business dealings or trouble over a woman? Alyssa? She intended to find out. Her plans included the ring she had found on the beach.

She left Gus to her quilting and returned home to prepare for the evening.

Like Alyssa, Hy had a piece of paper, folded up, tucked away.

When she got home, she took it out for the first time in years. She'd found it in her grandmother's jewellery box after she died.

"lady through whose profound and fragile lips
the sweet small clumsy feet of april came
into the ragged meadow of my soul."

It hadn't been from her grandfather. The penmanship wasn't his. Hy knew his scrawl. This writing was elegant, well-formed. And Hy doubted her grandfather had a soul, much less a ragged meadow of one. He wouldn't have known who e. e. cummings was. Not a man for poetry. No, someone else had given the poem to her grandmother. That was just as hard to believe.

Hy wondered how "meadows of the soul" and "sweet small clumsy april" could possibly apply to her grandmother. That stick of a woman with her tight-lipped disapproving mouth – "profound and fragile lips?" – the lukewarm eyes, the brittle voice issuing its terse instructions about conduct and chores. The woman who did her duty. What secret love had she been hiding? Had her smile, her warmth, her joy in life disappeared with her love, followed him and left behind just the shell, to carve out the mere outlines of a life? But that shell had kept this last scrap of who she had been, might have been.

It occurred to Hy then that she was not unique, having a lost love in the backdrop of her life. It seemed everyone had someone – her grandmother, Ian, with the ridiculous Suki, Gus and her teacher. Everyone had someone they'd lost – and there seemed no accounting for how one heart attached itself to another and why some held on so long.

"We will go to the ceilidh," Ed pronounced after Jamieson had left. He had to raise his voice above the noise of the vacuum cleaner Leone was pushing over the huge hand-hooked rug that dominated the main room. Curved like the walls, it had been custom-made to fit the dome's round shape.

Leone shut off the vacuum.

"What did you say?"

"We are going to the ceilidh."

"But you're not well."

"I am. You see that I am perfectly fit." He slapped his thigh. "Perfectly fit."

Leone wished it were so, but it was not.

Ed's mind was going, that was clear. And where his mind went, his body went, too. Leone had to pump him up every morning, for his daily walk – back and forth across the cape, from property line to property line, on what, Ed thought against all reason, were his own legs. They were as manufactured as the vacuum cleaner. But he had the ghost limb sensation, the feeling that his real legs were still there, and his eyes refused to see what his brain did not accept. Eyes and brain were in harmony. He had legs. Didn't Leone massage them every day?

He did, but only the thighs. Leone massaged mobility into him every morning, kneading his thighs and then his ghost limbs, the lower legs Ed thought were there, but he would never get back. They'd been amputated. The medical people and the army had been in a conspiracy of silence about it. First, because it was considered to be a part of the recovery process; then, because he became the poster boy for survival in medical and military circles; finally, because there was so much money riding on it, the secret had to be kept. Lord had been part of the tight circle who knew the truth. He had betrayed it. Lord had threatened to tell the secret and been silenced with land – and what did he, Leone, have for his loyalty?

The few others who knew the secret had kept it. A small lie, considering the remarkable mental recovery Ed had made. So much did they want to believe the miracle – and there was no doubt it was a miracle – that, over the years, the lie became the truth.

But the truth was that Ed could walk only with prosthetics, and was becoming less able to do so, as the threads he'd grown in his damaged brain had begun to wither and unravel. He spent most of his time sitting in his chair, which he refused to think of as a wheelchair.

"It will have to be in your chair." Leone wound the cord around the vacuum and stashed it in a closet.

Big Ed frowned.

"Well then, I won't go."

"I'll go instead," said Leone. "To let them know we have no fear of being seen."

"Exactly," said Ed. "No fear of being seen. Nothing to do with these horrible events. We have nothing to hide."

"Yes," said Leone. "I'll go. As your representative."

"My representative." Ed beamed, apparently satisfied, having already forgotten his desire to attend.

Billy had been looking forward to the ceilidh all summer, but didn't know if he could go. He felt he was in disgrace over the loss of Lord's body. But it had been found, hadn't it?

He was loading the washer on the back porch of his mother's tiny house. Like a little dollhouse it was, built so long ago that a lad as tall as Billy had to duck through the doorways and at the top of the stairs. The house was falling apart. Billy wasn't good like his father at keeping it in repair. Cars were one thing – at those he excelled, but houses? Downspouts, gutters, shingles, he couldn't fix any of them, and it showed. Shingles were missing on the outside walls and roof, the gutters were hanging down, partly detached, the downspouts bashed in, the lawn turned to weeds. Billy was his mother's only support. She was crippled with arthritis and couldn't even make a cup of tea, or so she claimed.

She was banging her cup on the table now, to inform him that she was ready for more. She insisted that she couldn't grip the pot, nor hold it steady, though there were times when he returned home to find that tea had been made, poured, and consumed. She'd say something about a neighbour coming over. Billy had never encountered anyone who'd been in the house, but he didn't question it. He was a good boy. He stuffed the rest of yesterday's clothes in the machine and set it going, then went to see about his mother.

Without filling her cup, he dashed back out of the room and slapped the dial on the washer. The sound of water streaming into the tub stopped. The sound of his mother banging her cup began again. He flipped the washer lid, dragged out his sodden jacket, and made a frantic search through the pockets. He pulled out the breath mint box. He had forgotten about it. He shoved it in a trouser pocket, then found what he was really looking for, the bunch of marijuana leaves, his own brand of tea.

He poured for his mother and retreated to the shed, where he rolled himself a spliff. Soon he was feeling good enough to decide he would go to the ceilidh. And the mint box he'd forgotten about? Jamieson would be livid. He'd give it to Murdo. Let him give it to her.

Hy saw Leone leave the dome at nightfall, heading in the direction of the Hall. Big Ed was not with him. *Good.* She'd approach them one at a time. She walked up the lane, leaning into a brisk wind. The wind was breaking up the cloud bank and allowing occasional glimpses of the moon. "A ghostly galleon," Hy whispered as it sailed behind the clouds, appearing and disappearing.

All the lights were on inside the dome, revealing a curious sight. In one porthole after another, in quick succession, was a face, looking out. She stopped and watched. Porthole to porthole, the head would appear, then glide away. After watching this happen half a dozen times, she approached the building and heard a rolling sound like a bowling alley. *Surely not?*

She knocked on the door. No answer. She peeked through a porthole, straight into the eyes of Big Ed Bullock. They were blank. He was drooling.

"Alyssa?" He croaked out the word. Hy couldn't hear him, but she read his lips and saw a glint of gold. *A gold tooth?* Then he disappeared from the porthole, and the rolling sound resumed. He was somehow rolling around the circumference of the building.

She waited for him to complete the circle, wanting to see his face again, to see if his expression remained blank, to see if he would call out for Alyssa once more. He did, looking straight at Hy. Did he think she was Alyssa? And around he went again, rolling along in some way Hy couldn't figure out. All she could see was the disembodied head of Big Ed Bullock.

Hy left to the sound of the rolling, around and around the dome. She turned and descended the cape, heading for the Hall, but her mind was still back at the dome, thinking of Big Ed.

That was the mastermind of Mind Over Muscle? A man who appeared to have no control over his own mind, no control of any kind?

Chapter Twenty-Five

"Alyssa."

Ed nodded his head, a small smile beginning to form on his lips, shaped with pain. Hard. It was hard to smile. He looked at all the photos of the women, with their endearments. *To my Big Daddy. Big Ed, Best in Bed. Muscle First, Mind Later*. He didn't notice that they were all written in one hand. Leone's hand. And now – they all turned into one woman. Alyssa. He hadn't had them, and he hadn't had her.

Big Ed was breaking down, just as Leone suspected. All the connections he had wired in his brain to make his big comeback were fraying, along with Leone's devotion, wearing thin. He had not been doing the upkeep necessary to keep Ed fully in the world, the tedious repetitions, the affirmations, the mental as well as physical therapy. Leone was becoming the master himself, making the decisions, running MOM, moving them from place to place whenever the secret of Ed's deterioration began to be known. A deterioration now so severe that secrecy wasn't the solution anymore. Leone had told Jamieson to keep Ed clear of suspicion. It was loyalty, but Ed had also become a means to an end. Alyssa.

"Alyssa," Ed said again. He wanted Alyssa, too.

Big Ed began to wheel himself again along the track that ringed the dome, looking out from all the portholes. Looking out at nothing. If Alyssa had appeared, he might not have known her. Hadn't he mistaken Hy for her? Or had he?

Big Ed could not be the killer, Hy thought – even though he had good reason to want rid of Lord, to be jealous of the reconciliation. If he couldn't be the killer, could he be behind it? She was trying to make sense of her different images of him. Yesterday morning, after the murder, he strode along the cape as he had done every morning, strong and sure. Tonight, he appeared to be a shell of a man, with only one thing on his mind. Alyssa. Hy looked at the ring she'd slipped on her little finger before she left the house.

Alyssa was at the centre of this. The ring would unlock more information. If Alyssa were the killer, what better way to find out than to confront her in a hall full of people? Would she show her face to publicly display her innocence? Hy looked down at Ben and Annabelle's house. All the blinds and curtains were closed. There was a thin crack of light from the parlour window and the outside light was on. Was Alyssa inside – or had she gone to the Hall?

The Hall was lit up, the parking lot jammed with cars, more cars parked along both sides of the road. Inside, Jamieson was finding it impossible to interview the people she was introduced to. They were all polite, smiling, pumping her hand, and then calling out to friends and charging across the room. She was studying Leone and Suki from her position by the door. Two, thought Jamieson. Now, if only Ed Bullock and…

The door opened. Hy came in, nodded to Jamieson, removed her jacket, hung it up, and bent down to take off her rubber boots, one hand holding on to the coat rack to steady herself. Every time someone opened the door, a gust of wind blew in, but now it was a steady stream of cold air, long enough for two or three people to enter, and Hy turned to see why.

Alyssa floated in, the wind wrapping her cape around her tiny body.

Three, thought Jamieson.

Bingo, thought Hy, pulling on her shoes. She felt a soft touch on her hand, on the finger that wore the ring. She looked up and saw a gleam in Alyssa's eyes.

"You found it." Alyssa's voice was so soft Jamieson couldn't hear what she was saying, and before any more was said, Ben and Annabelle came through the door. Ben was carrying a container of homemade ice cream. The cream came from his two pet cows, Liza and Rita.

"Clear the road," he called out, the great size of him forcing people to make a pathway.

In the commotion, Hy had grabbed on to Alyssa and disappeared with her to the back of the Hall.

"Yes, I found it." Hy made a motion to take the ring off her finger. "Do you know where I found it?"

"I have no idea."

"You don't?"

"It's not mine," said Alyssa.

"But – "

"Well, it was mine. It was my engagement ring, but it's not anymore."

"Ever since you lost it on the shore?"

A look of surprise on Alyssa's face. Genuine?

"On the shore?"

"I found it beside Lord's body."

Alyssa's hand came up to her mouth. She still had the wedding ring on.

"No," she said.

"Yes. When I found his body…I found this. Do you know why?"

"I have no idea."

"Isn't it your ring?"

"I told you, it was. It was my engagement ring." She took hold of Hy's hand and looked down at it. Her lips curled in contempt. "Small and ugly. I never liked it. I threw it away."

"When?"

"A long time ago. I wanted Lance to buy me a new one."

"And so how did it come to be on the shore?"

"You'd have to ask Leone that."

"Leone?"

"Yes. It's his ring. When I threw it away, he picked it up and kept it."

"Why?"

"You'd have to ask Leone that, too."

She turned away, leaving Hy with the ring. Alyssa weaved gracefully through the dancers over to the food table, where Leone was. They appeared to be ignoring each other, but Hy could see that they were talking as they filled their plates. They just weren't looking at each other.

Damn, thought Hy. I wanted to talk to him before she did. She played with the ring, circling it around her finger. She'd have to get to Leone next. Somehow. Or might he now come to her?

Everyone was talking about and staring at Moira and Suki. Suki, for her outrageous clothing and behaviour. Moira, for her new look. The makeup and more relaxed hairdo didn't make her look pretty, but certainly better, much better. Ron Dewey kept looking at her. Once, he winked. Perhaps there would be a way, he was thinking, an enjoyable way, to keep her silent about what she'd seen down at the shore in May. He sidled over to her and asked for a dance. She flushed with pleasure. She didn't like Ron, he disgusted her, but no one had ever asked her to dance before, not even Ian. She'd always asked him.

No one had ever touched Moira's breast before either, and she went hot with shame, and something else she couldn't identify, when Dewey, hand clasped over hers, brushed it up against her breast, his intent unmistakable. She was about to break free, when she saw Ian's eyes on them. Dewey was pressing her close. Let Ian see another man desired her.

He didn't see what Moira thought he was seeing. He was looking past her to Suki, dressed like no one had ever been dressed in the Hall before, not even the glamorous Annabelle. Suki's hair, newly dyed, glowed an unnatural blonde, tumbling down in abandon, looking as if she'd just gotten out of bed. Tons of cleavage. The front of the dress plunged below her breasts, revealing a tanned midsection and the slim white line of a bikini strap. The silky dress clung to her body, concealing none of her considerable charms. Her tanned legs looked magnificent on four-inch heels. Ian wasn't the only one looking at her. Dewey had circled Moira around, greedy eyes feasting on Suki, while his fist ground into Moira's breast, wishing it more ample, so that his fantasy that he was touching Suki would seem real.

In spite of her disgust, Moira felt a rush of warmth where she had never felt it before. She would have to consult *Cosmo*.

Even Harold MacLean, who was more inclined to cast loving glances at a piece of wood than a woman, was staring at Suki, his mouth agape. Many of the other husbands in the room were stealing quick glances – and getting sharp looks from their wives. Ian, dancing with Hy, was looking at Suki, too, and wondering what he'd ever seen in her and how he was going to get rid of her.

Annabelle and Gus watched Ian circle Hy around the floor. When the jig ended and a waltz began, Hy dropped her head on his shoulder, and he shifted so their bodies were touching from shoulder to knee. She melted into the dance and their movement together. He drew her closer. It was like last Christmas. They'd arrived at the Hall a bit tipsy, and had a long, slow dance that ended in a kiss – a real one, under the mistletoe. Something had started then, but it had subsided. It sank into the day-to-day, and their mutual desire not to ruin a friendship. They were both thinking about it now and about Suki. Hy – wondering why fight a lifelong dream. Ian – that his arms around Hy felt warmer, more comfortable than around Suki.

A tap on his shoulder. The moment was broken.

"May I cut in?"

Ian had no choice. He let Hy out of his arms, noticing the high colour on her cheeks, flushed with the warmth of the room and the pleasure of the dance.

She went into Leone's arms, and the warm feeling was thrust aside by the disturbing electric charge when he touched her. She didn't know what she would do if he tried anything. But that was not what Leone was after. While Hy was dancing with Ian, eyes closed, head burrowed into his shoulder, breathing in the comforting male scent of him, while Ian had been looking at Suki and thinking about the stupid choices he'd made, Leone had been riveted on Hy's hand. On the one small finger. On the ring. His ring.

Now he clutched her hand, crushing the ring into her flesh so that she winced.

He muttered into her ear.

"The ring. Where did you get the ring?"

Excitement shot through her. Alyssa had told the truth.

"I found it."

"Where?"

"Why do you ask?"

"Because the ring is mine." He squeezed her hand even harder. Ian, having been rebuffed by Jamieson – she didn't dance on duty – was now dancing quite happily with Annabelle, when he saw Hy wince and wondered what was going on.

"Mine," Leone repeated, and his fingers began to work the ring off her. She tried to pull away, but he gripped her. Mind over muscle, she thought. Use it. Mind over bloody muscle, as she tried to wrench free. Leone had worked the ring up to her knuckle, where it was biting in, too small to go over. She stomped on his foot. He let out a yell and released her, bending down in pain.

She fled across the room. Ian abandoned Annabelle as Hy sped by, grabbed her, and pulled her to him.

"What's going on?"

Jamieson was looking at them.

Through gritted teeth, Hy said, "Not now."

"When?" he said, holding on to her wrist as she tried to pull away.

"Later," she said. "Jamieson's watching."

"Okay, later. My house?"

"What about Suki?"

Ian looked across the room where Suki was entwined with Junior Johnson, a strapping young farmer with an eye for older women from town. Any town. He liked their slick glamour, their sophistication, their easygoing virtue. He'd never dated a girl from the village. The choice was limited, and none of the village girls would have been doing to him what Suki was now, moving with him, not to the music but to their own rhythm. A heated one. He whispered something in her ear and she smiled agreement at him. They'd be leaving soon.

"Somehow I don't think she'll be coming…," Ian almost said home "…back to my place tonight. So come. Okay?"

Hy nodded, and he let go of her.

Leone's baleful eyes followed her up the stairs, until she disappeared into the kitchen and the safety of the ladies bustling about, making tea.

Ian's eyes were on her, too. He wanted to know what had happened between her and Leone. Wanted to know very much. But even more, he wanted her in his arms again.

There was no one in Billy's arms. Tiny Madeline Toombs was staring at him from a corner of the room, too afraid to approach him, even when it was ladies' choice. Billy didn't even see Madeline, she was so small and hidden away in that dark corner. There was almost no one else of his age in the room. The young women of The Shores, those few who hadn't escaped to Charlottetown, Halifax, or Toronto, wouldn't deign to attend a ceilidh. They spent the evening instead at home, surfing satellite television, cell phones pasted to their ears or texting each other in their separate houses just across the road or down the lane.

Maybe he should go outside and have a smoke. He patted his shirt pocket, where he had two spliffs rolled up. Two spliffs, and, he remembered, the box in his pocket. Jamieson should have it, but he wasn't going to be the one to give it to her. He searched for Murdo and spied him at the food table, April popping a piece of cake in his mouth.

The band had switched to some sixties music. Billy crossed the floor, past eighty-year-old Elmer Gaudreau doing the Twist, Chester Gallant doing the Monkey and staring pointedly at Leone, and Moira and Ron Dewey glued together and hardly moving.

Jamieson had seen the struggle on the dance floor between Leone and Hy, but she'd been distracted by the exhibition Suki was putting on with Junior Johnson. Perhaps this evening wasn't a complete waste. The loud music banged in her head, threatening a migraine. She was staring at Suki, and thinking…thinking it through.

Suki read the will as angry voices shouted outside. Her eyes narrowed into two slits of pure hate.

Alyssa. He had left it all to Alyssa.

She shuffled quickly through the papers.

Then sliding them off the table, stuffed them in the wood stove, and set them alight.

The merry widow, thought Jamieson, as Suki and Junior pawed each other and sidled toward the door. She needed to know what, if anything, Suki could gain from Lord's death, what any of them could – Alyssa, Leone, and, quite possibly, Big Ed. She sat for a minute, and then climbed the three stairs unsteadily on her crutches to collar Hy in the kitchen.

"What was that all about?"

"What?"

"You know what. With O'Reyley."

Hy said nothing. Jamieson stared at her. There was silence. It worked.

"It was about this." Hy held up her finger.

Jamieson flipped through her mental files. The appraisal photo. This was the ring in Alyssa's photo.

"The stolen ring."

Hy flushed. "Stolen?"

"Well, missing. Alyssa reported it missing."

"She said she threw it away long ago. Why would she say it was stolen?"

Jamieson looked around. "If these ladies would excuse us." Olive MacLean and Annabelle quickly abandoned their food preparations and left the kitchen, looking behind them as they went. When they were out of range, Jamieson continued.

"I don't know. You tell me."

"How did you know this ring was hers?"

"I'm asking the questions. I saw the appraisal photo."

"So did I. In her jewellery box."

Hy had to explain how she knew about that. About it being thrown on the floor, its contents strewn around the room.

"But this ring? Why did you keep this ring? You're not a thief."

"I'm not. I found it."

"I don't think what you did counts as finding. More like taking."

"No. It wasn't in the room."

"Where was it?"

A long pause.

"On the beach."

"The beach? Where? When?" Jamieson ignored the sharp pain in her head that came with her excitement of at last having a clue.

"Yesterday morning. Beside Lance Lord's body."

Hy expected Jamieson to go ballistic on her, but it was worse. Restrained anger, tight and contained. The porcelain white skin blanched, the jaw stiffened, Jamieson's hands curled up in two fists, as if she were going to strike Hy. Her nails were digging into her palms to make her contain her fury. When she spoke, the words came out one by one.

"You…withheld…evidence?"

"Well, no. I only found it today, in my beach bag."

"I thought you said there was nothing in there."

"I didn't think there was. I collected the stuff elsewhere, but spilled it when I tripped over Lord. I must have scooped it up by accident."

"Why were you wearing it?"

"I thought I might find something out."

"And did you?"

"Leone says the ring is his. Alyssa says it's his, too."

"Then why did she report it missing?"

"Well, that's police business, isn't it? How could I be expected to know?" Hy took off the ring, set it on the table, and went back into the Hall, hoping that Jamieson would not lay charges against her. She didn't think she would. And Hy knew she couldn't stay out of police business.

In fact, she had every intention of finding out from Alyssa why she'd reported the ring missing. But when she got back to the dancers, Alyssa was gone. So was Leone.

Billy tapped Murdo on the shoulder. He held up the tiny box. Murdo, with the scent of April's butter icing in his nostrils, reeled from the smell.

"What in God's name is that?" he yelled above the music. Several faces turned to look at him. April flushed at the blasphemy.

Billy whispered in Murdo's ear. April studied Murdo's face. It was something important, she could tell, because Murdo stopped chewing the cake she had just slipped into his mouth.

"Jesus, man," he said. It sounded like "cheese 'n' ham" to April who, being used to people talking to her with their mouths full, started checking the sandwich plates.

"You should have – oh, never mind. Give it to me."

Murdo took the box from Billy's hand. He supposed he should tell Jamieson, but he dreaded the thought. Anyway, he couldn't see her anywhere. He'd wait until later, until the Hall had cleared. He slipped the box in his pocket, and forgot about it when April handed him a cheese and ham sandwich.

Chapter Twenty-Six

Gladys Fraser was sobbing hysterically. She was drunk. Everyone was so shocked to see her in such a state, and so blasted themselves, that nobody went to console her. Convulsions wracked her squat, square body.

Her husband Wally wondered what it was about. He'd been eyeing Suki all night, but she shouldn't care about that. They didn't share a bed anymore. Rather than go to help her, he went to help himself to more juice. He filled his cup to overflowing, brought it to his lips, spilled some down his chin, rubbed it off, and took another long haul on the drink.

The juice was better than usual. Much better.

Suki had spiked it.

Everyone had been drinking it. Some of them had never had a drink in their lives. Moira was one of them. She was so pickled she let Ron Dewey touch her breast properly, when he pressed her against the wall in the back of the Hall. So that's what it felt like. Disgusting. She leaned into him a little closer, and he slipped an arm around her waist.

Some had only ever had a drink for "medicinal" purposes, like Olive MacLean and Estelle Joudry. They were now having a great old laugh, slapping their thighs and cackling at…at…well, something. They couldn't remember later, only it had seemed funny at the time.

Gus had the odd glass of wine at family get-togethers, but nothing like she'd consumed tonight. She'd been parched. The juice hadn't helped. She was sure someone had turned the furnace on. Gus had given up hot flashes decades ago, but she felt as if she were having one now, and she stumbled across the room toward the basement door. The thermostat was at the top of the stairs. It was turned off. She'd swear it was on. She fiddled with it. It seemed to get worse – a blast of hot air and a sweet smell came from the floor vent. The furnace must be broken. Abel would fix it. Now where had he got to? She went looking for him, weaving unsteadily through the dancers, asking after him, but no one had seen him.

With her mucking about, Gus had accidentally turned on the furnace. The marijuana that had been in the kitchen had been moved to the cellar for the ceilidh, and when the furnace kicked in, the sweet smell of pot wafted up through the vents. There were only a few in the Hall who knew what it was; they looked at each other wisely, taking in deep breaths.

The juice and the scent of marijuana combined to get the Hall hopping as it had never hopped before. The band, a group of farmers and fishermen from up West, had knocked back a lot of juice and chased it down with more fuel from the mickeys tucked in their back pockets. They'd taken off, and so had their music, rocking the Hall like never before. Instead of the usual staid, shuffling two-step, the villagers were swinging and twisting and leaping up in the air. Chester Gallant had taught a few other old-timers his version of the Monkey, and Murdo and April were laughing and doing the Hitchhiker.

April's husband Ron was not laughing. Leaving Moira at one end of the room, he grabbed hold of April and told her to go home. Without him. He wanted to finish up with Moira. For once, April stood up to him and refused to leave. He went back to Moira, whose sour look turned into a smile at his return.

Gladys Fraser continued to sit on a chair below the stage, drunk and weeping for her lost love, Jim. When Hy came out of the kitchen, she was stunned to see the hard old bitch so vulnerable, and immediately crossed over to comfort her.

Jamieson was looking maudlin, too. She wasn't drinking – not even what everyone thought of as juice. But the emotion in the room had opened the door inside that she had kept firmly shut for years – still ajar from the night of her sister's wedding, when she had deliberately drowned her sorrows at the sight of Adam Buote, the last person she had expected to see. Muscle-bound – body and head, she'd thought with contempt. He'd come over and asked her to dance. She'd been giddy enough to accept, and she'd whirled around in his arms in a dream of what had once been and might be again. The dance ended. He bowed his head in a curt nod – and then ignored her for the rest of the night.

That had been humiliating. The one man she'd loved. The man who'd rejected her – twice. She should have known better than to open her heart to him. It had slammed shut when he dumped her. Now, she would have to put a lock on it.

Hy tried to comfort Gladys, but it was no use. She might as well not have been there at all, given how much attention Gladys paid to her soft words. Too soft, thought Hy. You'd have to hit Gladys with a truck for her to realize you were sympathizing with her.

Hy took another sip from her cup, went over to nuzzle Ian, and they began to dance again. Suki was doing indecent things with Junior Johnson by the coat rack. They hadn't made it to the door yet. Hy and Ian floated around in a pleasant physical and mental haze, out of step with the vibrant rhythm rocking the room. Ian was thinking he should take her home soon. His home.

"It's too late to go now."

"Mmmmm," Nathan murmured.

He and Lili had every intention of attending the ceilidh, but they went upstairs for a nap first. Now they couldn't get out of bed.

She was stroking his chest with her fingers, and planting little kisses on his cheek.

"You're doing it again," he said.

"What?"

"Mind over muscle."

"Heart over muscle."

"Whatever." He rolled over and enfolded her in his arms.

There would be no ceilidh for them.

Later, Lili lay awake, unable to sleep, a thought nagging at her.

"How's that feel?"

Hy was lying, spread out on Ian's floor, luxuriating in the warmth of the wood stove. He was sitting in the collapsing armchair. They were sipping brandy. They had been for about an hour. Hy had told him about Alyssa, Leone, and the ring – and about Alyssa reporting it missing. Was one – or both of them – the killer?

"It can't be Big Ed." Hy told Ian about her visit to the dome. "He's falling apart. He isn't lucid."

"But you said yesterday he strode the cape as usual."

"Yes."

"That was after the murder."

"Yes, I know, but – "

"He could be faking it."

"I suppose..."

"What about Suki?"

Ian groaned. "Not that again, although..." He stopped himself.

"Although what?"

"Never mind."

"Iaaaaan." She drew out the word in a way that always got Jasmine going. Soon they were both chanting his name in that irritating way. Ian was forced to cave in.

"Okay, I give up." Those were the signal words Hy had taught Jasmine to respond to. They both shut up.

"It's just that...nothing really..."

"There's no nothing about Suki."

"Well she made me a chowder..."

Hy sat up. "No...not...?"

"Yes. With mussels."

"Did she know?"

"Yes. Once..."

"Once upon a time. There goes the fairytale."

"Well, she would hardly try to kill me, would she. I'm..." Again he stopped.

"Her alibi?"

"I guess so."

"Odd coincidence."

They didn't get any further pursuing Suki than they had with any of the other potential suspects. Their discussion went around in circles. They tossed around names, mostly Alyssa and Leone, but couldn't decide on a killer.

"And then there's why. What motive?"

Ian shrugged. He was interested, but at the moment, wishing he could recreate the moment on the dance floor, that she might stay with him the night, that they might...

He polished off his brandy. Perhaps if he offered her another, sat down on the floor beside her...

He wasn't hopeful.

He poured them each another drink and slipped onto the floor. He took courage and twisted one of her red curls around his finger.

She smiled, stretched, and sidled closer to him.

He didn't know what to do next.

Neither did she.

Chapter Twenty-Seven

The next day was dead calm. A warm air mass shrouded Red Island, and the combination of the cold water and the warm air brought on a fog – blue grey and rolling in off the Gulf, over the tips of the waves, sea and sky like liquid smoke.

It settled in.

"RCMP are advising motorists to stay off the roads. Visibility is near zero. This unprecedented fog following on the September Gale has been wreaking havoc on island businesses and may severely affect the potato crop..."

Gus was nodding her head at the radio, and rocking her chair by the stove in harmony.

"You can't see as far ahead as your nose," she said, trying to warn Abel from going out. The back door slammed shut.

The fog made it hard to breathe – heavy, dense, intruding its way into the lungs. Hy had to fight not to panic. She felt as if she were suffocating.

Ian was suffocating, too, coming out of sleep, his face covered, covered with what? Hair. It was in his mouth, his eyes. She was on top of him, waking him. It should have been a dream come true, but it wasn't anymore.

She had come in last night just as he was about to put his arm around Hy. Suki. Sulky and dissatisfied. Junior Johnson had been a bust. He'd driven her to his house, one hand on the steering wheel and one on her knee. When she'd put her head in his lap, he had begun to weave all over the road. She'd come up laughing, gasping for air. He'd alternated between trying to get his hand up her skirt and taking hauls on his mickey. That was the problem. The mickey. He'd been pouring it into the juice at the Hall and was twice as pissed as he would have been otherwise. They had tumbled into his house – shack, he called it, and it was. Suki had sobered up instantly when she saw the inside. She should have known from the outside. A small bungalow, fully fifty years old and showing its age, paint peeling and siding falling off, no gutters. Car and motorcycle parts littered the driveway in front of a garage with a roof that sank in the middle.

The inside was littered with rum and beer bottles – covering every surface, including the floor. Junior had led her to a brown couch, its fabric worn and riddled with cigarette burns. It had smelled of nicotine and beer. Junior had burped, a big, smelly alcoholic burp, right in her face – as he wrapped his arms around her. Then another burp, and his face screwed up and Suki had thought he was going to vomit on her. She'd pushed away from him and jumped up, just as fluid projectile came out of his mouth, all over the couch. He'd groaned and slumped into it and begun to snore. She'd left the house, and though she had seen him leave the keys in his truck – all islanders did – she hadn't used it to drive back to Ian's. She didn't want to see Junior again. She'd walked.

Suki had struggled down the road, shivering in her flimsy dress and stumbling in her heels. She'd taken them off and plodded through the wet, cold grass up to her ankles, her dress clinging to her, wet through. There had been no chance of a lift. The few cars had been going the other way. As she'd approached the Hall, she had seen some stragglers still dancing inside. One of them was Moira, with Ron Dewey, holding each other up and hardly moving, just shifting their weight from one foot to another.

Suki had smiled.

She'd frowned when she had seen Hy and Ian lolling on the floor of his living room.

"Cosy, aren't we?" she'd said. It was well after midnight.

"Squawk. It's her!" Suki had pulled Jasmine's cover over her cage to silence her, then plopped herself down on the couch. She'd dropped her shoes, brought her legs up onto the couch, and stretched out with a big yawn.

"You youngsters been having fun while Suki was out?" She'd smiled, but her eyes did not. Hy, who'd been reclining against the couch, sat up.

"Just chatting." She'd reached for her sweater and pulled it on. "I better get going."

Ian had seen her to the door. He'd nearly planted a kiss on her forehead. She'd almost felt it.

"Ian, honey, bring me a towel." Suki, shaking her hair, rubbing it dry with her hands.

Ian pulled back. Hy turned and left.

Now morning had come and Suki was clinging to him and he couldn't shake her off. He struggled to sit up.

"What's wrong, lover?" Her tone was mocking. "Can't get it up?"

"Can't *get* up." He pushed her to the side. He could understand why Lance Lord might not have been able to satisfy her, her incessant demands.

"Come to Suki, sugar." She laid a hand on his shoulder. He shook her off. Actually shook her off. His dream woman. The love of his life. All he wanted now was to be rid of her, but he seemed to be stuck with her.

She pouted, and got out of bed. She flounced ahead of him to the bathroom. He went downstairs, and uncovered Jasmine.

"Silly bugger," the bird shrieked, piercing his ears. She did that whenever there were wine bottles or brandy glasses on the coffee table.

But Ian wasn't nursing a hangover. He was nursing regret. About Suki. About Hy. Would he ever get it straight? He made coffee.

Cup in hand, he looked outside. He couldn't look outside. There was nothing to see. Nothing but fog. He, with the best view in The Shores, could see the best of – nothing.

A shroud of fog. Red Island in funeral garb.

Looking at the thick, grey mist, he felt alone. Not just alone – lonely. He had to make contact. Not with Suki upstairs.

He hit number one on his speed dial. Hy.

The entire village had a hangover.

Moira Toombs had never been drunk in her life until last night, and had woken up with Ron Dewey beside her. It was a dream. A nightmare. So real she could smell the alcohol on his breath, then realized, with shock, that it was her own breath.

She'd realized, too, what a close call she'd had and knew now why they called it the demon rum. Her father had been what Gus called "death to drink," a rock solid teetotaler. They'd never had a drop in the house. She shouldn't blame herself. There had been something, something different in that juice. It had awakened feelings in her she'd never experienced before – not for Ian, but for that disgusting creature.

Had he been here in her bed? She couldn't shake the feeling that he had. Had she had what they call a blackout? Had he been and gone and done with her what he'd been doing to that blonde tart in Winterside?

And what about Madeline? What had she seen or heard? Moira got up and went to her sister's room. She opened the door, but Madeline wasn't there. The bed had not been slept in.

She tore down the stairs, pasty complexion flushed with anger and fear. Moira might think her sister Madeline was a useless mouse, but in those few moments she realized how tightly she was woven into the fabric of her life. The only one in the world who belonged to her.

Madeline had been drinking the juice, too, and had never got farther than the living room couch, where Moira found her sleeping with her thumb in her mouth. Moira was so relieved, her first instinct was to shake her awake. Then she softened, and let her lie there. It was the only tenderness she'd shown her young sister in years – and Madeline would never know.

Moira went to the bathroom to tighten up her hair, the same way she'd been wearing it for twenty years. She lacquered it with several coats of hairspray, as if that would erase last night.

Jamieson hadn't slept all night. She'd fallen asleep briefly, just before dawn, then woke, her head throbbing with the migraine that had been forming for two days. She groaned and rolled over in the cot, pulling the blankets above her head. It took minutes only for Murdo's loud snoring to transform from an annoyance to a rhythmical route to sleep.

Hy was up and feeling fine. She'd had only a bit of juice, and a couple of brandies at Ian's. Ian. It had been nice last night at the Hall – and after – but just as well nothing more had happened. It would have been awkward.

She pulled on her clothes, stuffed a muffin in her mouth, and daring the fog in her truck, headed to the dome. She wanted to meet Big Ed properly and decide what he was – or was not – capable of. She also wanted to know why that ring was so important to Leone. She was vibrating with excitement and fear, wishing Ian were with her.

Behind her, the phone rang in an empty house.

Chapter Twenty-Eight

Ed was not in good shape this morning as Leone massaged his stumps of legs. He didn't know how long it could go on. What would happen if the world knew that Ed had suffered a relapse? It could mean the collapse of his empire. Would anyone believe in Mind Over Muscle anymore if they found out that Ed had lost it, his grip on reality? It was all up to Leone now, and he had begun to think of Ed's business as his own. And Alyssa. Alyssa, too. How long could he prop Ed up? Did he want to anymore?

Leone wasn't sure Ed could go walking on the cape today. Especially not in this fog. He might go over the edge.

The idea flashed through his mind. He might go over. If he did go over – he shook the thought from his head. Ed was Leone's saviour as much as Leone was Ed's. But into that selfless loyalty, selfishness had begun to intrude. Ed was his means to his end. Alyssa. He would never convince her himself. But with Ed...

There was a knock at the door. Leone covered Big Ed with a blanket, peeked out a porthole, not meaning to answer, and saw through the fog that it was her.

A glint in his eyes, he went to the door.

"Alyssa?" Ed called out, pitiful, plaintively, and it was like a knife through Leone's heart. Ed. Lord. Lord, too, had loved and wanted her. And so did he. He was devoted to Ed, but in love, helplessly, with Alyssa.

"Alyssa?" Ed's tone was hopeful.

"No, no. Nobody."

Nobody. Hy frowned as Leone opened the door. She'd show him nobody.

He didn't want to let her in, held the door open only so far.

"Have you brought my ring?"

"Yes," she lied, "but please let me in out of the fog." She was as damp as if it had been raining. Scotch mist, she'd heard it called. Only this was thicker. Porridge.

He opened the door so that she could edge in. He held out his hand for the ring. Hy could see Big Ed lying on the table in the back of the big round room.

"Actually, I don't have it. Jamieson has it. She'll be wanting to question you about it, I'm sure."

He turned to look at Ed. Ed was preoccupied with a fly that was crawling across the table.

"She will think I killed Lord," Leone whispered between tightly clenched teeth.

"Did you?" She spoke up loudly.

He put his forefinger to his mouth.

"No, of course not," he hissed. Did it sound like the truth or a lie? Could he say one thing to her, and another to police? How long could he hold out before the inevitable? Not long, he knew, but it was no business of this one. He still didn't regret his promise to Alyssa. He would fulfill it. In time. There must be certain guarantees. For Ed.

"Why do you say of course not?" Hy was whispering now, too. She would get more with co-operation than antagonizing him, although he didn't seem antagonized so much as distressed. Genuinely distressed?

"Never mind. You wouldn't believe me."

"You don't have to make me believe you. You have to convince Jamieson. She'll want to know why the ring was on the shore – beside his body."

"Yes." He frowned. "Yes."

"Why was it?"

"That I can't tell you."

"How did you get it? When did you…?"

"She gave it to me."

"Alyssa?"

"Alyssa," said Leone.

"Alyssa," said Big Ed. He'd just killed the fly on the table and the name, her name, got his attention, brought him back. Her beautiful name. Soft and feminine, like her. He wanted to smile. It was so hard to smile.

Hy looked at him, surrounded by the photographs of women. Ed saw where she was looking.

"My women." Ed finally achieved the smile he'd been working on.

Hy smiled back.

"All your women?"

He looked confused.

They were – and they weren't. There was one other thing Big Ed lost in Vietnam, and he didn't get back. His fame, looks, and money lured the women, but it was Leone who had them while Ed watched.

"Our women," said Leone. He was Ed's eyes and ears, hands and legs, and…

Ed kept grinning. "Our women," he agreed. "All but one."

"All but one," said Leone.

There was no photograph of Alyssa.

"Alyssa," Big Ed called out.

"Alyssa." It stuck there in Leone's throat, and he had to say it again to get it out.

"Alyssa."

Like a broken record, thought Hy. Alyssa. These two men wanted her. So had Lord. That scrawny mean-spirited mouse with three men lusting after her. What was her secret?

"Why did she give the ring to you?"

"She didn't want it. She threw it away."

"Threw it away?"

"Tossed it across the room."

"When?"

"When she found out Lord had married Suki."

"But she kept her wedding ring."

He shrugged. "I know, but she didn't want the engagement ring. She said it was cheap and she had never liked it."

"And you did?"

"Yes."

"Why?"

He shrugged again.

"Love," said Ed. Was it a moment of clarity? His blank eyes said it wasn't. He was still in some dream about Alyssa that had nothing to do with their conversation.

"He's right," said Leone. "Love. She had worn it, so I kept it with me always on a chain around my neck, to have her near me."

"Then how," Hy returned to her original question, "did it land up on the shore next to Lord's body?"

Leone repeated his original answer.

"I can't tell you."

"Because you don't know? Or is it something you can't say?"

"I can't tell you," he said again.

"Is it your secret – or someone else's?"

He didn't answer.

The fog did not clear off early, as Harold MacLean had predicted it would.

It hung over The Shores, and most of the rest of Red Island, in a thick grey curtain with a layer of lighter wisps trailing across it. The surf was no longer pounding at the causeway, and it might have been crossed, if a driver could have seen where it was.

Nathan claimed he could. He couldn't see it, but he knew where it was, and was prepared to prove he could put his mind over matter and cross it today.

"It's a straight line," he said. "I can do it."

"No, you will not." Lili was the only one he would listen to. Besides, there was no reason to cross the causeway, and every reason to stay here with her, in their cosy love nest. That is what the big rambling old house felt like with the touches Lili had given it. Candles on the living room table, which shone with a paste wax polish. Pretty bits of material – found, Nathan knew not where – draped across the old, worn couch.

Lili was twirling the five-hundred-pound barbell in her delicate hands, not a muscle visible in her slender arms.

Nathan came out of the bathroom, a towel wrapped around his waist. With another towel, thick, white, freshly laundered that morning by Lili, he was rubbing his hair dry. She'd slipped out of bed and gone all domestic on him. His jeans and t-shirts were stacked neatly on the dresser in the bedroom. He finished drying his hair and dropped the towel to the floor. His hair, short and stuck up all over, was ready to face the day. So was he, with a big grin, and a warm feeling all over him from the night before.

Lili stood on her tiptoes to kiss him. He leaned his head down and nuzzled her neck. She was still holding on to the five-hundred-pound weight in one hand. He took it from her, and tossed it on the floor. He pulled Lili to him, the towel around his waist fell off, and he was ready now, not for the day, but to begin last night all over again.

The front door opened.

"Nathan?" Her call echoed through the house.

His mother.

Leone stood there, looking sorrowful, Hy thought.

She had thought him menacing on the dance floor, but now he appeared a pathetic creature.

"If you need to talk, need to tell someone, something..."

He looked up with a half-smile, gratitude in his eyes. No one had ever offered him anything. He was the giver; Ed and Alyssa the takers.

Hy shrugged, turned, and left. Ed was still smiling, reluctant to let the expression go once he'd managed it. Leone was in turmoil. What he had done he had done for her – and still she did not love him. Not him, not Ed, not Lord. The knowledge did not stop him from loving her and believing that she would come to love him. He dreamed nightly of the day they would be together, the day she would realize they were meant to be. Just the two of them. Ed was the carrot. A rotting carrot, but, nonetheless, the lure that would capture Alyssa.

Leone was convinced she had healed his damaged heart the day he met her. That was when it had begun to beat, truly beat.

They were on the television set for the first infomercial for Mind Over Muscle. Big Ed, in robust health, but for the loss of his limbs, sat behind a desk and talked of the miracle of his survival in Vietnam, a war hero selling a system based on his own miraculous recovery. A sure seller. Only there was the problem of the missing legs, which no one could mention, because Ed's mind could feel that the legs were there, but would not allow him to see that they were not. The prosthetics he considered merely braces to give him strength. The producer was happy to show close-ups of Ed's head – front and back – with the wound slicing down the middle, where only white hair grew, making him look like a skunk from behind. The producer didn't mind showing Ed's torso either – but wanted full-body shots. It was a muscle-building system after all.

Enter Lance Lord, out of work and in great shape, hired as a body double.

Enter Lord's wife Alyssa. The men on the set couldn't take their eyes off her. She'd floated in, a vision, her smile caressing each man individually, her eyes lighting on and lighting up theirs. That she was small, mousey, insignificant, they didn't see. She projected a different physicality when there were men around. No longer insubstantial, but transformed into every man's dream of a woman, no longer skinny, but achingly slender; her hair not a frizzy mass, but a golden halo; her eyes not glinting with purpose, but shining with possibility. It wasn't easy to do. She reserved it for entrances and exits and special moments. It was her own private version of Mind over Muscle, having nothing to do with muscle, but everything with appearances. It was so effective, men rarely noticed she wasn't good-looking.

While she and Leone watched the taping from the sidelines, Leone gave her his heart. She collected it up along with Lord's, and added Big Ed to the trio by the time they finished the first day's taping.

It was always good, thought Alyssa, to have an extra man in your pocket. Now she had two. She was content with Lord at present as he made no demands on her. She wasn't sure what Ed was or wasn't capable of, but she would find out if she needed to know. As for Leone, there were two strikes against him. He wasn't rich like Ed was or comfortably off like Lord. And he exuded sexuality. That she didn't like.

Jamieson pulled the covers off her head and squinted out the window at the thick grey fog. What a godforsaken place this was – The Shores, the whole island. She tried to sit up, and was walloped by pain across the back and then the front of her head. The migraine. She slipped back down on the cot, pain on both ends, her ankle throbbing and a deep buzzing in her brain.

She called for Murdo. Her voice was weak, the effort of making even such a slight sound stabbed at her head.

There was no response. He was fast asleep and, curiously, not snoring. In his dreams, he was eating April's white cake with the rich butter icing.

"Show me."

Nathan and Lili were at the kitchen table, having vacuumed up the better part of the fresh loaf of bread that Annabelle had brought them.

She was unloading a shopping bag full of groceries. Her homemade jam and other preserves. Beets. Pickles. Chester Gallant's cheese. Tomatoes. Her garden in back of the house was exploding with them – and carrots, lettuce, potatoes. She'd even dared to bring a zucchini. She wouldn't have for Nathan, but she expected Lili would like it.

She'd known there would be next to nothing in Nathan's fridge, except maybe a bottle of Gatorade and some left-over fast food. She'd been right. She wrinkled her nose as she removed food past its best-before date and loaded in the fresh stuff.

"All organic," she announced as she closed the door and put the jars in the cupboards.

Lili smiled thanks. She'd made tea. Organic green tea. Annabelle had coffee with Nathan.

The pair had hurriedly pulled on some clothes when Annabelle arrived, and come down to the kitchen before she could come up. Their cheeks were flushed. It was obvious what they'd been up to.

The three ate and drank – and then the young lovers began to argue. Their first argument. It was all nothing, really. How nothing could move mountains. All about Mind Over Muscle. It was what had kept Lili awake all night.

"There's something to it," she said.

"It's a bunch of bunk," said Nathan. "A scam."

"But look at Ed Bullock's life. Look what he did." Annabelle refilled their mugs, poured more tea for Lili.

Nathan stared into his mug, as if he might find the answer there.

"Yeah, it was pretty crazy what he did. What he was able to do. I just don't believe that." He jerked his head up the stairs, the five-hundred-pound barbell poised at the top.

"Do you suppose if it rolled down, it could kill someone?" asked Annabelle, with a grin, so like her son's that it startled Lili.

Lili's response was as serious as the look in her eyes.

"Maybe," she said. "You never know. If that rolled down the stairs at someone – and that person believed it weighed five hundred pounds, then, yes, they could die."

"From being hit by something as light as a feather?" Nathan looked at her in disbelief.

Lili sipped her tea and nodded her head. "If they believed."

Annabelle stirred more cream into her cup. "Mind over matter."

"Yes. I think it works both ways."

And then Lili said she could move objects with her mind.

That's when Nathan said, "Show me."

Chapter Twenty-Nine

Alyssa was packing. She wasn't planning to leave today – not in this fog, the causeway obscured, the ferry not running. But soon. All this would come to a head soon. She knew it would. Leone would admit to it. He'd said he would. And even if he didn't, she was sure they'd find him guilty. All the evidence was there.

As soon as they figured that out, and it would be soon, she'd leave The Shores.

She'd promised to take care of Ed. She hadn't mentioned that she planned to marry him, then put him away. Leone didn't need to know that. He'd be in jail, and it would be finished. When she left in a day or two, she would not return. When the legalities were sorted out, she would be free of Lord, Leone, and Big Ed, and their bothersome declarations of love. And she'd have Ed's millions. So many more millions than Lance, with no other wife laying claim.

There was only one person Alyssa loved wholly and completely. Herself.

"You said you could move a table."

Lili laughed. "Not this one. I don't think I could move this one. It's too big."

"Matter is matter. Why should it matter how big?"

"I think it does. And as long as I think so, I won't be able to do it."

Nathan shrugged. "Fair enough."

They got up from the big oak table and drifted into the living room. Annabelle cleared the dishes, rinsed a few, and followed them in.

“There.” Lili pointed at a side table by the couch. But when she touched it, she shook her head.

“What’s wrong?” Annabelle was wiping her hands dry on a dishcloth. It felt clean, not greasy. She looked at it, puzzled. Then smiled. Lili. Good for Nathan in more ways than one.

“Plastic. I’m not sure it would work with plastic.”

“It matters what matter it is?” Nathan enjoyed poking fun at her. She didn’t mind.

It seemed to Annabelle that Lili had been a very serious girl a day ago, but was opening up in the glow of Nathan’s love. Comments that might have made Lili bristle a day ago, today just made her smile.

She smiled now, a calm smile, indulgent.

“This will do,” she said, picking up a wooden tray from the coffee table.

“But it’s only a tray.”

“It’s wood. And if I move it with my mind, does it matter that it’s a tray?”

He shrugged, reluctant. “I guess not.”

“Now, I want you to sit down on the floor.”

That was, Gus would say, “easier said than done” in Nathan’s case. He didn’t quite know what to do with his long, gangly legs. He couldn’t pretzel himself like Lili. She was down on the floor and all wrapped up in the lotus position in an instant, as if it were her natural state. Annabelle was not so spry, but after yesterday’s yoga session she made a respectable descent.

“Now place your fingertips on the tray. Hands high, as if you were going to play the piano. Touch lightly. No pressure. Just barely touch it.”

Annabelle and Nathan did as she said. Both pairs of hands poised over the tray, fingertips skimming its surface. Lili placed just the tip of her baby finger on the tray.

"Shut your eyes. We're going to concentrate on sliding the tray away from me, so it would be impossible for me to be physically pushing it. You'll be able to feel it move with your fingertips, but remember, no pressure.

"Try to concentrate with me, and move the tray to the left."

Lili emptied her mind. Filled it with the tray. Saw its movement in her mind. Willed it to move.

So did Annabelle.

So did Nathan, in his way.

The tray didn't budge.

If anyone from the village had walked in on them, they'd have thought they were nuts. Annabelle thought that Lili had already accomplished a miracle just by getting Nathan to be still for more than a minute. They continued to sit, all three of them silent, eyes closed, concentrating on moving the tray.

The tray did not budge.

Annabelle's concentration began to wane. She wondered if Nathan was able to concentrate. Lili was struggling, struggling. She'd only done it a few times before, with like-minded people. It hadn't been this hard. Why was it now? She closed her eyes tighter, concentrated harder.

The tray shifted.

"Wow!" Nathan's eyes popped open.

"It moved." Annabelle's eyes were open, too.

Lili just smiled, her small smile, calm and confident.

"Of course," she said. "I told you it would. But it wasn't easy. Show me your left hand, Nathan."

He lifted his right hand.

"That's why it was difficult," she said.

Nathan looked puzzled. Knowledge shone suddenly in Annabelle's eyes.

"I said move the tray to the left," Lili explained. "But you don't know your right from your left. That means you were concentrating on moving it to the right. Annabelle and I had to struggle to make it go in the correct direction." Triumph lit up her eyes. "But it did."

Mischief lit up Nathan's. "Does that mean you're stronger than me?"

"Mentally, yes," said Annabelle. Mother and son grinned at each other.

Annabelle was still smiling when she left the house. She'd been impressed by the experiment, but mother love had her thinking, not about that, but about Nathan and Lili. Seeing them together, it was obvious they were a match.

Not physically. He so tall. She, half his size.

As she got in her car, Annabelle thought, she's the one. That it had taken less than twenty-four hours for the bond to happen neither surprised her, nor disturbed her, as it might some mothers. She understood. She understood that it had been instant, the way it had been with her and Ben.

Nathan and Lili would always be together. Joined at the hip.

But not, she thought, as she pulled out of the driveway into the thick fog, able to run a three-legged race.

Annabelle's car crawled along the Way. The fog lights only seemed to make visibility worse. She pulled in at Hy's to take a break and told her what Lili and Nathan had been up to.

Hy looked down at the old steamer trunk that was her coffee table. On it, were pages Ian had googled and printed about Mind Over Muscle.

"Mind Over Muscle," she mumbled, reading half to herself. She looked up, sharply, grabbed Annabelle's arm so hard she winced.

"What?"

"Mind over muscle."

Their eyes caught hold. Of course.

"Anyone could have done it," said Hy. "Anyone, no matter how small, crippled – mentally or physically – could have killed Lord."

"That's not exactly a solution."

"But it is an approach," said Hy, hauling Annabelle from the couch. She was triumphant, believing she held the key that would unlock the case. "We've got to go see Jamieson."

Jamieson had struggled to sit up, her head pounding. She dressed with difficulty, got unsteadily onto her crutches, and called for Murdo. When there was no response, she hauled open the stage curtains. His bed was empty – and not even made. Not that hers was, but she had an excuse. Where had he gone? And here, she couldn't even stomp down three lousy stairs to release her anger.

Murdo was in the comfort of April's kitchen. She'd invited him for breakfast. She knew her husband wouldn't be home. He never was after a ceilidh. She imagined he drank too much and stayed at Frasers' or Gallants'. At least that's what she liked to tell herself, and what he liked to tell her. They both accepted it as truth, but he was usually with that blonde piece of business in Winterside. He hadn't been able to cross the causeway last night, or today, but he still hadn't come home. Ron couldn't remember what happened with Moira, whether he'd had her or not. But he'd landed up in Wally Fraser's shed, sleeping it off.

Both Murdo and April had avoided the juice last night. April had brought her own fresh-squeezed juice that she shared with him. While Ron was sleazing around the dance floor, his arms and body wrapped around Moira, Murdo had taken April home. She'd protested, with a fetching smile, but he'd insisted, and had walked her the short distance to her door. He'd planted a small kiss on her forehead before she'd gone up the walk. Her smile had become even broader, and that's when she'd invited him to breakfast.

"That's ridiculous." Jamieson's lips were stretched in a thin line of disbelief. "It can't be done. It's just party tricks."

"But I was there," Annabelle protested. "I experienced it."

"It can't hurt to give it a try." Hy wanted to see it. It might make a good article for one of her website clients, the Mental Health Association, maybe.

"What will it prove?"

"It will prove that anyone could have killed Lord – weak or strong, small or large."

"So it busts the suspect list wide open. I'm trying to narrow it down."

"But you're not trying to exclude the person who did it, are you?" Hy challenged.

The thin line of Jamieson's set lips softened slightly.

"Well, all right," she said. "Bring her here."

Annabelle called Nathan.

While they waited for Lili, they looked around for something she could move. She'd insisted it had to be a natural product. The tables were out – steel legs. Ditto, the chairs. There was one wooden table, but it was oak, heavy, large. The piano was made of wood, but it was large, too.

It was the first thing Lili focused on.

"The piano," she said. "Perfect."

She took the three steps to the stage. Pulled out the bench. It was heavy.

Jamieson snorted. The child barely had the physical strength to move the bench. How was she going to move the piano with her mind? If she thought she could, it must be as feeble as her body.

"I can make it play."

Jamieson snorted again.

"So can I – but not very well."

Lili gave her a withering look. Annabelle smiled. Tiny, a bit kooky, but not weak, this Lili, able to stare down Jamieson like that.

"This will not be a concert. Not even music," she warned. "Just a note – or two, if I'm lucky."

A sour note, or two, thought Hy of the perennially out-of-tune piano.

Lili placed her fingertips delicately on the keys, poised in the same way she'd instructed Annabelle and Nathan to hold theirs over the tray. She lowered her head, closed her eyes, and sat still. Nathan, Annabelle, and Hy stopped breathing. Jamieson took a deep breath, her mind and stomach crawling with impatience. If…if she moved the keys, well…piano keys were one thing, an axe quite another.

Nothing happened. Nothing at all.

Please, Annabelle prayed, please let it work.

Hy was simply curious.

Nathan was hopeful and hopeless all at the same time.

Lili had emptied her mind. Filled it up with the piano. Focused on a note. "Heard" the note play. Nothing happened.

Something was interfering. *Someone?*

It was Jamieson. Jamieson's skepticism was as strong as Lili's faith. They battled it out, the vibrations of belief and disbelief.

Jamieson turned and began to leave the room, her crutches sounding like a metronome.

One note came out of the piano, the key descending on its own, Lili's fingertips poised but unmoving.

Another note.

One more.

Jamieson turned back. She saw, with the others, that Lili's fingers were not moving at all.

But the keys were.

"I wish you'd been there." Hy had returned Ian's call as soon as she got home.

Suki had gone back to bed and was snoring off last night. It wasn't an attractive sight or sound. Did she spend all her time in the bathroom or bed? It seemed like it. Ian was relieved when Hy called.

She thought there would be no way to convince Ian of Lili's mental powers, not unless he experienced it himself, so she was surprised at his reaction.

"I don't discount it," he said. "I wish I'd seen it, too. The more I've been reading about Bullock – and getting into some of the science on the brain – it's fascinating. Some say the mind is a separate entity from the brain. Religious factions suggest it may be the soul. Who we really are."

"The brain – physical. The mind – non-physical?"

"Something like that – or we just haven't found it yet. Don't know where it resides. In our head? Our heart?"

Hy grinned. "I could narrow it down."

"How?"

"Well, the part of Bullock's brain that he left in Vietnam is not where the mind resides, or he wouldn't have been able to come back like he did."

Ian smiled. "You're right about that."

They were silent for a moment. Ian broke the silence.

"He's not the only one."

"Huh?"

"He's not the only one who has that strength of mind. Others could have it, too – especially those around him. Any of them. Leone…Alyssa…"

"Suki?"

"Suki, I suppose."

"Does she have a mind?" Hy's tone was snarky. She could hear Ian's voice smiling back.

"Are you asking if she has a mind or a brain? There's a difference. We've established that."

"Okay, no brain then – but maybe a mind that could manipulate."

"Cheap shot."

"Ya, ya. Anyway, I agree, any of them could do what he did. That's what I told Jamieson." She paused. "And I told her that Suki fed you mussels."

"What? Are you trying to nail her?"

"I just think I should keep Jamieson informed of anything of interest. She didn't think it was relevant, but she wrote it down."

"You collaborated with Jamieson? I thought you were trying to outwit her."

"I was just letting her know I got there before her."

"But Suki? You don't really believe she tried to kill anyone…tried to kill me. I'm her alibi. You've said so yourself enough times."

"I don't know. Maybe you did hear her go out. Maybe you talk in your sleep. Maybe she thinks that maybe you know something."

"Too many maybes for me."

"But Suki has the height and the strength, even without the brainpower." Hy couldn't resist the dig. "But the others – they'd need Mind Over Muscle to have killed him."

"Alyssa and Leone. What about Big Ed?"

"He's a vegetable. I don't know what's with his mind or his legs."

"He strides the cape every morning."

"Not this morning. Or yesterday morning."

"Would you have in the rain and the wind and the fog?"

"I guess not. But I think he's losing it."

"Maybe it's a ruse. To make people think he couldn't have done it. And even if he is losing it, he could make a comeback. He's done it before. He's a very clever guy. His system is brilliant. Simply brilliant."

Something in his tone…

"Ian, you didn't?"

"Well, you can't say it didn't work."

Ian had been proudly strutting his new physique around the village for months. It had started when he came back from that university reunion. Suki! Suki was behind the new Ian. And so was Mind Over Muscle. Ian had responded to an infomercial. No wonder he'd never let on.

She scowled.

"I think I liked you better the way you were."

It wasn't just his physique she was talking about.

Chapter Thirty

The fog and gloom persisted past noon and through the day. The villagers weren't used to it hanging over them for this long. They liked to say, "Don't like the weather? Wait five minutes."

They were usually at the mercy of the wind, blowing across the slim strip of island, and the fragile finger that was The Shores. The wind, taking the weather with it – clement, inclement, dry, wet, cloudy or sunny, changing, if not in five minutes, very rapidly. But there was no wind and this fog had stalled over the entire island. Thick, grey, billowing, it cast a gloom over the village already suffering from a communal hangover and the fear that there was a killer loose.

No one was more conscious of that than Jane Jamieson. She'd left the others in the Hall, her brain aching from trying to rationalize what she'd just seen. Trying, but not succeeding. She'd had Lili repeat the experiment several times, and hadn't found a flaw.

She didn't know what to think. She went looking for Murdo, quite sure of where she'd find him. The cruiser sat in the parking lot outside the Hall, but she couldn't drive it. Her ankle was swollen to twice its size, and so sore that she was beginning to think it must be broken.

She swung along on her crutches, on the uneven, puddled lane towards April Dewey's house. She would find Murdo and they would question Alyssa about the ring. Jamieson could just barely see her bandaged foot as she hobbled along. She could see only a small patch of the lane directly in front of her. She would have to rely on gauging the distance, hugging the edge of the road, peering for signs of a driveway to her right.

She couldn't figure out where the edge of the road was. Finally she located it, feeling the difference between the clay lane and the grassy verge. One crutch on the lane, one on the grass, both feet becoming soaked through. The bandage began to unravel, slopping in the puddles and wet clay. She nearly tripped over it a couple of times. The grass was slippery under her crutches and they kept giving way on her. The banging in her head and the fog clouding her vision made it difficult to know where she was. It felt like a long way to April's driveway. She didn't know she'd already passed it. She began to feel disoriented. Panic set in, her stomach and head tingling with anxiety. She wanted to go faster, but couldn't with her crutches and injured ankle. To calm herself and try to stay focused, she thought about those other footprints. She, like Hy and Ian, had taken another look at the photograph of the sun reflecting in the water.

The footprints on the sand. Leone stepped into Jamieson's mind and slipped neatly into the prints, fitting them like Cinderella and the glass slipper. He was moving carefully, with the care a child takes not to "step on the crack, break your mother's back." Intent on obliterating the footprints and replacing them with his own?

Not the action of a killer.

Ahead of him, there could have been someone, someone who had left the prints and whom Leone was compelled to protect. Someone moving in the dark across the sand, eyes fixed on Lance Lord, breathing venom at Jim MacAdam for being in the way.

Someone who had killed them both.

The spiked juice had made her cry, but it was hard to tell if Gladys Fraser had a hangover. She was always grumpy. She did not emerge from her house until late in the day. She marched down the road, wincing with each footfall. Perhaps she did have a hangover, but it didn't cloud what she knew to be her duty.

She shoved through the door of the Hall, and was shocked to see what a mess it was in. The clean-up committee had been too sauced to tidy up. She was disappointed to find no one there to complain to or boss around. But that did not stand in the way of her mission. She flung open the cellar door and stomped down the stairs, the smell offending her nose. She hadn't wanted the marijuana put in the kitchen and she didn't want it in the cellar a moment more. She gathered up the plants, wilting and blackening, and hauled herself back up the stairs, out the door, and across the parking lot to the police cruiser. It was unlocked. Gladys was delighted in a mean-spirited way. She stuffed the plants into the back seat and slammed the door shut. The sound sliced through her head. A wave of nausea gripped her. She opened the driver's door, got in, arms folded across her chest, and laid her head back to stop it from pounding.

"We have to leave." Leone's vision was so poor, it had been no challenge for him to find his way to Alyssa's through the fog. He was a human compass when it came to her. She was his north, south, east, and west and he could always find her wherever she was.

"We?"

"You and me. And Ed. Of course, Ed." Ed wouldn't last long, anyway. It made Leone sad, but it was for the best. The best for him and Alyssa.

"We," Alyssa stretched out the word. "We aren't going anywhere, Ed and I. We have nothing to run from." Ed didn't. She didn't – as long as Leone stuck to his promise.

"You are safe because of me. I followed you…in your footsteps… I wanted to protect you…you wanted it too…" His distress had made him short of breath and he could only gulp his words out in short disconnected phrases. "The axe…the chain…I knew…you know I knew…and then I said I'd do it. That I would do anything to protect you."

Protect. The word was hollow. It had no meaning – from him. From her father, it would have meant something, but he had never protected her.

"We must go away. You and me."

"I don't know what you mean." There was a cold set to her lips.

"Come. Come away – " His words were choked off by the deep hate in her eyes, her contempt for him, his hope shattering like a glass that had splintered in his grasp and left him bleeding.

She stared at him, eyes unblinking, a hard glint in them, turning them from pale blue to icy green.

"I love you..." His eyes burned with his emotion. Hers remained cold green ice. "Don't you...love me?"

"What?" She spat the word out, reeling back.

He moved forward, a condemned man. One careful step. He reached out.

Was he going to touch her? She couldn't bear it if he did. That once, that once only, she had allowed it, and there'd been a reason for that.

Alyssa's hand slid across the counter. She couldn't bear it if he touched her. Her fingers edged toward a knife that lay there, as if in waiting.

His small, golden eyes swam in a pool of moisture.

"You said we would be together."

"Did I?"

He moved forward another step. "The three of us could be so happy together. He could be your husband. And I..." he dared another step, now close enough to touch her.

Her eyes froze. She touched the handle of the knife.

He put a hand on her arm. "...and I...could be your man." He pulled at her.

She shoved him from her, disgust in her curled lips and hate in her eyes.

"Man? Man? Monkey boy. That's all you are." She gripped the knife and slashed at him, aiming for the jugular.

His face screwed up in terrible realization as the knife sliced his ear. His hands flew up to protect himself, and he ran, whimpering, from the room and out the back door, and with his hope went his heart. It filled with her hate for him – the pain jagged, growing, exploding as he flung himself up onto the cape. The throbbing in his chest made his breath come in short swallows of anguish.

Not enough. Not enough breath, his heart swelling, head pounding the rhythm of her hate, her words thundering in his brain: *"Monkey boy. That's all you are."*

The playground insult, more wounding than ever, her words carving deep into him. He felt a sharp pain in his heart. This woman he loved was selfish, grasping, unloving. He knew it now and his heart was about to break.

Well and truly break.

Hy was not far behind Jamieson on the Shore Lane, but never saw her. She knew Jamieson would stop her trying to find out more, from interfering in police business. Hy was determined to prove her wrong, that she could be pivotal in solving this case.

It was creepy, walking in the fog, blind to everything but her own body, moving along the lane, tripping on the uneven clay, startled by sudden sounds. Like the whining of a screen door opening and slamming shut. Then slamming shut again because it hadn't caught. It was probably April letting her cat in.

The next sound wasn't so easy to explain.

A heart-wrenching scream came from Annabelle's house.

Alyssa?

Hy stumbled to Annabelle's door. She saw, through a tear in the fog, the shadow of Leone, staggering away from the house and stumbling down the cape, with his one arm swinging back and forward, beating the rhythm of his stride. The other was held up to his head. She wondered what he was up to. Another cry of pain came from the house.

Leone stopped when he heard it. Stopped for a moment, then disappeared into the shroud.

Hy ran up to the big double doors and straight in. The screaming had risen to a high pitch. She found Alyssa in the kitchen, a puddle of misery on the floor, weeping.

When Hy bent down to her, Alyssa looked up, tears drowning her eyes, her face red and raked with anguish.

"He…he…" Alyssa's voice was muffled in sobs. The knife lay on the floor beside her. And blood…

"Are you hurt…?"

Alyssa shook her head a few times, still unable to speak. Hy picked up the knife.

"What's wrong? What happened?"

"He…he…"

"Who?" Though she knew.

Alyssa gulped. Tried to speak. Dissolved in tears again.

"Lee…Lee…" was all she managed.

"Leone?"

Alyssa nodded. She hiccoughed. Once. And then a fresh set of tears, newly formed, spilled down her face.

"Leone did it." They both knew that Alyssa meant not just what had happened here, but Lord's murder. Perhaps both murders.

Alyssa regained her voice. "He did it for me." Hiccough. "He said he did it for me." She looked down at the floor, where the knife was, blood on it. "He attacked me, tried to kill me, too."

"Are you hurt?"

"No I…I…I don't know what…how…I grabbed the knife."

"I better get Jamieson."

Alyssa's hiccoughing stopped. Her tears dried up. Just like that.

"No," she said. "No. Not just yet. I need a moment…"

"But he's getting away."

Alyssa smiled. It did not match the expression in her eyes – a hard gleam.

"He won't go far."

"Then I'll go after him." Hy didn't know why she said it. Alyssa's hard gleam had melted into a pathetic appeal. She looked so…so fragile, so vulnerable. The words were out of Hy's mouth before she knew she'd formed them. This tiny creature was begging her protection and she felt compelled to give it. *Why?* What was tugging at her?

"He's dangerous," Alyssa warned, frowning.

Hy saw something, something in Alyssa's eyes, the birth of a small smile on her lips, something that pricked her with nervous fear. Somehow, for some reason she could not have explained because it made no sense, she felt danger in this room. She wasn't brave going after Leone, she just had to get out.

"Stay here." Hy still clung to the knife, only dimly aware that she did so. "I'm going to find him."

Jamieson entered the cottage for the first time since the morning after the murder. She turned on a light, and squinted as her eyes adjusted to it. It was good to be able to actually see things. What she saw wasn't good: her bandage unraveled, sodden, stained with red clay. She found some scissors, sat down on one of the kitchen chairs, and cut off the filthy length of gauze. Then she cut the end in two and secured it around her ankle.

She was exhausted. Two nights of poor sleep in the Hall, the injury, the pain, the painkillers, now the migraine had eroded almost all her strength. She negotiated her crutches down the three stairs and eased herself onto the couch. She looked at the woodstove. Lord's will. She pulled it out of her jacket pocket, the only place she had to keep it safe. Had either of them known which one it really favoured?

She leaned back into the couch. When she closed her eyes, vivid colours zigzagged in the periphery of her vision. The drumming of the headache became words, words that had been spoken in this room, the shattering of a glass on the tile floor, the whining sound of an electric guitar slicing through the air.

Jamieson shook her head to clear her mind and winced. The movement had sent pain rocketing through her brain. And Alyssa's screams, though imagined, went searing through her.

"You fool!" Alyssa waved the papers at Lord and slapped them down onto the table. Her forefinger dove down onto them and landed, like a knife, on the offending words.

"You fool." She read them out loud: "To my wife..."

"But you are my wife..."

She glared at him.

"Or were...and will be...again..."He put a hand on her knee. "Soon."

She shook him off.

"You didn't name me, idiot. You have to name me."

She watched as he wrote her name in.

She pushed him away. "A witness." She stood up.

"You're not leaving?"

"We need a witness."

"Now?"

"Yes, now."

Leone. The footprints in the photo.

Jamieson tried to get to her feet, but the effort sent more pain pounding through her. She sat down again and stared straight at the woodstove.

Suki had tried to burn it. She was the wife. Everything was hers, but had she known it? She had seemed genuinely surprised when she found out that the change in it made no difference at all. Everything was hers. If she thought Alyssa was to get it all, she'd have been jealous or angry. Jealous or angry enough to kill?

Jamieson didn't like Suki, but she tried hard not to let personal emotions enter into her police work. She didn't like her, but she didn't think she was a killer. Her prints were not on the axe. Nor were Alyssa's. The only prints on the axe were Leone's. She should arrest him. There was the ring at the crime scene. All the evidence pointed to him as the killer. But something was stopping her from accusing him. It wasn't that simple. Somehow she knew it wasn't that simple.

What of Alyssa? Pushing for that change in the will. It made it look like the murder was about possessions, but what if it was possessiveness, not possessions? Alyssa had said, *"Lance was always mine...we belonged together."* Suki's dislike of Alyssa and her hold over Lord made them both prime suspects. They might have more reason to kill each other than him, but he had been playing one against the other.

And what of Leone and Lord's "betrayal?" Was he not a possessor, too, a possessor of Big Ed and his legacy? And Bullock himself. He possessed everything – and nothing.

There were lots of leads. Lots of threads to gather up.

With renewed enthusiasm for a case that was in more tatters than her bandage, Jamieson stood up, forgetting her crutches.

She folded up in pain, clutching the will, then tried again, using the crutches, back on her original mission to find Murdo, and now Alyssa, to have a little chat about possession.

Alyssa went upstairs to the bedroom when Hy left. She took a long match from the box by the candles, and in a slow ritual, lit one, then another, then another. Their yellow flames flashed gold on the red tin foil covering the vanity, forming a bright circle around the picture of Baba. She didn't even know who he was. She hadn't ever studied Buddhism, only adopted some of its outer trappings. This was her own ritual, divorced from the Catholic upbringing she shunned, her own creation to trick what she wanted out of the universe. She stood hypnotized by the flickering flames, until, slowly, she lit another match, and put it to the incense, drawing the smell into her nostrils, the fragrance of desire. Her desire. She knelt down on the prayer mat and forced herself to be calm, smooth face, but tight lips and gritted teeth, not relaxing, not meditating, just trying to make the universe bend to her will. She was demanding what was hers, what belonged to her.

"Mine. Mine. Mine." She chanted the words, like Lili's om. But Lili's om was selfless. Alyssa's chant was all about Alyssa. Her mantra, herself.

"Let me be, let me be..." She couldn't think of the word. She couldn't think of one thing she wanted to be. There were many. Rich. Adored. Untouched and untouchable. Chaste.

Hy found Leone in the thick mist at the edge of the cape. He was huddled on the ground, moaning piteously. It was the sound that guided her to him. She couldn't see him at all until she very nearly tripped over him.

She crept up, knife still in her hand, not knowing what she would do if she had to use it, pricks of fear up her arms and legs. When he raised his head, and looked at her with those mournful eyes ringed with sorrow, she could not believe he was a killer. If he was, he was not a killer who scared her. The tension eased in her shoulders, the adrenalin stopped pumping through her blood. Still, she clung to the knife.

His body was heaving with unspent tears, his eyes dry with a sorrow that went beyond tears, stunned, robbed of expression, turned blank by the loss, the final loss of all his hopes.

"I did it for her," he said.

Hy could hardly believe it. Whatever it was he was confessing to he'd done for Alyssa? Then she remembered that small bundle of appeal on Annabelle's kitchen floor. Alyssa had, if not a physical strength, the strength to get others to do her will. Why else was she, Hy, out on the cape with Leone? She'd wanted to get away from Alyssa, true, but her first impulse had been to protect her.

To kill or be killed? For Alyssa? She gripped the knife.

"You killed for her?"

Leone said nothing.

He must be the killer. Hy shuddered with a mixture of fear and the cold, the damp fog swirling around them and seeping into her. They could just see each other, but nothing else around them, the coast and the village enveloped in white-grey mist as thick as nine-day-old porridge. Hy could not see the village, nor the dome, which must be nearby, nor the shore, not even the edge of the cape. How close were they to the edge? Where was it? Ahead, or behind? The sudden loss of any sense of direction put Hy into a panic. She felt as if the ground were opening up beneath her feet.

"I wanted to protect her."

"To protect her from Lord?"

He shook his head.

"Jim MacAdam?"

He shook his head again. Hy pulled back, her eyes drilling into his, his seeping with moisture – from the fog or emotion?

"For her. I did it for her."

"You said that."

But he could say no more. Alyssa had rejected him, but he couldn't tell the truth about her, about what she – and he – had done. He couldn't convict her with his own words, his own breath, not even if it saved him.

"Did Alyssa kill Lord?"

He was having a hard time getting his breath. She saw pain in his brown eyes. Emotional or physical?

"Did she kill MacAdam?"

Still he said nothing. Just stared at her with those wounded eyes, washed in torment and tears, his body heaving with grief at Alyssa's rejection, after all he had done for her, was still doing for her. He would tell this woman what he must tell her.

"No, no." There was a long pause. He breathed raggedly and spoke with effort. "I killed them." He didn't mind if they locked him up for life. His life was over without her, or hope of her.

"But you said before…"

He said only one more thing.

He clutched his hand to his heart, the pain in his face intense, the tears finally squeezed out of his eyes, pooling on his face. He gasped for breath, then let it all out on one word:

"Alyssa."

His last breath, spent on her name.

Chapter Thirty-One

"You could have woken me."

Murdo shook his head.

"No, I couldn't. I tried."

Jamieson's pearl-white skin flushed.

"The juice was spiked," said April. It was all over the village now, as people who'd never touched a drop of alcohol in their lives were waking up with pounding heads.

"Yes, but I didn't…" Realization dawned. The painkillers. Of course. They numbed one kind of pain but triggered the migraine. She was still feeling it – pounding, insistent. After the long walk on crutches to Lord's and back up the Shore Lane she felt…

"Do you mind if I sit down?" She was anxious to question Alyssa, but she had to sit for a moment.

"Please do." April helped her into the reclining chair, from which, once ensconced, Jamieson thought she might never be able to get out. The chair had tilted back, and April had worked the lever to bring the footrest up. Jamieson felt ridiculous, but that's how she had felt most of this long, long weekend.

Murdo had been tucking into a full English breakfast when Jamieson had arrived. Bacon and eggs, ham, home fries, fried tomato, and fried bread. Jamieson looked at it and wanted to throw up. She very nearly did when Murdo pulled the breath mint box out of his pocket and put it on the table.

Jamieson screwed up her face. "What's that smell?"

April opened the container and thrust it forward. The smell was overpowering.

"Tomalley," said April.

"Tomalley?"

"Lobster guts and poo," said Murdo.

"Actually, the liver – a few days old." April put the lid back on. "That's why it smells so bad. Lobsters are bottom-feeders. They eat garbage. That doesn't help."

"I can't imagine that it ever smelled good." Jamieson cupped a hand over her nose and mouth.

"Well, no." April handed the container to Jamieson, who looked puzzled.

"Why give it to me?"

"It's evidence," said Murdo. "Taken from the wound."

"How?"

"Billy. He took it from the wound, before the body washed away."

Well, he was good for something, Jamieson thought, as she inspected the container. God, it stunk. She felt her stomach rebel.

"Tomalley. What part of the lobster?"

"Arse end," said Murdo.

"Top half," April corrected, a look of prim disapproval at his language making his face go red.

McAllister had said she'd seen a lobster sticking out of the wound. This, perhaps, proved her right. But did it mean anything to what had happened that night? Other than that a bird had dropped the crustacean on the corpse and another one had plucked it away?

Leone O'Reyley lay dead on the cape, his dreams, his love and loyalty to Ed and Alyssa floating off on the fog.

Hy had known it was hopeless for some time now, but she kept giving him CPR, alternating between pushing on his chest and trying to breathe life back into his body, killer or not. She had to get help. It was time to bring Jamieson into this. She'd be furious, but it was Alyssa whom Hy now feared, Alyssa with her transformative power, the ability to make herself the vision that every man wanted. What more might she be able to do?

Alyssa had the mental skill to shift reality.

And an axe? Did she have the power to wield that as well?

"I should arrest you," said Jamieson, even though she felt stripped of her power, thrust back on the reclining chair in April's kitchen. They'd all been shocked when Hy had entered with the bloody knife in her hand. She'd had a long explanation.

"Arrest me?"

"For…for…" Jamieson struggled to sit up, fiddled with the lever and the footrest hit the floor with unexpected speed, the chair swung up straight, hurled Jamieson forward and smashed her bandaged foot to the floor.

"For obstruction of justice…" There was pain in her voice.

"Obstruction? I thought I was helping you out."

"I've told you before. Police business. You shouldn't get mixed up in it."

"I could hardly help it." Hy's head was high, her chin stubborn. "Anyone would have done what I did. There was a scream, and I responded…"

"How do you know he's dead?"

"Dead is dead," said Hy, and Jamieson, having seen her share of corpses, knew what she meant.

There was the question of what to do with the body. There was the problem of the wound, the knife, and the blood. Did that have anything to do with his death – or had he died from natural causes?

When Jamieson called Nathan, he swore he could take the body across the causeway in the fog because he knew it, as his aunt Gus would say, "like the back of his hand." He said he'd be there in ten minutes. Time enough, thought Jamieson, to have a little chat with the woman next door. She ordered Nathan to pick her up at Alyssa's on his way to the cape.

"Murdo, help me up." Jamieson hated to ask, but there was no way out of this chair and onto the crutches without help. "You're going up the cape to watch over the body. I'm going to have a conversation with Mrs. Lord."

"I'll go with you," said Hy.

"No," said Jamieson, and Hy bristled.

"No. Go with Murdo. Show him where the body is."

Hy put the knife down on April's table, covered in crumbs. Jamieson shook her head. She wondered what forensics would make of that. She got a plastic bag from April, put the knife in it, and left with Hy and Murdo, hobbling next door on her crutches.

As a police officer, Jamieson had to knock.

Alyssa wasn't there – or wasn't answering.

In the end, Jamieson just walked in, signaling Hy to continue on to the cape with Murdo.

"I should be here for Nathan," said Hy, "to show him the way. Three of us can search for her more easily. And I know the house – all the nooks and crannies, and there are lots of those, believe me. Besides," she pointed to the cruches, "you'll never get in the attic on those."

Jamieson caved in. Alyssa, so tiny she could be anywhere in the big house, couldn't be found.

Anyone else would have seen a skinny, undersized woman with the features of a spoiled child, but so great was Alyssa's power over Ed, that he saw the most beautiful creature he had ever seen – lithe, lovely, perfect, and the man in him came alive as she crossed the room, floating, pure.

She was close, so close that he should have seen she was just a little mouse, a spiteful, nasty woman, with nothing to offer. To him, she was a vision. Not a mere flesh and blood woman. A goddess come to life. Athena herself. Alyssa. Athena. Even the cadence of the name was the same. The goddess of love. Pure love.

In her own mind, she was a goddess. Not Athena. Diana, the huntress. Chaste and chasing. Not the man. His manhood. To destroy it and retain her chastity. Pure love was only for herself. *Amour propre*. Self-love. Ed? Him she hated for his desire.

"Marry me." Big Ed was lucid today. Or maybe not. Maybe that's why he could finally say it.

"Marry me," he said again.

It was what she had wanted. It was why she had come here. For him. And Lance. To keep what was hers. How she would have both, she had never worked out.

But now Lance was dead, it was perfect. He was hers in death – and Ed could be hers in life. Hers alone.

"I will – if you tell me what you've been keeping from me."

"Nothing. I swear. Nothing."

Her eyes beamed intent. A grim smile on her face. She was trying to look soft, but she did not feel soft. She felt hard inside; she had always felt hard inside. Hard and cold as marble. There was nothing soft or vulnerable in her eyes. They could have sliced the arm off a Greek statue. They were cutting through him now, wanting to know what he couldn't tell her, what he didn't know himself.

He held out a hand.

"Come to me, Alyssa." He wheeled toward her.

"Come to me." He became more insistent, grabbed her hand, desire – *My God, desire* – rising in him.

"Then you will know…"

She softened slightly. Perhaps he was finally going to tell her.

"You will know…" He pulled her down on him.

"How much I…"

He was swelling with desire.

An unwelcome desire. Physical. She hadn't thought he could.

It was worse. It was clear. Horribly clear.

There was nothing beyond his knees.

No legs.

"No legs!" she shrieked. "No legs!"

That was his secret. It sent her spinning from him.

"No legs?" He didn't know what she meant, but he saw the truth in her eyes. He looked down, his hand slipped below his knees, and they disappeared. His legs. For the first time, they weren't there. It hadn't happened in Vietnam or when he woke up from surgery. It hadn't happened, not once, in the years between then and now. It had happened in this moment. *Gone.* The hard gleam in her eyes had done it, the look that could slice marble had amputated his legs.

He looked at her in accusation, the knowledge flooding his brain.

He had no legs.

Confusion.

She had taken them.

His face crumpled, became a sack of wrinkles, tears trying to find their way down the ragged routes etched in the destruction of his face, his hope, his love for her.

Gone. Like his legs, it was gone, the love for her that had been his hope for so long.

Disgusted, with the force of someone more than twice her size, Alyssa toppled his chair. He smacked his head on the floor.

Gone.

Gone.

Gone.

His legs. His love. His life.

Gone.

Murdo was in the back of Nathan's ambulance. His eyes were closed. He wouldn't have seen much if he'd opened them – just the interior of the back of the van and Jamieson. Hy was up front in the passenger seat, giving directions, as Nathan negotiated the cape with abandon, thrilling at the bumps and the splash of the puddles as he carved through the dense fog.

He came to a halt when Hy shouted, "There!" and pointed at nothing.

"You sure?"

She nodded. She knew the cape as well as Nathan, and she would never forget the spot where Leone O'Reyley had died.

The four got out of the vehicle.

The fog surrounded them, circled around Leone. Clearly dead, thought Jamieson. Leone, looking, not at rest, but as if in some terrible nightmare, his lips pulled back in a grimace, his eyes wide open. Jamieson leaned forward as far as her crutches allowed. The wound to the ear was superficial, a slice taken off the lobe. So that hadn't killed him, but the shock, the physical effort? Heart attack probably, she thought. Not unusual in men of his age, especially if he'd had a shock, and he'd been running. She looked again. Had Alyssa aimed for the jugular and missed? Attempted murder? Jamieson closed Leone's eyes, nodded at Murdo, and he and Nathan lifted the body into the van.

While their backs were turned, Hy slipped away, soon hidden in the fog as she headed towards the dome, where she was sure she would find Alyssa. And Ed. She was thinking about the photograph. The photograph of the repeating suns and the footsteps planted down the shore beside them.

Two sets of footprints. Alyssa had said she'd followed Leone, but what if it were the other way around? Had he been following her, covering her tracks? Had he followed her and killed Lord, as she claimed he had? Or had he followed her, watched her kill Lord and then killed MacAdam because MacAdam had seen her do it?

"I did it for her." Is that what he meant?

Or was he protecting her by directing suspicion at himself? Lord and Leone were dead. There was a third man who loved Alyssa.

Was Ed in danger?

Hy herself might have been, had she not known the lay of the land so well. She skirted around the break in the cape, guided by the small outside light glimmering in the opaque night above the door of the dome.

"Where is she?" Jamieson's head whipped around from one direction to another, seeing nothing in the fog. "McAllister!" Nathan closed the van door as Murdo looked around helplessly.

Jamieson whirled around on her crutches – she was getting good at using them. "The dome. She'll have gone to the dome. Sticking her nose in police business again. Go after her. I'll follow you."

"I can wait for you."

"There's no time. I'd hold you back. She may be in danger." *From Alyssa? From Big Ed? From both of them?*

Murdo hesitated.

"Now!"

He began stumbling through the fog, in the direction of the dome. At least, that's what he thought.

"I'll come with you," Nathan volunteered as Jamieson watched Murdo disappear.

Night was falling. Darkness and fog. Danger. Jamieson could sense it on the air. Was it just a fancy?

"No," she said. "You take O'Reyley into town, if you can."

"Oh yes I can," said Nathan, with a grin at the prospect of daring the causeway again. But it wasn't quite the broad grin of a few days ago, before he'd met Lili. All he wanted now was to complete his mission and slip back between the sheets with her. Sooner done, sooner he'd be in her arms again. He jumped in the van and took off, Leone's lifeless body bouncing in the back as Nathan negotiated the bumpy lanes up onto the Island Way.

Jamieson regretted sending Murdo on ahead, as she made her

way towards the dome. She was not easily intimidated, but the crutches and injured ankle made her feel vulnerable, and the fog rolling in thick masses off the water was unsettling. When it thinned out, she would catch a glimpse of her destination, the dome appearing, disappearing, and reappearing at the will of the mist. That was unsettling as well.

It was frustrating, pushing herself along, the crutches sinking into the sandy soil. But Big Ed must be told. Alyssa might be there. And McAllister might be in trouble. She shuddered in the cold mist, all of her hurting.

She was in such pain that she almost didn't feel what hit her.

Her crutches were up from under her and she was sliding down, down the break in the cape, toward the shore, where hunks of jagged sandstone lay in wait for her, the waves washing over the rocks and beckoning her to slide into their cold grip. She was tumbling down, searching frantically for a foothold, and time moved in slow motion. She saw her hand, as if it were someone else's, grab an outcrop of the cliff, and watched her foot, her damaged ankle buckling as she came down hard on another support thrusting out from the cape. She winced in pain, but she had stopped the freefall. With one hand and her injured foot, she clung to life. Below was death, the jagged rocks reaching up to her, waiting for her to tire, to lose her grip, to fall. A clump of rock broke off beneath her foot. She hugged the cliff with her injured foot and one grazed hand.

She looked up, and thought she saw a scrap of fabric floating on the fog.

Chapter Thirty-Two

Murdo didn't know where he was. He was not on the cape anymore. He was not close to Cottage Lane or the Hall, or anywhere that might have restored his sense of direction. He was stumbling blind through a field toward an abandoned farm, its barn falling down, the terrain difficult to negotiate. He had burrs clinging to his clothes, panic on his brain, as he tore through tall grasses. His only certainty was that he was lost.

If he'd turned around, he might have spotted the light coming from the police cruiser parked outside the Hall. Junior Johnson had opened the car door to take back what was his – the marijuana plants. His plants. His and Jared MacPherson's. He began to stuff them into a large plastic yard bag.

In the driver's seat, Glady Fraser woke up.

Alyssa opened the door of the dome to Hy. Big Ed Bullock lay on the floor. Alyssa didn't know if he was dead or alive. Maybe brain dead but still alive, she thought. He wouldn't last long. She smiled. Hers. He, too, would always be hers.

Hy looked at Ed. What a machete in the jungle couldn't do, tiny Alyssa had.

Alyssa continued to look down at him and to smile.

"I didn't plan to kill him."

Hy thought she was talking about Ed.

"I was thinking about it when I came back along the shore, with Leone following like a dog behind me, thinking I didn't know he was there."

Lord. She was talking about Lord.

"No, I hadn't planned to kill Lance when I came back along the beach. But there he was, dressed like an idiot, staring up at the cape, his hands balled into fists, his vein sticking out in his neck. I could picture that vein bursting, his blood spilling on the sand, then he would be mine, he would be no one else's in death."

Alyssa's eyes were glittering. She was looking straight at Hy, but seemed not to see her. It was as if she were looking right through her to that night on the shore.

"I saw her, nearly naked, through the window."

"Suki?"

Alyssa nodded abruptly.

"I saw the axe. His neck, the vein throbbing. I grabbed the axe, before he knew I was there. I summoned all my strength, my inner strength, my fierce strength of mind the way Leone had taught me, and I brought it down."

"And killed him."

"No, I missed."

"Missed? So it wasn't…?"

"No, I missed." But Alyssa didn't look up. Was she telling the truth? The rest of it had sounded like truth. Was this?

"Then who?"

Alyssa looked up, eyes gleaming.

"You'd have to ask Leone that."

"He's dead."

She smiled. "Is he?"

Jamieson hung on to the cape by a thin thread of strength, a thread that was fraying. Every inch of her was aching. She had almost nothing to cling to, her body flat up against the wet sandstone, helping to hold her there. But she was slipping, slipping. Her fingers had begun to loosen on the rockface; pieces kept breaking off her foothold. She looked down to see if she could climb to the shore, but it made her dizzy. It was steep, too steep. She'd never make it down. If she did, she'd have to negotiate the slippery rocks at the bottom and the sand on the shore. Impossible, with or without her crutches. She looked up again. That odd, floating vision had appeared only once. Jamieson assumed it was drug-induced. She wished she had some of the painkiller now.

No, she thought. She'd never have been able to hold on so long. But she wasn't sure that she could much longer. She gripped harder. Something bit into her hand, broke the skin. It was a mussel shell, embedded in the sandstone.

Mussels. Suki had fed them to Ian. She had sucked on the tiny lobster legs one by one. She had cracked the lobster open. Tomalley.

Tomalley. The word echoed in Jamieson's overwrought mind.

She began to cry. Just one or two tears escaped. Then she gritted her teeth and hung on even tighter, the water pounding up against the rocks below her in a rhythm with the painful pulsing in her brain, as tomalley turned to mussels.

Mussels. Mussels. Mind over mussels.

A mantra to save her from falling.

"You said you missed."

"Yes, I did."

Hy wrinkled her forehead.

Alyssa smiled that smile that was small, hard, crystallized, a smile that could shatter in an instant and become what it really was. A scowl? No. A sneer, full of spite and hate.

"I missed. I missed that throbbing vein. But I killed him anyway. It turned out perfectly. Leone, you see, tried to stop me, so I missed my mark. But it left his prints on the axe, not mine." She raised her gloved hands. "They'll think he did it. He was prepared to take the blame."

"But it was you, not him."

"Yes."

I did it for her. That's what he meant. Agreed to shoulder the blame.

"And MacAdam?"

Alyssa shrugged and repeated, "Why don't you ask Leone that?"

"You know I can't. He's dead. I'm asking you. What happened? Detail by detail."

She did. Exacting detail that took Hy back to that night, to what had happened between Alyssa and Leone.

Alyssa turned to Leone. There appeared to be tears in her eyes – or were they just glistening with triumph? She flung herself into his arms, her brain working furiously.

They groped wildly at each other, falling onto the sand, so he never noticed – or so she thought – when she tugged the chain around his neck and broke it free.

As soon as she had done it, she pushed him from her.

"Not here. Not now. Later, darling," she said, standing up, smoothing her dress and disappearing like a spirit into the night, leaving him there, hungry on the sand, lying beside Lord, like two dead men.

"So that's how your ring got there."

Alyssa inclined her head, just slightly.

"Why did you say it had been stolen?"

"To draw attention to it. To point to the killer."

"Of Lord. Or MacAdam? Did Leone kill MacAdam for you?"

"You'll have to ask Leone that."

"You know I can't do that."

"Oh, that's right, you can't."

Ian was worried about Hy. The jungle drums, or coastal bodhrans, were beating in the village. Gus had phoned to tell him Nathan had gone rocketing down the road with Lord knows what or who in the back of his van. Ian phoned Hy and got no answer.

Annabelle called Gus to say it was Leone – dead or dying, she wasn't sure. Nathan had called Lili, and Lili had called Annabelle.

Some instinct told him to head for the dome, his fog lights on and a flashlight on the passenger seat. As he passed the Hall, the fog prevented him from seeing Gladys Fraser crossing the parking lot, holding Junior Johnson by the ear, as she had when she was his schoolteacher. Later, there was much speculation as to what she would have done with him if Billy Pride hadn't shown up and slapped a pair of handcuffs on Junior.

Ian knew the capes well, because he spent a lot of time there working with his erosion monitoring system, keeping track of how much of the cape was being worn away by the action of the wind and waves and the tiny South American swallows who drilled holes along the top to nest. Ian parked well back from the edge of the cape, and was about to mount the stairs to the dome, when he heard a yell.

"Help!"

Hy?

"Help! I'm slipping."

Crazy. She was crazy, thought Hy.

That gleam in her eye, the way she smiled with eyes full of hate.

"I didn't want Lance, but I did want what was mine. He belonged to me – and now he belongs to me forever. It was a clean death. Here on the shore. The ocean and the sand. A clean death."

As if that mattered. "It was a messy killing, though."

"Yes, bloody, but what killing isn't?"

Hy thought of Leone, dead on the cape. No blood. She looked at Ed.

Dead or alive? No blood.

"Oh, there are bloodless killings," she said.

Alyssa pouted, but her eyes smiled.

"How did you do it?" *Keep her talking*. "Lord, I mean. You said you killed him with the axe, but how did you do it? I can't believe you could kill him. Clean or messy. You're not tall enough, strong enough."

Alyssa straightened. Already she looked larger.

"Let me show you."

Ian looked down over the cape. In the fog, he could see nothing. Had he imagined it? A trick of the wind?

"Help!"

No. There was a woman's voice. Not Hy's, he thought with relief.

He went to the car, got his flashlight, and trained it down the cape.

Squinting into the beam was Jamieson.

"How'd you get down there?"

"Never mind that. Get me up."

How he would manage that, Ian wasn't sure.

Alyssa walked past Ed's body as if he were not even there, to the barbells cradled on racks in the back of the dome. She picked up a five-hundred-pound weight and strode across the room towards Hy.

Hy smiled. "That's nothing. Those weigh nothing."

"Oh, yes they do. These ones are real."

Hy didn't know whether to believe her or not.

"Very real. If you think I can't lift them, then how could I raise the axe that split Lance's head open?" She was boasting, smiling, but in her eyes – venom.

As Alyssa moved forward, she seemed to grow taller. Hy wondered if it was a trick of the light, or if her mind was playing games.

Alyssa's smile was gone. Her face was brittle, her expression chilling. Hy saw cold intent in her eyes. She was looking into the eyes of a killer. A killer who planned to kill her, too. The confession had been Hy's death sentence.

She backed away toward the door, left open when she entered the dome, filmy fog seeping into the room, a backdrop to Alyssa's deadly intent.

Alyssa loomed above her. Her shadow and the shadow of the barbells swept up the wall and across Hy's face.

She could have wielded the axe. She could have killed Lord. And MacAdam. Maybe Ed and Leone, too. Alyssa was no longer a woman, the vision she created to entrap men. She was a monster, menacing, her shadow growing as she advanced on Hy, casting her in darkness, making her feel small and ineffectual when was used to towering over others.

"Alyssa!" It burst from Hy's lips, she didn't know why. To try to destroy this ugly vision? Like pricking a balloon.

"Yes, Alyssa." The sound of the name no longer had that airy, silky quality. The "s" sizzled from the monster's mouth, searing.

"Alyssa." She spat it out again, as snake-like she unwound her body to raise the weight to full height above her head.

Alyssa. Able to lift hundreds of pounds, even though she was no bigger than a child.

Able to lift hundreds of pounds. Armed and dangerous.

The axe that struck Lord in the back of the head would have been nothing to her.

"Nothing," Alyssa said, as if she'd read Hy's thoughts, sliding toward her with triumph in her eyes.

"It was nothing to me." She held the weight over Hy's head.

Hy stepped back, fear buzzing through her. Alyssa stepped forward, arms still raised, the mouse now a stalking cat.

Chapter Thirty-Three

Ian had grabbed the rope from his trunk, the same one that had hauled MacAdam out of the pond. Jamieson had lost the sensation in the hand holding her to the cliff face. She tried to move the fingers one at a time, to work the numbness out. When she did, she slipped, the weight shifting to her injured ankle. She kept the palm of her other hand and her body flat against the wet sandstone, as if the contact would glue her there, hold her in place, prevent her from tumbling to death below. But it was not her body that was holding her there. Her mind was clinging to the thought that she would not fall. The moment she gave up she would be lost. She screwed up her face, eyes shut tight, teeth gritted together, hanging on to the thought with all her mental power. It was all she had now. And she realized then that what McAllister had said was true, what Lili had demonstrated had worth. Her mental state mattered in what she knew was a moment of life and death. She did not look down. She kept focused – and prayed for Ian to return. Fast.

"Lance, he was nothing to me." Alyssa held the barbell as if it, too, were nothing, her eyes intent on Hy.

"And Ed?" Hy took a slow step back. She wanted to raise her arms in defence, but held them steady at her sides, not wanting to provoke this – this – madwoman. Seemingly bigger than Hy. Stronger, too.

"Nothing. He was nothing to me except muscle. Mind Over Muscle." Alyssa took another step.

The doorway! Hy had to back through the doorway. Then Alyssa would have to retreat, three times, before she could go through it. It would buy time. She backed up two more steps, trying not to rush, to do anything that would set this woman off.

"Nothing. Ed was really nothing to you?" *Keep her talking.* A few more backward steps. Hy didn't dare look behind her to see how close she was to the door.

Alyssa's eyes narrowed.

"Never anything to me." She stepped forward.

From behind Alyssa came a whimper. Ed – a great lump on the floor, wounded by his own mind trick, by the love of his life – was still alive to know it. *Thank God.* But…what was he hearing? Understanding?

"Except he gave you power and strength." When she said it, Hy realized she could use the same weapon. *Fight fire with fire.* She needed to break Alyssa's concentration. *Destroy her confidence. Prick the balloon.*

Out of her peripheral vision, Hy could just see the side of the door.

Close. So close.

Alyssa glided toward her, showing no strain from holding the hundreds of pounds aloft, her little eyes glowing with triumph.

Ian was determined to bring Jamieson up the cape alive. She weighed less than half MacAdam's three hundred pounds, but he couldn't use the car. He'd thought about it, but it was too risky.

He threw down the rope.

"Loop it around your waist and I'll pull you up."

Jamieson grabbed the rope. The rock was grating the skin of her hand. With her other hand, she tried to loop the rope around her waist. She couldn't do it without letting go of the rock. If she let go, she would fall. Beads of sweat were trickling down her face.

"I can't do it. Not around my waist. I'll have to hang onto it and climb up."

She let go of the rock, grabbing the rope one hand at a time. She swung free, trying to snatch at something, anything that would hold her.

Ian had the other end of the rope around his waist, but wasn't ready for the tug of the full weight of her body, and he was yanked to the edge of the cape, only just stopping himself from going over. He stabilized, and so did she, digging in her feet to the cliff face, the pain knifing through her sprained ankle.

"Okay, start now. Climb up. I'll hold steady." Ian couldn't let her know the strain he was already feeling, the piercing pain in his lower back. Jamieson wasn't a heavy woman, but he didn't think he could hold her weight for long.

"C'mon, climb."

"I can't," said Jamieson. "I've got no more strength. Just let me go."

That's what he felt like doing.

"You have pig's eyes."

"What?"

Hy could see she'd shaken Alyssa. A step back.

"Yes, pig's eyes, but not a pig's nose. Worse than that."

Hy could see the weights droop, along with some of Alyssa's spirit.

"Say what you want," Alyssa challenged. She took another step forward. "Because you won't be saying anything soon."

Back two steps. The door frame.

"Pig's eyes, worse than a pig's nose, and – " Hy felt cruel even as she contemplated it.

She was on the other side of the door frame. Safely on the other side?

Alyssa loomed in front of her.

Too close.

"...and that ugly hand..."

Alyssa had reached the door frame. She took a step through.

"That ugly hand," Hy repeated.

Alyssa faltered. Torn between rage and the old superstition.

One step back.

"That ugly, ugly hand."

Alyssa came through the doorway again, her step now faltering, the weights lowering. She took a step back.

"I'm surprised any man would look at you."

A hesitant step forward.

"Or touch you. Who could bear to touch you?"

Sensing an advantage, Hy kept going.

"Who would put a ring on that scarred hand?"

Alyssa wavered, moved forward, struggled with what now seemed an overwhelming weight above her head. Her arms strained, she put a foot forward, tripped, and lost her grip on the weights. Hy watched, paralyzed, as the weights dove at her. She jumped out of the way and they glanced off her shoulder. Hy was forced to her knees by the pain that ripped through her. *Broken?* Was her shoulder broken? Blood seeped onto her shirt.

Alyssa folded to the floor. The weights fell on top of her, pinning her down. Hy pounced on them to pull them off her, but couldn't. They were too heavy.

Alyssa was unconscious. Possibly dead.

Not dead, thought Hy. *Please God, not dead.* She had the weight of her words on her conscience. Cruel words. Cruel words, not meant to kill, but to save her own life.

Mind over muscle.

Outside, Ian was fighting for Jamieson's life.

"Concentrate," said Ian. "Focus."

"I can't. I can't do it." Jamieson's body was tortured by pain unlike any she'd ever experienced. She couldn't last any longer. She was slipping, close to letting go.

Hy stumbled outside, shaken. In the weak light from the dome, she saw Ian, rope around his waist, grunting and heaving. What the hell was he up to? Then she heard Jamieson:

"I can't. I can't do it."

"Jamieson!" It was somewhere between a whisper and a shout.

Hy rushed forward and grabbed hold of the rope to take some of the weight off Ian.

"You can do it. Come on. Concentrate. Mind over matter."

Jamieson knew she was right. It was her mind, she knew, that had kept her holding on so long. She made a small movement.

"Yes," said Ian.

Then another.

"Yes," said Hy.

"Up you come," said Ian. And, an inch at a time, Jamieson climbed up the cape, with Ian holding steady on the rope around his waist and Hy taking up the slack, both encouraging her. Inch by inch, with all three minds focused on the task, all three carrying the weight of one, their muscles straining to the limit and beyond, they brought Jamieson up. They were rewarded when her face peeked over the top of the cape. Ian continued to hold steady on the rope, and Hy leaned forward to pull her up.

She slid onto level land, and rolled over on her back, exhausted. The front of her uniform was filthy.

Nathan was hurrying home. The causeway crossing had been a breeze. All he wanted now was to slip into Lili's arms. The grin on his face widened with each kilometre.

He frowned when his cell phone rang.

It was Jamieson. More bodies to transport. Half-alive or half-dead, depending on how you viewed the world.

He called Lili and delivered the bad news. He'd be another hour at least.

"Don't worry," she said. "We have lots of time. The rest of our lives."

A warm flush rose on his cheeks. They did. They had all the time in the world.

Ian helped Nathan carry Big Ed into the van. He was dense, heavy, muscular, and weighed a lot in spite of his missing limbs. It was a strange sensation carrying just a head, a torso, and a couple of stumps. Half a man. Ed was moaning and mumbling, his face white, his lips grey.

Picking up Alyssa was nothing at all. She was hardly more substantial than the clothes she was wearing. She remained unconscious. Even so, Jamieson had handcuffed her.

"Are you charging her?" asked Hy.

"With attempted murder of you, for starters."

After they'd seen Nathan off, it didn't take much to convince Jamieson to go home with Hy. She had no idea what awaited her at the Hall and she didn't care at the moment what had happened to Murdo. After her ordeal, she needed a long hot bath and a decent bed to sleep in. But after they got clean, both were too keyed up to go to sleep right away.

Hy told Jamieson all about her confrontation with Alyssa.

"She confessed to murdering Lord. And she set Leone up to take the fall – made sure his fingerprints were on the axe, his ring by the body. She didn't exactly say Leone had killed MacAdam, but she made it seem like it."

Jamieson didn't reveal what she was thinking. Hy persisted.

"He practically admitted it. He said, 'I did it for her.' More than once – to protect her, he said."

Jamieson warmed her hands on the hot teacup and looked into the woodstove.

"I need time to think. We'll sort it all out in the morning."

The next day dawned bright and clear, a beautiful late summer day, with a hot sun and just the breath of a breeze to keep it cool. Jamieson and Hy were both up early.

Jamieson made calls to Winterside before she would sit down to the cup of tea Hy offered her.

"And?" Hy dared to ask.

"Mrs. Lord's in the psychiatric ward for assessment. I don't expect she'll ever stand trial."

"Will she be charged?"

"Yes, but she's probably incompetent to stand trial."

"What will she be charged with?"

"A number of things, including the attempted murder of O'Reyley – and you."

"What about Lord? MacAdam?"

Jamieson's cell phone rang. "Yes…I'm sorry to hear that…yes… thanks for informing me."

She set down the phone and looked at Hy.

"And the murder of Ed Bullock."

"He's dead?"

"Another killing we can put at her door."

"And Lord and MacAdam? Will Alyssa or Leone be charged?"

"I can't say right now." Jamieson sipped her tea and they remained silent for a moment.

"Police business?"

Jamieson put her cup down and smiled – more with her eyes than her mouth.

"Yes. Police business." Her tone was softer than Hy had ever heard it. There was another side to Jamieson. She just didn't show it often.

Jamieson poured herself more tea. She was stalling. Something she had to say, but it was difficult for her.

"I have to thank you...," she began.

Was that a smile? The beginning of a smile?

"...for saving my life."

"Oh, c'mon..." Hy flushed.

"No, you did. I've no doubt." It had been the power of their minds – hers, Hy's and Ian's – that had brought her up that cape. She knew it was true. She was now a believer.

"I do have to thank you..."

"For interfering in police business?"

Now it was a smile. Wry. Apologetic.

"Yes. For interfering. You're good at it." Jamieson had made a joke. That was two.

"You're right," Hy smiled back.

It didn't help to be right, thought Jamieson. The case had been a mess. Four deaths and a killer who, if charged, would not be found guilty. But it wasn't over. It was not over yet.

"Drink up. I have a question about what happened last night. We'll have to go to the dome." Maybe this would confirm what she believed or didn't believe.

As they left the house, Hy returned like a terrier to her interrogation.

"But Alyssa confessed to me and you haven't charged her with murdering Lord?"

"Oh, there will be charges," said Jamieson.

Murdo woke up in the dilapidated barn. He'd gone to sleep the moment he literally hit the hay. He'd slept right through the night, his mind clear of any memory of what had been going on when he got lost. Now, waking up, he remembered it all. He bolted up and scrambled out of the hay. Spears of it were sticking to his uniform and his hair. The barn doors were crooked and they creaked as he pushed through them. He turned red when he saw how close he was to the Hall.

It was tougher to get to than it looked. The slope that had seemed gentle from a distance was steep, and Murdo had to climb on hands and feet, scrambling his way up. The cruiser was still parked outside the Hall. Would Jamieson be there? What had happened last night?

Chapter Thirty-Four

Wearing a sweater and jeans borrowed from Hy, and looking and feeling newly comfortable in them, Jamieson propelled ahead of Hy into the dome. She leaned forward on her crutches to look at the barbell Alyssa had hoisted, injuring Hy and knocking herself unconscious.

"Pick it up," she said to Hy.

"But I can't. It's too heavy."

"Try."

Hy bent down, braced herself for the strain, and almost fell backwards lifting the weight. Weight was the wrong word for it. It weighed almost nothing.

"It can't be the same one."

"It is. I took a good look at it last night. I have a mind for these things."

"Then how did it do this?" Hy slipped the shoulder of her sweatshirt down, to reveal a large, ugly bruise, and a scab formed on a bloody wound. "It glanced off me and did this. I felt it. It was heavy. It hurt. It still hurts. It pinned Alyssa to the floor. I tried to pick it up off her and I couldn't."

Jamieson shrugged, "Mind over muscle?"

"You mean it could work both ways – make something heavy feel light, and something light feel – and be – heavy?"

"Exactly."

"I thought you didn't believe that stuff."

"I didn't," said Jamieson. "But look at the evidence. I have to consider the evidence – and that I could be wrong." She was unsure about her next move. She hoped she wasn't wrong. She should wait for the lab results, but by then it might be too late. She hopped out of the dome, wielding her crutches expertly. Hy hustled to keep up with her as she headed down to the Hall.

Billy was asleep on Murdo's cot when Murdo entered the Hall. And Junior Johnson, sitting on the floor, his head lolling forward, his nose and mouth emitting a combination of mucous-filled and guttural sounds, was asleep, too. He was attached to the cot, the handcuffs linked through the springs.

Murdo shook Billy awake. He was startled to find out where he was. His first thought was of his mother. She would be raging, banging at the floor with her cane, waiting for him to deliver her morning tea. When he saw Junior Johnson, he remembered why he was here. He'd made an arrest. His first arrest. He beamed at Murdo.

"He was stealing the grass out of the cruiser." He didn't mention Gladys Fraser's part in it.

Johnson was awake now.

"That wasn't stealin'. That was my grass."

"Well, then, it was dealing," said Murdo. "We'll take him in and book him as soon as I find out where Jamieson is."

"You can book Jared MacPherson, too." Junior was red with rage. Jared had convinced him the cookhouse would be the perfect spot for a grow-op. Junior had taken all the risk and Jared had planned to take half the money. Well, he could take half the blame, too.

Nathan had dragged Jamieson's cruiser out of the dung and, apart from being filthy and smelly, it had suffered no ill effects. Jamieson dispatched Billy in the cruiser to take Junior to town, and ordered Murdo to drive her and Hy to Ian's.

Hy wondered why she was now being included in police

business. She didn't realize it was to be another thank you from Jamieson.

"I've come to make an arrest."

Ian looked puzzled. Jamieson was at his front door, with Hy and Murdo behind her. She came right into the living room. He and Suki were sitting on the couch having a morning coffee. He looked in question at Hy. She shrugged and opened her eyes wide to let him know she had no idea what Jamieson was talking about.

"Arrest?" he said. "For what?"

Jamieson turned to Suki.

"I'm arresting you for the murder of Lance Lord."

"What?" Hy, Ian, and Suki spoke in chorus.

Just the sort of sound Jasmine loved.

"What?" she added.

"But – " Hy looked confused. "Alyssa confessed."

"And she was telling the truth, what she thought was the truth. She did try to kill him, but Miss Smythe beat her to it."

"How?"

"You got me thinking, when you told me about the mussels."

"The mussels?" Ian looked confused.

"What's that got to do with it?" Hy was confused, too. It was hard to read Suki's expression, as if she were waiting to see how she should react. That wasn't lost on Jamieson.

"It was paralytic shellfish reaction. That's what killed him. Not the blow to the head."

"Para – what?"

Jamieson pointed at Suki.

"She stuffed a lobster in his head. There was tomalley in the wound. I'm betting he was allergic and she knew it."

"And that's what killed him?"

"In the immediate, yes. He was dying from the head wound – no doubt about that – but what killed him, almost instantly there on the sand, was the tomalley. I'm sorry I doubted that you'd seen a lobster stuffed in his head."

Hy shook her head. First jokes, then thanks, and now an apology.

"Suki, you didn't – " Ian had gone white.

Suki's head dropped.

"But I never meant to – "

"Then you shouldn't have done it."

"It was just…I was angry…"

"Angry enough to kill?"

"No. No, not really. He was already dead."

"Apparently not."

"But Alyssa is still the real killer." Ian laid a hand on Suki's shoulder.

"Technically, no."

"Morally, yes."

"Perhaps. But this is how I see it. Lord went out to confront MacAdam. You – " she pointed at Suki, " – got tired of waiting for him. You found him lying on the sand. Dead? No, not quite. You heard a low moan. Something that told you he was still alive. You wondered – worried – that he might survive this. That you might be expected to care for him if he does. A drooling idiot in a wheelchair, like Ed. No, you decided. You realized you had a weapon in your hand, his allergy. You were finishing off your lobster, and then you used it to finish him off. If he wasn't already dead, he soon would be, and you stuffed that lobster in his head, knowing it would kill him."

Suki looked horrified.

"No. No. That's not how it happened. I was angry, I admit, but…"

Jamieson made a quick, almost imperceptible signal to Murdo. He handcuffed Suki, almost before she knew what was happening. They worked well as a team.

"I don't believe in allergies. I didn't know what I was doing…"

"Save it," said Jamieson. "The Crown will argue that you knew precisely what you were doing – making sure he was dead." That was what the mussel chowder was all about. The final pieces of the puzzle were fitting together.

It had been a long case. First no body, then no suspect, then too many. Then dead suspects. And now this thin thread on which she hanging the case. She might be wrong, but she didn't think she was. Even so, she suspected she wouldn't get a clean murder conviction out of it.

All the bounce went out of Suki as Jamieson led her out of the house. And with the bounce went her beauty. She sagged into her age, her body deflating like a balloon slowly losing its helium, taut skin puckering, shiny swollen membrane becoming soft and thickened. The transformation happened right in front of their eyes. Hy and Ian watched out the front window as Jamieson helped Suki into the back seat of the car. She stared back at them out the back window. Pale, pathetic, every year her age. Ian wondered what he'd ever seen in her. So, of course, did Hy. And Jasmine.

"Silly bugger," she said, unlatching her cage door, flying out and landing on Ian's shoulder. Her beak caressed his cheek.

"Bloody silly bugger," echoed Hy. "You slept with a murderer."

"I believe you mentioned that before."

"And do you think she tried to kill you, too? With the mussels?"

"Just an honest mistake," he said.

"Maybe a subconscious mistake? A Freudian soup?"

"Well…"

"Well what?"

He hesitated.

"She did say she didn't believe in allergies."

Hy's eyes shot open.

"She was setting you up."

"Her alibi...," he said slowly.

"Twice over. Bet she asks you to testify on her behalf in court... that she doesn't believe in allergies."

"Well..."

"Well, you know it's true... Ian, you slept with a killer."

"Guess so," said Jasmine. "Killer. Guess so."

"Well," Ian winked. "The sex was certainly killer."

"Sure," said Hy. "Just muscle over mind."

"Muscle over mind," squawked Jasmine.

It would be a long time before either of them would let him live it down.

"Alyssa confessed to all of it. Lord. MacAdam. When they restrained her, she demonstrated it." Jamieson was back to The Shores the next day to wrap up the case. She was having tea with Hy and Ian. On duty.

"Her strength?" Hy rubbed her still-bruised shoulder.

"Yes, but it wasn't enough to overcome four beefy orderlies. And then she broke down, and admitted how she'd tried to put the blame on Leone, and how he'd agreed to shoulder it for her."

I did it for her – that's what he said. Not the killing but agreeing to take the blame. "I thought so," said Hy.

"That's what the footprints in the sand in that photograph of yours were about. Covering her tracks. He followed in her tracks. She got him to put his fingerprints on the axe, placed the ring by the body, just like she told you. Then she drew attention to it so suspicion would fall on him."

"What about Suki?" Ian asked.

"She'll get Lord's money. There's a lot of it." Lord had been as close with his cash as he'd been with his land. He'd made steady investments with half the money he earned. He was worth millions, something neither of his wives had known.

"That kind of money will pay for an acquittal." Jamieson's

expression turned sour.

Hy was finding victory bitter. She had been right about Suki; Ian had been wrong. But she felt sorry for her. She wasn't really a killer, just a very foolish woman.

"Do you know what killed Leone?" Ian offered Jamieson a fresh muffin, brought up that morning by Moira, a smug expression still on her face from having seen Suki taken from Ian's house under police escort.

Jamieson declined.

"Enlarged heart."

"Cardiomyopathy." Ian offered Hy the plate.

"Cardio what?" Hy bit into a muffin dripping with butter.

"A big heart," said Jamieson. "His heart was too big."

"I'll say." Hy thought about what Leone had been willing to do – had done – for Alyssa.

"It certainly was," said Jamieson, and Hy looked at her sharply. Jamieson was showing her human side. Again.

"When athletes die of a sudden heart attack…" Ian was on the Internet. "…cardiomyopathy is usually what they die of. Damage to the muscle."

"Right," said Jamieson. "He was being treated for it. His heart was as big as it could get. It was in a sort of a sling, well, a mesh sack that contained it."

"Until…"

"Until it swelled so much it burst the sack."

"Well, that's not exactly the scientific explanation." Ian looked up from the screen. The two women ignored him.

"Was it the strain of running across the cape?"

"Probably."

"He died because his heart was too big." Hy was shaking her head.

"Yes," said Jamieson, on a sigh. Something in her tone –

"And good," said Hy.

"No, bad," said Ian. "Or he wouldn't have died."

"You know what I mean."

"He died for love," Jamieson said. Hy wanted her to say it again, so she could believe what she'd heard.

Jamieson obliged. "He died for love." She straightened her jacket and became herself again, bursting Hy's bubble that she was becoming soft.

"What a waste – to die for love."

Hy had to agree. Lance, Leone, and Ed had lost their lives for love of Alyssa.

Love that hath no beginning hath no end?

For the three of them there had been an end. An unhappy, brutal end.

Epilogue

Red Islanders live and die by funerals, so they held the memorial service for Lance Lord as requested in his will, though most hadn't known him or liked him.

"...Purple haze all in my brain..."

Jimi Hendrix's signature song was emanating from the Hall, where distorted sound was usually young people scratching Celtic laments on fiddles. Toby and the other village dogs had gathered outside the building and were howling.

"Actin' funny, but I don't know why..."

Jimi Hendrix's whining, overmodulated guitar tones were a strange accompaniment for the journey of a man in his fifties to his eternal home. That was the sixties generation, refusing to grow old, unwilling to put on a mantle of dignity, clutching their rock 'n' roll mentality to the bitter and undignified end.

Moira stood up suddenly and marched out of the Hall. Estelle Joudry's eyes followed her, admiring her guts.

Moira's sister Madeline looked confused. Was she meant to follow? Stay put? She was sitting next to Billy, who was rocking to the music, knocking her with his knee. She began to tap her foot, too, and he noticed her. Pretty little thing. He smiled at her.

Hy found herself singing along. She didn't know why. She didn't know her mother had breastfed her to Hendrix. She'd absorbed him with her mother's milk.

The song whined to an end:

"Ooo, ahhh
Ooo, ahhh, yeah!"

"And not a moment too soon," said Gus.

They all trekked down to the shore to dispose of Lord's guitars. The guitars were worth a lot of money. Some were shocked at the plan to burn them.

But a last request is a last request.

Hy and Ian had stacked the instruments in a pile on the sand. The neighbourhood dogs, led by Toby, were nosing around the bags of marshmallows and packets of hot dogs and buns the village children had brought.

Moira arrived, wearing yellow rubber gloves, dragging two garbage bags, red tin foil bulging out of them from Alyssa's shrine.

She tossed the bags on top of the heap of guitars. Alyssa and Lance were about to create heat together that they never had in life.

Gus had caused a stir when she'd shown up. She hadn't been to the shore in twenty years. She'd brought the wedding ring quilt. A waste of good material, Olive MacLean declared, but for Gus, it was tainted. And too hard to complete. She threw it on the heap.

Ian squirted the pile with barbecue fluid, struck a match, and lit it.

The red tin foil caught in a flash of oily, rainbow colours. Nothing else did. Ian squirted on more barbecue starter, which slid down the shiny red, green, and yellow gloss finishes on the guitars. Paper and cardboard at the base of the bonfire caught fire and ignited them in an impotent smouldering burn, melting them into distorted shapes and colours, sending an acrid yellow smoke into the sky and giving off a pungent smell that made the children hold their noses and put away their hot dogs and marshmallows.

Nathan hauled a container of gasoline out of the back of his truck, motioned everyone to stand back and hurled the liquid on the pile, then jumped back quickly as Lance Lord's guitars went up in a fireball, a grand moment of Hendrix-style glory.

Someone found one of Lord's No Trespassing signs and tossed it on the heap.

And, as at any good bonfire, there was music.

Jasmine was singing:

"I have only one burning desire
Let me stand next to your fire."

And she went spiraling off into a rendition of a Hendrix guitar solo, weaving in and out of the sound of the crackling flames.

Stepping back from the heat, Ian wondered how Jasmine had learned the song. He had stood much too close to Suki's fire, and now he was going to pay for it. Hy had introduced Jasmine to Jimi Hendrix's greatest hits. They would become the winter soundtrack at Ian's house. Hy would just have to say, *"Jimi, Jasmine,"* and off she'd go. Like now, as the bonfire blazed in harmony with the setting sun, a streak of deep red over The Shores.

"Scuse me while I kiss the sky."

The fox, attracted by the heat of the fire, watched from the cape. She wondered at the strange ways of humans, who kill their own kind, but don't eat them.

An excerpt from *Good Will Toward Murder*, the next book in Hilary MacLeod's acclaimed Shores Mystery series

Prologue

A sparkle of light glimmered beside a deep blue coastline, like a diamond set in a sapphire sea. It was a still photo, but the light appeared to move, to radiate.

The tiny jewel was The Shores in a satellite photo called Red Island From Space, taken on a past December night. Now that Christmas was coming again, everything in The Shores that didn't have the legs or sense to get away was strung with lights.

Thousands and thousands of Christmas lights. More every year than the year before. The Shores was just catching up. Electricity had only arrived in the tiny community in the nineteen sixties. When it finally came, the villagers lost all their traditional restraint.

One year, the residents had put out so many lights, it had caused a province-wide power failure, plunging the whole island into darkness on Christmas Eve – except The Shores. The villagers were used to power failures. Almost everyone had generators. They fired them up and plugged in the lights again. A legal limit had since been set on how many they could install, but they ignored it.

There were decorative Santas, reindeers and elves crammed in every available space. Christmas angels and stars. The holy family, complete with creche and wise men, was proudly displayed on roofs, front lawns, on mailboxes and well houses, in empty lots and on boats parked on land for the off-season. The Hall at the centre of the village had lights sparkling on a massive spruce at the front of the building, and Santa and his sleigh and reindeer rode the green steel roof. Some houses dripped lights like falling snow; others had tossed clumps randomly up on their roofs, creating shimmering drifts. There was hardly a tree or plant of any kind – lilac, maple, dogwood – that wasn't strung with lights or a star or decoration of some kind. The Shores glistened in the night from every available source within plugging distance. Extension cord joined to extension cord, snaking around the village, causing potential hazards for pedestrians and drivers, and straining every household's fuse box. Breakers hadn't reached The Shores yet.

This overwhelming Christmas spirit was what had created the twinkling diamond seen from space. From the first of December until New Years, The Shores lit up the Red Island sky at night – and had become that tiny spark of light captured by chance in the satellite photo, announcing the existence of this forgotten village to the universe.

Apart from Ian Simmons' place, and he was considered odd, there was only one house in the village that wasn't lit up. It had been dark for years. That was about to change. Wild Rose Cottage was about to come to life, and death, once again.

Meanwhile, the villagers wished for snow to complete the Christmas portrait. When it came, they would regret it.

Chapter One

The house was weeping. That's what it looked like – except that the tears fell from its eyebrows, the high gables, and dripped onto its eyes – windows clouded and streaked with grime running like mascara over the sills, black streaks down the grey cedar shingles.

The name, Wild Rose Cottage, didn't suit the house. It was massive, ancient and nothing like a cottage, but in the summer, wild and domestic roses grew everywhere around it, out of control – so many they had become a tangle, an eyesore as unbecoming as the house itself, peeled to a faded rose, and deserted. Except for the vermin. And today one two-legged rodent.

Rats skittering across the wood floorboards, stained with their own excrement, competed with mice and ants for the remaining crumbs of human existence still to be found in the cracks between the floors and walls – so many had lived here for so long. In a hard winter, the animals sometimes ate the plaster and softened wood. There was no one to warn them it might kill them.

Certainly not the human parasite who was now tearing away at the walls and floorboards. He wasn't looking for nourishment, but he was finding plastic bags of rodent "treats" that someone had left in the walls years ago. Whenever he found one, he flung it across the room and the rats scrambled for it, tearing at the plastic, wolfing down the contents, soon to be dead.

The man was looking for something, and becoming increasingly angry that he could not find it. The rats didn't bother him. He had them at home. If one or more of them got in his way, he kicked them off. Every time he did, the squealing would rise suddenly, and then die off.

The plaster was peeling away from the walls in big chunks, baring the lathe made of fish crates. The first owner, a young architect who had designed homes for the very wealthy, couldn't afford the expensive supplies when he built his own house. The skeleton revealed his cost-cutting measures, but the house, when it was first finished, had been magnificent. That had been more than a hundred years ago.

Now the floors were littered with the discarded remains of lives lived – broken furniture, clothing, old books, toys, hockey equipment, now all chewed and covered in rat excrement.

Jared MacPherson stood up and planted a big dirty boot right on top of a plastic place mat featuring the infamous satellite photo of The Shores, now covered in red clay and old urine. The diamond had lost some of its sparkle.

Jared had plenty of warning of the new owners' arrival. He was still in the house, up on the second floor, from where he could see well down the road. He happened to be looking at the hill when they crested it. He couldn't have known they were coming here, but something told him that they were – a ragtag bunch, just the types to fall for this old place. Damn – he'd only searched a handful of rooms, and not all that well. It might be found under the floorboards, in the walls. And he didn't even know what he was looking for. The Sullivan Legacy. What the hell was that supposed to mean?

"You'll know it when you find it," he'd been told.

He didn't think he'd find it here. It was an old library, cradled in the large middle gable of the house. It had built-in shelves and benches, and rotting books – eaten away and pissed on by rats, mildewed by the damp air, a fuzzy white mould growing on them. Jared kicked a few books around and began to sneeze.

He finished his cursory search of the room– and then scurried down the stairs, out the back and through the ripped tarpaulin. There was no snow, and the red clay was frozen solid, so he left no tracks.

Perfect conditions for thieving. But what was there to steal?

Acknowledgements:

Thanks to all the usual suspects:

My friend Janet Campbell for her terrier-like support.

My daughter, Kirsten MacLeod, for never losing faith.

The Acorn Press publisher Terrilee Bulger and former publisher Laurie Brinklow for their faith in the series. And editor Sherie Hodds for her intuitive and sensitive approach.

Matt Reid for his inspired cover art, which everyone comments on, and his overall design talents.

And to some new partners in crime:

JoAnne Wilson for her guerilla publicity strategies.

And to my internet agents Nikita and Red.